THE WOLF BOSS & HIS DARLING

MAFIA, MURDER, MAYHEM SERIES
BOOK 3

ELM JED

The Wolf Boss & His Darling

Underground Edition

© 2023 Elm Jed

Cover Art by: S.Wolf.Art LLC

EBook ISBN- 9781967019021

Paperback ISBN - 9781967019090

❀ Formatted with Vellum

To my Marine Brethren,
You're not alone.
And I'm glad you're here.

CONTENTS

CONTENT WARNING

Explosions, gunfights, slight gore,
Family death/loss, talk of sexual assault, death on page, and
discussions of PTSD and depression

BOOK PLAYLIST

"Enemy" – Imagine Dragons, JID, Arcane, League of Legends
"Big Bad Wolf" – Roses & Revolutions
"Hurt" – Johnny Cash
"The Only Thing Worth Fighting For" – Lera Lynn
"Shipping Up to Boston" –Dropkick Murphys
"Welcome To Wonderland" – Anson Seabra
"Wicked Game" – Lusaint
"Barrels of Whiskey" – The O'Reillys and the Paddyhats
"Flowers of the Red Hill" – Orthodox Celts
"Neverland" – Kyla La Grange
"So it Goes…" – Taylor Swift
"Rose Tattoo" – Dropkick Murphys
"You're Somebody Else" – flora cash
"Lion" – Saint Mesa
"Up Down" – Boy Epic
"Wild Side" – Roberto Cacciapaglia
"Sunlight" – Hozier
"TRUSTFALL" – P!nk

CHAPTER 1
WHO'S AFRAID OF THE BIG BAD BOSS?

I'm gonna be late for brunch.

The gun goes back into my holster as I glance down at the body bleeding on my office carpet. I look at Gunther, then at one of my newer members, Finn, staring wide-eyed at my reason for being late.

"Call cleaning," I order him. "That damn stain better be out of my carpet before noon."

I move toward my office wet bar as he removes the dead half-breed named Ralph out my door. I pour myself a glass of whiskey and down it. Day has barely started and already I'm fucking drinking. Great start.

"Boss?" Gunther inquires in a low tone.

"He had it coming since last spring. His fault for coming inside the zones."

"Not disagreeing." I walk over to my desk. "Just thought you'd have *persuaded* more answers out of him before placing a bullet in his head. Maybe cut his hand off, the classics."

I scowl at the shorter werewolf with reddish sienna skin and hair and bright hazel eyes. Gunther's the most reliable beta wolf I've worked with since he joined the Pack a century ago. Some didn't agree with me making him my head beta given how young he is, but his quick thinking saved my ass more times than a left hook. His easy-going personality and patience balance out my prickly, stubborn mood on bad days. Like today.

I sigh, picking up the thumb drive Ralph had on him. "Ralph said this was supposed to go to DiNardi. And I'm damned sure Antoni will talk more than a two-buck con man who owed me lives and over fifty thousand dollars." Should've shot Ralph earlier for that shit.

"Wasn't questioning that either."

"Then what is it?"

"Lil sis it out front."

"Fuck." Blood isn't even dry on my carpet. "Tell Victoria to keep her out there. Don't let her back here."

He turns away with a low chuckle. "We both know she's probably already smelled—"

"Gunther," I warn. "Tell her any damn story you want, but don't let her back here."

He chuckles, closing the door behind him.

I look back down at the thumb drive, moving it around in my fingers. Guess I'll find out what Ralph was delivering to DiNardi from the mob boss himself. All the human mob bosses knew *never* to send their messengers, henchman, or whomever they tossed bills at through my territories. I decreed to DiNardi and Boston to hand Ralph over if he ever showed up after disappearing for nine months. Instead, my wolves find him sneaking through my turf smelling of *my* recent missing explosives saying he was hired by DiNardi. Other human mobs have muddied their relationship with the Underground Mafia this past year, but DiNardi hadn't been one. I've worked with his family for generations and never had any issues.

Until now.

I toss the thumb drive onto my desk and pull out a clean flannel from my closet, catching sight of myself in the small mirror. My tired, deep green eyes contrast against my deep umber skin and fur trailing down my neck and shoulders. I graze over the closely shaved sides of my head and wince when my long nails scratch my skin. I yank off my bloodied shirt and put the new one on, noticing the great kilt hanging in the back for the last decade. I shake my head, shut the closet, and grab the thumb drive.

There's a knock, and Gunther pokes his head in. "Victoria gave her coffee, but we both know she'll down that."

I adjust my hip holster and toss him the thumb drive. "Find whatever the fuck is on there. I want to know what was so important for DiNardi to break our bargain."

Gunther raises a brow, looking down at the drive as I pass him. "Which one? Not handing over Ralph? Using our territories for spy games?"

"All of the above."

Two of my cleaners appear as I give them a nod and walk down the hall into my restaurant, *Donny's*, a steakhouse my grandfather built decades ago. It's exactly how he envisioned it: wood paneling, low amber lighting, dark carpet, booths, and the smell of eggs, steak, and whiskey. Despite the time shift, werewolves sit throughout the venue for late breakfast or brunch.

Up here on Topside New York City, where *Donny's* sits, it's early evening hours for the humans, but for us Paranormals, our day's just getting started. Most of my Pack live in the Underground of New York City, while those only in the Wolf Mob were above where I've spent most of my time over the past decade.

I catch sight of Victoria's pearl-white skin, fur, and shimmering blue eyes. The werewolf smiles brightly and looks over at me, winking briefly. I look over to who's making her laugh, leaning over the counter with a mug of coffee in her hand.

Brenda Cuorebella, my lil sis, turns and beams before running over with her mug and punching my arm. I scowl and ruffle her hair with my hand.

"Hey!" She shouts, punching my arm again. "You're five minutes late, Lassie. Better have a good explanation."

"Don't worry about it," I say, ushering her forward, hoping she doesn't smell the blood. Known as the scary Wolf Mob Boss, and my biggest worry at the moment is my lil sis learning about my morning... "business transaction." Even if she *has* encountered worse.

"Someone beat you with a couple of sixes or something?"

"What?"

"Who'd you shoot?" Never fucking mind, her nose is worse than a bloodhound's. "And your Smith & Wesson? Must've been twos."

I grumble as we sit down at our usual rounded booth near the back, "You sure you ain't wolf?"

"Jealous, Lassie?" She smirks, sliding in beside me.

"Not when you're the first one to smell puke."

"Or that you've been drinking?"

I frown. "*Now* you can quit it."

She opens her mouth, and I put my hand over it. A trick I learned from her brothers. Brenda mumbles against my hand as Victoria sets down a pot of coffee and a mug for me.

"Warned you, lil sis," she says. "Want whiskey, boss?" I glance over at lil sis, who raises her brows. I nod once. "Coming up," she giggles and walks away, her jeans tight across her thighs and...

Brenda pushes away my hand, and mumbles, "You also need to trim your nails."

"You done?"

"Only if you get me in on that Irish Coffee."

"Deal." She smirks as I give her a side hug, kissing her cheek briefly. Our brunch dates had a way of making the bloody messes in my life disappear. Even without coffee.

Brenda rubs my head and chuckles as I scowl at her, causing murmurs nearby. I turn and glare at the wolves a few tables over, instantly looking away as I curl my lip. My gaze finds two other groups, who quickly find something else to do. Brenda's my "adopted" sister, a half-breed who grew up in a family of incubi and succubi. She used to be a head librarian for the New York Public Library, but now she works at *The Vault* in the Underground, an even larger library for the book nerd.

Victoria brings over the whiskey and smiles at me warmly. "Food will be out in a moment. Behave, lil sis," she says.

"I am an angel," Brenda retorts.

"Depends on which angel," Victoria teases, walking away. I watch her help a few patrons at the bar and she flashes a smile at me before I look away.

Brenda reaches for the whiskey. "Is there something you wanna tell me?"

"No," I reply a bit too quickly.

"Uh-huh."

"Don't start."

"I'm not the one staring at Victoria's ass."

"Wasn't staring." Brenda pauses mid-pour with a look of disbelief. "Tried it two decades ago and it didn't work out. Not risking the Pack dynamic for a *maybe*."

"But that was decades ago."

It still feels like yesterday some days. She pours the whiskey into my mug with a quizzical eye, and I counter, "So were Zane and I, should we try *that* again?"

She snorts. "You'd kill him."

"See? Some things aren't meant to be, like me and relationships."

"That doesn't mean—"

"You been hanging out with your Ma again?"

"Look, past few months, I've learned how right my Ma can be, so don't give me a reason to bring her into this."

"Then let's just drop it." I lean back in my seat, and take a sip of the coffee. Damn, lil sis does know how to make a good cup of joe. I take another gulp of the Irish Coffee, hoping to calm more of my nerves. I've been uneasy since Ralph was found slinking through my territories. And talking about relationships wasn't helping the unease, not when I've got missing explosives and mob bosses going behind my back.

"What's up, Rodney?" Brenda asks, swirling her coffee and watching me with her violet eyes through the red-tinted glasses. Her dark hair is pulled back, revealing her undercut and the two large facial scars across her face. The rest of her scars hide underneath her leather jacket. The jacket that used to be her Mate's and still smells of the bloodsucker.

Of course, fate would have it that'd she'd end up with my archnemesis, Vincent Dracultelli, AKA Vinny the Vampire, Blood Mafia Boss of the Underground Mafia. Fate has a fucked-up sense of humor.

A growl forms at the back of my throat, and I shake my head to keep it at bay. "Just gotta deal with DiNardi later. Usual business."

"Over in Brooklyn?"

"The Bronx." Brenda freezes, and I realize my mistake. Shit.

The servers come and lay out brunch as I anxiously watch her put her mug down. I nod as they leave and try to speak, "Lil sis—"

"You going there?"

I exhale sharply. "I have to. He broke a bargain, and if I let him get away with the fuck up, I'll have bigger problems." And find out what was worth hiring Ralph for.

"Bigger than being arrested by PSB or the police?" She hisses, glaring at me now. "The Bronx is still crawling with them, and if they grab you—"

"It's cleared up some," I argue. "And you know what entails—"

"Just cause I know the mob can be dangerous, doesn't mean I'll agree when one of you asses decide to get into the thick of it." She scowls, crossing her arms as she slumps back. I rub my head and wince. "And trim your damn nails."

I grumble at her, taking my coffee and practically down it.

The chaos of the last few months flashes across my mind. PSB, the Paranormal Security Bureau, existed to help protect Paranormals from injustice within the United States. If I wasn't a mob boss, we'd probably work together to help protect Paranormals, but they hate the Underground Mafia's guts. Surprisingly, the government dislikes us. Maybe it's due to us doing their fucking job half the time, like stopping a mad scientist from creating a ghoul army. In the past six months, we've lost neutral zones to PSB hovering everywhere, caught in stings, and the police toeing boundaries with their trigger-happy asses. The entire Underground Mafia lost a lot of ground. Hasn't been good lately. Not to mention the many times Brenda almost died from getting involved in mob affairs. If Brenda found out DiNardi hired a half-breed who smelled of missing explosives, no doubt that pattern of her almost dying would continue.

Not on my fucking watch.

My stomach clenches at the thought, and I clear my throat. "I'll be careful. Don't worry. In and out, simple shit."

She looks at me, and I give her a small smile, hoping she can see it. Sometimes her glasses don't help her eyesight much, and she can barely even notice a smirk. I bump her shoulder, and she bumps me back, giving me a tight smile.

"Enough about my boring business ventures; what you been up to, smarty-aleck?" I ask refilling our mugs as I put extra bacon on her plate.

"You really want to know?"

"Try me."

"Last time you practically snored, ya old dog."

"Did not."

"Did, too."

"You were talking about vampires and their history with the witch trials of the 1600s. Excuse me if my favorite subject isn't those vamp tramps."

She laughs, and I smile. "Oh, cause you'd be interested in about historical anecdotes on the development of socioeconomics with shifters in Germany and France in the 20th century that I've been cataloging at *The Vault*?" She muses, and my smile falters. "Or something lighter like the rise in profit of gold and cocoa in Nigeria after vampires laid claim to half the territory in the 19th century?" I scrunch my face, my smile completely gone as I snort my displeasure. "Damn, least Vinny hides his reactions."

"Unlike the bloodsucker, I wear my heart on my sleeve." She rolls her eyes, laughing at me. "What?"

"Keep telling yourself that, Lassie, especially during poker."

"Yet never lost to you," I retort, and she scoffs, grabbing her coffee. "Does Beckham just give you all the hard materials?"

"I ask for it," she mumbles around a mouthful of eggs and toast. "Keeps me busy, especially if Joey and Vinny are off playing mob boss all the time."

I notice her playing with her food a little, and I start feeling like a shitty brother keeping secrets.

"The human mobs are nothing to worry about. Annoying but harmless," I say softly. "Nothing's gonna happen to us. I'm a big wolf and can take care of myself."

"Even you're not invincible, Rodney," she murmurs.

It feels like there's lead sinking in my stomach. I swallow hard, pushing away old fears and pain as I move closer, putting an arm around her shoulders. I hold her close to my side.

"Shit hasn't been safe for *anyone*," she whispers. A part of me wants to tell her it never has been, but guilt stops it. I squeeze her tightly, kissing her temple and she lets out a sigh. "Just worried about you."

"And I'm thankful for you but have a little faith in me. Been doing this for centuries." I pull away, lightly hitting her chin.

She kisses my cheek briefly and goes back to her food. "That's why I worry. What if your old bones start breaking the next time you jump two stories?"

"It was one story."

"Two! It was over thirty feet."

"Hey, I had a cool landing," I argue playfully, biting into my steak.

"Yeah, and how'd your knees feel the next day, Lassie?"

I pause and glare at her as she starts snickering. "I was thinking about getting you new guns for your birthday, but maybe—"

"Wait! Wait! Truce!" She drops her fork and starts waving her hands in surrender. "I'm down a few good guns."

"Whose fault is that?"

"Police were chasing me."

"Uh-huh."

"My reasonings are solid."

"Like when you threw a handgun at a sewer rat?"

"I was twelve, and that's not what we're discussing."

I laugh, letting our time together melt away the trouble of this morning. Through brunch, Brenda almost persuades me to get her one of the new Desert Eagles she saw released. Every so often, wolves glance our way, but Victoria quickly distracts them before I can snarl at their lingering gazes. They aren't Pack, making Brenda a conundrum for them as to why she's here.

I ignore them as we finish our meal, Marcus coming over, glaring at Brenda with his usual disproval as he lets me know we're ready to roll. Lil sis tries to pry more info from me, but I wave it off, distracting her with a tight hug before I send her on her way back home. I watch her walk away into the night and look up at the skyscrapers surrounding the block. The ease of the past hour slips away as I huff, readying myself for the role many expect me to be.

The Big Bad Wolf of the Underground.

CHAPTER 2
BOOM. BOOM. POW

It's fucking freezing for the end of November.

I adjust my jacket and shift uncomfortably in the confinement of the car, wanting to burst from my skin. This is why my ancestors lived off in mountainsides or the hills of Ireland. Cities are too damn small for werewolves, and even being in my humanish-form, this car feels too small. It's been years since I've shifted into my full animal form, and my inner wolf seems a bit loud tonight. I clench my jaw, trying to shove away the wanton feeling. I roll my shoulders and look out the window as we head to DiNardi's club, *4D*.

"You good, boss?" Gunther asks, cautiously eyeing me in the next seat.

"Fine."

He snorts, then cracks his neck. "Could've fooled me."

I growl under my breath, but he only shrugs. The only problem with good betas, they know when you're bluffing.

I catch a glimpse of Marcus driving upfront, his sharp blue eyes quickly returning to the road with our two other cars ahead as we drive through the city, approaching the Bronx zones. Cars were an extra precaution with the movement of police lately. I adjust again, still hating being inside one.

"Wolves will scope the place before you enter," Marcus says, disrupting my thoughts. "Zane's taking lead."

"When did he come up Top?"

"An hour ago. Heard we were knocking on DiNardi's door and wanted to join," Gunther answers.

"Don't need three alphas for this," I mutter.

"Taking all precautions with recent events," Marcus comments.

"Lil sis' concerns rubbing off on you, *Balto*?" I grin wickedly as his gaze darkens at Brenda's nickname for him. The grey alpha wolf hates it. "Yanking your chain, so relax, Marcus. We're all tightly wound, and it's just a fucking nickname."

Marcus snarls low, concentrating on the road again. Gunther snorts under his breath, and I see him hiding a grin. "The day she finds one for you, I'm using it the whole damn time," I tell him.

"She does come up with good ones, a lot like how Cl—" He stops and looks away with a mournful expression. I keep my gaze from Marcus' reflection in the rearview mirror.

In about a month my younger sister, Claudia, would've been turning two hundred, instead, the anniversary of her death recently passed. She and my mother, Cassandra, were murdered twenty-six years ago, but it only feels like months. A gift for being Paranormal is a longer life, although it seems more like a curse with loss. Their deaths left a gaping hole in the McLycan Pack. The emptiness was somewhat filled when Brenda came around, who showed up soon after becoming the "little sister" of the Underground Mafia. She's a wild child like Claudia was.

But she still wasn't Claudia.

I clear my throat, adjusting my weapons as we pull up to *4D*. Marcus grumbles as the other cars park along the block, "Who the fuck names a club that anyways?"

"Humans," Gunther replies as we step out of the SUV.

I glance over at the bright neon lights of the club and look around the area. We're on the cusp of a neutral zone past 2 AM, and there's no sign of Paranormal life. Don't blame them, the zones have been heavily patrolled by PSB. Mob or not, better staying on certain sides of invisible lines. I look at the other wolves checking their weapons as Zane makes eye contact with me. He's a light-grey wolf who flashes his teeth in an excited grin. I glance down at the kilt he's wearing with nothing else. I give him a look, and he shrugs, waving for wolves to follow him before kicking down the club door, prompting people inside to scream as wolves swarm the club.

"Remember you promoted him," Gunther mutters next to me.

"He gets the job done," I answer with a sigh, shivering from the breeze. "Even if he's only in a kilt with these temperatures."

"Because he's nuts, even for a grey wolf," Marcus grumbles. I glimpse at him, and he scowls at me, daring me to comment on his own ancestry.

"Pretty sure, it's cause he hates clothes," Gunther says.

"A wolf who hates clothes, groundbreaking," I say deadpan, shifting my gaze back over the club as metal screeches and more screams sound.

Said wolf who hates clothes, comes out with a nod, and we walk toward 4D. Zane growls at the other wolves to stand by as we enter the neon establishment.

I inhale deeply as cigarettes, cheap alcohol, and coke slams into my nostrils under the pink, red, and blue lights. My stomach churns from the stench as I glance over at the people pressed against the walls and huddled by flipped tables and shattered glasses. Wolves guard every entry, watching the wide-eyed and drenched in fear humans.

I stop in the middle of the dance floor, look around, and find DiNardi in his usual spot in the back VIP section. I flex a singular finger, and Gunther announces, "Just business, so if you're not a worker...go party somewhere else."

Patrons immediately rush for the door, tripping over each other as some of my wolves stop them and check for weapons before letting them go. A few bartenders start to move, but two wolves jump over the counter, blocking the exit as they raise their weapons and snarl.

I walk toward the VIP section, where a few gun-wielding men clad in shabby suits sit beside Antoni DiNardi with a limp cigar in his mouth. The mob boss has red-rimmed eyes, messy black hair, and badly done tattoos down his neck. I inhale again, detecting no silver bullets. He's still got some smarts. Wouldn't know it from the rumpled clothes, and the white powder on his fingertips. I flick my eyes to the rows of white on the glass table and snarl.

Fucking humans and their vices.

I'm kind of glad his father is dead; he'd be disgusted with his son today. I blame Charlie Boston for getting the young mob boss onto drugs.

DiNardi clears his throat, forcing a smile, "McLycan, what a surprise—"

I pull my gun out, shooting the coffee table as it shatters into a million pieces. People scream, and Marcus loosens a growl behind me, silencing everyone as DiNardi's guards shift their weapons. My wolves respond with snarls.

DiNardi tightens his mouth, swallowing hard, and keeps his hands in front of him. I raise a brow, something feeling off as I glance over at the workers behind the bar. "You all just serve drinks?"

One of them in a white tank, splattered in pink, replies, "We on-only work for... for the club—"

"Get the fuck out," I growl. "But if I find out any of you work *personally* with Antoni here, well, we're wolves. We'll hunt you down. Zane." I jut my head toward the exit.

I turn toward DiNardi as Zane ushers them out when a peculiar scent catches my attention. Lavender, citrus, and honey tickle my nostrils and my heart clenches with longing, and I freeze. I glance back at the last group escorted out, but Zane's moved them out already. No one there. I narrow my gaze as my chest floods with emptiness. Odd.

"Boss," Gunther murmurs beside me. I quickly bring myself back to the present. Drugs in the air must be getting to me.

"Now we can talk," I say, turning back to the VIP group.

"What...what is this, McLycan?" DiNardi asks as one of my guards comes up with a cloth bag. "We've always worked well together, whatever you need—"

I yank the bag open and toss Ralph's head onto the glass, his goateed jaw open with wide eyes staring into nothing. DiNardi stares at the head, mouth gaping.

"Remember what I told you? Bring him to *me* if he came

looking for a job," I snarl. "Instead, you sent this fucker through my territories to do *your* dirty work."

"I'd never break our bargain," he argues. "I know better than to touch your territories."

"Sure about that?"

"McLycan, I would never hire him," he pleads, holding his hands up. "After what he did, Ralph wasn't worth—"

"Then why did he say he was delivering to you?" His eyes suddenly go wide, flicking to the bar. I follow his gaze, seeing only the dirtied bar and my wolves keeping their guns trained on his guards. "Got an answer, *Antoni*?"

It looks like all argument is out of him, looking nervously at his guards beside him. My brows pinch slightly, and that feeling of something off worsens. My gut twists, uncertain.

He quickly switches demeanor, standing with a forced cocky demeanor as he adjusts his suit. "He was lying to you, obviously. Ralph played the mobs all the time, did anything for a buck," he says, clearing his throat then flicks his gaze to the bar again. "I'd never cross you, *ever*...I learned that lesson well."

I smirk as my wolves chuckle darkly, remembering how we put him back in his place after a botched attack on the feds' buildings.

"Perhaps this is a private conversation?" he gestures toward the back of the club. He can't think I'm that stupid. "Talk like gentlemen?" Or maybe he does.

I pull out the thumb drive, and his hands freeze over his lapels as I look down at the decapitated head. "Said the delivery hadn't happened, maybe he was lying about that, too," I say in a dark tone.

He pales as all confidence leaves him. "Did...did he show you what's on it?"

"No, should he have?"

"I didn't hire him," he says with a steady tone. "So, I guess we're both curious."

"You know it was curiosity that killed the cat. Not the dog."

His scent shifts into a primal fear, his gaze meeting mine and that's when I notice. They aren't dilated. And although the place reeks of drugs, it's lacking on his breath. There isn't even a hint of alcohol on his breath. He's sober. DiNardi is never sober.

His gaze stays with mine and he says, *"I never hired Ralph."*

I cock my head, unsure what he's playing at, but my gut is telling me to listen. I put the drive back into my pocket, and say, "Maybe that *private* conversation ain't a bad idea."

Marcus snarls low behind me and I hear the click of metal. Something shifts in the air as DiNardi gestures toward the hall again and swallows hard. "We can talk in priv—"

Metal scrapes, a gun pops off, then chaos erupts as bullets fly through the air. My wolves roar and shift into hybrid form to take down the guards shooting at us. Glass shatters as the cacophony of bullets destroys the club. DiNardi yells and pulls out his gun as a guard shoots me in the chest. My body immediately rejects the normal bullet, pushing it out as I growl and shift into hybrid form. My size grows as my body becomes covered in fur; my skull turns into a wolf's head as I charge forward. All hell breaks loose as blood and gunpowder fill the air.

Gunther kills the guard who shot me as I go after DiNardi huddled against a wall. I snarl in his face, pinning him underneath me. He cries under my grip, "You-you were—"

"Were you planning to ambush us?" I bark at him.

"No! N-no…Rodney…listen, they said—"

"Boss!" Zane yells over the chaos. "The club is rigged!"

I glance over, inhaling deeply, and pick up the weak scent. Explosives.

Shit.

I order in Noctora with a thundering growl, *"Everyone out!"*

Zane and Marcus howl in response as my wolves evacuate the club, smashing through windows as they kill the last of the guards. Fear tugs at my spine as DiNardi begs under me, "I did…everything….no—"

For a moment, everything becomes a blur as my chest tightens, lost in the noise as horror writhes inside me. I can almost hear the ticking bombs, remembering her screams over the radio, *"You have to scatter! Get below! Now run!"* Burning flesh fills my nostrils again. Fuck.

"Rodney!" Marcus shouts from the present as DiNardi pleads beneath me. I look down, noticing the crimson that now covers his torso. Move, Rodney. *Get out.*

DiNardi rasps, "They…promised…the deal…"

"Who?"

"Not…I swear…they…*they promised—*"

An explosion pops off in the back of the building, and the walls start to crumble with the ceiling. I look at DiNardi one last time and turn as a loud whistle pitch hits my ears as the explosives start going off. I punch through the unstable brick as the blast rocks the building, rubble blowing past me as I fall out into the smoke-filled street. Gunther grabs me, dragging my ass toward my crew as the building implodes. Heat encases my back as glass pops off and the ground shakes as another explosion rocks the earth.

"Everyone's accounted for!" Zane yells through the mess.

I turn toward the carnage, snarling as I take a deep breath of the familiar napalm. It's mine. Those explosives were *mine.* The missing shipment from weeks ago which Ralph smelled of. Damn it!

Gunther holds my shoulder as I growl in frustration. "Boss, are you—"

"Check for survivors, and bring them to the Underground," I order. "Scavenge anything left for the explosives. I want to know why DiNardi had our shit! Now!"

A cacophony of barks and howls sound off as they set to work under Zane's lead into the smoke. The fire begins to spread toward the other buildings, causing a new wave of screams from people. 4D, what's left of it, burns to a crisp as I talk to Gunther.

"Get everyone in the tunnels before the police show up," I rasp.

"Don't worry, we will," he says as a car pulls up to the curb. My heart thunders in my chest, not able to take my eyes off the fiery blaze. "Boss."

I shake myself and shift back into my human form. My body screams at me, angry at the bruising and heat it's taken on. Old bones my ass.

"Still have that drive?" Gunther asks as he opens the car door. I pull it out, then back into my pocket. "Maybe DiNardi knew it was wiped?"

"From the look on his face, no," I say as I get in, nodding at Marcus behind the wheel. "Either Ralph wiped what DiNardi gave him or he really didn't make it to DiNardi, whatever his side of the exchange was he got rid of."

"Exchanging Information?" Marcus asks. "Like what?"

"Whatever it was," I say, nodding toward the carnage. "It's burning to a crisp with DiNardi."

"We'll look, boss," Gunther says.

"Clear out before the sirens get too close, burned shit ain't worth any of you dying," I instruct, shutting my door.

Marcus peels off down the street as I watch Gunther disappear into the thrall. I glance over myself at the small gashes and dried blood, then check where the bullet hit me, already healing. Silver and I'd be a dead wolf. I'll thank my lucky star later.

"You think DiNardi was hiding something?" Marcus asks.

"Definitely was, but he might have been willing to tell me if someone hadn't shot that damn weapon."

"He didn't give the signal to attack?"

I shake my head, recalling the shock on his face. "He seemed surprised as we were. Guard probably got trigger-happy, which may have saved our asses with finding the explosives in time."

Marcus shakes his head, snarling low as he takes a sharp turn. "Something's not right."

"We're not being targeted," I say automatically, watching his brows furrow.

"Didn't say that."

"Your face did."

He growls again. "Almost blown up by our own explosives? Weeks after they went missing and Ralph smelled of them? You don't think that's a coincidence? Maybe DiNardi was luring us there."

"DiNardi was hiding something, but not that. I don't think he knew they were there."

"How the fuck do—"

"Because of the way he pleaded before he died," I interrupt, rubbing my chest above where the bullet hit. "If you'd seen his eyes, Marcus, you'd see he was betrayed. Those explosives… someone crossed him *and* us."

Marcus goes quiet, turning the car and going down into the Underground as sirens wail behind us in the distance. "Those were the same explosives we used at the center," he mutters.

"Yeah."

"Someone knows it was us."

A piercing sensation slices at my lungs, and I rub at my chest again, stopping when Marcus glances over at me. I watch as we take the ramps down into the Underground, the scenery shifting to familiar stone and brick walls. The lingering scent I caught earlier drifts under my nostrils, causing my jaw to tighten.

Another day in fucking paradise.

CHAPTER 3
WELCOME TO THE UNDERGROUND

I rip my shirt off, glower at the bullet hole and toss it into the trash. I go for a bottle of whiskey as Marcus stops at the doorway, crossing his arms and muttering, "Brenda's a bad influence on you."

"Been drinking long before she was born," I reply, taking a long swig.

We made it to the Underground to *Mountain Edge*, my tavern built into one of the pillars that keep Topside from crumbling above. We're in my office, designed much like the one on Topside. I'm rarely down here, so everything is covered in dust, and the gun rack is mostly empty. The three leather chairs, adding to the woodsy motif, are the only well-looking things here.

"Updates yet?" I ask.

"Gunther and Zane pulled everyone out in time," Marcus replies, checking his phone. "Delilah's updating Skylar and Victoria on taking care of Topside. Police are crawling everywhere with the fire department. No sign of PSB yet."

Makes sense, the club wasn't technically in a neutral zone. "How far did the explosion spread?"

"Almost four blocks."

"Shit. Casualties?"

"None for us, not sure about outsiders, yet."

I glare at the whiskey bottle in my hands. I have my fuck-up moments, but I hate when innocent bystanders get caught in our mob dealings. Paranormal or not, they don't deserve to be dragged into our shit.

"Put the word out for the Pack and the rest of the Wolf Mob to watch their backs," I say. "Stay in the neutral zones. We've got no idea who they may be after next."

"What about the rest of the Underground Mafia? Dracultelli have any issues lately?"

I grunt. "Like I keep up with that bloodsucker."

"You keep up with his Mate." I turn toward Marcus as he glances up, scowling. "And she might be right about shit getting dangerous for all of us." He frowns deeper, and mutters, "Don't tell her I said that."

"Agreeing with your archnemesis, maybe hell froze over," I muse, putting the bottle down.

"We only agree when it comes to your life. Which someone just attempted to take yours."

"Don't know that. Could've been after DiNardi instead. Wrong place, wrong time."

"Fuck that," Marcus snarls and bares his teeth. "*Our* explosives? Rigged the place to rocky mountain high after we found Ralph, leading us to DiNardi? Only shit that adds up is someone was out to kill you."

"Got evidence there, Scooby, or only a hunch? Cause that's all you got."

"We designed those explosives to kill Paranormals and any magic we produce. Making them just in case—"

"I know why, I was with you!" I snap back, yanking my undershirt and pants off. "Don't lecture me."

"Then admit there's more wrong here than just some *coincidence*."

I stop and loosen a long breath. "We can't point fingers unless we have *proof*. Shit is already unstable."

"Then you come Underground." I raise my arms, gesturing at the office, which makes his scowl worsen. "Meaning *stay here*. No Topside until we have answers."

"Can't tell me what to do."

"Stubborn arsehole," he mutters.

"Marcus," I warn as I slam open the closet door.

"I know you, ya fucking gobshite, which means you'll be itching to go back up in a day's time. And get yourself killed fucker."

"Watch it." The growl I emit echoes in the office, and my long-time friend takes a step back. His blue eyes blazing in anger, while I snarl at him.

He's always had my back, since we were pups, ensuring my safety and the McLycan Pack. The anger rises in my chest, almost overwhelming me as I push it down to keep from doing something stupid. It's been a long day, and he's just doing his job, but something primal in me snaps at the insults.

"Don't forget who you're talking to," I warn. "I'll watch my damn back and stay down here, happy?" His brows stay furrowed as he crosses his arms and grunts. "Been a while since you called me that."

"Haven't acted like one."

"Yeah, well, push like that again I may give you scars to match lil sis," I snort, pushing aside old shirts in the closet and Marcus moves toward the door.

He pauses and asks quietly, "She going with you again?"

"Her turn for alcohol," I answer, glancing over my shoulder. "You could come—"

"No." He walks out, slamming the door behind him.

I exhale loudly, leaning against the desk as I stare down at my bloodied nails. I try to shrug off the heavy feeling and go back to the closet, coming face to face with my great kilt. It hangs up much like the Grey Wolf one on Topside, but this is my family's tartan, the McLycan Pack. My grandfather's old kilt. The blue threads mesh with the light gray and deep black between them. The red lines cut through like veins, while the small lines of green give a lasting reminder of Irish hills. The ache in my chest worsens as I trail a finger over the wool.

My mother always wanted to go back to Ireland. She was over six hundred years old when she died, a long life with my father and the mob. And she hated both profusely. Death was probably her freedom. It's what I told myself, anyways. Making the hole not feel as vast.

But Claudia.

Her death festered like old wrath boiling in my gut, each year got easier but then again, it didn't. I grip the tartan, letting go before I tear it to shreds, pulling out pants and a shirt before slamming the closet shut. The heaviness weighs deeper as I remember the shattering glass and the aroma of burning flesh and fur as I grab the whiskey bottle and chug. It barely helps push away the horrible memories.

Too late. I'd been too late and failed.

My memory plays like an awful movie as I try to get dressed, remembering falling to my knees on the charred pavement. The building burned to ash, flames devouring everything as shrieks filled the air, echoing off the broken walls. Gunther yelling for help, pulling me away from the flames as Zane dragged Marcus, keeping him from burning himself alive. It was the last day Marcus had shown any true emotion as he witnessed the death of his Mate, my sister, consumed by fire.

My throat constricts, and I reach for the bottle again to shake away the awful memories. Even after we found the fuckers who'd done it and ripped them apart with most of Queens...it wasn't enough. We had our revenge, but it never helped the pain. It never brought them back.

My hands shake a little, and I take a deep breath, feeling the familiar emptiness. "Just the past," I murmur and finish the bottle. "You've got a Pack to protect. Just like she wanted."

There's a knock at the door, and I finish getting dressed as Gunther peers in. He flicks his gaze to the bar and torn clothes on the ground. "We're all back and found two survivors." Do I thank my lucky star now or later?

"DiNardi's men?"

He steps in and leans against the door, wearing his Pack kilt. "One is. Kind of shaken but kept spitting and calling us slurs."

"Any new ones?"

"Nah, same old with mutt, flea-infested creatures, and beasts. All unoriginal material." He shrugs, grinning a little. A part of me relaxes seeing my head beta at ease, an indication my Pack is safe.

"Said there's two," I say.

"A female, who claims to be a bartender before Zane caught her," he says as we walk out of the office.

Catwalks frame the walls of the building, opening into an atrium over the tavern on the first floor. My office is located on the second with other bedrooms, while the third holds more rooms including my apartment. Pillars hold up each walkway and there's a spiral staircase in the far-right corner. I look over the railing at the bar in the middle of the room, mimicking the layout of the building while tables and chairs are sprawled out. All in cherry wood or walnut, creating a warmer atmosphere than it deserves some nights. Like right now.

I see the two humans, blindfolded and tied up in chairs, surrounded by the Pack from the Underground and a few from Topside. Gunther leans against the railing and I give him a side glance. "Blindfolds?"

"He stopped spitting. And she didn't faint."

"What makes you think she'd faint?"

"They always seem to faint."

"Being cliché and shit," I grumble, rolling my eyes as I make my way down the stairs.

My boots hit the wood hard, which makes all the wolves look and back away as I approach. Zane sneers at the man, backing up toward the bar where my bar manager, Delilah, a black timber wolf with haunting green eyes, stands. Her hair is pulled back into a braid, and she flicks it over her shoulder as I give her a nod, and she leads the staff out back for a 'break.'

Marcus watches the entrance as my wolves circle the survivors. I stop before the humans, looking over the male first, who has patchy light skin with red burns, dark shaggy hair, and a tattered button-up and slacks. I glance at Gunther, who quirks a brow. He might've been one of them in the VIP section.

I take a deep breath, looking for any leftover scent of the explosives, but instead find the intoxicating scent of lavender, citrus, and honey.

My heart thunders in my chest as I bring my attention to the female survivor tied up before me. I move my eyes over her thick thighs covered in ripped jeans, the curve of her stomach partially exposed from the rising hem of her pink-stained white tank top. I steady my breathing and try to keep from staring at her full, ample breasts pushed further out from how she's tied up. My lip curls involuntarily over her being tied up in such a manner, but I school my expression as I continue moving my gaze up. Her mahogany hair falls past her shoulders in waves, contrasting against the pink undertone of her skin.

The tightening in my chest moves down to my groin as I see the sheen of sweat over her light skin, and I tear my gaze away to find Gunther with a look of uncertainty. I gesture for a chair, and someone brings it over as I glance back at the female, my mouth going dry, making me ache to touch her.

What the fuck is wrong with me? No human has ever...

"Take it off," I say roughly toward the male's head, and Zane rips off the blindfold. The man blinks harshly, then looks at me and sneers. He spits, and it lands near my boots. "If I wanted a spit shine, I'd tell you." Some wolves chuckle as I attempt to ignore the female's scent. *Fucking concentrate, Rodney.* "Been told you've been a pain coming down here."

"Go back to the woods where you belong, inbred!"

"Inbred?" I look at the other wolves, all baring their teeth. "You're talking about the wrong species there, fucker."

He spits again, hitting my boot that time. Zane punches him across the jaw while Josh, a beta wolf with dark brown fur and eyes, yanks his head back to look at me. I take my chair, flip it around, sit down, and lean forward on the back.

"It'll take more than your racist shit to offend me. Been around humans like you far too long, but my wolves..." I say, looking around, "...may feel differently. Especially after almost being blown up. Know anything about that?"

The man struggles against Josh's hold. "No."

"What did you do for DiNardi?"

"Dishes." *Cocky humans are* really *pushing my patience tonight. At least it wasn't another dog insult.*

He flicks his gaze around the place, frowning heavily in disgust. "Don't like my place?"

Blood in his teeth shows as he grins. "Looks like a doghouse." Never mind.

I sigh and nod, letting Zane and Josh work him over with a few hits as I pull out my revolver and shoot the man in the foot. He screams, thrashing as Josh yanks his head back again. The female barely flinches, not making a sound apart from rapid breathing, but her scent isn't drenched in fear. Bartender, huh?

"I won't tell you shit mongrel!" The male yells. "Stupid dogs!"

I look over at Gunther, who shrugs. "I mean if he isn't going to help..." he says, crossing his arms, "...might as well *release* him. Finish what we started. Otherwise, he may become my next reason for drinking."

"And mine," Zane mutters. "Yaps louder than a pup."

Josh kicks the bullet-filled foot, and the man screams again. He nods with Zane while the other wolves snicker.

I watch the man yell profanities, then gaze at the female again. I stand up, put my gun away, and walk over. Her chest rises heavily, and the hairs on her skin rise as human nature tells her to run. Barely, I smell fear on her as I stop and tower behind her, leaning forward until my mouth is inches away from her ear. Her intoxicating, torturous aroma tickles my nose, making my breath hitch. Her sharp inhale makes me pause and look closer at the tinged cheeks beneath the blindfold.

"Your friend isn't quite helpful," I whisper, and she shudders. "Between the spitting and yelling, not sure what's worse." She breathes hard, not daring to turn her head. "Would you be willing to help?"

She swallows hard, taking a shaky breath. "Depends on what you need."

"Is that so?" She nods stiffly. "Know anything about the bombs that went off?"

"Maybe."

Amusement dances across my mind at the small defiance. I'll take it over the dog insults. "Maybe?"

"He...Antoni didn't put them there."

"Is that so? Do you know who did?"

"Maybe."

"Maybes aren't going to save you, darling."

"What will?" Her fucking scent, for starters.

I move to the other side of her head. Bringing my mouth barely an inch from her ear, I whisper for her only to hear. "Names."

She shivers again, and asks, "What if I don't know names?"

"What about faces?" For a moment, she doesn't move or say anything as I glance at Gunther. He flicks his gaze to the panting man, held still by Josh's hand. Finally, she nods, and I hum to myself, wondering if it'll be enough.

"Are you going to kill me?"

I flick my gaze to the Pack around me, watching intently before I look back at her, noticing her soft chin.

"I'll make you a deal, darling," I murmur, and her breath hitches as my lips graze over the shell of her ear. "Help me find who blew up your boss, and I'll help keep you alive."

She swallows hard again. "Promise?"

"On my grandfather's grave."

The spitting one thrashes and yells, "Keep your mouth shut, bitch! You fucking snitch! I'll kill you! I'll fucking kill—"

Zane punches him. The female shifts in her seat again and loosens a quick breath. "Deal."

I stand to full height and nod once at the fucker tied up. Josh moves out of the way as Zane pulls out his gun and I place my hands over the female's ears. She jolts at the contact, then flinches when Zane pulls the trigger on the screaming man. Blood splatters across the floor, dripping from the back of the human's head. She shivers as I let go and walk away, my skin thrumming from the touch of her.

"Bring her to my office," I order, moving past everyone. "No one goes Topside until I say so!" I glare at Marcus who glowers back. "Spread the word to every Pack member to watch their backs!"

Growls of obedience echo behind me as I climb the stairs, glancing behind as they start cleaning up the mess. Zane begins to walk the female toward the stairs before Marcus growls to take over. I roll my eyes and nod, gesturing for him to take off the blindfold.

I enter my office and sit on the edge of the desk, crossing my arms as I wait for them. The coiling heat in my gut presses toward my groin. I get up, adjusting myself, and growl, "For fucks sake… she's just a human—"

Marcus knocks and opens the door, moving to reveal the female next to him. Her large earth-brown eyes remind me of the forests of Ireland, and her tinged pink cheeks send another jolt through my body. And I can't seem to stop my eyes from roving down her voluptuous curvy body. My breathing becomes shallow as our eyes meet.

I'm in fucking trouble.

CHAPTER 4
DEAL WITH THE DEVIL

Marcus sits her in the chair, and I give him a nod to leave. He glances between us and quirks a brow and closes the office door behind him.

I bring my attention back to her, finding wide brown eyes as she watches me. Worry lines her scent, but not much fear. Her expression holds an intriguing look of determination on her face. This should be interesting.

"Why don't we start with your name?" I ask, leaning back on my desk.

She clears her throat, hesitating. "Meg."

I raise a brow. "That all?"

She shifts in her seat and glances around the office. "For now."

I suppress the laughter in my chest and walk around my desk to the bar. Her steely attitude is refreshing from other humans, compared to the dead man below. She's not mocking me but being careful.

"Do you know who I am?" I ask nonchalantly.

"Should I?" Movement behind me makes me look back to watch her go still in her seat, then settle back into the chair.

The corner of my mouth moves up as my insides tug at me, pulling me towards this woman. I ignore my body and ask, "Ever hear of the 'Big Bad Wolf' of the Underground?"

"Thought that was a myth."

"What are myths but stories based on history and unexplained events?" I smirk, pouring myself a glass of whiskey. "Nowadays, I usually go by Rodney McLycan."

I turn again and see her gasp as she jolts in her seat looking up from my body and straightens. She grips the seat of her leather chair. She swallows hard, quiet for a few moments as I watch her and she finally whispers, "You're the Wolf Boss, then."

"Uh-huh."

Meg moves her eyes to my desk, while I sip my whiskey. She loosens a sharp breath and looks back at me, asking boldly, "Are you going to kill me?"

I cock my head at her. "Made a deal, darling. You help me, and I keep you alive." And I'm old-fashioned and don't kill females and children outright, but she doesn't need to know that bit. "You drink?"

"I'm a bartender."

"Doesn't mean you drink." She purses her lips. "What's your poison?"

"Anything clear," she answers, and I finally chuckle. "What?"

"Don't expect a mojito or martini…*Meg*," I say, pouring some old vodka into a glass. It's the only clear stuff I have up here.

Her brown eyes narrow, watching me as I walk over and offer the glass, and she carefully accepts it. I return to my desk and watch as she takes a sip, pursing her lips in disgust. The bottle was old and opened for a while. And un-iced.

I smirk, drinking from my glass and placing it on the desk next to me. "Let's discuss the details of our deal then, darling."

"I don't know names, but I do remember faces. I can describe them to you."

I raise a brow. "Do I look like I employ police sketch artists?"

"I'm terrible with drawing if you expect me to."

"And here I was about to pull out the 64-pack," I say, moving to sit in my chair, putting my boots up, and lounging back. "No, you're going to ID everyone we find connected to DiNardi who may have had it out for him. Shouldn't be a long list, he rarely pissed people off."

"You seemed pretty pissed tonight."

My eyes flick to hers, noticing the hardness in her gaze. I ignore her statement, and continue, "You'll tell us if they were at the club the last few weeks. Those bombs couldn't have been there long."

"Less than two weeks," she murmurs, and I pause mid-sip. "We deep clean the bar every three weeks…would've noticed the place was rigged."

I grunt in response. Two weeks' worth of people going in and out of a busy club owned by a mob boss. Odds were slowly going out of my favor.

"Do you have pictures of people?" She asks, and I shake my head. "Video footage or phones?" I shake my head again. "How am I supposed—"

"I bring the fuckers down here, like a good ole' police lineup. Or if they're unlucky, show you their obituary."

Her lips tighten as she stares at her drink, tries another sip, and coughs a little. I keep from smiling as she leans forward to put her glass on my desk. Her breasts push up from the movement, and my hand twitches along with my dick.

Shit, I'm acting like a damn pup. And here I thought explosions killed your libido.

"When you say bring them *here*, do you mean—"

"Here," I answer, pointing at my desk. "In the flesh."

Meg stares at me, her brows pinching together, and her hands rub over her thighs. "How will you know they may be the ones who did it?"

My gaze goes to where her hands move over her jeans, tugging at the material. I down the rest of my drink.

"I have my hunches. Knew DiNardi long enough to know who else he may have pissed off, like me." Her hands stop and she meets my gaze again. "Don't worry about how we find them. You'll be my confirmation or informant; whatever title works for you."

A peculiar emotion flits over her gaze and her jaw clenches. "Should I expect to be at your beck and call? Or will you drag me down here when you need me like the rest?"

I snort. "Oh, you're not leaving."

"What?"

"You heard me."

"You're not…you can't expect me to…I'm not, not some… some—"

"Animal?"

Her cheeks turn red, her eyes widen, and I can now smell a bit more of that fear. Her voice is a rasp, "That's not what I…I…"

I get up and walk around the desk to perch on the edge. "I don't know you, *Meg*, so I can't trust you to not disappear on me."

"I won't."

"Forgive me if your word isn't trustworthy yet."

"I keep my promises."

"So do I," I murmur, keeping her eyes with mine and the fearful scent mingles with the citrus, honey one. "Keeping you alive will be a priority for me unless you go above where DiNardi's crew is, who'll do whatever they want to you when they realize you've talked. Made a deal with me." She gulps and sinks back into her seat as I stand up and lean over her. "Then there's the other mob families, who may want a piece of whatever DiNardi was hiding. And whether you did more work than a bartender or not…you should already know what lengths they'll go to get it."

Meg's breath becomes shallow as her dark eyes stare up into mine, the lingering scent of fear coming back full force. Her natural aroma disappears. Interesting. She's more scared of them than me.

"Whoever that fucker was down there," I continue, now fully intent on scaring her into staying willingly. "He's the least scary of who's out there. Not to mention what would happen if PSB or the FBI got a hold of you. And take it from someone who's been around a long time, *that's* the cruelest fate, cause you'll never have a real life again."

"I'm just a bartender," she whispers. "They won't care."

"Oh, they will. You're all that's left of *4D*, and whether you like it or not, there's no getting out." Tears fill her hard gaze, and my chest tightens as she tries to blink them away. I need her, but she'll need me more if anyone finds her. Whether she knows anything viable or not, they'll tear her apart for *something*.

Then again, what I'm doing doesn't feel that much different.

I push away those feelings as I watch a single tear move down her cheek. I ask softly, "Which will it be, darling? Death, a cell, or Wolf's den?"

Meg loosens a shaky breath and looks around my office again. Her brown gaze comes back to mine, and I almost smile at how she unabashedly is willing to look me in the eye. Finally, she answers, "I'll stay."

"Smart move," I say, standing up fully and taking her discarded glass. "I'll help make sure you see spring arrive in Central Park."

"Am I...staying *here* then?"

"There are other rooms. None of my wolves touch outsiders without my say-so, and if anyone does, you inform me, Marcus, or Gunther." I pour the vodka out and see her furrow her brows. "The grey wolf and the—"

"I remember."

I raise a brow, then smirk. "You have my word; no harm will come to you from my Pack."

She exhales sharply. "And what exactly is your word worth... *McLycan?*"

Now she's mocking me.

My lips curl, and my hackles raise from the tone of her voice as I growl low. "More than any human you've known." Her back straightens as she visibly swallows, not taking her eyes off me. "You made a deal with the Big Bad Wolf to keep you alive, so you better hope it's worth your entire life, darling."

———

THE SCENT OF SANDALWOOD, passionflower, and sex hits my nostrils as I enter *Unbound*, the strip club owned by the Cuorebellas. Vibrant tango music plays under dim, sensual lighting of violets and reds, matched perfectly with the suede seating surrounding four stages displaying pole-dancing strippers. I look up to see Gina, a succubus well-known for her skills and long onyx hair falling over her deep maroon skin, exposing her ample breasts as she dances.

The pheromones heighten in the club as people cheer as she reaches the pole and spins with her legs out. As she does a move with her hanging upside down, she finds my gaze, trailing her tongue across her bottom lip. I chuckle to myself at the tantalizing Paranormal, give her a nod, and walk toward the back of the club. I told Gunther I was meeting Joey alone and would be back late. He grumbled more when I told him to call Vincent about the development on Topside. Besides I wanted this conversation to be private, even in a strip club filled with patrons and dancers.

This one was different from others, owned by an incubus mafia family who prided themselves in providing an open club that regulates emotions and pheromones for the safety of the workers and patrons alike. A centuries-old goal achieved by the ex-mafia boss, Alanzo Cuorebella, the most powerful incubus in the country and Brenda's adoptive father.

I sit on a couch and watch the main stage, noticing something above it that makes me snarl. "You gotta be fucking kidding me."

"Hung them up three days ago," Joey's voice comes from behind.

I turn to see the mischievous smile on the incubus' face, his violet eyes glowing against his dark maroon skin. Joey Cuorebella, the oldest of the siblings, is the spitting image of his father with black moused hair and short horns protruding through. He's wearing an open black satin button-up to show his chest.

He nods towards the dark boxer briefs hanging next to Brenda's underwear as he joins me. "He lost a bet to baby sis. Ma was elated to have another pair up there."

"That vampire hasn't been a virgin in centuries," I grumble. A server comes by handing me a whiskey, and I give her a half smile as she leaves.

"More for a 'welcome to the family' kind of blessing. Should've seen the party for it, maybe baby sis can give you details." He leans back, sipping his drink as the music thrums under pulsating lights. "Speaking of, she had brunch with you earlier, aren't you supposed to be Topside?"

"Shit came up."

"Such as?"

I knock back my drink. "Hear about the bombing?"

"Yeah, feds have been crawling all over the Bronx again and now into Manhattan. Heard it was just the human mobs."

"Mostly...but DiNardi's dead." Joey freezes, and his laid-back attitude disappears. "It was his club that blew up."

"And how do you know that?"

"Because I was there when it blew up...well, got out before it did." I feel his powers tickle over me like smooth leather and honey whiskey. "Pack is fine, and so am I."

"Oh well, then excuse me for worrying about you almost *dying*."

I glower at him. "You chastise lil sis after she almost got—?"

"Yes, and Pops grounded her for a month."

Joey's violet eyes search mine as I shut down my emotions, cutting him off from sensing them. Except, in the back of my mind, I hear the bombs and screams over the radio from that night at the center.

She's fine. As Joey said, she came home and was grounded. Perfectly fine.

"I didn't come here to get a vibe check," I say roughly. "I'm telling you this because the explosives used were from a missing shipment of mine from a few weeks ago."

"Yours?"

"Thought it was just some punks or con guys wanting leverage. We were wrong."

He furrows his brows as the server comes back, but I shake my head, putting my empty glass down. She looks at Joey who nods and gives a quick smile. Once she's gone, he asks, "Was it an attempt on your life?"

"You sound like Marcus."

"You almost get blown up at a *human* mob club, and you don't think it was an attempt? It was even your explosives."

"Doesn't mean it was meant for me."

"Yet here you are sitting in my father's club telling me *personally* about it. Choose a damn lane." Joey scoffs as the server comes back, serving his drink. He kisses her cheek, thanking her as she winks, then walks away. "You only come to those outside the Wolf Mob when you think it goes outside your borders, and this time, you confide in me. I'm touched."

"Closest thing we got to an HR rep."

"No, that's Gina's job."

I look over at the succubus who's doing the spread eagle. "Maybe next time," I answer, and he scoffs again, leaning back. "I thought you were the best to share the news with."

"Or you don't want my Pops, Beckham, or Vincent to know, which tells me...you *do* think something is wrong besides a human mob boss being dead." He smirks, sipping his drink. "If it was another 'darn these humans,' I'd have only gotten a phone call. Again, pick your lane."

"Maybe I didn't need Vincent telling me 'all dogs go to heaven.' Not all of us have patience for him," I mutter, glancing at Lola, a younger succubus with light pink skin and black hair with blue streaks twirling around a pole. She sees me and wiggles her ass before going toward a patron holding out tips.

I haven't gotten a rise from her or Gina like I usually do. This long in the pheromone-induced club, my dick would be saluting them. Today must be really getting to me.

"Distracted?" Joey asks.

I turn back to him, shutting my emotions off again as he eyes me. The cocky incubus' powers have become almost as precise as his father's in detecting certain emotions. I may be able to sniff out fear or arousal, but incubi and succubi become walking lie detectors if taught well.

"This stays between us for now. I don't want to cause a scare," I say in a low tone. He narrows his gaze, leans back, and waves for me to continue. I don't remember being this smug or cocky at a hundred like him. "They were the explosive types we used on the center for Traloski."

A spark of cold steel hits my nostrils, making me tense. "And you're thick enough to not think it was an assassination attempt?" I scowl at him. "Why didn't you say anything when the explosives first went missing?"

"Were you initiated into the Pack without me knowing?"

"Don't play that card with me, otherwise I could ask if you told baby sis," he counters, and I growl at him. "Thought so." He knocks back the rest of his drink, letting out a hiss. "Who knew it was us?"

"Supposedly only the Underground Mafia," I say, crossing my arms. "That's why I don't think it was an assassination attempt, just a warning. Someone sending a message that they know." Or DiNardi made a deal with the wrong devil.

"Freyja?" Cue the wrong devil.

My thoughts flit back to seeing those angry green eyes while blood trickled down my face, and the glint of silver on her hands. My throat constricts remembering those tear-stained eyes, and regret fills me. "She's conniving, but not dumb enough to outwardly kill me."

"Maybe DiNardi knew, planted them, but didn't get out in time."

"He didn't know," I say, shaking my head as he raises a brow. "If you were there, you'd agree. It had to be whoever he was working with or thought he could trust."

"So, another mob family?" I shrug, and he rolls his eyes. "Well, aren't I glad you came to me with this valuable information? Next time I'll stick with the gossip column."

A growl forms in my chest. "All I know is that someone used *my* explosives to blow up 4D, almost killing me and my Pack, but they did succeed in killing DiNardi. It could've been just for him, and we got caught in the mix, but I'm gonna find out who took my damn napalm. Until then, thought I'd be nice in giving you the heads up to watch your damn back. The kind of courtesy I learned from *your* father."

I get up, walking away with a snarl. No sense of relief I'd hoped to get here finds me, and I'm prickly more than I was before. I reach the door, but Joey stops me and gestures for the main bouncer to walk away. His violet eyes flash, and he whispers, "Fine, thanks for the heads up."

"You're welcome."

"Here's what I don't get no matter who took those bombs, they still planted them in DiNardi's club. Who the fuck would want him dead?"

"Don't know yet, but that's where the rag-tag group of teenagers will come in."

Joey smirks. "Baby sis' comebacks are rubbing off on you."

My jaw tenses and I flex my hands. "Don't tell her about the bombing."

"She's gonna find out."

"Don't care. Do *not* tell her what happened."

"I'm her brother, she'd want to know if something happened to you."

"Nothing did. Got out. No Pack member was killed either."

"Rodney—"

"Don't," I growl as he scowls at me.

Suddenly, he gives me a wicked grin and holds his hands up. "Fine," he says. "But when she comes to shoot your ass, don't blame me I tried to warn you. In fact, take pictures."

"I'll handle her, always have."

He snorts. "Just be careful, 'cause if you upset her…you'll have her territorial Mate to deal with, too."

"Don't remind me," I mutter, leaving the club and inhaling the outside air. I glance up at the club's neon sign, contrasting against the warm flickering lights of the Underground which illuminate the brick of the city beneath. A part of me wishes Alanzo was still the boss, not that Joey wasn't good at it, but his father always seemed to know what to say. Always had advice that helped. I stare up at the fake stars and loneliness fills me as I gaze upon the night here.

"Heavy is the one who wears the crown," I mutter, and I start walking back to *Mountain Edge.* "And lonely is the devil who walks the streets of hell."

CHAPTER 5
EMPIRE OF CHARCOAL

Mountain Edge is dimly lit and quiet for the night, a relief after the last twelve hours. I climb the spiral staircase to the third floor when a door opens. Meg carefully peeks her head out, her dark hair falling over her shoulders. I stay in the shadows, curiously watching as she starts checking doors and pulling at their door-knobs. Each one remains shut until she reaches my unlocked apartment door. I rarely lock it because no one's either brave or dumb enough to go in. Not sure which category she falls into, yet.

I cross my arms as she peers in and call out, "Narnia isn't that way."

She jumps and covers her mouth as a small yelp escapes before stumbling back against the rail. She spins to face me, gulping down breaths. "I-I wasn't...I'm not...I-I was looking for...for—"

"Bathroom?" I step out of the shadows, and her gaze widens.

"No."

"Glass of warm milk then?"

The wide eyes disappear as she purses her lips, then quickly straightens herself. "No. And you're not as funny as you think you are."

"It was pretty funny. Almost as much as how far you jumped."

"You startled me."

"I was out in the open."

"In the shadows."

"Not my fault you have human eyes," I retort, approaching her. "Or that you were distracted with sneaking around."

"I wasn't…sneaking around," she says, crossing her arms. I quirk a brow as I stop a few feet from her. "I *wasn't*. Just couldn't sleep."

"Need a bedtime story?" She glowers. "Maybe another time, but you'll have to get used to the time change."

"What if I'm not down here that long?"

"Then consider it jetlag." I take another step forward, but she doesn't move as I crowd her space. She tilts her head back, staring at me with pinched brows. I glimpse at her hair, and then move my gaze down to notice she's still wearing the clothes she arrived with. "Didn't like the pajamas you got?"

"What?"

I gesture to her tank top. "Or do you prefer dirty bar clothes over clean sleepwear?"

She looks down at herself. "I didn't get any."

"What?" My head snaps down to glare at the bar. Delilah and Gunther should've known better. I grumble under my breath, "Stay here."

"Why—"

I lightly growl and she closes her mouth, pressing against the railing to stay put. I walk into my apartment, enter my bedroom, and look through my dresser and closet for something that will have to do. And maybe, just *maybe*, a part of me wants to mark her, but I ignore that odd nagging at the back of my mind. I pull out some flannels, shirts, and lounge pants; all clothing I usually wear in my hybrid form. I'm already a large wolf, tall and burly even in human form, so these should fit her fine. And better than ripped clothes.

I take it all out to the catwalk, where she still stands. Good to know she can take instructions sometimes. I hide my smile and hold the clothes out to her, which she just stares at. A minute ticks by and another, and slowly the last of my patience begins to wear thin.

"They don't have fleas."

"I wasn't thinking that!" She exclaims under her breath. "I

would ...never would I—"

"I was joking."

Confusion flits over her face and she admits, "It's just...those are your clothes."

"And?" I cock my head at her. Please tell me she doesn't know about werewolf courting.

"I don't exactly wear other people's clothes." Crisis missed.

"Does it offend you wearing mine?"

"What? No."

"Then you prefer looking like something the rats dragged in?" She gapes at me in horror, looking down at herself. Okay, not helping my argument. "None of that can be comfortable, let alone sleep in."

She clears her throat and adjusts her tank top until she finds a hole. And then another. Meg sighs, closing her eyes tight. Almost reluctantly, she holds her hands out in defeat. I place the clothes in her arms. My hand brushes against hers. Something jolts down my spine as I straighten and clear my throat.

I need a stiff drink and someone to knock my ass out with a baseball bat.

"You sure these will fit?" She murmurs, looking over the pants.

"The pants will be long. I'm usually taller in my hybrid form, but the shirts should fit more comfortably. The pants stretch."

"Hybrid form?" She asks, glancing over me briefly. "Isn't that this?"

"No," I answer, gesturing at my nose. "I'll have a longer snout."

"Oh," she hums and flicks her gaze down my front. I smirk, noticing how she lingers. "I heard *this* was your hybrid form."

"Second lesson of the Underground, darling; forget everything Topside humans have told you about Paranormals."

"What's the first?"

"Do everything I say, like staying on this landing at night for your safety. No matter how restless you get," I whisper as I cock my head at her. "Need anything, you knock on my door first."

She frowns. "I thought you guaranteed my safety, what happened to that word of yours, McLycan?"

I find some amusement speaking with her, but she sometimes

pushes too far. I wouldn't consider myself having a fragile ego, but I don't like having my integrity on the chopping block. My lips curl as I lean forward until her face is inches from mine.

"I keep my promises, darling. But I won't pretend my wolves aren't trigger-happy after the past twenty-four hours. If they see you as a threat, they'll take their job very, *very* seriously. Loyalty is imperative down here with me." Her jaw clenches. "My word is my word."

"So just...trust you?" Her dark brown eyes search my face.

Keeping the distance close between us, I whisper, "I may be an animal to some, but I have better morals than most humans. Remember that."

Her gaze softens, her shoulders dropping. "Noted."

I breathe in her citrus and lavender scent, my hands flexing at my sides as her earth-brown eyes don't waver from mine. "This is the part where you do as you're told and go to bed, darling."

Meg clears her throat as she straightens and holds her head a bit higher. "You need to move."

I step to the side, allowing her to walk past me toward her door. She pauses before disappearing inside with the lock clicking shut.

She's got balls, I'll give her that. But something's telling me she's hiding more than she shows. I shake it off and head into my apartment, keeping the door unlocked.

My apartment takes up most of the third floor, wrapping around like the perimeter. The living room contains a small bar area, a couch and chairs, and an old table. On the left are my kitchen and main bathroom, and to the right are my bedroom space and studio. Open floorplan, apart from the studio hidden behind a locked door. I strip off my shirt, guns, and knives and toss them onto the bed as I head to the bar. I pour myself a glass of brandy and sit on the chair next to the round window overlooking the Underground.

Nothing is reminiscent of Topside like neon lights and billboards. The colored reds and blue lights are soft instead, glowing. I've spent so much time lately up Top, it's odd seeing the calm Underground. Quiet.

I pull my phone out. No messages.

I toss it aside. Don't know why I'm checking. If anything, my father would just start complaining about the shit job I'm doing as boss rather than making sure I'm alive.

The brandy is smooth as I take a sip, remembering those hard lessons from my father decades past. He had priorities, and they only consisted of the Pack or the Wolf Mob. It's why he showed up for that Mafia Head meeting months ago, but then again, Bruno called it. My father, Fredrick, usually stayed further north. Honestly, the more time passes, the more I preferred it that way.

A yearning grows in my chest as a memory drifts forward.

CLAUDIA LEANS BACK against the window, holding her glass of rosé to her lips. Her dark brown hair, braided down her back, contrasts with her bright green eyes. Just like mine. We look like our mother.

Her expression is soft as she looks over at me. "It'll go better next time."

"You say that every time," I say, finishing my drink. I reach for the bottle, but she swipes it from me. I groan and lean my head back. "It's been a long day, Claw, let me have this."

"You've already had half the bottle," she argues, hiding it behind her. "You can day drink tomorrow."

"Always the worrier."

"Someone needs to," she murmurs, gazing out the window.

I sigh and sit on the windowsill next to her. My hand falls into hers, gripping it tight. This has become our weekly tradition: sit, drink, talk, and act like she's not turning 200 soon. My little sister is growing up.

"I know you're gonna be the best boss," she says. "But I still worry you'll keep trying to impress dad and just…get yourself hurt."

"At this point, I doubt he'll ever hand over the title. So, you got nothing to worry about."

"Rod, you're already a great leader and the whole Pack trusts you. Dad would be insane not giving the title over officially."

I look up at the sparkling lights outside. "They believe in Marcus, too."

Claw laughs lightly. "Except my Mate doesn't have the…skills to communicate well with others. Encouragement is not in his wheelhouse. He'll always be the scary brooding one. Perfect side-kick alpha."

"That works for being boss." *It does for dad.*

"Not if the Pack is scared of you. Fear doesn't lead a community; compassion and fairness do. Loyalty. Pack before Mob." She raises her fist like grandpappy would. "McLycans stand tall!"

"And Pack is Pack," I whisper, and she grins at me. "I'd give Marcus the position if he asked."

She shakes her head, still grinning. "He'd never. He believes you were made for it. Even if you don't have faith in yourself yet. He's got your back."

"You're just saying all this 'cause you don't want Marcus as boss. Want him all to yourself."

"I won't pretend I have my own motives," she giggles behind her glass and lightly shoves my shoulder. "Everyone has faith in you because you've already shown what you're willing to do to protect them. They know that. You can delegate, you care, you're not controlling like…well…"

"Dad."

She sighs, staring at her glass. "He's just stuck in his old ways. Old New York before the agencies—"

"And keeping mom here," I mutter. Claudia sighs, finishing her glass. "You know I'm right."

"If mom didn't love dad, she'd leave. We both know that."

"I know mom doesn't hate it here that much, but…" I exhale harshly, take her empty glass to the bar then adjust my kilt.

"Well, you'll be boss before we know it, and I'll be there to tell you 'I told you so' at least twelve times a day for centuries."

"Just cause you're younger doesn't mean you're right," I say, washing her glass and then setting it on the shelf with the others.

"I was in naming the tavern," she argues playfully. "Including that we should decorate it without empty bottles, as classic as it is."

"Fine, I'll put flowers in them." We laugh. "No touching my apartment."

She scoffs, heading for the door, and gestures around the space. "I've given up trying to change your Clint Eastwood obsession a while ago, your place is safe from me," she says, looking over her shoulder. "For now."

"Go downstairs to your Mate before I give him a job tonight, just to spite you."

She gives me a wicked grin. "Want me to put a sock on our door?"

"I'm telling him you said that."

Claw laughs loudly. "If you hear howling—"

"Don't you dare finish that."

Her laughter disappears through the door as it closes behind her.

TEARS FALL DOWN MY FACE. I wipe them away as I stare at the dusty wine glasses, untouched for almost thirty years. My throat tightens at the empty void in my chest.

I put the brandy away and look at my phone on the dresser. I start dialing lil sis' number but stop myself. The sounds of glass shattering and screaming echo in my head as I feel the heat on my hands and back, memories merging.

"This place isn't falling into anyone's hands! Scatter—!"

"Claudia!"

"Boss! The place is rigged!"

"Lil sis, no—!"

"Claw!"

My chest aches and I drop the phone as I clutch the dresser's edge. Shit. I shudder and decide not to call her. If I do, I'll have to tell her what happened. Just thinking about it makes my hands shake.

"I'll tell her...later," I rasp, rubbing my head as I walk through my bedroom to the studio.

I open the door, walking into the sea of parchment pinned up on the walls filled with faces from the past. I clip a new piece of paper to the top of my easel, grab a piece of charcoal from the messy pile, and sit before the blank canvas. I close my eyes, taking a long breath before I quietly sketch out her face from memory.

The lonely hours tick by as I draw her looking back at me, forcing the hurt to disappear in silence. I draw the memories, trying not to forget the young eyes looking back at me with hope. The only light is the twinkling lamps of the Underground, finding some solace in the quiet.

[illegible]

CHAPTER 6
TRUE WEREWOLF GRIT

Zane props his elbow on the railing outside my apartment as I drink my coffee. I stifle the moan at the back of my throat, regretting staying up late. He smiles at me. "Rough night?"

"Almost getting blown up should warrant it," I mutter, leaning forward on the railing.

"Want cuddles tonight?" I glare at him as he gives me a feral grin. "What? Thought maybe you miss me in your bed."

"Haven't for fifty years, and don't make me regret not castrating you."

"I'm a stellar ex and the best *hound* in finding you shit," he retorts. I glare at my coffee, wishing it was stronger. Maybe Delilah will let me chew on the coffee beans instead.

"Not going to open that box, but what did you find?"

Zane's eyes scream delight, warning me of his usual mischief. He's wearing his Grey Wolf tartan today, the great kilt swept over his shoulder with nothing else besides his boots. "Boston's on the move. Seems he and O'Reilly are scared they may be next on the bombing list."

"Any word on survivors?"

"Apart from the patrons who ran out? Nah, but some did cause trouble. Took care of it."

"Get me pictures of every single one. Any of them DiNardi's crew?" I ask, downing half my coffee.

"Nope. Burned with DiNardi and the rest. Only ones left would be runners or bottom of the pyramid as it were."

"Find and grab them. I don't care if they once washed his car or some shit."

"Got it, boss," he says, looking toward the bedroom Meg's staying in. "Really keeping her down here?"

"She's the only one alive who might've seen who placed those bombs, which includes who stole them. And not spit in our faces." Zane raises a brow. "Long as I don't leave her alone with you."

"There go my evening plans," he says deadpan.

I roll my eyes, finishing my coffee. "And I promised I'd keep her alive."

"Well, aren't you a softie?"

I glare at him, and he winks. "I haven't had enough coffee to deal with you."

"I gave you a cup."

"Exactly."

"That hurts."

"Boo-hoo."

"Can you not annoy him before we even have breakfast?" Gunther asks as he comes up the stairs. He's wearing his kilt, but it's the Pack one, and at least he's wearing a shirt.

"Hey, I'm updating him like the good alpha that I am," Zane replies.

Gunther juts a thumb at Zane, frowning at me. "Tell me again why you agreed to that?"

"I'm cute." Zane grins.

"Do you want him being a beta?" I ask, and Gunther glances at the smirking grey wolf and grimaces. "I rest my case."

Gunther glares at Zane, who winks at us, jumps over the railing, and lands on the first floor. He calls out to Delilah to make more coffee. I grin, somewhat missing his chaotic energy. He's in charge of taking care of the Underground portion of the Pack and the Mob. Since I've mostly been Topside these past years, I haven't seen him as regularly as I used to.

"I still don't know how you dated him," Gunther mutters.

"Trying to be his next partner? I could give you some tips," I smirk, and Gunther gives me an exasperated look. "Honestly, because—"

"Please don't," he pleads, pressing his fingers against his temple.

"Sounds like you could use coffee, too."

"More like a valium." I raise my brows, and he sighs. "Phone call with Vincent last night was lovely, by the way." I snort, not all sorry for having him talk with the vamp. "But the highlight of my evening was being berated by your father for thirty minutes."

I freeze. "He called you?"

"Yeah," he huffs. "Angry that we instructed the Pack to watch our backs and stay below. And something about being pups."

"Pack before Mob. Not endangering them."

He goes silent and looks down at the bar, then down the catwalk. "So, this Meg—"

"Any reason why she didn't get new clothes?" I stand fully and cross my arms. "And my gut tells me she didn't get food either."

Gunther holds his hands up. "Hey, Delilah showed her the room, not me. Delilah said she locked it and wouldn't come out, and I wasn't about to force her. Don't blame her for not trusting-… hold on, how'd you know that?"

"Caught her walking around," I say.

Gunther looks past me as a door opens, and I look over my shoulder to see Meg peek out wearing one of my flannel shirts. His hazel eyes narrow on me. "Rodney, I swear—"

"Nothing happened," I hiss. "I can keep my dick in my pants."

"I'd rather you slept with her," Gunther whispers harshly as I look back to see her slowly approach. "Instead, you gave her your *clothes?*"

"Keep your trap shut." I can hear her come closer and switch to Noctora. Fingers crossed she doesn't know the language. "*She was covered in grime and alcohol, what was I supposed to—*"

"*Get clothes from the linen closet.*"

Meg's footsteps stop, and I glance back to see her straighten, holding herself close as she watches us carefully. She's wearing her jeans, but with the flannel, my scent lightly mingles with hers.

Gunther groans, "*Zane and Delilah are gonna have a field day with this.*"

"*Calm down, it wasn't my fucking kilt or tartan I offered.*"

"*No, you just marked her as yours.*"

"*I was trying to be nice.*"

Meg clears her throat behind me. Gunther flicks his gaze toward her. She asks quietly, "Excuse me…is something wrong?"

"No, just wolves being nosy," I mutter, turning toward her. "You look more comfortable than you did last night."

She looks down at her herself, meets my gaze, and folds her arms over her chest. "I am." I raise my brow. We stare at the other for a few beats and she sighs. "Thank you."

"You're welcome, darling."

I glance back at Gunther, who's flashing his eyes between us. I glare at him, and he takes a step back as I ask her, "You hungry?"

"Do I have to make a deal for it or just beg?" Suddenly, Gunther growls behind me and Meg's eyes go wide. Her face pales, and she quickly adds, "That's not…not what I meant, just yesterday—"

"Ignore him, he hasn't had coffee," I say, gesturing for her to follow me. At first, she doesn't, but quickly skims past Gunther and comes up directly behind me as we head down the stairs. "Remember what I said, you're not a threat, but don't push them."

"Uh-huh."

I stop briefly and find her at eye level with me from the stairs. Her brown eyes are wide, and that hint of fear lingers with her aroma. I'm not sure if I should ease her fears. Tell her that Gunther and the others down here would never touch a female without permission. Or have her willingly help more out of fear of being torn apart by wolves. Usually, I'd stick with the scary persona, but I'm finding it harder each second with her; hasn't even been 24 hours yet.

"He's had a long night," I say finally.

"Him and me both," she whispers. "You know…jetlag."

"Got plenty of coffee," I smirk, continuing back down.

When we approach the first floor, she asks quietly, "What language were you speaking?"

"Noctora, the Paranormal language."

"Sounds lovely." My steps falter a moment, realizing she's genuinely intrigued.

We go through the tavern's back swinging doors to the dining area. Booths line the walls, and tables spread out toward the back-room with a large table where my main alphas, betas, and family eat. I pull out a chair near the head of the table and gesture for Meg to sit. She pauses before taking her seat next to mine, keeping her hands in her lap.

"Really like the John Wayne motif, huh?" She asks, looking at the wood paneling.

"Wolves aren't meant to be in cities."

"Then, why live here?"

Delilah comes in and flicks a gaze between us as she sets the coffee down. "Heard you needed more."

"Thanks," I say, filling our mugs as Delilah leaves. Josh comes in, puts food down, and heads out as Gunther meets him at the doorway, pulling him aside. "Real world doesn't give a shit about what's supposed to be or not," I finally answer her.

I clink my mug with hers, and she picks hers up carefully. "So… you're stuck here, too." Her voice is barely a whisper, and I look over as she sips her coffee, grimacing at the dark roast.

I drag over the sugar bowl and creamer, putting them in front of her as she looks over at me softly. For the first time since she arrived, a small smile rises on her face. My chest tightens, stealing my breath almost.

"Boss!" Edward, the young tawny werewolf, rushes in with alarm. "Fredrick's here, and he's pissed."

Fuck. I get up and Meg begins to follow, but halts when I growl, "Stay."

She remains seated as I head out with Edward close behind. Like Gunther and Josh, Edward's one of my main betas, who meets me at the double doors. We walk out into the tavern to find Delilah scowling at my father.

He's a shorter deep grey wolf with dark, judgmental brown eyes that look at the tavern in disdain. Like me he's got broad shoulders, but a thicker middle from age and more silver in his hair. He wears his Pack kilt, glares at my jeans and button-up with disgust, and says, "This place looks like a shit hole."

Delilah grunts under her breath, and I step in front of the rest of the growly wolves. "Haven't seen or heard from you since the meeting," I state. "I'm guessing you must be busy up north. Run out of females?"

His gaze darkens as he stalks towards me, trying to challenge my presence. Yeah, that tactic hasn't worked in over sixty years.

"You're *ruining* this Pack! What right do you have to tell anyone—"

"If you haven't heard, some of us were about to be six feet lower than the Underground. *That* validates my decision to protect the Pack."

"By making the Wolf Mob look weak! You're getting fucking soft from being on Topside too long."

I snarl, ignoring the old hurt as he chastises me. "Unless you're here to check on the Pack or even your own son, go back up north."

"And let you destroy my reputation? You'll make us the laughingstock—" He stops and sniffs the air. He levels his gaze, bringing his face inches from mine. "*Why* do I smell human?"

I won't budge, even as I feel the heat of his breath along my cheek and his nicotine stench. "*Mountain Edge* is a haven to *anyone*, including humans."

"You're helping a—"

"She's helping *us*," I say as he growls in my face. "Unlike you, she's here to help."

He cackles maliciously and something in my chest cracks when he speaks, "Help? You've sunk so low to ask a mere human's help? And what help can she be when *you're* involved? There'll be causalities for sure."

My stomach drops as he steps around me as my throat goes dry. Fucking bastard. I go to stop him, but Gunther and Josh stand in his way at the doorway. Both flick their gaze at me, and I shake my head once.

"Let me through, *beta*," my father warns them.

"Not letting you touch her," Josh says.

"She doesn't belong here."

"Doesn't matter what you think, not the boss anymore, Fredrick," Gunther argues.

"And the *boss* says she stays," Josh snarls.

"I may not be the boss anymore, but I'm still a damn alpha in this Pack," Fredrick warns, stepping forward and snarling at them with command. *"Move aside."*

"And I'm the *head* alpha of the Pack," I state. "She's been promised my protection from any threat, which includes you."

My father eyes me. "And when have you ever been good enough at keeping beings alive?" Guilt gnaws at my heart as I picture closing Claudia's tomb. "You'll get her killed just like—"

"Enough," Marcus snarls, slamming through the doors. I catch a glimpse of Meg through the swinging doors, ducking behind Edward. Delilah and Zane join Marcus at the doorway, moving the betas aside.

Fredrick takes one step before Delilah bares her teeth and her claws punch out. "No touching," she warns.

"Pack law is Pack law," Marcus warns in Noctora. *"No harming females or children."*

"She's human," my father growls.

"Still female."

"And will you keep this one alive, then?"

Marcus and Zane shift into hybrid form, snarling as they bite at Fredrick with challenge. They're direct Irish Grey Wolf descendants, larger than anyone else in the Pack. Marcus towers over Fredrick and his jaws open to reveal his long canines to the ex-boss.

Fredrick looks us all in disgust as my Pack takes up defensive positions. The hurt fades as I watch in pride of the loyalty I've garnered over the past few decades. All of them willing to stand against my father. He sneers at the three alphas before him and turns away finally.

"You're a disgrace," he spits at me. "Your decisions will destroy everything and take you down with it. I won't be surprised when she betrays you and there's more blood on your hands, including hers."

Marcus and Zane shift back as my father leaves, slamming the door behind him. Delilah grumbles with a light warning, "No one else better diss this place or no breakfast for you."

"It's cleaner than the bloodsucker's main stead," Josh mumbles. "Hell, our showers are better." A few of the wolves chuckle, the heaviness in the air lightening.

"Get back to whatever you were doing," I say heading toward the dining area. My appetite is officially gone, but I still need caffeine. There're some murmurs of confirmation behind me as I find Meg in her seat with Edward in his. I take mine with Marcus on the other side of Meg, Gunther next to me, then Josh, Delilah, and Zane.

"I'm starving," Zane says, sitting down and grabbing the platter of pancakes.

"It's what you get for shifting," Delilah comments, taking the bacon and passing it onto a few other plates. Everyone follows suit as I rub my forehead and look at the clock. Fucking hell, it's not even 9 yet. I snatch my coffee mug and down the contents.

Gunther pours me more coffee as I catch a glimpse of Meg watching me carefully. He shakes his head and says, "If I'd known he was coming—"

"Not your fault," I grumble, stabbing at my bacon. "Let's just forget it happened."

The table is quiet until small conversations begin, making the room buzz, but Meg quietly plays with her food. Once again, I'm unsure what to say. I need her to trust us, open up and be honest, but after hearing my father yell like that...I'm surprised she's not cowering in a corner.

I keep thinking of *something* to say, but Marcus surprisingly speaks gruffly, "You've barely been around Paranormals, haven't you?"

She pauses and looks at me. She then slowly turns toward Marcus. "I...I grew up in a human town and spent most of my time in New York in...non-neutral zones."

"When'd you move?" I see Gunther frozen with a fork just before his mouth in shock. Zane blinks and looks over at Delilah in confusion.

"A few years back, but uh, I met my first Paranormal soon after."

"What species?"

Delilah flits her eyes to Marcus and back to me. Josh mumbles something to Edward, who shrugs as Zane leans back with his mug and observes like he's Sophia from *Golden Girls*.

"Incubus," she answers, sipping her coffee and watching Marcus curiously. He's listening and talking like he does this on a daily basis. He doesn't even talk during meals with *us*. "I'd been taught to stay away growing up," she says softly, and he nods in interest. "But I've met more in passing, just never…uh, talked."

He grunts, and bluntly asks, "How old are you?"

Gunther drops his fork, Delilah facepalms, and Zane snickers behind his mug. I scowl at Zane and his grin gets bigger. Glad he's enjoying this, while I'm confused about my own personal episode of the *Twilight Zone*.

Meg looks at me with uncertainty. I clear my throat, and say, "Marcus…"

He huffs at me and says, "It's a legitimate question. None of us here are under a hundred anyway. When has age ever mattered to us?"

Meg's eyes go wide, moving her gaze down my chest and back up. I smirk at her reaction. She blinks quickly and looks around the table. "None…none of you, I mean…wait, you all look…what?"

"We reach puberty same timeframe as humans, but then aging slows," Zane says with a wink.

"You haven't answered my question," Marcus mumbles over his food.

Gunther sighs heavily as Meg shifts in her seat and whispers, "Thirty-two."

Marcus looks at her briefly and shrugs. "So, still pretty young."

"Comparably to a Paranormal?"

"To anyone," he says.

I find Delilah smiling as I sit in shock over what's just happened. Meg is talking, even after my father's little interruption, and Marcus is talking. He's talking…to a *human*…*without* growling.

Huh, miracles can happen.

[illegible] her eyes to circle and back to me [illegible]
something to Tara and whispering [illegible] Zane leans back
[illegible] and observes like he's Studite in the Colosseum.

"Marcus?" she asks, wiping her coffee [illegible]
[illegible] He's sweating and talking like he's just
[illegible] you talk during meals, you are [illegible] I been
[illegible]

He grins quickly and replies, [illegible]
[illegible]
[illegible]
[illegible] of the [illegible] Zone.

Meg looks at me with amusement.
[illegible]

He braces himself and says, "It's a disaster [illegible]
[illegible]
[illegible]

Meg is [illegible] pouring herself [illegible]
[illegible]
[illegible] is human [illegible]
[illegible] Zane says with [illegible]
[illegible]
[illegible]

[illegible] thirteen.

Marcus looks at her [illegible]
[illegible] to a Paranormal.
[illegible]

CHAPTER 7
THE GOOD, THE BAD, AND THE GROWLY

The tavern's quiet as I come down from my office after hours spent going through old ledgers and footage. Even with the information Zane and Gunther had, I couldn't find any leads or what was on that damn thumb drive. Screw this detective work bullshit.

I approach the bar as Delilah cleans and pours me a glass, flicking her green eyes over me. "What?" I ask, quirking a brow.

"You good?" She asks, setting the glass of whiskey before me.

"I'm fine," I grunt, downing the shot, and clearing my throat once the spiced liquor hits. "Thanks for earlier."

She snorts. "Would've done it anytime, boss. And with more bloodshed, if you asked nicely." I smirk at her, scratching my head, and wincing at the sharp nails. She shakes her head, taking my empty glass. "Just cause you've been on Topside more, doesn't change anything. You're our head alpha and boss for a reason. Pack is Pack. We trust you and your decisions."

My throat tightens and I clear my throat again, looking out the windows. "And if it's the wrong decision? My father is right?"

"Wrong or not, least you're trying and in the trenches with us. You've always been that way." She puts the glass away, rearranging bottles. "Speaking of Marcus showed Meg around a bit."

"How does that pertain—?"

"I brought her behind the bar for a bit. She seemed impressed with the setup and said it was better than *4D*. Even better than other places she's worked. Boosted my ego a bit."

"Course you're already trying to hire her," I grumble.

"Look, good bartenders are hard—"

"Wait." Her words catch my attention. "Where else did she work?"

"Ask her yourself," she says, and I follow her gaze to Meg coming down the staircase. She keeps a hand on the railing, looking around until she finds me and freezes, straightening up. Her chin rises slightly, glancing at a couple of wolves.

"She may end up being more important than you think," Delilah whispers.

"What are you talking about?" I mutter.

"Known you a long time, Rodney, and can practically smell it on you."

"Get your nose checked."

"What about the clothes?"

"She's not Dobby."

"Still your clothes. You didn't even do that for Zane, Victoria, or—"

"You can stop now. And her stuff was torn and dirty."

She gives me a knowing look, leaning over the counter. "How long you gonna tell yourself that?"

"Until you get off my back, you're smelling nothing." My body almost shudders as I sense Meg come closer.

Delilah smirks and says, "Stubborn alpha."

I glare at her as Meg stops a few feet away, fidgeting with her sleeves as she says, "I was hoping we could talk."

Delilah grabs a tray and walks away with a nod. I cock my head at Meg and lean an elbow on the bar. "Get a better look at the place?"

"Yes," she answers.

"Won't have to worry about you getting lost in the coming nights then?"

Her gaze narrows. "No."

"Just checking," I smirk as she tugs her flannel sleeve again. "You wanted to talk?"

She looks away, pinching her brows as she says softly, "I agreed and plan to uphold my end of the deal." My smirk falls, unsure where she's going with this. "But it seems I may be causing more trouble being here than helping."

I scoff, and she brings her gaze back to me. Her scent tickles my nose, making my hand twitch.

"Deal's a deal, darling, whether trouble comes or not. Besides danger and trouble comes with this kind of business. But you already knew that…didn't you?"

Meg takes a long breath in and walks around the bar. "What's your poison, McLycan?"

"Avoiding the question?"

"Trying to show gratitude for you and your people, I mean, Pack from protecting me from…that *other* werewolf."

I snort involuntarily, and she stops. "That was my father."

"Oh," she says with brows shooting up. "He sounds, um, well—"

"He's an asshole."

"You said it, not me." She glances back at the rows of alcohol. "Double it, then?"

I give her a half smile as those brown eyes search my face. "Show me what you got, darling."

She turns and grabs a few bottles and a shaker. I watch how comfortable she suddenly becomes, mixing the drink with…is that Irish Whiskey? My head tilts when she flinches at the sound of a chair scooting back and the cock of a gun. She pauses, takes a breath in, and continues mixing the drink.

Yeah, she knows the dangers.

She places the cocktail in front of me, and I pick it up detecting a hint of something sweet. I scrunch my nose at the scent, and she smiles at me, then whispers, "It's not gonna bite you…big bad wolf."

Something flutters in my stomach, seeing the genuine, soft smile. I take a drink and the taste hits the back of my throat, and I'm surprised at the brighter finish. Don't usually have cocktails, if ever, and… I don't hate it. I'll be damned.

"What is it?"

"Secret," she answers, grabbing vodka, a shaker, and a glass for herself. I sip some more, becoming impressed as I find myself craving the taste. "So...how old *are* you?"

She didn't take conversation advice from Marcus, did she?

"320."

Meg almost drops her glass and catches it before spilling. Her eyes come to mine with shock. "Are you serious?"

"Think I look older?"

"No!" Her voice reaches another octave. "No, no that's not... what I mean, you don't—"

"Quit while your behind, darling." I hold back a smile as her expression goes sour, pursing her lips. I point at the fur along my neck. "Was it the fur that threw you off?"

She stares at me a moment, then sighs going back to mixing her own drink. After she's done, she begins cleaning up as I take another sip of the mystery cocktail. Her lips are tight together and whatever she wanted to talk about, doesn't seem important to her anymore. Or maybe that's why she's thinking so hard.

I hold the drink up, catching her attention. "Hear you bartended in other places than 4D."

She nods. "A couple."

"All on Topside?" She nods again, now refusing to make eye contact. The scent of lavender and citrus diminishes. "Where? Probably know it."

"I...I doubt it."

"Try me."

She gives a blatant fake smile, not reaching her eyes as she shakes her head. "Nowhere near the Bronx. I moved a lot when I came to the city, well Topside that is, trying to find my footing, and it was just..."

"Meg."

"...not the place, but the city...isn't as big as you think it is," she whispers. My lungs feel like a fire, not liking how defeated she's just become.

"Meg, look at me," my voice deepens, and she freezes. Slowly, she does as I say, and her eyes are glistening with unshed tears and...terror. "Meg—"

"You ever wish you can rewind time?"

I want to rear back at the sudden question, almost slamming into me. "What are you—?"

The front doors slam open, and Gunther walks in, calling out, "Boss, we've got company!"

"If it's Dracultelli, tell him fucking later," I growl, keeping my gaze on Meg. "I'm busy."

"It's Boston." Meg's eyes widen while her scent becomes rampant like tainted flowers. Horror.

I growl, then get up and face Gunther. "Get rid of him."

"He's already two blocks away. Someone let him through."

"Tell him—"

"He's mentioning NIIA and PSB, fucker's playing dirty."

Damn it to Atlanta and back. "Get Zane and Marcus. Everyone into positions."

Gunther nods and disappears, while other wolves start setting the place together and awaiting orders. I turn back to Meg, who's frozen in place, staring out the front windows of the tavern. I move into her line of sight, and she jolts back to clutch the bar. She stares up at me, breathing harshly.

Her chin quivers and she whispers, "Don't give me over to him…please."

"What?"

"*Please*. I'll do anything."

I growl low in response to her plea, but Meg closes her eyes as she shrinks within herself. I crowd her space, watching her shake as her fear runs rampant. She winces as I lean close and order, "Go upstairs."

Her eyes snap open. Her mouth works a little, but no words come out. I whisper, "Now."

She stiffly nods as I step out of her way to disappear upstairs. I grab a bottle of scotch and two glasses as Delilah comes over, clearing off the bar as I go sit at one of the tables. Marcus takes point at the front, while Zane stays near me along with Gunther. More wolves position themselves throughout the tavern. Marcus flicks his gaze above, scowling in confusion. I shake my head just as Boston comes to the front door with two bodyguards, dressed in black suits and ties, and wearing shades over their eyes like they're from *Pulp Fiction*.

Charlie Boston is in his late forties, deeply tanned from playing golf, and balding with wispy grey hairs on his chin. His sunglasses are wired-rimmed, wearing a dark suit that doesn't hide his ever-growing beer gut. He gives Delilah a crooked smile, who sneers back at him, jutting her head toward me. Boston looks over as I hold up a bottle of scotch.

He grins as he walks over. "McLycan, good to see you up and kicking, given recent events."

Kinda hate this fuckwad mentioning me being alive. See, dad? Not that hard.

"Know anything about that?" I ask, kicking my boots up.

"We know I'm not that stupid." He gestures toward the empty seat across from me, and I nod as he continues. "Like others, I learned my lesson years ago after what you did, where was it, Brooklyn?"

"Queens."

"Right, right." He sits, still with that crooked smile. He folds his hands in his lap, not saying anything and my expression darkens.

"Why'd you come down *without* invitation?"

"Can't have a little chat?" I frown deeper, dropping my feet to the ground. "Alright, alright…I've got business with you."

"Can't call?"

"Not for this." The greasy look he gives me makes my skin crawl.

There've been humans in the past century who've made my inner wolf want blood. He's one of them. A con man at heart, Boston has been a mob boss for almost two decades, in control of Staten Island and parts of New Jersey. Still no clue how the fuck he took over, but he's a cocky S.O.B. worse than Dracultelli, which is saying a lot.

I pour a half finger of scotch, then push the drink toward him. He sniffs it and puts it down with disgust. "Maybe a beer—"

"Explain what the fuck you want before I choose one of your guards to be Marvin." He scrunches his brows, looking back at his men. There are approximately five wolves watching them, hovering and waiting.

"You have something I want."

"Do I?"

"Yes, but I should remind you about those pesky laws with humans being down here against their will, not to mention being unclaimed. It'd be terrible if PSB found—"

"Your negotiation skills are shit," I mutter, knocking back a shot of the scotch. "Already threatening shit before I even know what you want."

"Who said anything about threatening?" I scowl at him, wishing to tear his throat out, but I've learned to be a patient wolf. Babysitting does that to you. "Rumors are, you picked up the last survivors of the bombing."

"I did."

"Where are they?"

I grin ruefully at him, and respond, "How do you feel about swimming?"

The grin stays on his face like he's got me pegged, then shakes his head. "You didn't kill them."

"I'll send you their heads next time, just like how I warned DiNardi."

His expression falters, his mask falling away when he states, "I know you have the woman."

"Woman?"

He chuckles, waving a finger in my direction and Zane growls under his breath. "I know you, McLycan, and your old laws, which include you not willy-nilly killing women...females," he says, looking at Delilah. "Your moral code forbids you. So old-fashioned."

"It's hard to teach an old dog new tricks."

"Apparently," he mutters. I tap my fingers against the table. Finally, he says, "Let's cut to the chase. She's *mine*."

A dark emotion engulfs my senses, catching a whiff of her scent from above, most likely watching. The fearful scent yesterday in my office connects now, why she agreed. The rise in fear. The reason is sitting across from me.

Well, isn't my last 24 hours filled with *peachy* people?

"Is that so?" I ask casually, glancing over at Gunther who watches Boston cautiously.

Boston glances at the others, his conniving smile coming back. "She was my mole," he says. "Bartenders are good at it, especially if there's nothing much noticeable about them."

Delilah snarls lightly, making Boston's men tense. I glimpse at her, and she goes still as I ask, "Why have a mole within DiNardi's operations?"

"Does it matter now?"

"If you want her back, it does."

He looks over the wire rims. "Antoni was selling parts of his operations to someone, near my territories without telling me. Didn't give me a chance to offer. He was always naïve, paranoid, and fidgety, probably the drugs."

"You gave him those drugs."

He puts his hands up in surrender. "Business is business, McLycan. He wanted to get high, and I gave him what he wanted. Not my fault he was a lightweight," he defends himself and I scoff. "Even so, I needed ears on the inside. It's all just Topside, human stuff, nothing to include the Underground Mafia, I assure you. Squabbles you'll forget in fifty years, right? So, just hand over the girl and no worries."

"DiNardi's dead, why do you want her back?"

His jaw tightens that smile of his cracking a little. "She owes me."

"What exactly?"

The laughter that comes out of him makes my spine stiff as he gestures nonchalantly. "This and that, you understand. People have to pay their dues, and she hasn't." I frown and Boston loses the smile, leaning closer. "How about this? I'll pay to have her back, it'll add to her dues, but she'll *work* it off. I get what's mine and you don't have to be involved in frivolous human matters. Fair deal, right?"

Not that stupid, huh? He's trying to play a dangerous game of chess.

I stare at the mob boss before me, slowly trailing my tongue over my canines. Boston's smile comes back, settling back in his chair as if he's won.

Gunther speaks, "Boss, I don't think—"

I hold my hand up and grin wickedly at Boston. "Let's hear his offer."

There's a stifled gasp from above, and the scent of her fear plunges deep into my soul. I don't break character, tilting my head in curiosity.

"Look who's moving into business ventures," Boston says, then shrugs. "Why don't we start with her worth, let's say about...50 grand? Probably worth less, but I'm being generous today."

"Are you?" I ask, moving a hand down to the table, and placing two fingers on it. Zane shifts on his feet and Marcus' claws come out.

"Oh, fine I'll add another—" I rap my knuckles on the table twice.

In a blink, his guards are taken down and shoved to the floor, while Zane pins Boston to the table, claws pricking his neck. All three have their weapons pulled from them, barrels bent and emptied of bullets. A twinge of silver hits the air, and I glare at the ones near Boston's feet.

Is it kind of stupid to start something with another mob boss soon after another has been killed? Maybe. But he did just try to buy a human from me, and mobsters are a dime a dozen. Except, I can't fucking kill him, not without causing more turmoil on Topside. What I can do is remind him to stay in the damn sunlight.

I move to look up at Meg, who's gripping the railing tightly as she stares down at the scene. I yell up at her, "He telling the truth?" She nods numbly.

"First for him," Gunther comments, giving me my Colt revolver.

The *Pulp Fiction* rejects sputter, trying to move, until the wolves on them snarl. Boston whimpers, "McLycan, what-what are you d-doing? We go b-back. I can give you—"

"You came into *my* Underground and *my* tavern," I speak low. "Trying to con me into selling a human." I gesture for Meg to come down, and she slowly she starts moving. "I wonder what the Cuorebellas would think about that."

Boston begs, "Wait, wait…this-is between you—"

"Joey has had a rough couple of months," Zane comments, pushing a rag into Boston's mouth. "Could use some practice."

"Besides, when was the last time two bosses died within days of another? Could make history again," I mention, glancing at Marcus.

"36', I think."

"The Dillinger wannabe?"

"Kid from Detroit," Gunther adds.

"What about that guy from Cleveland?" Josh asks as I grin at Boston, who's gone very, very pale. "Alanzo tore them up good."

Meg reaches the first floor, approaching carefully as my wolves chuckle darkly as we taunt the mobsters. I close the distance between us, threading my fingers through the end of her hair. Meg's eyes widen as I place my hand on her shoulder. I cock my gun back and ask her, "Was Boston ever in 4D?" She gulps and shakes her head. "The guards?"

Her chin quivers, flicking her gaze to Boston who grunts in protest. I squeeze her shoulder, and she brings her eyes back to me. She steadies herself, and whispers low, "The one on the right was my contact. The other came in months ago."

"Would they've been able to place the explosives?"

"No."

"Smuggle them in?"

"No."

"Brought anyone else who could?"

"No. Just them."

"Thank you, darling." I step away to crouch before Boston, holding my gun up as I look him in the eye. "She belongs to the Wolf Mob now, Charlie. Whatever she owed you, that debt is repaid with you walking out with all your limbs and dick intact. But next time, you *ever* come onto my turf trying to buy someone, I'll replace you with someone who has better taste in liquor."

He nods once.

Zane lets go, while the others are released as I tower over

Boston. He spits out the gag and adjusts his suit, beginning to leave the tavern. His guards follow, but one goes to snatch a gun from one of the wolves, almost aiming it at Meg before my Colt goes off, hitting him in the head.

Meg gasps as the body hits the floor. Boston freezes. I snarl, "He's Marvin. Take the trash with you."

Boston orders the guard to grab the body, and they flounder a bit as they leave.

Rage pulses through me, half-tempting me to go out and put a bullet in both men. Except, I can't add another dead boss to the slew of issues. Not yet anyway. The wolves are silent as I order, "I'm going back to Topside."

Marcus' eyes flare, baring his teeth in aggravation as I ignore him. Gunther interjects, "Boss, you can't—"

"*I want every connection to Boston pulled out,*" I growl, switching to Noctora in my red-vision anger. "*And someone get me anything on our missing explosives. Because if one more self-righteous prick comes down here, making demands in my tavern, I'm spilling more blood. Understood?*"

Wolves nod and start moving, listening to my orders. I look at Meg, and she takes a step back, watching me with wide eyes, and swallowing hard. I should question her; see how deep the secrets go, but I'm too damn pissed to care. In the last century, *no one* has tried to buy someone from me. Something doesn't sit right, but my anger is so consuming, bruising my pride, that I ignore the fear in her eyes. Seeing the emotion in her eyes, I don't want to face it. Not now.

I turn toward Delilah, and point at Meg, "*Keep her the fuck here.*"

"Boss—"

"*Gunther, tell Skylar and Victoria to meet us at the docks.*" I turn, ignoring the pain in my chest as I head out of the tavern.

you out of here like that, so

He has promised not to let me freeze. Warm. Like me that such you

guard to put the bow and may hand. Else as they have.

miles through the ballroom, me to go out and get her. Heart and another

not yet away. The

I'm going back to tonight.

Maybe she'll be

Doctor Prince? Thus you

in my veins or some

Voices rose and removing the

Me, and she take a step, be watching

to care. In the

conversation blurred in pride, the

Her now

and quick vice.

CHAPTER 8
MORE THAN YOU BARGAINED FOR YET?

The docks are quiet as I look at the false walls and floors. Every few years I rotate our explosives between warehouses along the shipping docks. This one's barely been used for a year.

"Well, one good thing," Gunther says as I rub my temple. "Nothing's been stolen since that missing shipment."

I frown and he shrugs. Fine, he's not completely wrong. A yawn struggles to get out as I walk toward the exit as Skylar approaches us.

"Need a pick me up, boss?" The wolf has piercing yellow eyes, which glimmer against the sun beginning to fall on the horizon. Skylar's a lighter cinnamon shade of fur and skin, taller than most with long hair pulled back into an intricate braid. They've been an alpha for Topside operations before I took over as boss.

"Wouldn't happen to have coffee beans to chew on?" I ask, and they pull out a thermos from their utility pants. I take the offering and drink some of the coffee stashed inside, and mumble, "You're my new favorite alpha."

"Careful, Marcus may hear you," Skylar comments, walking beside me.

"He'll live."

"Hear what?" Marcus asks as he comes in from the harbor doors.

"You're not the favorite," Gunther answers.

"I'll live."

"See?" I say, and Skylar snorts taking back the thermos.

"Pulled everyone out of Boston's territories," Marcus informs. "Talked to some contacts and seems that Boston was right. DiNardi was planning to sell part of his operations."

"Great," Gunther mutters, leaning against a crate.

"Any idea who?" I ask.

"Nope," Marcus answers. "We nabbed a few runners of his, Zane took them below, but they don't know anything. If Meg IDs them, Josh will contact Gunther."

"Which reminds me to ask, since you've cooled down over the past eight hours," Gunther says, and I scowl at him. "Why didn't you stay to question Meg?"

My jaw works, noticing Skylar flick their gaze to Marcus for answers. He just frowns at me, waiting for my answer as well.

"She did what I asked, said if they were there or not. They weren't. End of."

"Even though she worked for Boston?" Marcus asks.

"She begged not to go back to him before he arrived," I tell him, and he grunts. "Whatever they had, it's done. One employer was fake, and the other tried to buy her, so I doubt she'll risk losing her protection."

"Oh, I don't think she was lying about helping us," Gunther says. "Just may have insight into Boston's shit."

"Don't care, but I do want to know *why* DiNardi was selling."

"If she was a mole, she could have that answer," Skylar says.

"You really think DiNardi would let a *bartender* know his business?" No offense to Meg, but the other mobs weren't like mine. They didn't function as a collective but as a *selective*.

Marcus grunts. "Not wrong."

"Whether we find the why and who he was selling to," Skylar starts. "We need to find the rest of the explosives. What was used wasn't nearly as much taken. They could do it again. Go after another boss."

"Good, they can get rid of Boston for us," Gunther mutters.

"You're supposed to be the cool-headed one," I tell him.

"Look, I'm just as pissed that he tried to buy a human from us. Like, what the fuck?"

"Some men will do anything to keep what they think is theirs," Skylar comments, sipping from the thermos next. "That includes owning humans, some of us remember the slave trade all too well, young one."

Gunther scowls at them and I snort. Skylar's over four centuries old. They've seen some shit before they joined the Wolf Mob and the McLycan Pack.

There's a shout and we look over as Victoria jogs up to the group, giving me a reassuring smile, and holding up papers. "Did some digging and found footage of Ralph a few blocks down where the explosives disappeared. It seems he found a tunnel of ours and that's how he got in unnoticed."

She holds up a photo, and I see the man I shot, sneaking down an alley. "How did we not find this before?" I ask.

"Scent was masked, no other trail, and footage is from a non-neutral zone," she answers.

"How'd he find it, is the next question," Gunther says.

"Maybe old contacts?" Victoria suggests. "Could've been doing deals with ex-Wolf Mob; spite Rodney and the rest of us."

"Friends with a common enemy," Skylar mutters, meeting my gaze.

"It'd have to be someone freshly cut off," Victoria says. "Less than a year to know about the new routes."

"Really trying to earn beta status, huh?" Gunther smirks.

She crosses her arms and says, "I'm a good bartender, and know when to listen. And keep contacts *outside* the Wolf Mob just in case."

I pat her shoulder, and she winks at me. "Keep listening to those contacts," I tell her. "See if you hear anything about ex-members helping the human mobs." My phone starts buzzing, and I start walking out of the warehouse. "You'll be a Topside beta before you know it."

Gunther murmurs as Skylar chuckles at the two. My phone rings again, and I scowl at the caller ID, then answer, "I'm busy."

"You should get a secretary, that way you have someone to

distract you on long nights and answer phone calls," Vincent speaks over the line. "Or is that Gunther's job?"

Why is this pain in the ass bloodsucker calling me? "What do you want?"

"I thought you were busy? Clearing your schedule for me, how thought—"

"What do you want, Elvira?"

"Moody, aren't we?"

"Coming from the drama queen."

"Excuse you, I have classic tastes," he taunts with a cockiness that makes my hair stand up. "How do you feel about pink polka dots? I think it'll bring out your eyes."

"That's it, I'm hanging up." I pull the phone away but stop when his voice questions through the air.

"Who killed DiNardi?" I bring it back to my ear. "PSB and FBI are crawling all over the Bronx, *again*, and now Manhattan. I've had to reroute half of my supply chain, so, *Pongo*, wanna tell me why?"

"You talked to Gunther."

"He wasn't much help."

"Cause the rest ain't your business."

"Yes, *it is*. I had a deal with DiNardi, and that bombing cost me blood and plasma donors, including an exchange spot. If buildings keep exploding, vampires will start taking people off the streets."

"Just how your father wanted."

"Reason 42 why he's dead."

"Aren't you lucky," I mutter.

"We're on the same team, remember?"

"No. We're not." I worked with him *one* time for that sting, and shit went sideways. I won't count the center cause it was Brenda's idea. "Just stay on your side of the fence. I'll take care of it."

"Not if it concerns the whole Underground," Vincent warns. "Or my Mate." I freeze, staring at the blood-red, violet dusk. "I know you were there when it blew, and I don't give a fuck if you're trying to play hero, but you won't lie to—"

"Don't you dare tell her!" I warn under my breath.

"Tell me what's going on in…hmm, how about three days, little mermaid? And I'll rethink telling her. And maybe, *just* maybe…I won't bring the popcorn when she realizes you ordered her brother to lie, too."

He hangs up, and I grip the phone until it cracks. "Fucking bastard."

I breathe heavily, trying to ignore the distant screams and lingering smoke as my body trembles. By all of Ireland, I *hate* that vampire. I reign myself in as I hear Marcus approach, and he asks in a low tone, "You good?"

"Fine," I answer, putting my phone away and jut my head for the others to follow down the docks. A cold breeze blows, and I shiver away the last of the emotions. "We'll head to *Donny's*."

"Then *Mountain Edge?*" Marcus asks in an inquisitive tone.

"Probably should," Gunther says, coming up beside me. "Make sure our *informant* is in one piece."

"Informant?" Victoria asks. "Did I miss something?"

"We have a witness from the bombing," I answer. "Keeping it on the down low, since she *was* Boston's mole." Gunther raises his hands at me. "She'll help us identify who rigged the bombs."

"What if she's lying to stay alive?" She asks bluntly. I stop and give an exhausted look, she shrugs and whispers, "Look, in this macho-mob world females will do whatever we can to survive, boss. How do you know to trust her?"

"I don't," I state, and the others go still. "But my gut says give her a chance."

My stomach twists at the idea of throwing Meg back into the hands of Boston. I keep walking and Marcus catches my gaze, narrowing his eyes, then shakes his head as he walks ahead. And then my gut tells me, whatever Delilah scented, Marcus had, too.

CHAPTER 9
DEAL ME OUT, DARLING

Gunther trails behind me, grumbling about wanting dinner and a shower as we enter *Mountain Edge*. It's been a long couple of days on Topside from placating parts of the Wolf Mob to not listening to my father, going through DiNardi's connections, rerouting, and just usual business. Marcus and Victoria at least found some who may be connected to Ralph, but that's it.

I wince, scratching my head as myself and the group I'm with enters the dining area. Delilah greets us, getting dinner together with Josh on her tail, Zane comes in after us, holding his kilt and naked.

"How's Topside?" Zane asks, laying the kilt on a table. Delilah swats at him, pointing to the floor. He goes where instructed.

"Frustrating," I answer.

"That's reassuring."

"Didn't get blown up, does that count?" Gunther adds as Zane kneels down to start pleating his great kilt. "Found a few contacts that could connect to the explosives, but we'll need confirmation if they were in *4D*."

"Needle in a haystack," Josh mutters.

"Dead ends for the others we brought down, by the way," Zane says. "Meg hadn't seen them in weeks to pick up their shit."

"Where is she?" I ask.

"Upstairs," Delilah answers.

"She coming down?" I sit down, groaning in relief.

"Won't," she answers, and I freeze. "She helped identify the men and hasn't come out of her room for nothing."

"Has she eaten *anything* since we left?" Delilah shakes her head. I slam back my chair, heading out to the tavern.

Zane calls out, "Figured she'd give in, and come—"

"You don't know that!" I bark back, others following at a distance with Delilah directly behind me. I grumble at her, "I don't care if you don't trust her, I do—"

"That's not why." I stop and turn, facing Delilah who's barely inches away from my face. My brows pinch in confusion, and she snorts. "She jeopardized herself by choosing you over Boston, even with how terrified she was. Course, she's secluding herself."

My jaw tenses and I glance up at the third catwalk, my heart pounding in worry. "She didn't hand over Boston," I say. "Perfect time to lie and say he *was* the one who did it, and she told the truth. She kept her promise, so why would she hide—?"

"Cause the only one *she* trusted left, yelling in a language she doesn't know, after almost being *bought*," Delilah tsks me, and crosses her arms. "And no alpha is gonna touch another's *Gae*—"

"Stop," I growl, and she eyes me. I'm already furious and tired, not adding the acknowledgment of that damning truth to the mix. Even if my alphas can presumably sense it.

I head up the stairs to Meg's room as my anger fades into exhaustion and plain worry. I glance down to see others gathered near the bar, pretending they're not watching. Nosey-ass wolf pack. I rap my fist against the door lightly. Nothing. I do it again. Still nothing.

My breathing becomes erratic when the image of her being dead hits me. Smoke fills my nostrils, making my head throb. *Failure.* My arm shakes this time as I knock. "Meg. Open the door."

I'm on the verge of breaking it down when she answers, "No, thank you."

I gulp in air, relief finding me and soon replaced by frustration. "Open the door."

"Not now."

You gotta be kidding me. "Open the door, Meg."

"I'm busy."

"Rearranging furniture?"

"Maybe." I groan, leaning my head back.

"Hey, boss!" Gunther calls, and I scowl at him over the railing. "Ask nicely."

"Don't forget to say 'please,' always a cincher," Zane comments. Marcus snarls at them, to which they respond with wide eyes.

When did my life turn into a rom-com?

"Go do something else, you mongrels," I snap and the wolves scatter. Gunther gives me a thumbs-up before disappearing.

I knock again. "You haven't eaten in days, so come down to eat...please," I say rolling my eyes.

"I'm not hungry."

"That's bullshit and we both know it."

"Maybe." Her and those *damn* maybes.

I lean against the doorway, thinking of something to get her out. I remember one of Claudia's pranks. "Fine. Tonight, while you're sleeping I'll take your door off. Do you prefer wooden beads or plastic?"

The door slams open, and she glares at me. "You wouldn't dare—!"

I give her a rueful grin, and her eyes widen realizing I'm yanking her chain. She gasps and tries to shut the door, but I easily catch it with my arm. She struggles, then stops with heaving breaths and I see how pale she's gotten. There are dark circles under her eyes, her hair a mess, and she's in her old bartending clothes. My grin is quickly gone, anger replacing the mirth.

"Why haven't you eaten?" I ask gruffly. She steps back and hugs herself, not meeting my gaze. I step forward, and she takes another back. I pause. "Meg."

"I'm not hungry," she murmurs. "If I recall correctly our deal does not include me coming down for—"

"But we did agree with me keeping you alive, nourishment includes that." She won't look at me, staring at the ground. "Meg, just come down—"

"Were you actually thinking of selling me?"

"What?" Her gaze meets mine, filled with exhaustion and defeat, which makes my chest tighten. An overwhelming need washes over me, wanting to bring her in close and reassure her. "Fuck no," I growl.

"But you asked to hear—"

"I needed his guard down. He's distracted easily by the prospect of money or illusion of control."

"By *pretending* you'd sell me?"

"Worked didn't it?" She shakes her head in disbelief. "Look—"

"You left and I thought…"

I go to step across the threshold, and she backs up. An invisible force keeps me from stepping over the threshold. My voice softens and I say, "You upheld your end of the deal, and so will I."

"What if I lied?"

"About?"

"Boston and if he was there."

"Did you?"

"No."

"Then I'm confused what's the issue."

She scoffs, looking at me incredulously. "I was Boston's mole and didn't tell you."

"Don't care."

"You…you don't *care*?"

"Can't blame you for not blatantly telling me you worked for one mob boss to spy on another, saving your own ass," I say with a shrug. "Myself and the 101 Dalmatians down there don't give a damn about how the other human mobs conduct their business. Unless it pertains to us, so do you know anything in that area?"

"No…nothing with the Underground."

"Then I *definitely* don't care. What matters now is you helping us find who blew up your… 'fake' mob boss." It's almost impressive how many she's worked for, but also unlucky.

Her hands rub over her arms, lips pursing as she stares at the ground. I lean back on the railing, waiting for her to willingly come with me. I'm half-tempted to throw her over my shoulder though when my stomach grumbles.

"How can you already trust me?" She asks.

"You begged me," I answer without thinking. I stare at her, partially folding in on herself, not at all resembling the woman I first met. Quietly, I ask, "How long did you work for Boston?"

Her gaze meets mine. "Two and half years."

"He abused you?" She swallows hard. After a few moments, she nods, taking a deep breath like she's stopping herself from crying. "What—"

"I don't want to talk about it."

"Fine." She watches me quietly. I take a deep breath and lower my head to appear less scary. "Meg, you won't be abused here. My Pack doesn't operate like that. Long as you don't backstab us, and I doubt you're here to spy on us—"

"I meant it, not knowing who you were," she says, keeping her gaze on me and a bit of that spunk of hers comes back. "And what I know about DiNardi, has nothing to do with…anyone here."

"Then we're good," I say, and her body relaxes. "Let's head down to dinner, we'll talk business tomorrow." Meg nods and runs her hand through her disheveled hair, and I notice specks of rubble still in it. "Have you even taken a shower since you've been here?"

"Excuse me?" I gesture toward her hair and then rest of her. She glances down at herself with a frown.

"Once again, you look like a rat pulled you in from the sewers, worse than the first night here somehow." Her mouth opens in shock, staring at me in horror. "What? I didn't say you smelled." She gasps. Shouldn't have said that.

She covers her face in her hands and lets out a long groan, "Mob boss or not, what is wrong with you?!"

"Not insulting you."

She drags her hands down her face. "I swear, you men are all the same."

"Hey. Wolf."

"Then explain how even being over 300 years old, you just—"

"I've barely slept for four days," I argue, and she scowls at me. "So, pardon me for worrying about you endangering your health. Or that you could have napalm residue on you or starve to death."

"Then just *say* that."

"I'm understanding that now, darling."

Her brown eyes meet mine, causing my heart to ache. The lavender and citrus scent invades my nostrils, no longer diminished, and helping ease my frustration.

"You have an odd way of showing worry," she says.

I huff, admitting defeat. "Sorry. Will you please come eat, so I don't *worry* about you becoming a wraith?"

"Are those real?"

"No, just scary bedtime stories for children…and humans."

She gives an exasperated look, then goes to shut the door. I yank it open, and her face comes close to mine. She exhales sharply, and I can practically taste her scent. "I'm changing," she whispers. "Give me five minutes. I'll be down. Promise."

I linger a moment, then let go for her to close the door as I step back and lean against the railing. I rub the bridge of my nose, debating going for a run after dinner or strangling something. Zane's probably the safest to strangle, he does have a kink for breath play. Then again, Marcus and I haven't grappled in a while…

Still debating options, Meg opens the door and jumps when she sees me, clutching her chest. "Why are you still here?"

"Not giving you a chance to hide," I answer, and see she's wearing my lounge pants and flannel again. My chest swells seeing her in it, a sense of…no, no thinking that 'Rodney the Pup.'

She rolls her eyes, following me. "I would've come down."

"Before or after becoming dehydrated?"

"Very funny."

"Dehydration is no laughing matter."

I glance back, noticing her glare as we head downstairs. She comes closer to me as we enter the dining area, wolves already chatting and getting plates filled. Some glance our way but keep to themselves as we head into the backroom. Everyone's seated, and I pull out the empty chair next to mine for her to sit. I give the table a nod, and they start passing food around which consists of fried chicken, collard greens, cornbread, and fruit. Marcus places chicken on Meg's and mine.

Meg begins to protest, "Wait, you don't need to…I'm—"

"Don't even try it," I tell her, putting cornbread on her plate as she stares at me. "What's ours is yours."

"That's not...I mean, this is just—"

"Quit while you're behind, darling," I murmur, and she scowls. Something sparks inside me seeing the small defiance in her eyes. After a moment, she relents to the food being placed on her plate.

I start eating, and she exhales sharply but follows suit. I don't miss hearing the small moan she makes when she takes a bite. I glance up to see Delilah smiling behind her water glass, then get distracted by Josh nuzzling her neck. Dinner isn't quiet, filled with gossiping wolves and their jokes. They've never been a quiet bunch. Down here it's a livelier atmosphere than what I've grown used to on Topside. Up there it's just Mob, while here it's Pack first. Home.

Not all in the Wolf Mob were Pack, those not granted into the family stayed on Topside, overseen by those part of the Pack. Most in the McLycan Pack were born into it or granted membership by the alphas and betas, once meeting certain criteria. The mob was business, Pack was family.

I remember the nights spent alone in my office in *Donny's* or just with Gunther and Marcus. I look up to see Gunther has already changed into his Pack kilt, along with Marcus. I glance down at my jeans, ignoring the emptiness as I bring my attention to Meg. She watches the others carefully, even as we clean up and others peel away for the evening.

Delilah brings over some whiskey, while Josh adds cigars and a pack of cards. He asks, "Care for a game, boss?"

"Once ya'll clean up, you smell worse than bloodsuckers tanning or ghouls after a fresh shed of skin," I answer, lighting a cigar. I glance at Meg, who eyes me. "You, too."

"I think your verbiage needs improvement," she says.

"I'm blunt and honest."

"Oh?"

"I'll take lessons from the bartender later."

Edward chimes in, "Maybe she's—"

"Careful how you tread, Scrappy," I warn the young beta.

He holds his hands up, and Josh pushes him out of the room. "Come on, pup."

"Delilah, make sure Meg gets everything she needs to shower," I say before the wolf disappears.

She gestures for Meg to follow, and Meg gets up and asks, "What game are you playing?"

"Poker."

"What kind?"

"Strip poker," Zane comments.

"Are you serious?" She rasps.

"Only when he behaves," I grumble. "Usually Texas Hold'em or Seven-card stud."

She flicks her gaze over the dining area. "Why am I not surprised about one of those?"

Zane snickers and I glare at him. "You play?" I ask her, and she shrugs. "Guess could bring in a new player, keep you from hiding." She scoffs gently, leaving with Delilah and Zane.

Marcus and I are left, who puffs his own cigar as his jaw works. His blue eyes are distant, staring at the doorway. I watch the empty space and can almost imagine Claw bounding through naked cause she "won" at strip poker. Zane directly behind, somehow wearing her bra, and Delilah with Zane's kilt. I smirk, looking down at the cigar in my hands.

"You trust her," Marcus murmurs.

"Yeah," I sigh. "Even if I probably shouldn't."

He sighs, tapping his cigar on the ashtray. "Well, Claw always said your gut was the better moral compass."

I look over at him as he chews his cigar a little. I take a long breath in, and chance in suggesting again, "You should come with me on her—"

"No."

"Marcus."

"No," he states roughly, taking a long drag on his cigar. "Unless you're gonna admit *why* you trust her."

"You just said—" I stop when his disappointed gaze finds me, and I shake my head. "You're wrong. She's human and it's a myth. Like you said, following my gut."

He snorts, "Sure."

"She's here to help, after that, she's gone," I snarl, not willing to let him finagle the words out loud. I'm not giving myself that delusion, not as fear trickles up my spine and the flash of burning bodies comes over my mind's eye. I'll trust her, take her help, then get her out. Simple and done.

"You that scared—"

"She's all that's left of DiNardi's club and Boston came to *buy* her," I argue. "It'll be dangerous keeping her longer than needed, cause I may not care what she knows, but the other human bosses will. Not to mention if Freyja wants her next as a pawn."

"Then get support," he snarls. "The Cuorebellas will back you, and the Blood Mafia because of Brenda. Take the damn help, you're not your father."

"That was always the problem, wasn't it?"

"You *not* being him was the answer," he says, pointing at my chest. "That's why you were head alpha before being boss. You choose—"

"And look what happened, Claudia's dead and then I gave Brenda the means to do the same. Who knows how'll I destroy Meg." His expression falls, all fight leaving him. He puts his cigar out as he gets up and prowls for the door. I swear, calling out, "Fuck, Marcus, wait—"

"*Don't,*" he snarls, blue eyes piercing into my soul. He leaves, slamming the doors behind him.

I fall back into my chair, putting my cigar down as I rub my chest harshly. My hands tremble as I take a shuddering breath, the crushing guilt weighing on my shoulders. I won't be my father. The part that's haunted me for almost thirty years comes back, wishing Claw was here instead. Maybe she'd—

Zane walks in, and I stop rubbing my chest. He glances over to me, and asks softly, "You okay, Rod?"

"Just need a couple bad rounds of poker," I say, grabbing some whiskey. He sits in Marcus' old spot, takes the cards, and shuffles.

"Sure, you don't want cuddles? You always hated being alone," he murmurs, and I look over at the grey wolf.

"Stop trying to get me back into your bed, you pain in the ass," I joke, but my words sound hollow.

He claps my shoulder. "Fine, I'll just snuggle with Edward, he's better as the big spoon anyways," he teases, which gets me to chuckle. "There's the Rod I know."

The others trickle in, settling in for the first round with me, Gunther, Edward, and Zane. Edward sits beside Zane, who puts his arm over his shoulders and tells him, "Looks like I'm bunking with you tonight."

Edward frowns at him and replies, "You hogged the blankets last time."

"Did not!"

Gunther deals out the cards, and laughs, "*Acquires* is his word for it. Aces are wild."

"*Borrow*," Zane grunts, ruffling Edward's hair before snatching his cards. Delilah walks in with Josh close behind. "I gave them back."

"With a price," Edward and I say in unison. Zane groans, while the rest of us laugh as Meg walks in.

I peer over my cards, barely helping myself to gaze at her generous curves. She looks pretty, wet hair and all.

"Playing next round?" Gunther asks her, and she nods sitting beside me.

"Do I look like a rat?" She asks quietly.

"I said *dragged* by a..." I pause as her brow raises, "...fine, I'll work on the banter."

She smirks as Gunther deals, and we play the next round. I watch as she plays, the first round not going far. The others chuckle, as she says it's been a while. I hide my amusement, then see a pattern after the third round as her pot slowly gets larger. Not much, but a controlled gathering of chips. Her brown gaze flicks to others and calls with tiny smirks. I watch the human with my complete attention as she beats every single wolf at the table.

"Beginner's luck!" Josh shouts, throwing his cards down.

"Just mad she got you with a pair of eights," Zane chuckles. I see a gleam come over Meg's expression, and a spark of excitement goes through me, wanting to know every single facet of her. Mafia or not.

CHAPTER 10
RUH-ROH

Meg shakes her head. "Never came in."

I crumble the picture of the dead man, tossing it. It's mid-afternoon, and we've been in my office for hours going through every connection we have to DiNardi. Apart from Boston, there's Oliver O'Reilly, Malcolm Greene, and Johnny Calhoun, all of whom have gone quiet since the bombing. They're more likely staying out of the spotlight from police. They can cover their own asses, I just wanted the fuckers who hired Ralph, killed DiNardi, and took my explosives. Easy enough wish list.

I've learned how much Boston used Meg in almost three years. Only this past year was she at *4D*, before playing as "patron" for the other bosses. A few times she'd grown distant in conversations about certain individuals, and I stopped pushing. I knew a bit too well remembering things you don't want to. No point making her relive her own traumas.

Gunther pulls out a few snapshots from those in Greene's operations, and she shakes her head. "No one from the other mobs visited, I'm sure of it. At least not since summer."

"Apart from your contacts," Marcus comments, folding his arms over his chest, and leaning against the door. Zane pours himself a drink at the bar, while Gunther tosses the pictures before settling back into his chair next to Meg.

"Yeah," she mutters, grabbing her water. Her gaze becomes distant as she bites her bottom lip.

"Hey," I murmur, and she looks up at me. "Need a break, darling?"

She shakes her head as Zane brings me over a drink. "I don't think the human mobs planted the bombs," he says. "Someone outside of them, willing to risk more."

Meg leans back in her chair, fiddling with her flannel sleeve.

"For once, I wish it was one of them," Gunther says, shuffling photos in his lap.

Meg abruptly grabs his wrist and points. "He was in *4D* three weeks ago. Talked to Antoni for almost two hours and I don't recognize him from the other mobs."

"Timing doesn't fit," I say.

"Maybe not, but he could've been whom Antoni was making deals with. Selling to that Charlie mentioned."

Zane looks over her shoulder, and snarls, "You gotta be *fucking* kidding me."

Gunther joins in disgruntlement, handing me the photo as I come face to face with an old "acquaintance." The black and white picture doesn't show his crimson eyes, but I know the vampire anywhere. I look at Marcus, and mutter, "Sebastian."

He scowls and asks Meg in a calm, soft tone, "Are you positive?"

"Yeah, the others wouldn't stop whispering about the Blood Mafia being there," Meg answers. "That's him, right? Their boss?"

"Unfortunately, no," I say, dropping the photo.

This just got worse. If Sebastian was talking to DiNardi, this just became a bigger problem, because it means the she-devil may be involved.

"If it was *her*," Gunther says, sitting back. "What would she have gained killing DiNardi?"

"Unless they were meant for us," Marcus mutters, and I meet his hard gaze.

"Could be, Rod," Zane whispers.

Meg whispers to Gunther, "Who is *she*—?"

There's a loud bang from outside. Marcus snarls as he opens

the door and goes out to the catwalk with shouts below. And then a very familiar voice screams, *"RODRICK ROWAN MCLYCAN!"*

Marcus shuts the door, while the other two give me exasperated looks. "Didn't tell her, did you?" Gunther asks.

"No," I grumble, getting up as there's more shouting and I hear Marcus snarling. "Been a bit busy."

"Is it you father again?" Meg asks.

"Nah, scarier," Zane replies.

"An angry lil sis," Gunther chuckles under his breath.

"Watch it or I'm throwing you out to her," I warn.

"RODNEY!" Brenda yells.

Zane laughs and I growl grabbing the door handle. "Quit it."

"Should I be worried?" Meg asks.

"No," I mutter, opening the door and closing it quickly. Marcus stands between me and the fuming half-daemon, her eyes glowing violet behind her glasses.

She orders, "Talk. Now."

"Office is occupied."

"Fine. Your apartment has better alcohol." She spins on her heel and heads for the stairs. Marcus frowns as I pass, following her, and glaring down at Delilah. She cleans like nothing's happened, while Josh and Edward avoid eye contact with me.

Brenda storms into my apartment and I close the door as I turn on the lights. She spins to face me. She breathes heavily, eyes still glowing. "You lied to me!"

"Technically, I didn't—"

"Fine! You made Joey lie to me!" She yells, pointing at my chest.

"I forgot—"

"Bullshit!"

"I had business," I growl.

"That you couldn't call me, and say, 'hey almost got turned into dog food?' You've called me for less. Vinny had to tell me after giving you *three* days!" She snarls and something crackles at her knuckles.

Oh, she is *really* pissed, and I realize I should've listened to Joey. "Lil sis—"

"You promised not to keep secrets from me. You said you'd never do that to me!"

"That doesn't mean I tell you everything, I can't sometimes."

"Almost dying is worth telling me."

"Like when you didn't tell me?" I accuse.

"I apologized!" She growls. "We're not discussing that again."

"Then don't come yelling at me in *my* tavern!"

She groans in exasperation, yanking at her hair. "Hours after I saw you," she rasps. "Fucking *hours* after brunch and me telling you to be careful. You said it was an in-and-out job. Are you fucking kidding me?"

"We had things under control."

"Dead mafia boss and rubble say otherwise."

"And I'm not dead!" I yell, anger flourishing in my chest. The heaviness on my shoulders worsens, guilt like a stone in my gut. "I'm fucking alive. So, what, I didn't tell you. Are you so pissed—"

"Because I almost lost you!" She screams, tears forming in her eyes, and the glowing stops. She gulps harshly, and her shoulders shake as her chin quivers. "You almost died...and didn't say anything, couldn't fucking tell me *yourself*—"

"Brenda."

"I can't lose you," she pleads as tears fall down her face. "To bombs, vampires, mobsters...please, I can't..."

The anger is replaced with heartache as my mind flashes to months ago. Hours Marcus kept me in his room as I ripped shit apart, not knowing if she was alive as the Underground shut down. Report after report on the inferno above. I thought I'd killed her, crying as Marcus kept me from killing myself. I couldn't stop. "*I can't do this again! Don't make me bury her! Don't make me bury her!*" I only stopped when Garrick called, and she'd showed up at his place. I then locked myself in my apartment and studio.

In avoiding my own past, my own fears...I'd broken a promise and made her go through similar hurt.

"I'm sorry," I rasp. "I'm sorry, I shouldn't—"

Brenda slams into me, hugging me close as I wrap my arms around her, burying my face into her shoulder. We both tremble, holding onto each other. She squeezes tighter as she nuzzles against my neck. Tears go down my skin as the apartment becomes eerily still.

"I know I wasn't around much these past few years," she whispers. "Maybe you don't think you can talk to me—"

"That's not it, lil sis."

"Please don't feel like you can't. Please talk to me when this shit happens."

"I know I can," I say, my throat tightening, remembering the rumble of the explosions. "It's...it's complicated."

Minutes tick by with more silence as we hold onto each other, my arms loosen, and I kiss her head. "Again, sorry."

"Just don't hide shit from me."

"Kettle calls the pot black."

"Okay, maybe I deserved that," she winces and pulls back. "And I'm sorry for yelling at you in front of the Pack. Kind of." I snort, ruffling her hair. "I'm angsty from lack of sleep and caffeine."

"I can help with one of those."

"Hell yeah, nap time."

"Coffee, lil sis." I roll my eyes at her.

She rolls her eyes back at me, kisses my cheek, and steps back with a serious expression. "Fine, but you're telling me what the fuck is going on. Especially since Vinny's been going Topside to deal with mobsters."

"Blood problems ain't mine." I head into the kitchen and pull out a Moka pot. I glance back, and her face is scrunched up as she cocks her head. "What?"

"Why does it smell like human?"

"What?" I ask again.

"Dumb is a bad look on you." She's worse than a succubus.

"First, you gotta promise not to yell at me again, I'm a delicate flower." Brenda snorts sitting at my short counter. "Two, apologize to Delilah for disrupting the tavern, and three, come back sooner for brunch. *Then*, I'll tell you."

"You drive a hard bargain," she says, pursing her lips playfully. "Fine, beam me up, Scotty." I look at her incredulously, and she points at the coffee. Right. As I make the coffee, I explain what's happened, including what we've found so far. She listens quietly, furrowing her brows as I put a mug before her.

"How many ex-mob would've been willing to work with Ralph?" She asks.

I shrug, "Maybe a dozen? Victoria and Skylar try to keep them under tabs, but if they leave the city, we don't track them anymore."

"And why you rotate routes," she murmurs, I nod, leaning on the counter in front of her. "Considered you have your own mole?"

"No, and I won't."

"Even Topside?"

I sigh, sipping from my own mug. "Three alphas, including myself, almost died. It would've devasted the entire Wolf Mob and would've only benefited my father." She gives me a look. "He's an asshole, but not Bruno."

"Touché," she murmurs. "Well, you're dealing with someone smart enough to use Paranormals *and* humans to get what they want. If it's the same explosives we used, then it tightens the list of who it is."

I look out toward the round window as my jaw tightens. Brenda clinks her mug against mine, bringing my attention back to her.

"If it's ex-mob, fine, we'll find them and gut them," I say and pause. "Don't tell your Pops I said that." She snorts and waves for me to continue. "If not, then it may mean it's someone *else* who may be on that list."

"Meaning?"

"Sebastian was talking to DiNardi," I say, and Brenda swears under her breath. "I may have issues with Freyja, but—"

"She wouldn't."

"Except she's not the same from twelve years ago," I say, rubbing my temple. A truth I hated to accept years back. My relationship with Freyja was…complicated.

"Even if she knows it was us who blew that center, why target you? The entire Underground Mafia was involved." I shrug, and she grumbles under her breath.

"Probably not her, Sebastian visiting doesn't fit the timeline."

"Hired someone?"

"Low possibility?"

Brenda takes a swig, and comments, "Guess I could pay a visit—"

"Nope, don't go near her with a fifty-foot pole."

"But—"

"No."

"But—"

"Not letting you get involved, *again*." I glare at her.

"Newsflash, *I'm a big kid now*." I hate it when she mock sings.

"You forget a certain vamp?"

"He doesn't control me."

"Not saying that, just..." I huff, straightening my back. She narrows her eyes as my gaze flits to the metal ring on her right index finger, signifying her Mating.

"You said being Mated to him didn't change anything," she whispers. "I'm still loyal to *every* being in the Underground Mafia, especially the Pack. Or were you lying about that, too?"

I want to tell her it changes everything, because of *whom* she Mated. She'll always be Pack, but I can't ignore the decision she made. I didn't give two shits that she Mated a vampire, but did it have to be *Vinny* the Vampire? But none of that's why I don't want her involved. *"Don't make me bury her!"*

"Just don't want you getting hurt," I murmur.

She sighs, touches my hand, and says, "At least let me take the blame if Freyja is behind this. I pressed the button, not you. I got you into this mess, let me help."

"Alanzo said no mob business."

"Then as a Pack member, I should help," she smirks, knowing she found a loophole.

"Conniving."

She rolls her eyes. "Brat by nature. What if I got you a contact in the NYPD? See what they found in the rubble."

"So, nothing? Those were the good explosives, lil sis."

"But could help find who planted the bombs."

I pinch my brows and ask, "How?"

She clears her throat, tapping her finger on the rim of her mug. "Genevieve. The Head of the Hive Mind of the ghouls that Traloski experimented on, said she saw suits. Federal agents. And footage was found weeks ago of two agents near the center."

"Now who's hiding shit?"

"Fine, we're even," she grumbles. "*But* Midnight told me forensics can track napalm recipes, including yours. Could be in the system, and the agents followed it back to you."

"You've *already* been looking into this."

"Not with *4D*," she mutters, putting her mug in the sink. She looks at her hands, the titanium claws punching out, engulfing her fingers. I watch carefully as she stares at them, and says, "Traloski was days away from creating a serum that could control Paranormals. Whoever hired him to do it, they're still out there. And I'm not letting them finish what they started." Something wrenches in me as she swallows, claws disappearing. "I know you don't want me involved, but I *need* to be if they're connected."

I've thought to ask her what she saw below that center, but I understand keeping some things in the shadows. I glance at the wine glasses, and my throat constricts. I hate letting her help, but I was running out of options.

I nudge her shoulder. "Your contact any good?"

"He's been useful so far."

Something tells me it's the detective who's almost gotten her killed. *That* conversation I'll let Dracultelli or Alanzo have with her.

"Fine," I cave, and she grins. "No telling him about Meg. It'll be easier to keep her safe and squash any more cockroaches coming out of the woodwork, in case it was mob-related."

"Conniving works on me, weird with you." I tussle her hair, and she pushes me away. "You're the classic, straight-up whiskey kind of boss, Lassie."

I snort, putting my mug in the sink, then put my arm over her shoulders. "What does that make Vincent?"

"The cocktail you don't ask what's in it and hope it doesn't kill you." I think about what Meg made me, and I think fate is screwing with me again.

I hug her to my side, walking toward the door. My side feels cold when she steps away, heading out to the catwalk as I flick my gaze to the studio.

"Is that her behind the bar?" Brenda asks.

I join her on the catwalk, catching Meg's scent immediately. I see her with Delilah, mixing drinks for the early evening crowd.

"Yeah, that's her," I answer, leaning on the railing. "Thought you'd smell her on your own."

She waves me off, cocking her head in curiosity. "You didn't say much about her, any idea if she has a family?" I shake my head. "Friends?" Another shake. "Where she lived?" And another. "Oh, come on, favorite ice cream?"

"Chocolate?"

"That's a cop-out," she snorts. "Probably haven't even asked her if she likes Pina Coladas or being caught in the rain."

"She's here to help, why would I prod her about personal shit?"

Brenda frowns. "What about missing her friends? Wanting a phone call home? Did she ask for *any* of that?"

"She worked for Boston for almost three years, undercover at 4D for one," I explain. "He only recruits those who can disappear easily. So, I'm pretty certain most of those answers are dead or don't exist." The words feel sour in my mouth. "Not everyone is the Underground Mafia, lil sis."

"Well, if she was Costigan or Sullivan deep, probably better down here. I'll start the adoption papers."

I shake my head. "I'll have Joey get her out of New York when we're done, but she's not staying."

I clamp down on my emotions, feeling Brenda stare at me. She's no succubus, but she's been trained well with her blood-hound nose to detect hormone changes. Don't need her on my ass along with two wolves. Meg obviously wants to get out, and I won't stand in her way. Even if my inner wolf acts like a damn pup around her and makes my heart pitter-patter. The idea of getting her killed, making her stay, injects a coldness down my spine.

Her pocket vibrates, and she pulls her phone out to answer, "It's not my turn to set the table." Must be Joey or Ricky. "I did it last night and the night before because you were *lounging* about downstairs." It's Ricky. "Yeah-huh, Gina told me. And quit touching my stuff with glitter on your hands...it does not add character! Ricky, I swear I'll tie you up in *The Vault* and make you listen to ghoul anatomy from the 18th century! Yeah, yeah I'll be home soon."

She hangs up and I ask, "How does he obtain so much glitter?"

"Probably has a dealer," she grumbles. She turns to me, pulling her glasses down to stare up at me with pleading eyes. "Can I stay with you…please?"

"No, Donkey."

"But we'll stay up late, swap stripper stories, and make pancakes in the morning."

"No way am I explaining to Carmen why you're not home for dinner. Playdate's over."

"Cruel, cruel world," she complains overdramatically.

I smile, yanking her into a hug as I take a deep breath in. She squeezes back, making the flash of memory disappear. Even with the hint of Vincent's scent lingering on her leather jacket. Always a damn shadow over her, even when trying to say goodbye in peace, hugging her. I kiss her head, hoping my scent will piss him off.

"Sure, you're okay?" She asks.

"Yeah."

"Better tell the truth or I'll starch your socks *and* your pillow."

"He already declined cuddles, so he can't be that bad," Zane teases, walking up to us.

Brenda lets go and points at him. "I have a bone to pick with you."

"What did I do?" He asks as I step out of the way.

"Could've told me what happened, Krypto, you live down the street. Okay, it's a few blocks, but still."

"Want a hug or not, munchkin?"

"Do I get to braid your hair with butterflies?"

"That's Delilah's job."

Brenda grins ruefully, and asks, "Kilt check?"

"You mongrel," he laughs, pulling her into a hug as she groans, then relents. He lets go and shoves her shoulder. "Anyone else coming in like that would've gotten their ass beat."

"And grounded," I mutter.

"Take it up with Pops, it can roll over with the other days."

Gunther comes up the stairs, leaning against the wall with arms crossed, and laughs, "I'm letting Marcus eat you next time, little red riding hood."

"Delilah! Don't let Marcus eat me!" She calls out as Zane puts her in a chokehold.

"Don't barge into my bar!"

"Fine! I'm sorry! Zane, you better not tickle me," Brenda warns, struggling in his arms.

Meg looks at Delilah, then me, confusion lining her face as my grin widens watching Brenda. On Topside, she'd never have gotten away with this shit. Most above, Wolf Mob that is, don't know Brenda's importance, that she's considered direct family with me. Brenda could be a full-time Pack member if she wanted, and probably be an alpha in a few decades. I'd be insane to let her be a beta, even with her smarts.

Brenda rips out of Zane's hold and goes to rip his kilt off. He howls in laughter, jumping out of the way. As great as it'd be to see them grapple, she needs to get home.

"Lil sis, you're gonna be late for dinner."

"Shit!" She yells, clicking her tongue and racing down to the first floor, where she waves to Delilah. "I'll make it up to you!"

"You better!"

Wolves laugh and holler as Brenda disappears. I close my apartment door and go downstairs with the others. I approach Meg, who stares at where Brenda disappeared.

"She'll say hello next time," I say. "She's gotta get home for dinner."

"She's your sister?"

"Adopted."

She suddenly laughs, bringing her hand to her mouth. I stare at her, the sound vibrating through my core. It's the first time I've heard it, and I want to hear more of it. *Laugh again.*

"What?" I rasp.

Her gaze shimmers, dimples showing on her cheeks. "I see the family resemblance."

CHAPTER 11
OF WOLVES AND MEN

My mother's eyes stare back at me before I smudge the charcoal across them. I sigh at the half-finished portrait and put the charcoal down, noticing how much I've gotten on my white t-shirt. Why do I wear white when I'm drawing? Maybe to remind me when it's time to stop or get a drink. I glance at the clock, noticing it's two in the morning. Nightcap it is.

I leave my studio and apartment into the eerie calm of the empty tavern. Amber light creates shadows as I head down to the bar, quietly searching through the bottles. It's been some time since I've been behind here. Delilah has changed where she keeps the good whiskey.

I rifle through the lower shelves where Delilah used to hide the good shit and find hidden pictures. The first makes me smirk. It's when Brenda turned thirteen, all of us sitting at the bar with her lounging across my lap and Gunther's. Zane stands off to the side with Delilah and Josh behind the bar. Victoria is on the other side of Brenda, and Skylar's giving a thumb's up. I smile at Brenda's earlier years and flick my gaze to the kilt I'm wearing in the picture.

My smile falls when I find another snapshot from fifty years ago that makes my stomach drop. Delilah and Josh are behind the bar next to Skylar holding up a beer. Zane leans on my shoulder while Gunther stands off to the side, smiling softly. I sit in the middle in front of the bar next to Marcus, and Claudia sits on the bar between us, elbows on our shoulders. Marcus holds her hand, and there's a faint smile as she rests her head on his.

My finger traces along her face down to where she connects with me. I put the photo back and find a bottle of whiskey and a couple of glasses. I pour two shots, putting the second at the seat across from me. The glass clinks against mine as I tap them together, remembering a time further back.

I sit at the bar looking at reports. The dining area doors open to Claudia entering and looking a bit too suspicious. "What have you been up to?" I ask.

"If anyone asks how noodles got on the ceiling...I have no idea," she responds, jumping over the counter into the bar area. "It's late. Why the hell you up working?"

"Cleaning up your mess from putting hot peppers in the whiskey barrels we smuggled in."

"It made them taste better!"

"Do you know how much it costs to get that shit over the border? Not to mention making sure we don't get caught by the feds?"

She blows a raspberry. "That prohibition act is for humans."

"Still affects us, Claw," I chuckle as she takes away my bottle and puts down a glass of water. She then leans on her elbows and grins. "What do you want now, hellion?"

"I need you to ask dad to take Marcus off the roster next week. It's our anniversary and I want us to take a few days off. He's beat and needs a break."

"I'll cover for him, but you should ask," I say, staring at the numbers before me. "Dad likes you better. He'll do what you want."

She puts her hand on mine, and I look up into her soft gaze. "He loves you, Rod. He just...sucks at showing it."

"Doesn't seem that hard for him when it comes to you." Her face falls a little, and I pat her cheek briefly. "It's fine. I'll ask, and when I mention it's for you, no way he'll say no. What are you planning anyway?"

She lets it go, and hums, "Just visiting Central Park."

"The Underground's not done yet." She smiles mischievously. "You better not cause—"

"Claw, why are there noodles on the ceiling?" Marcus' voice interrupts, and I turn to see him scowling with folded arms.

"No clue," she answers, moving around the counter and winking at me.

He snorts at her and then gestures upstairs. "I'm heading to bed. You coming?"

"Right behind you, cutie pie," she tells him, and he grunts. How those two work, I have no idea. She kisses my cheek and hugs me around the neck. "Hey, I love you, Rod."

"Love you, too Claw. Go annoy your Mate."

She turns and asks Marcus, "Do I annoy you?"

"No."

"Rude is a bad color on you." She punches my arm playfully and then runs toward Marcus. I turn to see Claudia already flung over Marcus' shoulder, she grins and waves at me before biting his ass.

Marcus swats her own playfully. "No biting."

"Don't put my face near it!" They go up the stairs, and I turn away. There's a scuffle from them, and I peek over my shoulder to see Claudia wrapped around Marcus's front. Her legs wrapped around his middle, snuggling his neck as he smiles. I go back to work as his laughter echoes in the tavern.

A SOFT SMILE rises on my face. I pause with my drink when I hear creaking from the stairs. I look over to see Meg coming down and quirk a brow as she stops before the bar. She tugs the cardigan Delilah gave her closer.

"Didn't we discuss you staying on the third floor at night?" I ask.

"More like you ordered." I give her a look, and she purses her lips. "The bar's not exactly the West Wing," she comments, and I snort. "Besides, didn't you promise to protect me...*Rodrick*?"

"One, don't use my words against me. Two, don't call me that." She smirks, "Too formal?"

"Too similar to my father's name." Her expression softens, and I clear my throat. "Could even the playing field, tell me what Meg is short for."

"Hmmm, not yet."

We stay there in silence, and I find myself roving my eyes over her soft curvy figure. The way the light makes her skin glow with her hair pulled up. A feeling churns in my gut, pulling me toward her like a storm's current.

Her brows furrow, and she asks, "Have you been rolling around in a fireplace?"

I glance at the dust on my shirt. "Charcoal."

"So…yes?"

"No. Drawing."

"You draw?" Her brows shoot up.

"Hard to believe?"

"Yes," she replies, and her eyes go wide. "No! I mean… of course, you could draw or—"

"Quit while you're behind, darling."

She scowls, folding her arms over her chest. "In my defense, you haven't alluded to having a hobby outside of playing poker terribly and give, what you deem, *blunt* and *honest* remarks."

"I'm not that bad."

"For which one?" Her deadpan tone makes me snort suddenly.

"Why you up?"

"Jet lag." This time she smiles a little through the sarcastic tone.

I hold a bottle up. "Alright, sassy pants…" I say, and her jaw drops in amused shock, "…want a drink?"

She glances above, then back to the bar. Her gaze catches mine, assessing me before she carefully sits across from me at the bar. "Just not vodka, please."

I chuckle and grab another glass. I turn to see her looking at the shot of whiskey still on the bar. She looks back at me, folding her hands in her lap. "What's your *actual* poison, darling?"

"Red wine," she answers, and I look at her in shock. Wasn't expecting that. "What?"

"Didn't peg you as a wine drinker, let alone red."

"Wine isn't exactly a… *mob* thing. Especially within DiNardi's and Boston's organizations, so, I stick with martinis and mojitos."

"They didn't have wine listings at their clubs?" I switch out her glass with one meant for wine, and glance at what we have. "Cabernet, Merlot, or Shiraz?"

"Shiraz," she answers. I pull out a bottle and pour her a glass. "And probably no wine listings, because it would've clashed with the scent of coke and dried beer on the floor."

"Can't have that, what would the clients think?" I grab my drink and raise it. She does the same, then sips it. "To your liking?"

She gives a thoughtful expression and says, "I'll take it over the vodka."

I grin and so does she. Dimples appear at the side of her mouth, creating a beautiful expression. In my head, I can imagine how I'd draw her on paper, contrasting the light on her paler skin and dark hair. I breathe easy, unable to pull my gaze away from her. She stares out the windows, tilting her head in a gentle way. And that deep voice from inside says gently, *tell me to hold you.*

"I'm kind of sad I never came down here before," she whispers. "How much I've missed from..."

Her voice trails off, and I follow her gaze to the twinkling lights of the Underground outside. "Where did you live on Topside?" I ask, and she looks back at me. "Could check on it until it's safe for you to go back." She shakes her head. "If it's in a non-neutral zone, I still—"

"I lived above 4D."

Oh. "Shit, I'm sorry—"

"It's fine, wasn't much anyways." She sips her wine again. "So, this has been an upgrade."

"So, you agreed for the amenities?" I ask, and she snorts. She quickly covers her mouth. I smirk at her. "Oh, it must've been your curiosity about wolves then?"

"You know, I never saw Paranormals when I worked at Boston's bars," she says, her gaze flicks to the windows as a couple of shifters pass. "But I saw the most by 4D, I thought Paranormals could go into any zone?"

"We can, but you were just on mob turfs that don't allow Paranormals, well...we could, but won't. There are places Paranormals just don't ever enter. Boston and Greene are two we steer clear from, mob wise."

"Like some humans not entering neutral zones?" She asks, and I nod. She purses her lips, taking another sip, brows pinched. "I thought I knew how the world operated enough, but I guess not."

"Because of how you were raised?"

She shrugs. "I learned the essentials like where Undergrounds were, Paranormals you were likely to meet, and such. I could compare it to learning about a foreign city, something I thought I'd never see."

I hum, finishing my drink and pouring another small glass. "Where was the town?"

"Small one in Vermont."

"First part of my life I lived in Ireland," I talk, opening up as she watches me. "Small town, only werewolves, so I understand that upbringing. From a different view." Meg smiles gently at me, and I give her one back. "Why come to the big city?"

Her expression becomes sad, including her smile. "There was nothing left for me to stay."

An emotion I recognize flits over her gaze, something mournful. The weight of the past. The weight of death. "Want to talk about it?"

She leans back, swirling her wine. "Not really, it's been almost six years, and I've moved on. Closed the chapter, which I presume you're used to. With the longer lifespan? You must get used to moving on while the rest of humanity just…well, leaves."

Yeah, one would think that, except most of us hold grudges longer than human lives. Not that I'm speaking from experience. Not at all.

"What a decade is to you, can be a month to us," I answer, leaning on the counter. "Over time some memories blend, and you become used to living on while others…disappear."

"So, you live down here with those who don't disappear as quickly?"

"Sometimes," I say, looking at the whiskey still sitting next to her. Meg follows my gaze. "We live here mainly for safety. Even Paranormals have things that scare us in the dark."

She props her chin on her hand, and asks, "Such as?"

"Death for one," I say gruffly, looking at her and finding our faces only inches apart.

"What else?"

"Angry sisters." She giggles, and I grin at the delightful sound. "What about you?"

"You've mentioned one, already."

"Oh, so you have an angry sister, too?"

"Very funny, but no," she whispers. Meg gazes at me, still smiling softly. Her scent drifts under my nose, teasing with lavender, honey, and citrus. I remain still as I watch her smile fall and her lips tighten. A tendril of her hair falls, and I want to stroke it back from her face but find myself frozen. Her calm expression becoming weary and unsure.

"What are you scared of Meg?" I ask. She leans away, grabbing her wine. She swirls the glass then sips it, taking a deep breath.

"Being caged." My heart pounds in my chest as I freeze, guilt beginning to creep up my spine. "Yet, I've not felt that being here. Not truly."

"Meg—"

"Boston once locked me in a closet for three days," she whispers, her eyes meeting mine. "That's nowhere near the worst of it. But you've not once locked me in a room. Not once taunted me that the idea of freedom is futile."

"Yet I'm the one keeping you Underground," I murmur, my stomach twisting.

"But I believe in your word," she whispers. "Even with your gruff and bluntness, you've been kind, something I've grown unaccustomed to the past few years. And your morals *are* different from humans, at least those that I've known." She looks away, tracing her finger around the wine glass. "And you're not as...as scary as I first thought you were."

"We all play a character to survive," I reply suddenly. Her brown eyes meet mine, holding my gaze. A piercing feeling hits deep, remembering my mother pleading to my father to leave, letting them be done. Let her go. My throat constricts as I battle at the idea that I've already become my father, keeping her against her wishes. Even if she doesn't appear angry. Like I'm not some ruler, locking her below ground.

"I'll get you out," I rasp, and her eyes widen. "You won't go back to Boston, whatever is left of DiNardi's organization…I'll help you leave."

"He'll still come for me," she whispers.

"I've dealt with worse men," I state, and her shoulders drop. "I promise, you'll never go back into his hands or anyone like him. You have my word."

Her eyes glisten with unshed tears, and then she touches my hand. My breath hitches as her soft skin meets my rough hands. "Rodney, I promise I will help find whoever tried to kill you. You have my word, too."

I glance down at her hand over mine, and she starts to pull it away, but I quickly grab it. I don't want to lose that small bit of warmth. Her touch makes my head clear but makes my heart thunder.

"Then we have another accord, darling," I say quietly. "You believe in my word, and I'll trust in your help."

I force myself to let go, grab my whiskey, and hold it up. She stares at me for a few beats, then blinks rapidly. She smiles, clinking her drink with mine. "Agreed."

I finish mine, trying to get rid of the dryness in my throat. It becomes quiet and I start to clean. I'm putting bottles away when Meg asks a question that makes me pause.

"What do you draw?" I look over my shoulder at her. "Or we could continue talking about fears?" Yeah, cause that subject change will do it. Not.

"Portraits," I answer.

Her brows pinch and then points at me. "Thought you said you don't hire police sketch artists?"

"Do I look like police?"

"Could you've drawn those men the entire time?" Well, her belief in me went out the door quicker than a cheater through a window.

"I only draw faces I know."

"The Pack?" I shrug. "Then who do you draw?"

"Memories." The word comes out before I can stop it.

She's silent as I clean my glass. "Memories?" Her eyes flick to the whiskey still beside her.

"The ones that haven't blended."

"Such as?"

I sigh, close the cabinet doors, and collect her glass and the other. I dump the one for Claw. The outside lights shift to darker shades of violet and blue as I wash them, pausing to look at the glass I had out for Claudia. "Long life also means you hold on a bit too tightly to things you shouldn't."

She hums as I toss the rag into the sink. I clear my throat, "Alright, you know about my hobby, what about you? Turnabout is fair play, darling."

Meg smirks. "Florals." My brows raise in surprise again. "I worked in a floral shop in my hometown, and I loved it. Occasionally, I'd go to Central Park and see the gardens. Less in the past two years."

"Flowers don't mingle with mobs, either?" She purses her lips playfully and shakes her head. I look around the tavern. "Can't argue."

"Could spruce up the place," she says, getting up. "Add a daisy or two."

"Volunteering?"

"Are you asking?"

I chuckle and flick the light off over the bar. "We'll talk another time," I say, stopping at the stairs and gesturing for her to go first. "If you make that cocktail again."

"Maybe." She winks, walking past. I follow her up the stairs silently and down the catwalk to her bedroom door. She stops and turns with a soft smile.

"It's Megara," she whispers, and my muscles go slack as her brown eyes shine. "My parents had a thing for Greek mythology."

"I'll be sure to use it wisely," I murmur, leaning past to open her door. "Good night...Megara."

She stares up at me and my breath becomes shallow when hers opens slightly. I can practically taste the citrus and lavender, the warmth of her only inches away. Her eyes flick down, back up to my eyes as she swallows hard, chest rising heavily. The heat inside begins to pool into my stomach and a tingling sensation runs down to my fingertips, itching to touch her again.

Meg suddenly blinks. She clears her throat and disappears into her room.

A possessive growl threatens to break free as I prowl to my apartment, the heat unrelenting. Once I shut the door, my claws punch out from mid-shift and a snarl escapes as I rake my claws into the wall. A need writhes inside me, and I close my eyes concentrating to keep control. I take long breaths, trying to clear my nostrils while also remembering her scent.

Megara.

CHAPTER 12
AND I TAKE A DEEP BREATH—

Someone pounds on my door, jolting me awake. You gotta be fucking kidding me.

It's barely six in the morning. For shit's sake, today was supposed to be a break day. I've already slept like shit in the past week. Worse the past two nights from being plagued by feverish dreams involving Meg and waking up alone. And I didn't want to run my wolves into the ground working. Me included.

They knock again, and I growl, throwing off the blanket. I open the door with a snarl, greeted by Brenda sipping her thermos. "Looking adorable with bedhead, Lassie."

"Why are you banging on my door?"

"I have work, needed to see you first."

"What time do you start?"

"Seven." She really does run on coffee. "You're usually up by now."

"Break day."

"You choose today?"

"Yup."

"Oops."

"Yeah, *oops*, lil sis. I should tan your hide for knocking that loudly at *6 AM*."

"If I had good news, would ya forgive me?" I scowl at her. "I'll bring over one of Ma's pies."

I grumble, scratch my "bedhead" and wince at the sharp nails. She frowns and cocks her head. "Seriously, what's it gonna take for you to trim your nails?"

I roll my eyes and glance at the obvious empty tavern below. "Who'd kill me first if I threw you over the railing? Vincent or Alanzo?"

"Ma. Cause she'd have to stitch me up." Might be worth it.

I hear another door open, and we turn as Meg steps out in leggings and a loose sweater. Brenda gives a feral grin. Why does shit happen before breakfast? Before *coffee*?

"Hello there," Brenda greets.

Meg stops and quirks a brow. "General...Kenobi?" I roll my eyes. Great.

Brenda holds her hand out to Meg, and introduces herself, "Brenda Cuorebella, nice to meet you."

"Meg." She shakes Brenda's hand.

"Also known as annoying, *loud* lil sis without a sense of decency," I grumble.

Brenda snorts over her thermos. "Look who's talking."

Meg looks at me, eyes widening as she looks down and gapes in shock. She squeaks, quickly covers her eyes and turns away. She makes another distressed sound as Brenda chuckles.

I glance down. I'm naked.

In my human form, there's some fur on my shoulders and it runs down the middle of my back and part of my chest. I'm built like a human man, but bigger than any average human. My dark umber skin and hair don't hide anything from the imagination, including my free-swinging dick at the moment.

"Not even a kilt," Brenda tsks teasingly.

"Rodney...you...you're *naked*," Meg hisses, peeking over her shoulder, showing her *very* cherry complexion. I detect a twinge of arousal as she looks away. Yup, ego still intact.

"After the first couple of naked wolves, you'll get used to it." Brenda waves off flippantly.

"What are you talking about?" Meg asks.

Brenda looks at me with confusion. "Have you all *actually* been keeping your clothes on?"

"Mostly," I shrug.

"Someone please explain," Meg hisses as Brenda leans on the railing casually.

"Can I?" Brenda pouts dramatically. "Beckham will be ecstatic that I'm late because I'm lecturing."

"Lecturing?" Meg asks.

"Not a full one," I tell Brenda as I go back into my apartment and pull out my werewolf great kilt.

"Spark notes then," Brenda says. "Werewolves function similarly to animal wolf packs, surviving as a community or collective. Down here mostly, like a family, unlike above with the Topside Wolf Mob, where—"

"Straying!" I call out, lay down the fabric, and start pleating. I glance over my shoulder and notice Meg watching before she quickly looks away.

"But then I could go into the existence of other lycanthropes found in remote places, and their different living habits..." she protests, and I growl, "...fine. Another time. Basically, wolves don't give a shit if you're naked. Clothes are a nuisance to shift within. Being nude was normalized until werewolves encountered humans and then technology came in, which now there are clothes that'll shift with them. Except, some wolves choose not to conform and go 'au natural' or they stuck with other traditions, such as kilts."

"I thought it was because of their ancestry?"

"Somewhat, not every Pack wears them. Werewolves were introduced to kilts by humans who lived in what would become Scotland and Ireland. Donny, Rodney's grandfather, implemented them because it was easier to shift without ripping clothes or being naked in front of humans all the time. Kilts are adjustable to the larger sizes of werewolves, and he was trying to integrate with humans."

"What are the tartans?"

"The one he's pleating is the standard werewolf or Grey Wolf tartan," Brenda explains as I finish pleating. "The other you'll see is the McLycan Pack tartan, only those accepted into the Pack family can wear them. Your first is gifted to you by the alphas or the head alpha."

I fold over the kilt and lay down, buckling my belt, and catch sight of Meg watching me. Her eyes flick down, and she turns away as I chuckle softly.

"I thought Rodney was the alpha," Meg comments.

Brenda looks at me excitedly and I nod as I stand up. "Go ahead."

"Alphas and betas are titles," Brenda, well...lectures. "Alphas are the warriors of the Pack, the first line of defense to protect. While betas are the advisors or consultants; think before kill. Or football standards, alphas are the defensive lineman and betas are the quarterbacks. Gunther's a beta but could be an alpha if he wanted to, *but* it's harder being named beta than an alpha. Plus, you've gotta be granted that position within the Pack by more than three alphas."

"Marcus is an alpha," Meg mentions.

"Yeah, and so are Delilah and Zane, who's the newest," Brenda says as I tuck the corners of my kilt. "Rodney's just the head alpha of the Pack, due to being from the main lineage. But Pack is Pack, no matter who or what you are, long as you pass the trials." I lean in the doorway and smile at her in pride.

"Got excited there," I tell her. "Been a while since you've ranted about werewolves?"

"Daemons and ghouls for six months," she grumbles. "And archaic vampires."

"Your decision, lil sis."

"You sound like Pops," she mutters.

"If you're his...adopted sister," Meg says slowly, her eyes roving over my chest. She's gonna give me a damn hard-on if she keeps doing that. "Are *you* in the Pack?"

"Accepted at sixteen," I answer, and Brenda grins smugly. "Young even for those outside any lineage, but she knew her stuff."

Meg's brows furrow slightly, tilting her head. "How come this is the first time I've seen you in a kilt?"

My heart falters, and I glance down at the dark grey tartan, missing the other. I clear my throat, ignoring Brenda's inquisitive expression. "Mostly an Underground thing to wear them, and I've been Topside lately. Hard to break some habits."

"Still shocked she hadn't seen Zane naked first," Brenda comments.

"So, you're just used to it? The nudity?" Meg asks her.

"I grew up above a strip club," Brenda says deadpan, while I snort. Meg gapes, recovering quickly. "Raised by incubi and succubi, another species who'd rather be naked. Honestly, vampires and ghouls are the only main Noctis Immortalis who don't normalize 'communal' nudity, and that's due to assimilation with humans. I can explain more when I'm not telling you why he looked like Larry Talbot on a midnight stroll."

"Pain," I call her.

"Panic."

I snort laughter, lightly shoving Brenda's shoulder as she chuckles. I notice Meg's confused face and add, "Lil sis is a librarian and has a master's in Paranormal History and Literature. She used to work at the New York Public Library. If you want to learn beyond the essentials, she's the one to talk to."

"Impressive," Meg whispers, glancing at Brenda and then me, where her gaze flicks over my torso. She blinks rapidly and clears her throat. "I'm helping Delilah with breakfast, trying to keep busy until you drag the next mobster down here."

"And here I thought you were a civilized mob boss," Brenda taunts.

"Hey, you got a better idea, smarty-alick?"

"Well, you—"

"Actually, don't tell me." Meg laughs abruptly, and my senses lift at the wonderful sound. "What?" I ask playfully, giving her a half grin. She smiles back, biting her lower lip.

Suddenly, I hear Brenda intake a deep breath and go still. Her eyes start to glow. Damn it.

"*Don't,*" I warn in Noctora.

"*Then why do I smell—?*"

"*I said don't. And doesn't concern you.*"

"*Lassie.*"

"*Lil sis.*"

"I should go downstairs," Meg interrupts. "It was nice meeting you, Brenda. Maybe I'll see you around."

"Oh, you will," Brenda replies, keeping her glowing eyes on me as Meg passes her. "By the way, heard you're a bartender. What's your specialty?"

"Why do you want to know?" Meg asks, pausing near the stairs.

"May want to try it."

"I've had it," I say. "It's a secret cocktail, apparently."

"That wasn't it." I swing my gaze to Meg, who eyes me mischievously. "Something else entirely, but it's been years."

"Is that so?" I ask.

Delilah clicks the lights on in the bar, and Meg smiles softly before heading down the stairs. Her scent heightens with citrus and lavender, slamming into my nostrils and I'm glad I have the kilt on to hide my semi-erect cock. Well, fuck me.

"She got you to drink a cocktail?" Brenda asks, and I nod. "You liked it?" I nod again, my gaze following Meg as she disappears with Delilah. "*And* you gave her clothes?" I glare at Brenda, annoyed. "I'm right!"

"Quit it. She's just here to help—"

"Not with how her scent and yours just skyrocketed. And my eyesight may be shit, but even I can tell she practically eye-fucked you."

"Who gave you that mouth?"

"Mad scientist. Technically."

I groan, close the door behind me, and cross my arms. "We made a deal, which includes me getting her out when all is said and done. She wants out of the mob, Brenda. If you haven't noticed, I'm a mob boss."

"But you're an Underground Mafia boss, not the same as the Capone or Costello wannabes Topside."

"Doesn't change things," I say softly. "Sometimes the lines between Topside, the Pack, and here blur."

She sighs, and glances down, sipping from her thermos. "Fine, but I'm gonna tell you what Pops always told Joey before he took over."

"What's that?"

"At the end of the day, behind closed doors, take away the title yourself and others gave you...*that's* who you are. Forget the mafia shit. Then again, Pops has had six centuries to figure out who he is."

The exact opposite of what I've been told my whole life. The Pack was a priority, but the mob was everything else. It *had* to endure according to my father through titles. And a firm hand.

"Didn't you wake my ass up for something?"

"Oh, right." I roll my eyes. "My contact can meet wherever you want, but I have to be present."

"Who's the contact?"

"Detective Drauper," she answers, and I snarl instinctively as she holds her hands up. "He's good at finding intel. Trust me."

I sigh, knowing I don't have many options. "Fine. When?"

"Two days."

"I'll let you know where tomorrow."

"Get some coffee," she chuckles. "By the way, want a sock for your door?"

I growl, and she waves me off, disappearing downstairs and out the door.

"Hey, boss!" Delilah calls up, and I lean over the railing to see her pointing at her phone. "Victoria says we're gonna have company!"

So much for a fucking break.

CHAPTER 13
AL, BUGSY, JOHN, VITO, MICKEY...

"Put your kilt on," I order.

"I'm sweaty," Zane replies.

"Put your kilt on."

"But—"

"Put your *damn* kilt on, before I yank your dick off." He gives me a wicked grin, and I snarl.

"Alright! Alright!" He holds his hands up, storming upstairs as I glare at the other nude wolves. They soon follow behind. They'd gone on a morning run, in wolf form, which usually they'd just stay uncovered. Except, Meg's extremely red face needed a break.

It's late morning and Meg, Gunther, Marcus, and I sit at a back table in the tavern. Delilah shakes her head, attending the bar with Josh.

"Well, thank goodness for Brenda this morning," Meg murmurs.

"Yeah, her timing is a bit too on the nose," I grumble. I sip more of my coffee and glance at the clock. Victoria is escorting Johnny Calhoun down, who at least had the smarts to ask permission first. The past few hours I've been going through Calhoun's people, double-checking with Meg if he had anything to do with the bombing. He's in the clear. Even so, I don't like it and it smells of bullshit. No movement from him or the other bosses for a week, and *now* he shows up? My brows furrow as I glare at the front.

"He's covering his ass," Gunther says as if reading my mind. "Probably doesn't want to get caught in the middle of everything. He'll be in and out."

"Hopefully," Marcus grumbles.

"I'm normally right," Gunther retorts, and I give him a look. "I am and you know it."

"Want her out of sight?" Marcus juts his chin at Meg.

"No," I answer and look at her, who raises a brow in question. "Just sit there and look pretty."

She scoffs at me. "Should I get a fan to look demure?"

"Next time," I smirk. "This time no speaking, sit here, and keep Marcus company."

She motions zipping her lips tight. Marcus just frowns at me. I snort as Josh approaches, hanging up his phone. "Victoria's a block away."

"Get Zane back down here, clean or not, but covered." Josh motions at Edward, who bounds up the stairs.

I stand, having Meg stay put with Marcus. Gunther follows me to the bar. I lean against the counter, my foot propped as Delilah grabs some whiskey and pours some into my mug.

"Figured you'd want it," she comments.

"Remember when they used to be scared coming down here?" I ask.

She scoffs, "Yeah, cause the ceiling kept falling."

I snort and glance toward the front. Members from Topside Wolf Mob stand near the windows. All were passing through for route changes, now staying for the show. I murmur, "He may be in and out, but not without causing a ruckus. Make sure we keep up appearances. Don't need anyone tattling to my father."

Delilah and Gunther glance at the wolves. "Got it," she whispers. "Good to see you in a kilt again, boss."

I glimpse down at the button-up I put on, matching the grey tartan. Delilah walks away, and Gunther tries to hide his smirk. I mutter, "Don't even."

"Said nothing."

"Your face did."

Zane hits the first floor hard, prowling toward the Topside

wolves with Edward trailing him. You wouldn't know he was the same wolf complaining about having to put clothes on. A few minutes later Victoria comes in. Johnny Calhoun, mob boss of Brooklyn and New Jersey, who shares turf with Boston trails behind. He has two men with him, wearing black v-necks and slacks. Calhoun is a man in his late thirties, fit like a gym junkie who lives off protein powder. He has dark-tanned skin, coiffed brown hair, and almost black eyes. He's wearing a black v-neck with slacks, but with a velvet jacket and gold chain around his neck. Not to mention a cocky attitude.

I miss Bugsy and Al.

I move to the middle of the tavern as Victoria approaches, staying near the bar with Gunther. Calhoun walks towards me, bringing his hands up in mock surrender and a smile. His guards start to follow, but Zane and Edward pull their guns on them. Zane smirks, cocking back his revolver as a guard looks at him wide-eyed. "Last visitors pissed in my cereal."

Calhoun glances back at them, and I ask, "Wouldn't want to continue a pattern, would we?"

"Not at all," Calhoun replies with a shrug. "Guards don't come cheap." He snaps his fingers, and they move back. Zane and Edward lower their weapons. "Not as cocky as Charlie."

I snort, glancing at Gunther, who scowls. "What do you want?"

He looks around, then asks, "What about privacy?"

"No," I state, crossing my arms. "Let's try again. What do you want, Calhoun?"

"Just wanted to assure our relationship is intact, given how, well...chaotic Topside is at the moment," he says, pointing at the ceiling. "Boss to boss as it were. See, I've gotta do what I can to protect future assets and relationships, and you're one of them."

I frown deeper, a warning ticks down my spine, not liking where this is going. If it feels like a trap...probably damn well is. I raise my brows, nodding for him to continue. He flicks his gaze to all the wolves around us, watching with hungry eyes.

"Why don't we cut to the chase?" He asks, moving to the bar, but Delilah snarls at him and he stops.

"That would be a relief," I mutter.

"I just want to show you some good faith," Calhoun says, putting his hands in his pockets. "That I won't get in your way, whatever objective you may have with Topside and other businesses. Again, I want to make sure *our* relationship and businesses find success, unlike DiNardi who seemed to play the wrong cards, but it happens. Pity, I liked the kid, and we were on good terms."

These mobsters are making me miss Dracultelli.

"What was that about cutting to the chase?"

"What I'm saying is that in the past couple of days, I've had to...realize how to move forward for future endeavors. Certainly wouldn't want to make the same mistake as DiNardi. Trusting the wrong people."

"Get on with it, *Johnny*."

He cocks his head, keeping his suave presence. My senses tingle, telling me he thinks he has something on me. A low snarl hits the back of my throat, and he finally says, "Thought we could come to an agreement of some kind. Boston and Greene are moving turfs, and see, I could use the territories DiNardi had, which *you* have access to. Anything you're not using from his old territories, I'd gladly take—"

"I don't," I state. "Our territories were close, but they're not mine. Never have, never will, even after death. An agreement between me and his grandfather. You all can fight over it if you want."

Calhoun narrows his eyes suspiciously, and says, "Was told DiNardi was selling to you. Everything in the Bronx and north since you lost so much to the feds lately." The insinuating tone in his voice starts to make my blood boil. I exchange a glance with Gunther.

"What the fuck are you talking about?"

"Rumor is that he was selling to you, that's why he died. He double-crossed you or was backing out. Although, I *never* believed you'd be someone to blatantly kill another boss over territory. You have more class than the rest of us humans, but it was *your* explosives that killed him..."

Anger writhes inside me, hating that myself and my Pack are being dragged deeper into this. Whatever truth was out there is being twisted, the gun being pointed back at *my* mob. After *we* almost died. Fuckers are blaming us now.

My claws begin to grow as I partially shift, and growl, "Who the fuck told you these *rumors*?"

Calhoun's eyes widen at the small shift, and Gunther warns, "Suggest you tell him."

The boss clears his throat and adjusts his jacket. "Boston."

"Is that so?"

"He said one of his 'little' birdies told him weeks ago, warning him that DiNardi was selling to the Underground Mafia. Actually, just you. They knew about the explosives, and that you were taking back zones from DiNardi into Manhattan—"

"That's not true!" Meg shouts.

I spin as Meg is yanked back by Marcus, holding her against his chest. "He's lying! DiNardi wasn't—"

"And how would you know?" Calhoun sneers. "Unless you're said bird, which makes sense." She glares at him, held back only by Marcus' arm. "If not the Wolf Mob, who else would've he been selling to?"

Meg starts to pale and the drift of her fear wafts under my nose. "A…another mob. Human mob."

"Yeah, right," Calhoun cackles. "Although, I heard you're the only survivor, and you seem to know a few things…wouldn't have planted the bombs yourself, would ya, girl?"

My stomach drops when Meg's wide eyes meet mine. Betrayal and failure begin to rise at the back of my mind. "No…no, no, Rodney…don't listen to him…"

"They always get squirmy when they get caught, huh?" Calhoun continues as my skin crawls while my stomach drops.

"That's not—"

"Come on, McLycan," Calhoun says smugly. "We both know how traitorous some people are, especially for the right price."

"No…I never…please, *please* listen to me!" Meg pleads again as some of the wolves in the tavern adjust their stances, growling low.

My head starts to swim as I look away from her, trying to decipher through the torrent of emotions and thoughts.

A loud growl emanates from my throat, stopping her and other noises in the tavern. I can't look at her as anger engulfs my chest. My father's disappointment echoes in my head, warning me of my failure. *Your decisions will destroy everything.* Finally, I gaze into her eyes. Hearing my father's voice mixed with screams and the smell of napalm I struggle to believe her.

"Moles you can't trust them, McLycan," Calhoun comments, and I swing my glare at him. "He warned me about her, that's why he wanted her back. Conniving. Will play you. Well, I could take her back—"

"*No.*" The word echoes in the tavern, flourishing with my anger. Calhoun takes a step back as the snarl that comes out next shakes the glasses, something primal snapping inside. I step forward, and Calhoun backs up again.

"She's *mine.* And I'll remind you as I reminded Boston." I bring my face close to his, and he gulps, losing his cocky attitude. "Do *not* come into my territory demanding deals."

"Wait, I was just proposing—"

"And *I* propose you stay the fuck out of my way, go back to Jersey before I *do* become that one who blatantly kills bosses."

He steps back slowly, nodding. "Course, we're good McLycan...we're good." My head cocks slowly, like a predator assessing his prey as I feel myself on the brink of shifting. Calhoun visibly shakes. "Want nothing to do with you and Boston. Swear."

"Get out. And careful where you get your *rumors* from," I tell him, narrowing my eyes. He nods then tries to walk out like he didn't just piss his pants as he leaves. I flit my gaze to Marcus, and order, "Take her to my office. *Now.*"

Marcus' face darkens, and I bare my teeth at him. The entire tavern becomes deadly quiet. A moment passes with harsh tension, before he starts taking her up the stairs. My heart pounds, unsure how badly I've fucked up. The air is heavy, and I keep my snarling expression as I look at the Topside wolves.

Victoria gestures to something in her hand. I motion her

forward, and she stops next to me. She grabs my hand and puts a piece of paper in it. Close to my ear, she whispers, "He was found prowling near Freyja's borders."

She presses it into my hand, and I glance down at the name, snarling low. Travis.

"How long ago?"

"Few weeks. Same time as Ralph."

"Track him." She nods, about to leave, but stops. "What?"

"Be careful." I snap my head, finding her face close to mine. "I know you have a soft heart, but please...be careful."

Victoria touches my arm gently and walks away, following the mobsters that just left. I jut my head at Zane, who orders all the Topside wolves out. They all disappear, leaving only me and a few of the Pack left. Once the doors shut behind them, I head for the stairs. I feel like I'm going to burst from my skin, bristling with churning emotions.

Delilah chases after me, "Rodney, there's no way she—" I bare my teeth at her, and she does it back, keeping her ground. "Calhoun's messing with you, along with Boston."

"She's right," Gunther adds. "We know Meg's been helpful, don't listen..."

My head becomes swamped with guilt, not hearing any of their voices. *You're getting fucking soft. Rodney! Your decisions will destroy everything. Scatter! You're ruining—*

"Rod." Zane's voice strikes through the voices in my head. His light green eyes find mine. My lungs hurt, squeezing harder and harder. His expression falls, and he shoves past Delilah and Gunther. He snaps at them as they back away as he brings his head close to mine. "You're better than them. Including Fredrick."

"Zane—"

"Don't let those gobshites into ya head."

I try to calm my fury coiling under my skin, warping with betrayal, guilt, and failure. I nod once and he steps back as I head up the stairs. Zane keeps the others below. I come to my office door, where Marcus stands, scowling as he crosses his arms over his chest.

"You're not Fredrick," Marcus murmurs, echoing Zane.

"I'm only talking with her."

"Doesn't mean you won't hurt her." I bare my teeth, and he brings his face close to mine. "Don't condemn her before you know her story. Survival is survival."

A flicker passes over Marcus' gaze, but his hard scowl remains. I take a calming breath, and order softly, "Move...Marcus."

His blue eyes search mine then steps aside. I open the door, walk in, and lock it behind me as I face Meg. She stands near my desk, watching me carefully.

"They're both lying," she says, and I just watch her. The warning sensation at the back of my spine is gone, seeing the worry in her eyes. Not fear.

Emotions thrash inside me, yanking me in every direction as I try to make sense of everything. If I'm better than my father, then why do I feel like I keep failing? Not seeing the obvious, not interrogating her, or forcing what she knows? What could've helped or if *she* had been the one who'd done it? Smoke drifts in the back of my mind, burning memories as I fear what else I'll fail. Keeping my Pack safe. The pressure builds on my shoulders, and it feels like forever ticks by in silence. We stare at each other in the silence as my fear stretches across my chest, threatening to break me.

"You promised you'd never give me back to Boston, correct?" She asks gently. "Will that include others?"

"Depends on what you lied about," I answer, and she straightens. "What you hid."

The way she swallows harshly is answer enough. I fall back against my door, wanting to disappear into my studio. How much did I fuck up by trusting her? *Assuming* she wouldn't backstab me after Boston?

"Promise me you'll keep your word. Keeping me safe," she pleads, reminding me of that first meeting.

It takes all my willpower to not let tears form in my eyes, aching and wrenching in my heart. I'm confused with anger and hurt bristling, while her eyes and scent taunt me. One part says to trust her, while the other threatens to tear her apart.

"Yes," I rasp.

She takes a long breath and admits, "Antoni found out I was a mole. For the last seven months I've been feeding Boston false information."

"You became a double agent," I murmur.

"I was helping Antoni, but I swear *nothing* had anything to do with the Wolf Mob or the Underground Mafia. He wouldn't dare touch any of you. It was between him and the other human mobs."

"What were you helping him with? Selling his territories?"

"Kind of," she whispers. "He was getting out. I helped obtain information on Boston and Greene, which would guarantee my freedom, too. Only he and I knew that he...was talking to police. I didn't even know his handlers. He met with them, I think, in SoHo. He was giving up everyone, *everyone*, including his own organization. He was selling everything to the feds."

"I'm supposed to believe a *mob boss* from a well-known mafia family of the last *century* was defecting?"

"He was. You *have* to believe me."

I stand fully as I try to think. Questions flit over my mind, and then pieces of memory come forward. That night. I could scent DiNardi was sober. "How long until he was supposed to get out?"

"A couple of months? He'd been working toward this for years, compiling lists of names, accounts, and businesses. I didn't see most of it, but he had information that went back years."

"And it wasn't you who blew the place?" I ask, and her jaw goes slack. "Afraid he was going to—"

"Something happened weeks before the explosion," she interrupts, glaring at me. "He stopped going to SoHo, and then two individuals, whom I'd never seen before kept appearing. They wore suits and I never learned who they were, but *they* were there long enough to plant the bombs." Meg tightens her jaw and swallows hard. "I think...I saw them bring it in."

It feels like lead has fallen into my stomach, dragging me down.

"You *knew* it wasn't mob, wasting my—"

"I didn't know *who* it was," she argues. "But it wasn't me, I swear to you." I stare at her as she wraps her arms around herself. "I'm sorry, I didn't tell you the whole truth, I wasn't trying to deceive you. I don't know who they were, but maybe *you* did. But if...you'd known I was working with police...that..."

"DiNardi and you were defecting, I wouldn't have helped you," I finish for her. Her eyes meet mine and she nods. "You used me and the Pack as your bodyguards."

"Antoni was still talking with others, like Sebastian, who could've known or realized. The police didn't know I was helping Antoni, and they may not have believed me. You were all I had left, and so...I...I made the deal with you."

This is why it's a bigger mess on Topside. The feds lost their key to the steal of the century. "Do you know where DiNardi kept everything?" She nods stiffly. Fuck, if the mobs find out Meg was involved, she'll be on their Most Wanted list.

"Rodney, I swear the Underground Mafia wasn't supposed to be involved," she murmurs, as she steps closer. "I swear, it wasn't about you. I thought Antoni was getting ready to get out with the bombs, but when they blew...and he died, I thought..."

I move around her, tearing my shirt off as it feels like I'm overheating. Meg stays clear as I toss ragged clothing, breathing heavily, unsure what to believe. She could be telling the truth, that a mob boss was turning everyone in. Or lying to save her own ass. I thought I'd conned her into a deal when it was the other way around.

"Anything else?" I ask gruffly.

"No, but Rodney please don't be mad—"

"For some damn reason, I'm not. Not about that," I say, stalking back to her. "You were neck deep into a spider web of the worst human beings to cross in the city. If they found out what you know or were planning, there'd be nothing left of you. Nowhere is safe for you in New York, maybe even the Underground. So, I would've done the same as you, but that doesn't mean you didn't hurt me. *Lied* to me."

I tower over her, but she doesn't budge, staring up at me. Her jaw tenses as her scent rises, swamping me in her aroma. A growl escapes my throat. "I'm sorry," she murmurs. "Truly. My word still stands in helping you. Just like I know you'll keep your word. You'll keep me safe from them. I'm safe with *you*."

"Is that so?" I snarl.

"Yes."

"You're riding a lot on a deal made on lies there, darling."

"No," she states.

"No?" I step forward, and she backs up to press against the door. My hands above her head, bringing my face close to hers.

Her gaze doesn't falter with mine as she takes a deep breath in. "It's because of the mercy in your eyes."

It feels like my chest is being throttled. The weight on my shoulders is minuscule in comparison. Suddenly, all twisting emotions disappear as I stare into her eyes as if I'm staring into evening morning hills. Hope. Freedom. Any sense of betrayal or lies is gone, consumed by the woman's gaze below me. I try halting the tremble in my limbs, flicking my gaze to her lips.

Get your shit together Rodney. She just revealed a fuckton of info.

I take a long breath in, which partially makes things worse as I taste the citrus of her scent. I exhale harshly, making strands of her hair flutter.

"Honesty here on out," I rasp. "No more dancing around. No more hiding. No more *maybes*...Megara." A hardness comes over her gaze. "You're not going anywhere, but I am someone who deals in absolutes, and you're gonna start doing the same."

She brings her face closer to mine, barely inches apart. "Anything else?"

Her scent is heavy as I bring my face to her ear, and growl low, "Anything you want or need, tell me. No more fucking secrets."

Her entire body shivers as she shudders a breath. I step back, giving her space as the heat continues to build in my gut. My hands twitch, wanting to grab her and press my body against hers. What the fuck is wrong with me?

"Don't tell anyone about DiNardi," I mutter. "Go show Marcus you're in one piece."

She turns away and whispers, "You'd never harm me, and not because of a Pack law."

"Why not then?"

"Deep down...Rodrick Rowan McLycan..." she murmurs, glancing back at me, "...you have better morals than most. I think *including* Paranormals."

I'm left standing in my office, frozen as she slips out. I take a few steps and fall back into a leather chair. I feel fucked up from emotions raging inside me, betrayal twisting my gut, and my head pounding trying to make sense of it all. I rub my head as it starts to throb. She may be the end of me in more ways than one.

And I don't think I care.

♡ Honey Lavender
Cupcakes

Flour
Butter
Sugar
Powdered sugar
Eggs
Milk
Baking powder
Vanilla
Salt
Honey
Lavender extract
Lavender flowers

CHAPTER 14

PIB: PARANORMALS IN BLACK

Marcus grumbles next to me as we walk through Central Park on Topside at the brink of twilight. The early winter is already closing in with its cold chill and light snow. Something you don't have to worry about in the Underground. It's not freezing. There aren't many people out as we approach the meeting point.

"You agreed to up here, why?" Marcus grumbles.

"The detective will be more open on his turf," I answer. And being below has been stifling the past 24 hours.

I haven't spoken to Meg since Calhoun showed up, staying mostly in my office. I told Marcus and Gunther about what Meg told me. Apparently, they believe her about Antoni defecting. Honestly, so was I, even if it sounds unbelievable. Except all we have is her word.

"It's freezing," Gunther mutters.

"Not *that* cold, Lucky," I say.

"I have sensitive skin."

I roll my eyes as we head down a path toward the Balto statue, and smirk glancing at Marcus. He grumbles more, making his scowl worsen. "You've *got* to be kidding me."

Gunther snickers as we stop. Marcus crosses his arms in annoyance. Okay, so maybe, I didn't tell him exactly where we'd be meeting because I wanted to see his reaction. It's been a rough couple of days, and I needed the chuckle.

We see Brenda and the detective approach. He has dark copper skin, a close fade, and a shadow of a beard. Comparably to other men, he'd be tall, but not to a couple of werewolves pushing past six and a half feet. His brown leather jacket is like Brenda's, and I notice he's not wearing his badge.

Brenda nods away from the path, and we follow into an area covered with some fir trees and a boulder. Marcus snarls at her, and she smirks. "Enjoying the scenery?"

"You're a smartass," he growls.

"What? Great scenery around here and history."

"You didn't choose it because of history."

"I didn't choose it, *Balto*," she says, glancing at the detective whose brown eyes go wide. "He did."

"*You* did?" Marcus questions.

"Thought it was neutral enough," the detective answers, staying close to Brenda.

"Ignore him he's just grouchy when his joints get cold," Brenda says. "Let's start introductions. Detective Louis Drauper, my NYPD contact, and the Brady Bunch are Marcus, Gunther, and Rodney McLycan."

I cross my arms as Louis stares at me. He takes a small step back, whispering to Brenda, "You said we were meeting the Wolf Mob, not the *fucking* boss."

"That 'fucking' boss can hear you," she chuckles.

"Brenda, we agreed—"

"We've already had breakfast if that's what you're worried about," I say, and Brenda snorts. His scent mingles with passionflower and lotus with a hint of fear. Good.

"They're the good guys, Drauper," Brenda says. "They want the truth, too. Our endgame is the same; keep the innocent safe. Trust me, Rodney knows how the mobs interact on Topside and Underground the most."

"Not by choice," I mutter, and Gunther flicks his gaze to me.

"It'll be fine," she reassures.

"Not your badge on the line if anyone sees me standing here with them," he retorts.

"Is your badge worth beings' lives?" I question, and he swings his gaze to me, tightening his jaw. "Your fear of losing your *replaceable* job is how you get people killed." Or caught up in the damn mob, like Meg.

"Like you know anything—"

"About six times your age, try me."

"As if that—"

Marcus snarls. Louis steps back while Brenda gets between them. She gives Marcus an exasperated look. "Can you not?"

"He started it."

"Seriously?"

"Look, I'm *actually* the good guy here," Louis says.

"Not this again," she mutters. "Don't make it worse."

"Worse? We're talking to a mob boss."

"So?" Brenda shrugs.

"Exactly," I interrupt. "So, how *good* are you, detective?"

Gunther grabs my shoulder, and then Marcus', speaking in Noctora, *"We're here to find solutions, not more problems. If lil sis trusts him, we can, too."*

"You didn't see her that night," Marcus snarls.

"We move on," Brenda chimes in, and my gaze meets her. *"Give him a chance."*

I look at Gunther's bright eyes, advising Marcus and me to keep our cool. If what Meg said is true about Antoni, and the feds are involved, he's our only trustworthy connection to Topside.

Marcus and I exchange a look, easing up as Gunther moves forward stepping between us and the detective. He holds out his hand and smiles. "It's been a long week, but we trust lil sis, so we'll trust you. So, why don't we put differences aside to achieve our end goals? Helping those we care about."

Louis looks at Brenda, then back to Gunther. His jaw works but shakes Gunther's hand. "Fine."

And thus, why Gunther's my main beta. Somehow getting two alphas to back down and begin an agreement with a human cop.

"What do you got?" Gunther asks. Brenda steps back, giving the floor to Louis.

He shakes his head and pulls out his phone. "PSB took over the investigation of the bombing of 4D about three days ago. NYPD and FBI were in charge until they found traces of explosives they thought belonged to your…mob."

"They were," Gunther says, and Louis narrows his gaze. Gunther smiles. "Someone else used them, almost killed us, too. People are cheeky like that."

"Uh-huh." Louis clears his throat. "Well, they traced it. Didn't quite confirm it's yours, but it was enough for PSB to make a statement and take over the investigation due to Paranormal involvement."

"But PSB and NIIA haven't come knocking," I say.

"They're saying they are." I exchange a look with Brenda, who gives me a weary expression. "A few weeks back, I found footage outside the center you all blew up," he says, bringing his gaze to me, and I smirk. "A couple of people dressed like feds walked toward the center a few nights before it blew. But that footage is gone now."

"Did you get copies?" Gunther asks.

"No, someone wiped it clean before I could. Not even a footprint. Whoever they are, they can cover their tracks well, but Brenda asked me to dig again, and I found something." He holds his phone and shows footage pointed toward a street a few blocks from 4D. It's grainy, but I can make out two men dressed in dark suits walking down the street away from the camera. Faces mostly hidden.

"How'd you find this?" Gunther asks. "We searched for days and got nothing."

Louis doesn't answer and Brenda nudges him. "They're not gonna give away your secrets," she murmurs. He gives her an exasperated look, and she grins.

He sighs, and admits, "This traffic camera was decommissioned about two years ago. It's still working, just not connected to the system. You have to go through some old firewalls to get to the feed, but it's doable. It's about four blocks from the club, dated the night before the bombing. They didn't come back the same way, and I tried the same trick with other decommissioned cameras, but nothing."

"DiNardi could've smuggled them out," I suggest.

"Any car with tinted windows you wouldn't be able to see shit," Gunther mutters. "Drop the explosives off, hightail out of there."

"The men aren't carrying anything," Louis says.

"Wouldn't need much to blow one club," Brenda huffs. "Their jackets are all they need to hide it, get into the club, and get out."

"And we didn't sniff out the explosives until it was almost too late," I mention. "They were trying to hide it. Anything closer to the club?"

"I was able to get into the club's security system, but everything was wiped and pulled five hours before the explosion," Louis answers. Is this detective fucking MacGyver?

"Same time frame we caught Ralph," Marcus mutters to me.

"Is there a way to get a shot of their profiles?" I ask.

"Low probability, but this is all a hunch anyways."

"We have a way to ID them, make sure it was them."

"How?" Louis asks.

"Got an inside man," Gunther jumps in, reaching back to pat my shoulder.

"Heard all of DiNardi's guys died. Not true?"

"Oh, his *guys* are dead," Gunther answers, and Brenda rolls her eyes. "We got someone else who was there the night before. Can help confirm and figure out who they are. You know, without traipsing through PSB's employee appreciation posts." Louis flashes his gaze between us, narrowing his eyes. "So, if you could send the footage."

Louis exhales sharply, then types on his phone. Brenda's goes off, and then she sends it to Gunther. "Use whatever you want, but just know I have copies."

"Like any good cop," Gunther smirks, relaxing his stance more. "Find anything else?"

Louis glances at Brenda. I'm not sure what their deal is, but something keeps nagging me every time he looks at her. Maybe the lack of sleep is getting to me or not feeling the best with trusting anyone outside the Pack. Not to mention the man almost got Brenda killed a few times, used a warrant to barge into the Underground, and almost got an incubus murdered.

It's probably that.

"Tell them. May be connected and why those agents showed up," she suggests.

"I told you it's top secret," Louis mutters.

"Won't tell your bosses," Gunther comments. "Promise."

Louis adjusts his coat, and sighs. "Antoni DiNardi was talking to NYPD for two years. He was leaving the mob. For good."

Meg was fucking telling the truth.

Marcus and Gunther give me a quick glance as I keep my expression neutral apart from my racing heart. A part of me hoped she'd been lying; it'd have been easier getting her out. Keeping her alive. But now…shit just got more complicated.

"What was the deal?" I ask.

"Bring in Charlie Boston, Johnny Calhoun, and Malcolm Greene, including his own operations. Then he'd get immunity. He played the long game but had another two months left. Tops. He was willing to get rid of everything. There was also talk he was selling to the Wolf Mob, but never confirmed."

"He wasn't."

"That's what I said," Brenda adds.

"Didn't say I believed it," Louis says, looking at her. "I wasn't part of the operation, but a buddy was. Two years down the drain once DiNardi stopped contacting his handler about 4-5 weeks ago. Didn't show up for his meet, phone went dark, and the two inside people we had disappeared."

"Two years and he just stops?" Gunther asks.

"Could've got caught," Marcus mutters. "Not by police." Our eyes meet, and my stomach drops. Sebastian. This just keeps getting lovelier and lovelier.

Brenda taps his shoulder, and Louis glares at her. "I'm getting to it," he says and continues. "I tapped into the burner phone he used before he got into contact with police. It was activated a week before he was killed. Five phone calls, all encrypted to government-related numbers rerouted to shell companies."

I narrow my gaze at the detective. "How did you even get access to that number?"

Louis meets my gaze, tightening his jaw. "Deal was to provide you with information, not the how." For someone who claims to be the good guy, he sure knows how to get intel. The detective switches his attention back to Gunther. "Whoever he called; they weren't our guys. Maybe mob?"

Gunther shakes his head, and says, "Not with government numbers. Too risky."

DiNardi's begging last words echo in my head again. *They promised. They promised.* Was someone offering a different deal, better than the feds were giving? It could've been Freyja; she's been known to use encrypted numbers. Whoever made DiNardi stop promised him something. In my gut I knew Meg was more involved than what she even believed. If someone *did* realize what DiNardi was doing, they'd be after her next. Maybe those explosives weren't meant for us, used as a red herring from who really was after DiNardi...but that feels too easy.

Gunther crosses his arms. "Will have to find who, but...damn you're good, detective."

"And earned the name Sherlock again," Brenda says, patting Louis' back.

"Thanks," he mutters.

"Can you track those numbers?" I ask.

"I'd need time. And luck."

"What about the investigation, who are they pushing toward?"

"As I said, you all."

"Who gave that announcement?" I continue pressing, while Gunther gives me a weary look.

"Director of the PSB Alliance Branch for New York."

"Why the Alliance Branch?" Marcus asks suddenly.

"Because napalm presumably made by Paranormals to destroy a *human* club is against International Paranormal Law. You should be familiar with it." Marcus snarls and Louis leans away.

"Careful," I warn.

"Just because those men could be PSB agents, doesn't mean the agency is part of this."

Marcus snorts in disbelief.

Gunther intervenes gently, "We could speculate all day, but how about we don't go accusing the detective who's helping us?" He then looks at me. "I'm sure he can look into any connections, including the phone numbers, let's give him time. We'll need to recalibrate if the other bosses scramble for DiNardi's territories and if they point fingers at us."

I try to keep my cool as my head starts to pound. Saying I'm on edge would be an understatement, more than usual. I don't like any of this, and my gut is filled with dread. Gunther shifts, finding my eyes and I nod. "Yeah."

"And we'll protect our own, right, boss?" I nod again, listening to my beta. He squeezes my shoulder, reassuring me. "Detective, I'll keep in contact with you. Let us know when you find something."

"Hold on, he's still my contact," Brenda says. "You go through me first."

"Afraid I'll tell him stories about you?" Gunther teases.

"Gotta compare notes," she smirks. "He and I will search through more footage and push out the radius to see what else we can find. And I'll talk to Midnight on—"

"You're not getting any more involved," I growl.

"Rodney, we talked about this. I'm helping."

"To bring in the detective, that's it." I take a step toward her, and she crosses her arms. "You've been through enough."

"Again, I'm a big kid now. I decide what I'm involved in. Not you." Louis steps back, along with Marcus and Gunther, knowing this is between her and me.

"And I decide who's part of the business. *You* are not."

"This isn't just Wolf Mob; this is the Pack and the Underground Mafia. If those agents are the same—"

"No."

"I'm part of this whether you like it or not," she argues, pointing at her facial scars.

"Your want for vengeance is blinding you."

"Look in the mirror, Lassie."

I snarl at her, bringing my face close to hers, but she doesn't budge. Her eyes glow as she stands her ground against me, and my body starts to shake. Slowly, the drifting of smoke invades my mind with the smell of burning flesh.

"You didn't argue when I went into the center or the Bronx to investigate," she counters, and it feels like the smoke is choking me.

"Because you had protection."

"I can protect myself! You even said I'm the best shot there is in the Underground."

"Brenda."

"Or how about that I can slice people in half now?"

"Those abilities won't always save you."

"Like yours didn't at 4D?" She jabs my chest, and it feels like she's placed a stake in it.

"Brenda," Marcus warns. "Stop."

"Of course, you're siding with him!" She yells at him. "I'm sick and tired of being told what to do. Fuck! Even Vinny compromises with me, *trusting* me to take care of myself."

"'Cause he's there to help you," I rasp.

"Oh, but you'd get angry if I brought him into it, huh?" She questions as my heart pounds. "Can't fucking put your pride down for once and ask help from others like Vinny. You're fine using people like Drauper, but only on *your* conditions, even when myself...*right here,* is offering. Why? I've proven I know what I'm doing. I took care of Traloski, didn't I? Even Bruno!"

"Lil sis, stop," Gunther pleads.

"I can help take care of business, so trust me to do this," she insists.

"*I've got business to finish.*" It feels like my chest cracks as the past roars back. Screams echo in my head as Claudia waves goodbye one last time and Brenda walks down the tunnel. Last goodbyes. Gone. Flames devour the memories, replacing hope with unending pain. All the anger dissipates from my body, agony replacing it with horror, making my breathing shallow. I try to focus on her eyes, but I keep seeing only hollow ones. Dead ones. My vision darkens as I hear Brenda's screams, "*Scatter and get below! Run!*" And then my own screams echo, "*Don't make me bury her! No—!*"

"Rodney." Brenda's voice reaches me, and I blink. Through my darkened vision, I see her worried expression. She reaches for me, but I turn and walk away. "Rodney!"

"No, let him go," Gunther says, keeping her there.

My body shakes, aching as the gnawing in my gut worsens as I stalk through the snow-covered park in silent agony.

———

I STORM INTO *MOUNTAIN EDGE*, slamming the door behind me and heading for the stairs.

"No disturbances," I say darkly to Zane in passing. "Gunther will catch you up when they get back."

"Rod—"

I loosen a snarl and he quiets. I prowl to my apartment, shutting the door loudly as I rip away my jacket and shirt as the memories come flooding back. My body shifts into hybrid form as I toss a table at a wall, shattering it. It feels like fire engulfs my coiling, throbbing muscles as I rip my claws into the carpet, trying to make the memories go away. I can't stop hearing their voices, scratching at my mind. Screams invade with shattered brick. I shake my head in agony as tears fall, loss weighing heavy with guilt.

She should be turning two hundred, making Marcus laugh, and helping Delilah run *Mountain Edge*. It was hers. Always hers. My little sister is dead. I can't lose...

Joey's voice echoes in my head, *"She's dying. Baby sis is dying, something about—"*

My entire body tenses as I fist my hands, hitting the floor. Make it stop. No. No...

I let out a strangled roar and claw at the floor, trying to control my rage and not destroy my apartment again. Until I see a picture of Claudia and me together. A soft whine leaves me, echoing in the unforgiving emptiness as I slump on my hunches. Tears gather which make my vision blurry.

There's a soft knock at the door, and I snarl, "Not now!" They do it again, and I roar, *"No!"*

I heave strangled breaths, trying to focus, until they knock *again*. I get up and swing the door open with a vicious growl. Meg stares up at me. My heart stops as her scent changes, and I start to back away.

"Wait," she says calmly, and I stop as she holds up a plate. I look down at five cupcakes with pink icing and small pearl-like beads. Her citrus and lavender aroma blossoms. "It sounded like you needed a cupcake."

I tilt my head as saliva trickles down my jowl, and quickly wipe it away. She smiles, and my instinctive reaction is to curl my lips, which doesn't deter her. She grabs a cupcake and holds it out. "My specialty."

I stare into her gentle earthen eyes. For all I know, this is the first time she's ever seen a werewolf in hybrid form. Here I am snarling with bared teeth, twice her height. And she's offering me a cupcake…with pearls.

I take the dessert, which is extremely tiny in my large hands. I poke it with a claw.

"It doesn't bite," she murmurs, and I huff at her. "And make sure you come down to dinner."

"You telling me what to do?"

Meg's eyes widen at my deep, timber voice, then smirks, "I'm telling you what I want, no maybes. And I don't think your Pack would appreciate you withering away."

She flicks her gaze down my front and walks away. I see Zane leaning in the stairwell, watching in awe. I scowl, look at the cupcake and sniff it. Looking at the pink frosting, I take a small bite.

"Is there champagne in this?" I ask as she reaches Zane.

Meg looks over her shoulder. "I didn't have shitty vodka."

CHAPTER 15

MIDNIGHTS AND AFTERNOONS

I went down to dinner.

Marcus and Gunther updated the others, handling business accordingly, not mentioning what happened with me. I remained quiet throughout dinner as Meg spoke with the others, while my brain felt like mush. My body was heavy as if I'd been hit by three trains. I left for my studio soon after, leaving behind the talkative group as they set up for cards. They're still playing as I come down, hours later, covered in charcoal dust.

I head to the bar, reminding myself to restock booze in my apartment. The back doors open as I grab a bottle. Meg steps out into the tavern, stopping a few feet from the bar. "Want me to make you something?"

I stare at her, wanting to disappear, but the weariness in my bones makes me put the bottle back. I gesture toward the bar, walking around the counter to sit. She skims past me, grabbing the Irish whiskey. I smirk.

"You did kinda ask for me to make it again," she murmurs.

I nod stiffly. "I did."

"Drawing?"

"Uh-huh," I grunt, watching her mix the cocktail. I'm unable to stop myself from staring at all her alluring curves. Her hair is in a messy bun, strands framing her face. Within the fog I'm in, a small delight grows, looking at her. A very, very small sense of peace.

She grabs two glasses, equally pours, and puts one in front of me. I nod my head at the other glass. "Is that so I don't think you poisoned it?"

"No," she says, placing a napkin at the spot next to me. She sets the drink down carefully. "It's for whomever you drink with."

Meg grabs a bottle of Shiraz as my throat constricts, staring at the other drink. I inhale sharply, sipping the mystery cocktail. Yeah…still good.

"Ever gonna tell me what's in this?"

She leans on the bar. "Will you get mad if I say maybe?"

I snort, and she laughs under her breath. "Might be best if I don't know."

We sit in silence; the only noise is the wolves in the back. Meg sips her wine, and whispers, "I am sorry for deceiving you, Rodney. I never meant to hurt or use you."

"No, I proposed the deal. Seems hypocritical to be angry when I was using you, too." She opens her mouth, but I continue. "And I'm sorry for accusing you…and not fully believing you about DiNardi."

"I didn't help by…tiptoeing around the truth," she says. "You were just doing your job."

I stare at the drink, and mutter, "Yeah. The *job*."

Meg moves back from the counter as I keep my gaze from hers. She mentions, "Gunther showed me the video." I grunt in response. "I recognize them as the men who came to—"

"Later," I mumble, my head beginning to pound as the heavy depression sinks me deeper. "Talk later."

Meg sighs. She puts her glass down and disappears into the dining area. There're howls and I shake my head at the ruckus. I look over at the drink, wishing with everything that Claudia was here. Or mom, who'd tell me to brush it off and get back up. All I can seem to do is wallow in the darkness that doesn't relent. Not wanting to be here.

The back doors swing open again, and my senses tingle as I smell warm lavender, honey, and citrus. Meg goes behind the bar and sets a cupcake in front of me with dark chocolate frosting. I look to see her with her own, taking a bite with a hum.

Carefully, I grab the cupcake, and bite into it. It has a rich taste with a twinge of…Kahlua?

"Like it?" She asks, then smiles gently when I nod. "You'll have to tell me your favorite flavor sometime."

I take another bite, holding back a moan at the rich taste. "So… liquor cupcakes?"

"Uh-huh, something different and I liked baking with my mom growing up."

Tears press at my eyes, and I blink quickly, staring down at the counter. I look over at the drink beside me, doing everything I can to not cry in front of Meg. Not to lose control.

"Is that who the drink is for? Your mom?" Meg asks gently, and I slowly shake my head. "You don't have to tell me. I won't push you if you're not ready."

I look at her with tired eyes and say in a hushed tone, "Thank you."

A caring look comes over her as I gaze into her eyes, becoming lost in the dark brown that reminds me of ancient forests and mountainsides. Calmness washes over me, pushing back the darkness like I'm staring at…moonlight.

It's not a myth.

My throat constricts knowing I can't keep fighting this, and I'll succumb to fate. I should be elated. Happy. Yet, all I feel is dread.

"Rodney?" Her voice brings me back to reality.

"I'm sorry," I say suddenly.

"For what? You've already apologized."

I'm not sure what for either. I clear my throat and yank my gaze away from hers. "For being a scary asshole."

"Said yourself we all play characters sometimes," she says over her wine glass. "And I did keep secrets from you."

"You were just protecting yourself. Surviving." I drink, swallowing the contents harshly.

"Maybe," she says slowly, and I look up to see a small smile. "But I think I'd rather survive with someone, than alone. You know? Like how your Pack does." There's a shout in the back about someone being a poker shark. "Even when they sound like a group of hyenas."

"I'm telling Delilah you said that."

She gapes at me in mock shock, and her expression gets a smile on my face. "Even after giving you a cupcake? Two, actually."

"Didn't know they came with terms and conditions."

"Fine print," she says, raising her glass.

I pick up the wrapping paper and glance at it. "Still don't see it."

She swipes it from me, throwing it away with hers. "Very funny."

"You seem to think so."

She smirks, then clinks her glass against mine. "The bluntness is improving."

"Guess, I'll try harder, darling." I finish my drink.

"Want another...*boss?*" She winks at me, and I shake my head.

"You should rejoin them. Josh needs *actual* competition in playing," I say, getting up.

Meg takes my glass and the other drink, putting them in the sink. She grabs her wine and walks out to meet me by the counter. "Sure, you don't want to join?"

"No, they don't need my money tonight."

She nods, flicking her gaze up toward my apartment. "What memories are you drawing tonight?"

I pause, my heart beating harder as she tilts her head in curiosity. I want to grab her, pull her close and bury my face against her neck. Instead, I shrug and answer, "Times before the Underground."

"You were here for that?"

"Age, darling."

She hums, then reaches up slowly and places her hand against my cheek. I freeze as the warmth spreads through me while her thumb strokes over my skin gently. She whispers, "Don't look a day over a hundred."

Tell me to hold you.

She drops her hand and disappears to join the others who shout through the doors. I remain in my spot, touching my cheek. "...*the mercy in your eyes.*"

I drop my hand when the doors swing open and Marcus walks

out, stopping a few feet from me. He cocks his head, frowning, and juts his head at me. "You gonna finally admit it? Make it easier on yourself?"

I'm on the verge of admitting he's right when I notice his scowl. The permanent one that never seems to leave. I look at my friend of almost three centuries and I can't remember the last time he smiled. Fully. Or even laughed.

My emotions shut down, the walls going back up as I head for the stairs. "No."

I'm halfway upstairs when he calls up, "I'm going to Topside. Gonna check on *Donny's* and other imports."

There's a finality in his voice, prompting me to turn and look. His arms are crossed, still scowling at me. "Coordinate with Victoria."

"You're allowed to be happy," he says suddenly. "Your mother would've wanted that, including Claw."

"Can you say the same about yourself?"

A shadow covers his face. "There's still hope...for *you*."

He leaves *Mountain Edge* and disappears into the Underground.

CHAPTER 16
SHIPPING DOWN TO UNDERGROUND

I walk along the dock with Zane and Gunther, Edward directly behind as we approach the warehouse entrance. It's early evening on Topside with the sun just below the horizon, prompting lanterns to flicker over the icy water. My gaze catches Marcus with Skylar near the entrance. It's been five days since I've seen him. It's been quiet below as mob business went back into a routine. Marcus and Victoria set up a 'sting' warehouse, trying to lure anyone out of the woodwork. And it worked, someone broke into the tampered weapons and dummy C4.

"They broke off the locks," Skylar says as we approach. "They got out quickly across other shipyards, heading back to the city. Tracking them now but keeping a distance to see where they lead us."

"What they target first?" Gunther asks as we walk into the building.

"The rifles," Marcus answers.

"Left them and grabbed the dummy C4 instead," Skylar says. "No other imports were touched. Didn't make it past the first shipping containers."

The first half of my warehouses were decoys, fronts for shipping companies of mineral goods. Apart from importing guns and napalm, I also deal in silver, iron, and medical equipment. My grandfather started the legal side of the Wolf Mob before it was that, importing untainted and sustainable materials to Undergrounds, Neutral cities, and Paranormal businesses across North America. And sometimes I ship weapons to help those materials stay in the proper hands. Shit isn't as dire as it was when my grandfather started this gig, but some things never change.

"Victoria's heading the tracking," Marcus reports. "She recognized one of the scents but we called you up for this."

We move around shipping containers, coming up on a back wall where a container has been pried open. Rifles are scattered, bent, and tossed like leftover party favors. There's damage to nearby containers, but not much else.

"They got in through old tunnels we closed off a year ago," Skylar says, pointing to a grate that comes up from the sewers.

Zane heads over, pulls it open and disappears into the hole, and pops back out a few minutes later. "The locks had to have been opened from the inside. No way can you get to them from the other side. Someone let them in."

"We got a rat," Gunther mutters.

I glance at the mess, something not sitting right, including the air. There's no scent *here*. I walk over to the containers, pick up an M-16, and look it over. Unless they knew we took out the firing pins and shit, why'd they leave them behind if they broke the locks? They targeted the weapons first but didn't take them. If they only wanted the C4, why destroy the weapons?

"How long were they here?" I ask.

"Ten minutes tops," Skylar answers.

My gaze meets Zane's, and I ask, "Can you smell anything down there?"

He wipes his hands off. "Human, shifter, and werewolf."

"Victoria must've recognized the werewolf one," Gunther says.

Warning crawls up my spine as my gaze meets Marcus'. His glare tells me he doesn't smell them up here either. His and my hackles raise as I slowly draw my pistol, moving my sight toward the far darkness of the warehouse.

"Boss, whoever showed them those tunnels, they knew we weren't using them," Gunther murmurs, moving closer.

"Which neutral zone do they lead to?" I ask, as the others go on alert. They start moving into a defensive formation.

Skylar swears under their breath. "Chelsea."

Edward whispers, "Isn't that near—?"

"*Freyja*," I growl as Zane snarls along with Marcus, both getting in front of the betas as Skylar comes up next to me. I step forward, gesturing for them to hold as they unsheathe their claws.

"Come out, vamp! Fuck off with your dramatics!" I'm slammed by the smells left over from the intruders. Fucker cloaked the entire warehouse from smelling anyone.

A dark chuckle responds, and I almost choke on the scent of velvet and spiced rum. The vampire wears a long trench coat over a tailored suit. His long black hair is pulled into a braid, contrasting against his pale skin and red eyes that flash with delight. He smiles, showing elongated fangs as he saunters forward, acting like he owns the place, and stops a dozen feet away.

"Sebastian," I snarl.

"Been some time, McLycan," he greets.

"Not long enough," I say, straightening as I flash my gaze to the containers. "Missed me so bad you had to trick me back up here?"

"If I'd known that's all it took, I'd have stolen your toys weeks ago," he answers, flicking dust off his lapel.

"Surprised your mistress let you out this far, didn't know your chain stretched."

"She's not my mistress." His eyes darken.

"Could've fooled me."

Sebastian Crimsworth belongs to Freyja as her enforcer, body-guard, servant, or whatever she wants. When she came back to New York, he came under her control, and everybody including the Vampiric Society hates him. Problem is, he's still an aristocrat, so I can't tear his throat out without starting a war with the vampires. He's a cocky bastard with the demeanor of a demented demi-god. Only vamp I hate worse than Dracultelli.

"Well, good news, your sticky tack will be found in a warehouse in Jersey. You'll find it easy enough, right, pooch?" Sebastian asks, looking at Zane. The grey wolf steps forward, and I stop him. He's baiting us, and I'm not gonna let him win damn it.

"What does *she* want?" I growl.

Sebastian smiles.

Marcus snarls along with Gunther as the vampire looks at his wristwatch. He hums and then pulls out a piece of paper. Slowly, he unfolds it, clearing his throat before reading, "*I warned you. Stand in my way and I'll follow through with my promise years ago.*"

My stomach drops as my heart clatters in my chest. I look at Gunther, whose hazel eyes blaze in worry as his breathing becomes shallow. Ice fills my veins. She wouldn't fucking dare.

"I didn't break our damn deal," I snarl.

Sebastian ignores me, continuing the letter. "*I've spoken to associates and have agreed to help, given our* mutual *interests are aligned. You've garnered some anger toward you, including your own beasts. And as delighted as I'd be seeing you, I'll have others remind you who owns Topside. Besides...*" he looks up and grins as Gunther's phone buzzes, and then Edward's, "*...I had silver to spare.*"

"Sebastian," I warn.

"Boss," Gunther says in a shaky voice, and there's faint shouting.

The vampire smiles maliciously, and finishes, "*Signed, Freyja.*"

"*Mountain Edge* is under attack," Edward rasps.

Zane roars, aiming for the vampire before Skylar and I stop him. "Grab the others!" I bark, pushing him toward the entrance. "Go!"

Everyone runs for the dock as I glare back at Sebastian. My finger itches for the trigger, wanting to shoot him, bleed him out. He tsks me, "Wouldn't want to piss off the vampires next, would we?"

"Go to hell," I snarl, running for the entrance as he cackles behind me.

"Should've agreed to what she wanted, McLycan!"

I put the pistol away as I get to the rest of the group, Gunther and Edward still on the phone. "They're using silver," Gunther growls. "Two wolves already down."

"Tell Delilah to get out—"

"They're surrounded," Edward interrupts. "Every pathway is blocked, more than two block diameter."

Skylar calls over more wolves as my gaze flashes to one of the Underground tunnels far end of the dock. "Skylar," I order. "Catch the fuckers who took the C4 and drag them back to me when you do." They nod, running off and taking wolves with them. "Everyone else, down below, *now!*"

Zane takes off, shifting into hybrid form as the rest of us follow, howling as we run toward the Underground. The safety gates are practically ripped off as we descend under the river to the city below. It'll take more than twenty minutes to reach them.

"Vehicles are steel-plated," Gunther reports. "All gunmen smell of half-breeds."

"They're skirting Paranormal laws!" Marcus growls.

"They're Boston's!" Edward yells from behind. "Meg's identified three...five of them!"

Mutual interests. Fuck, they want Meg. Dead or alive.

"Tell them to hold until you get there!" I order.

"Boss—"

"Take Cuorebella's south tunnel, take out vehicles, and use the steel to barricade the tavern. I'll be right behind you."

Zane protests, "Boss—"

"Go!" I thunder and they all bolt, disappearing into the tunnels. I pause, grab my phone and dial, hoping for once he picks up fast enough. I breathe heavily as terror makes me run again and turn down another way. Another exit to help flank them.

Vincent finally picks up. "Do you know how early—"

"Boston's goons are attacking *Mountain Edge!* They're using silver!"

"Are you—"

"I'm giving you permission to intervene!"

"How long can you hold them off?"

"Don't know. I'm still fifteen minutes away!" There's a pause and I almost ram into a wall. "Damn it, Vincent, I need—"

"Stay alive until I get there." He hangs up.

I push down the path faster, reaching the brick alleys of the Underground. I head toward the tavern and hear howls and screams echoing. The first vehicle comes into view, and there's a flash of Marcus jumping, ripping someone's head off.

Then I smell it. Blood. *Wolf* blood. Pure wrath engulfs my senses, wiping away the fear as a roar rips from my lungs.

I jump, grab railings, and race across the rooftops. With a heavy rumble, I land on a couple of gunmen. Teeth and claws rip into their bodies, tearing off limbs as they scream. I roar slamming into a vehicle and pushing it over. A gunman shouts from inside, and I reach inside snapping his neck. I run into the chaos engulfing the tavern, seeing most of the front shattered and torn apart with a car driven into it. Fire sparks underneath the vehicle, threatening to burn next. Shops nearby have shattered windows, holes riddling the brick.

Delilah leaps over a vehicle, shoving the burning piece away from the tavern. She's in her hybrid form, wearing only her kilt, hanging barely over her hips and chest. The black werewolf snarls, blood dripping as she lunges at a gunman while I dodge bullets as I aim for Marcus.

We use the element of surprise, tearing apart the vehicles and snapping off the steel plates as we toss them to Gunther and Edward. They barricade the tavern, getting others inside as more gunmen shoot from the remaining vehicles, stuck behind the downed cars. I storm forward, hot silver grazing my shoulder, and slam into an SUV. Men scream as Zane leaps out of the smoking carnage, helping me tear it apart before it explodes. Metal snaps, then burst as I glance over to see Josh and Delilah destroy the last vehicle.

"More incoming!" Edward shouts.

I turn to see vehicles bumping over the brick, and silver rains down. Did she send a fucking small army? Everyone takes cover inside the tavern, bullets pinging off the steel. I look over and see Meg behind one of the steel plates, holding a gun.

"Get further inside!" I yell at her.

"You need back up!"

"Meg—"

"It's Boston! This is my fault!" She screams as vehicles screech around a corner. Everyone ducks behind the disjointed barricade. The cacophony of flying bullets fill the air, shattering glass and splintering wood that's been exposed.

Edward howls, going down with his shoulder and thigh hit. Josh moves him back as another wolf is hit and then another. I hear a grunt, and Gunther tumbles to the ground, crouching low. The smell of silver, sulfur, and blood fills the air. It threatens to choke me as crimson fills my vision. My head begins to feel fuzzy as the noises converge into a horrific symphony.

Meg runs to Gunther, ripping her flannel, and ties off his thigh. My ears twitch as I hear clicking and then the smell of gasoline hits through the fog. Meg gets up, moving toward the scent unknowingly. Instincts scream as I charge her, taking her down beneath me as a vehicle explodes, burning my back. She clutches me, stifling a scream as I cover her with my body as another explosion rocks the ground. The heat blasts across my back and I wince as it burns me.

No. Not again. Please—

"Reload!" Delilah shouts.

"More in the left alley!" Zane calls. "They've got us pinned!"

"We need backup!" Gunther yells, limping further into the tavern.

"Get down!" Delilah screams, and everyone ducks as bullets ricochet, blasting into the tattered walls of the tavern.

My heart is in my throat, shaking as I try to keep myself from losing it. Come on, Rodney, think!

Meg trembles beneath me, and my mind goes blank as I look down. A fog of horror overwhelms my senses, and all I can concentrate on are the eyes that remind me of mountains. Home. Realizing, they may be lifeless in a few minutes because I couldn't protect her. Failed her.

You'll get her killed just like—

"Rodney," Meg rasps, gripping me. "I'm—"

"*Meg.*"

There's shooting in the distance, and then the familiar roar of Vincent Dracultelli aka "Vinny the Vampire" shakes the Underground.

CHAPTER 17

THE LIGHT OF ALL LIGHTS

My head snaps toward the vampire's roar. I look down at Meg and order, "Stay."

I stand and thunder, "*Alphas!*"

They respond in howls as others provide cover from behind, all those unscathed poised as another roar echoes from Vincent. There's a lull in the rain of bullets. An opening. We charge past the barricade, attacking just before the next hellfire of silver comes. Killing a gunman, I catch sight of Vincent ripping into throats, blood covering his jaws and hands. Suddenly he points his gun toward me, shooting just past my head to hit a man coming up from the alley. I snarl and race past the vampire, charging one of the vehicles with Marcus, and slamming into the steel. Men scream as I notice Samuel, Vincent's right hand, dart past and kill more down another alley. Gunmen begin trying to escape, realizing who else they're up against.

There's a shout and I turn toward the tavern, seeing a destroyed vehicle that begins to spark flames. My heart stops when I see Meg trapped behind it about to be caught in its explosion.

"Meg!" I yell, running for her, but I'm pushed to the ground as two bullets almost hit the back of my head. Marcus keeps me down as an explosion erupts, silver threatening to kill us, and my vision blurs. "NO!"

Suddenly, the burning vehicle flies toward another, crashing and exploding into flames. I peer past the smoke, seeing Vincent stand in the vehicle's place. He towers over Meg as he snarls, causing lamps to flicker down the path. More of his vampires arrive, blasting the last of the gunmen trying to run as they come up behind them. Adrian and Matty, two vampires, shoot into slumped bodies as Marcus finally lets me up. Another vehicle explodes and Delilah yells to put out the flames.

I look at the destruction of destroyed bodies and burning vehicles. *Mountain Edge's* front is almost obliterated, along with other storefronts nearby caught in the attack. I breathe heavily, looking at Meg who helps Gunther stand. An ache tangled in wrath makes me snarl as I look at the mess in disbelief. Blood is everywhere, more than just those who were sent down here.

Freyja…what have you done?

"Your morning promenades are more eventful than mine," Vincent comments as he slicks back his black hair, revealing his pointed ears and lightly tanned skin spattered in crimson. He adjusts his leather jacket like he's just gone to dinner.

I snarl in response, looking at the destruction my Pack just endured. They begin to check on others throughout the neighborhood.

"Now then, how'd Boston get firepower like this?" He asks.

Marcus prowls up next to me, blood dripping from his jowls as I answer, "Don't know."

"Bullshit." The pureblood vampire narrows his eyes.

"Not your problem."

"A human mob boss sent a shit ton of silver and gunmen into the Underground, it's *my* problem. So, you better—"

"You can go. Thanks." I start to walk away, but Marcus snarls at me and I do it back. My anger heats under my skin, wanting to break free and keep killing.

"You better talk, hound." Vincent grabs my shoulder, and I bare my teeth. I tower over him, but you wouldn't know it from how he glares at me with glowing red eyes. "You're keeping a human he's obviously after. He practically sent an armada. She needs to get the fuck out of here if you want her to stay alive."

"How do you know about—"

"*Someone* knows how to relay information." His eyes blaze. Brenda.

"No."

"Don't be a stubborn asshole."

"*No.*"

"She's not safe here!"

"I'll protect—" My throat closes up as my eyes flick to the dismantled vehicle Vincent threw. Saved her from.

"How are you gonna protect her?" Vincent asks, gesturing to the tavern. "With *that?* You need time to regroup and not worry about her safety."

Marcus snarls at the vampire to back off. Vincent gives him a look but listens stepping back. Marcus grabs my shoulder and mutters, "*Unbound.* She can go there."

"No one will touch her if she's with the Cuorebellas," Vincent adds. "They'll take care of her while you get your shit together."

I stare into the blue gaze next to me as my inner wolf thrashes with rage. *Don't let her go…don't…Mine. Mine.* I grip my hands tight, piercing my claws into my flesh. Marcus narrows his eyes and takes a sharp breath. He says low in my ear, "Focus on her safety. Alanzo won't let anything happen to her."

My breath becomes shaky as I look back at Meg again and order Vincent, "*Unbound.* Not vampire territory."

"Fine," he says in a softer tone. "I'll take her now—"

"Wait," I warn, stalking toward the destruction of *Mountain Edge.* Delilah helps Edward to a table as Josh and Zane move rubble. Paranormals from the neighborhood come out to help where they can with the Pack while the vampires stay near their vehicles.

Meg is with Gunther, and I motion for him to help the others. He obeys, limping a little as Meg remains in her spot, staring wide-eyed at the destruction. Her gaze meets mine as I approach. "Are you okay?"

She nods, looking me over. "Are you? You're really bloody."

I look down at the blood on my fur. "Mostly not mine. I'll be fine," I answer, and she holds herself close, swallowing hard. I go to touch her cheek but stop and clear my throat. "Meg, I need you to listen and do what I say."

Her brows furrow. "What is it?"

"You're going to leave with Vincent. He'll take—"

"You are *not* sending me away," she argues, pointing at my chest. "You promised to protect me, that I stay—"

"Our deal was to keep you alive," I argue, the guilt eating away at my insides. Against the need of keeping her here. With me. But I failed her. I *watched* as I failed her. "He's taking you somewhere safe while we clean up and figure out next steps."

Her eyes search mine. "Then you'll come get me? Bring me back?" I nod. "Promise me."

"I promise," I rasp.

Her chin quivers, and I can't keep myself this time from touching her face as a tear rolls down her cheek. She glances past me. "That's him, isn't it? The *real* Blood Mafia Boss?"

"Yes."

"But he's...he's another boss...a vampire."

"He'll keep you safe." The words sting, hating the truth in them. Fear begins to seep into her aroma, and I step closer, shielding her vision of Vincent and the carnage. She looks up at me as I clutch her face carefully. "He's Brenda's Mate. He's not like the other bosses. Trust me, darling...I promise I'll come get you. Do as I say and go with him."

Her eyes stay with mine, slowly nodding as I inhale her scent deeply, memorizing it. A part of me wants to take her, hide her away from the world and let us be in the dark where I'd keep her close. *Mine.* The force of the voice deep within shakes me to my core.

I force myself to step back and nod at Vincent. He approaches with a soft, charming smile. "It'll be good to know whom I threw a burning car for," he says, and my gut twists. "Promise no hanky-panky, I'm a taken male."

"To Brenda...Rodney's sister," Meg says.

Vincent flicks his gaze to me, smiles at her, and winks. "That's my sweet cheeks, so you'll be safe with me."

She quietly follows Vincent to the other vampires and gets into the car. She watches me through the window as they drive off into the day of the Underground. The distance that stretches between us places a stake through my chest.

"Boss!" Josh yells, and I turn to see wolves coming down from Topside. They drag a wolf between them with Skylar in the lead. They drop the wolf in the middle of the destruction as more of the Pack show, circling the traitor. I approach, looking over the light-brown fur and the new kneecap he was granted after I shot him.

"Travis," I growl. Victoria was right.

"He was the one who let them in," Skylar growls, saliva dripping down their jowls. "Distracting us."

"The others?"

"Take care of," Skylar's yellow eyes flash.

I glare at the wolf bent before me. "Why?"

His piercing eyes come up, and he growls at me in challenge. Zane punches him across the face, blood spattering across the ground. Travis bites back, but Josh yanks back his head as Zane punches him again.

"*Why?*" I ask again.

"Freyja understands the order of things!" Travis grinds out, spitting blood. "You let *anything* come into the Pack! Instead of wolves—"

"Not your decision," I seethe. "You were never part of the Pack, not even close to being accepted by a *single* alpha or passing the trials."

"Yet you choose half-breeds! A *human* over us!"

My vision goes red as I stare at the degenerate before me. "They've done more in protecting this Pack than you. *You* turned your back on the Pack *and* the Wolf Mob! On every Pack member and Paranormal down here! Brought *death* to our door!"

"I—"

"*Every member is worthy in the Pack!*" I thunder in Noctora, and the group goes still, watching in anticipation. Travis bares his teeth again, and I look out toward those gathered. "*Werewolf, shifter, incubus, half-breed…it does not matter who enters, long as they pass the trials. Aye?*" Wolves howl and bark back in agreement. "*Is Brenda Cuorebella part of the Pack?*" Beings shout "aye" in return. "*Are the*

Magix's?" The walls echo with the same answer. *"Is Wanda? Dean? Yuki? Pavel?"* They get louder as I yell names within the Pack, spanning from species to species. My gaze flicks to the faces of those I call, shouting with others.

"Pack is Pack!" They scream back, thundering through the Underground. They all defend the Pack, their fury rising through the smoke-filled air.

Travis watches me, becoming drenched in fear as I step closer baring my teeth. Josh holds him still as he starts to shake, a whimper escaping Travis. I growl in bloodthirst as the need to kill pulses through my veins. Vengeance.

"Alphas, what say you for his betrayal of the Pack?"

"Death," Zane mutters.

"Death," Delilah sneers.

"Death," Skylar growls.

I look at Marcus, who curls his lips, whispering, "Death."

Travis tries to back away, but Josh shoves him down against the ground.

Marcus calls out in Noctora, *"No matter the blood!"*

"Pack is Pack!" The crowd shouts.

"What do we do when someone betrays our Pack?" Delilah shouts.

"We defend!"

"With what?" Zane snarls.

"No mercy!" The Pack resounds with a deafening cry, hurt and betrayal lining their voices as blood coats the brick. Josh steps away, leaving Travis alone before me.

"No mercy," I mutter, grabbing Travis' head and ripping it back. My teeth tear into his neck, and he thrashes, gargling a howl as I rip out his throat. Weak claws grab at me just before I snap his neck and decapitate him, tossing his head. It thuds against the ground before everyone, rolling into the fires.

I breathe heavily, catching my reflection against a shattered window. My dark wolf's head is covered in crimson blood, dripping down my jowls and across my chest. Green furious eyes scream back at me, writhing in agony and betrayal.

Not a glimmer of the mercy that Meg said was there.

Rum cupcakes

Flour
Brown sugar
Buttermilk
Vanilla
Sugar
Butter
Salt
Baking soda
Baking powder
Eggs
Cinnamon & nutmeg
Spiced rum

CHAPTER 18
STRAWBERRY WINE

"You've got blood on your nose," Delilah says, tapping hers.

"Thanks, Lady." I grab a napkin to wipe it off.

"Can't have you looking like a pup who forgot his manners," she smirks, wrapping Josh's arm.

It's been a few hours since the attack, and the tavern is a fucking mess. Most of the front is gone with shattered glass, splintered wood, and fire damage. *Mountain Edge* took the worst of it, but a few other buildings were damaged, too. Bodies are being disposed of, while Shannon and Victoria are placating the NIIA and PSB on Topside, keeping them away from here. The Pack is taking the vehicles to scrap for metal and parts. Might as well get something out of this shitty situation.

Skylar gets off the phone and reports, "Shannon's NIIA contact is telling the agencies it was a ceiling collapse and issues with the pillars. They'll stop by later. Beckham agreed to sway others to stay above."

I nod, sitting at the bar of the tavern with all the main alphas and betas. Edward has been sent to Charlene, a succubus physician for the Underground Mafia, along with others who've been badly injured. No dead. Thank fuck. We're all spread out on what's left of the chairs, back into human forms.

"Warehouses are sealed," Marcus says.

"Could try again," Zane mutters, and Marcus grunts, shaking

his head. "Technically it worked, caught someone...just not who we thought." I scowl, flexing my hand from the last remnant of wrath I had hours ago.

"What do we do about Freyja?" Gunther asks.

"What about her?" Josh says, wincing as Delilah tightens the wrap.

"She's the one who provided Boston with the silver," Gunther replies, and Josh snarls.

Zane mutters, "And probably bankrolled the gunmen to come down."

Gunther grumbles, adjusting his leg where he'd been hit. He refused to go to Charlene's, saying it was a "flesh wound."

"We can't go after her," I say, and the others grumble. "We'd be starting a damn war with Topside, not to mention she may drag the government agencies down here anyway."

"She crossed a damn line, boss." Zane adjusts what's left of his kilt.

"I know, but she agreed to help Boston knowing she has immunity. *That's* why she did it. She has pull that we don't have."

"Including Sebastian," Marcus mutters.

"Don't remind me about the Twilight reject," Zane groans.

"He still smell like an antique shop?" Delilah asks, and Skylar grimaces with Zane. "Over two hundred years old and reeks like it, too."

"The bloodsucker cloaked his scent and the others," Skylar says. "Distracted us with a stupid letter, smiled when you called. Fuck his scent, he still doesn't have a heart."

"Can't touch him, that's why Freyja uses him," Marcus mutters.

"He knew there were kids near here," Zane snarls. "Innocents. They attacked the entire block—"

"Let's stay on topic," I say, giving Zane a look as he slumps back into his seat.

"Yes, let's," Delilah says, patting Josh's shoulder. She walks around the bar and grabs a bottle of whiskey, taking a swig. "We know why Boston agreed. He obviously wants Meg back, either because of what she knows or just pissed off you didn't sell her."

"Probably the latter," Josh mutters.

"That doesn't explain *why* Freyja would agree to sell him the ammunition needed to attack us," Delilah continues. "Or even bait Rodney and the others, past differences or not, why now?"

"The letter Sebastian read mentioned something about mutual interests...presumably with Boston since it was his people that came," Gunther adds. "They both want something, and the connection could be DiNardi. Meg saw Sebastian at *4D*, maybe he knew DiNardi was defecting, and Freyja's personal shit was on those lists. Boston gets revenge, she gets what DiNardi collected."

"If DiNardi was smart enough not to fuck with the Underground Mafia, why fuck with her?" Marcus asks.

"Just a thought, and she's vindictive. She could be in cahoots with the agents who showed up. That letter insinuated we broke a promise and blowing that center might be it."

"She broke that deal herself the moment she harbored a mad scientist testing on beings," Zane growls.

"Perhaps," Delilah says. "That won't change her mind about it. Today obviously showed she's willing to toe some boundaries to get what she wants, question is...what is it?"

My mind clatters around with questions, finding dead ends and more problems. There were so many hands in the damn pot, you couldn't tell who was who.

"Everyone started scrambling when DiNardi was killed," I mention, and everyone looks at me. "He *is* the main denominator here, but we may not find answers until we find out *why* he was killed. We're not the only ones wanting to know, which is why they're probably after Meg."

Everyone becomes quiet, thinking as a few take a swig of alcohol and adjust in their seats. DiNardi's death doesn't make sense, being killed before he handed over the information. No one knew about his defecting, Meg seemed sure of that. But it was painfully obvious Boston and Freyja wanted her for something. *Mutual interests.*

"Boss?" Gunther asks.

I shake my head, trying to think clearly as I look at my alphas and betas. They're looking to me for answers and leadership even after today's events. My head pounds with my heart, not entirely sure of how to move forward, but protect what I could.

"Until we come closer to answers," I start. "Those above think Meg has what they want, they may not stop until they do."

"You're not thinking of sending her away?" Zane asks. "We still need her."

"She saw the agents who probably took the explosives, the answer to *who* killed DiNardi," Gunther adds. "Which could lead to—"

"I know."

"You promised to keep her safe," Marcus states.

"Sending her away can do that," I answer.

"She's safer protected by the Underground Mafia. By *us*." Marcus scowls.

"Even after today?" I get up as he stands and faces me head-on. "We almost lost—"

"We didn't because of the Pack and *you* asking for Vincent's help," he argues. My gut twists as he mentions Vincent, his blue eyes piercing through me. "Promise was kept. We all will help keep it."

"Freyja won't stop," I murmur. "If Meg is who she's after, we both know—"

"That she-devil isn't invincible," he whispers. "We just need to find a weakness or some kind of leverage. And Meg could help with that."

"We'll defend her against any of those fuckers," Zane chimes in. "Anything to wipe that smirk off Sebastian's face."

"Boston will stay back," Skylar adds. "He's lost too much, and the Blood Mafia showing up...he knows he's Public Enemy Number One for the Underground Mafia."

"We can't touch Freyja but can keep Topside where it belongs, in the sunlight," Josh says. "Until we find answers."

"We'll stay Underground as you ordered weeks ago," Delilah says casually, meeting my gaze. "Even if this place looks like the Ghoul Civil War, we have an advantage down here."

I glance at every one of them, each covered in blood, grime, and ash. They appear war-torn, but their eyes are focused. The thundering of my heart eases but worry still digs at the pit of my stomach. I loosen a breath, easing back as I meet Marcus' gaze.

"Pack is Pack," he says. "We're a Pack before a mob business, and you've led us as such. It's kept us strong. We've depended on you, now depend on us to protect Meg."

"Ya'll seem a bit hell-bent on keeping her here."

Delilah snorts, sharing a look with Zane, then Josh. Gunther looks guilty, and I scowl at him. He raises his hands. "Didn't say nothing."

"Your face did."

"She stood up to you, knocked on your door, and gave you a cupcake," Zane says, grinning. "Even told you to come to dinner. Pure poetry."

They snicker, and I glower. "And *who* gave her the champagne for cupcakes?"

"Me," Delilah answers slyly. "Wasn't about to turn down alcoholic cupcakes, and she promised to use whiskey soon."

"Now, *that's* a bartender," Skylar laughs, and I grunt at them. "Hey, been Topside covering shit, least you could do is give me sweets. Don't deprive us of dessert, we'll start whining."

"Is that how easy it is to stop ya'll from yapping? Cupcakes?"

"Pretty much," says Delilah.

"They're tasty," Gunther adds.

"Always down for carbs," Zane comments.

"Weren't bad," Marcus murmurs. I give him an exasperated look, and he shrugs.

I rub my temple, unbelieving of this new revelation. Within a few days, she's got them wrapped around her finger. "I'm not keeping her here because you want her cupcakes."

"Fine, then the real reason?" Delilah asks softly.

Her sharp green eyes meet mine, and that inner voice calls again. *Mine.* I try to ignore it, but the longer Delilah keeps her gaze with mine, the louder it becomes. The need for Meg pulses through me, tingling up my spine like a lifeline.

"We know, Rod," Zane says, and I look at him as he shrugs. "Hoped you'd finally admit it, even though it's been weeks."

"What?" I rasp, furrowing my brows as I look at Gunther. "You knew, too?"

"After you thought she was hurt from not eating for two days, it was hard *not* to smell it," he says. "Even on her."

"What are you talking about?"

Marcus walks over to Delilah; she places a hand on his shoulder as he drinks from the whiskey bottle. "You both smell like an old Mating scent, dim and aged, but there. It's similar to Marcus's and Claw's," Delilah explains quietly, squeezing his shoulder. "Even though you haven't Mated, yet…it's gotten stronger."

"If it helps, took me a few days to realize," Zane adds.

"Not a myth, boss," Gunther says quietly as I meet his hazel eyes, and he smiles gently. "We'll follow your lead, but…she should stay, we all believe she belongs here. That is if she decides to come back to this disheveled joint."

"She just needs some love," Delilah grunts, flicking her gaze to me.

"You all done?" I ask, crossing my arms, and hoping to shut down any conversation about me and Meg. They all mutter stuff, shrugging while Marcus averts his gaze.

"I'll check on her in a few days," I say, clearing my throat. "In the meantime, what happened to that thumb drive Ralph was carrying?"

"Forgot about that damn thing," Zane grumbles.

"Should still be in your office, haven't touched it since the attack, why?" Gunther asks.

"We'll try again to find what was on it, could be the leverage we need or answers," I say, holding out a hand for Josh to put a bottle of whiskey in it. "And that detective seems to know how to get intel from places he shouldn't, maybe he can crack into the thumb drive."

"Damn thing is what got us into this mess," Zane says. "Go back to square one."

I take a swig from the bottle, and say, "Louis is already sifting through footage, let's see what else he's capable of." Gunther grumbles, nodding his head. "What? Find out he owns a cat or something?"

Marcus murmurs, "He gave him a nickname and it stuck with Brenda."

"Wait, finally?" Josh asks.

"Please, share." Zane gets up as Gunther scowls at him. "After all this shit, make our day. Might as well tell us before we ask the little daemon ourselves."

Gunther mumbles and we all gesture for him to speak louder. He sighs, "Clifford the Big Red Dog." I snort, while others chuckle.

"Seen you shift, has he?" Josh asks.

"Watch it," Gunther warns.

"Okay, okay…Clifford," I smirk, and he frowns at me. "Check if he can help with the thumb drive, see if DiNardi was in deeper shit than defecting. Maybe he dug too deep, and that's why he was killed. Then ask if we can visit the bomb site."

"Why?"

"Zane's right. Gotta start at square one, and that's 4D. We'll start looking for answers there."

"How do we keep Freyja away until we do?" Skylar asks.

I exhale sharply. "I ask another favor."

I WALK INTO *Unbound*, four days later, while Josh waits for me. It's odd not having Gunther, but I had to force him to stay home and rest. Darius stays outside with Josh as I walk into the quiet club, lights turned on as beings clean the stages. Crates full of alcohol are stacked behind the bar and the place is underway of being restocked and sanitized.

Ricky, the middle child of the Cuorebellas, stands near the bar with a clipboard. He's smaller in stature with long black hair, pulled into a bun showing his horns, and a cherry complexion with bright blue eyes. He's wearing a loose shirt and leggings with thigh-high boots. It's a joke amongst his siblings that he got the "legs" of the family, and his dancing on the poles proves it with his heels.

The incubus sees me, smiles, and calls to the back, "Pops! Got company!" I approach, raising a brow. He shrugs. "Joey said you'd show."

"Still don't want part of the family business?" I ask as he checks labels.

"Oh, I am, just not *that* one." He winks. "Not a gig for me. The club is my domain."

A hollow feeling gnaws in my chest, and I respond, "Perfect for you, I guess." His powers start to wrap around my senses, teasing with sweet rose and orange blossoms. "Not today, Ricky."

"Seemed stressed, and you haven't been by lately."

"Just long couple nights." Ricky narrows his eyes until Alanzo approaches.

"Ricky, Gina needs to speak with you," his father says, keeping a calm expression as he strokes his son's head. He nods toward the dressing rooms. "Dispute over schedule shifts."

"Only breaks were adjusted."

"I know. Run through it again, give them peace of mind."

"Sure, Pops." Ricky walks away, disappearing down the hall.

I'm left with the ex-mafia boss as others disperse. He gestures toward the couches, and I follow. Alanzo Cuorebella has dark maroon skin, slicked-back onyx hair with horns sticking through the strands, and sharp violet eyes. He's lived over six centuries, older than most below, but looks forty by human standards. His calm demeanor is controlled and thoughtful. You'd never know he could cause thousands of beings to lose their sanity in a moment within a fifty-mile radius. He's easygoing until you touch his family.

By now, it's spread throughout the Underground the Wolf Mob was attacked. I wasn't worried about the Cuorebellas, but I need his help and that means telling him where Boston got the silver.

I sit across from him as pulls out a cigar, and lights it. "Sounds like you've had your hands full. But you handled it well enough, even called back-up. Put your pride down and it paid off."

Not gonna think what I owe the bloodsucker. "How's Meg?"

"Upstairs, baking with Carmen. She's planning to have Meg stay for dinner unless you're taking her back." He puffs his cigar, watching me carefully.

"She should stay longer. We're still rebuilding, and things are… not as stable as I'd like them to be." Did I mean the mobs or myself? Yes.

Alanzo narrows his gaze, and the scent of cinnamon trails through the air, relaxing me as I sink further into the couch. He taps his cigar, asking, "If you're not here for her, what is it?"

"I need a favor."

"Not the first time with me. Why you cautious?"

"'Cause, you're not the boss."

"Mob favor, then?" I nod, and he sighs. "All of you will have—"

"I know, Alanzo, but Joey doesn't have the same pull as you."

He considers me. "Care to elaborate?"

I clear my throat, then explain, "Freyja supplied Boston with the ammunition to attack us. It was deliberate because she thinks the Wolf Mob broke a deal with her. She even involved Sebastian."

"Freyja usually has her reasonings."

"And has a knack for revenge and long grudges."

"Like her father," he grunts. "What deal did you supposedly break?"

My history with her was complicated, only seeming to worsen over the past decade as I stayed on Topside to keep her hands off my Pack. Grudges were an understatement for her. I refused an agreement with her once, and ever since I've had to watch my back. How Vincent got away with his own gigantic deal was beyond me, even with cards up his sleeves all the time.

"Deal was keeping our territories separate," I tell him, hoping it *was* the promise Sebastian was referring to. "I stay out of hers; she stays out of mine. That center we blew was hers, and she may have realized it was my explosives that destroyed it. It belonged to one of her 'clients,' but she may harbor ill will."

"It was a joint operation of the Underground Mafia, why go after you? And my baby girl pushed the button."

"Not many know it was lil sis," I answer quickly before the memories can trickle back. Last thing I need is to lose it in front of Alanzo. My mouth becomes a tight line, keeping my emotions in check. "Could you talk to Freyja?"

"Years ago, I told you to take care of your own business. You've got a good head on your shoulders, always have."

I sigh, defeat pushing on my shoulders. "Alanzo, I need—"

"Didn't say I wouldn't," he says, leaning back. "She aids in attacking the Underground, that's *my* business. I just wish you'd come sooner."

I blink rapidly, trying to process his words. He's always been helpful, but...I feel like I'm missing something.

"She's young and still learning," he explains. "And she does hold grudges longer than her father had, but she's not stupid. Whatever she believes you broke, I suggest you find what it is, and see if you can mend it. Your business is your business. But when someone gives the means to send those down here to kill, maim, and destroy...well, perhaps, I'm the best to help remind them of the consequences of doing so."

Alanzo examines his cigar, his eyes darkening as they begin to glow. His expression is stern as I smell cold metal, a chill running up my spine. "You helped my baby girl destroy her monsters, including that low-life who tried to take her from me."

"Alanzo—"

"I'll have a chat with Freyja. Remind her she best stays on Topside for her own health until she remembers which lines never to cross. And certain deals should never be made, especially when it was *her* decisions that housed the man who tortured my daughter."

The sharp scent of steel slices through like his quiet, wrathful voice. I remain still, hoping it doesn't strike me, knowing what comes next if his powers do. The scent disappears and I breathe easier.

"Thank you," I rasp. "I owe you."

"No. You aided my family, and I'll give that aid back."

"You already have by taking care of Meg, and I owe you for that, too."

Alanzo smiles knowingly. "Help doesn't require a price." I look toward the apartment door to his home. "Besides, Carmen has gained a new friend. You've given joy to my Mate, and there's no owing in that."

I smile softly, imagining Meg giving Carmen recipe ideas and vice versa. The longing I've felt the past few days strengthens, aching for her. It's been hell without her. I want to run up there and bring her back with me, but I can't ignore my failings. The past screams at me that it'll happen again, fear crawling up my spine and making those soft emotions fragile. Easy to lose.

"Rodney." Alanzo's voice pulls me from my thoughts. He leans forward, tilting his head, then whispers, "How long have you known she's your *Gaelach*?"

My heart stops, realizing my scent has betrayed me, tumbling out for him to know every emotion. "You know about them?"

"Been around many communities," he chuckles at my surprise. "That includes werewolves, and what many of you presumed was a myth. It never was, just rare."

"Did you meet ones in the past?"

He nods, taking a long draw of his cigar. "Two couples, a few centuries ago. Norway and India."

"Wolves?" I ask, and he nods. I shake my head as I rub my neck. "She's human, Alanzo."

"Doesn't matter, fate is fate." Yeah, but fate's a bitch with a sick sense of humor. "Have you talked to Meg about it?"

"No." He raises a brow curiously. "Been busy."

"You should. Not just your fate, but hers, too."

"She can't stay, it's becoming too dangerous for her."

"Topside and the world outside from here are just as dangerous, there'll always be something." I shake my head, and he sighs, tapping his cigar on the ashtray. "Take your advice from me, Rodney. Don't fight it and waste time. You'll regret it. She's your *Gaelach* for a reason, just like you are for her."

"It's barely been weeks."

"And I asked Carmen to be mine after two, knowing she was my Mate fifteen minutes after meeting her. Your point?"

Okay, maybe I should listen to the one who's had a successful relationship for six hundred years. Yet, I'm still feeling stubborn. And scared.

"She wants freedom, and this may not be what she had in

mind," I say quietly, and he goes still. "I watched what happened to my mother, I don't want the same for her."

"Give her the choice, don't make it for her," he says, putting his cigar out. "Don't give up your happiness at every whim to protect others...because your own joy matters. You haven't lived this long to not deserve some. So, if you know she's the one, tell her. Maybe not today or tomorrow, but don't waste precious time."

"And if it's a mistake?"

"Finding a part of your soul is never a mistake. For when the darkness comes, they'll be the light to guide you back to the living." I stare at my hands, the words echoing as they press against old scars. "You're not your father," he says quietly, and I meet his gaze. "Your life is your own, not his."

I swallow hard as the incubus gives me a warm expression. How many times have I wished for him to be my father? To have affectionate conversations and understanding, instead of being yelled at? Not this pressure that keeps pushing onto my shoulders, and the constant worry of failure? I wonder if things would have been different, for Claudia and me. For mom.

He pats my knee as he stands, motioning toward the apartment. "You should at least come say hello, whether she leaves with you tonight or not."

I follow him as he opens the door, pausing to look back with glowing eyes. "One last piece of advice," he says carefully. "My baby girl will belong to the Pack as long as she wants, but she is *my* daughter. I'll tell you what I told Vincent *and* Anita." Cold steel chills my bones, stopping my breath. "Don't give me a reason to remind you."

I swallow harshly and nod once.

He hums thoughtfully, the warning scent disappearing as I let out a sigh of relief and follow him up the stairs into his home. I smell fresh baked pies and bread, the warm space engulfing me as it always does with tender care. Alanzo walks through the foyer, disappearing into the kitchen as I stop in the living room. I see an arrangement of flowers on the dining table that looks new.

Meg walks out, wearing a ruffled apron that hugs close to her front, while her hair is in a messy bun. Her eyes light up when she sees me, and if I wasn't standing still, I'd trip over my own damn feet. She smiles, rushing forward but stops briefly. I watch her drop her shoulders and mutter, "Screw it."

She hugs me, and I freeze. She's warm and I want to melt into her embrace as I carefully put my arms around her. I inhale deeply, breathing easily again. She pulls away, and I want to yank her back into my arms.

"I'm...I thought maybe, perhaps...it'd be longer, or that you didn't—"

"Quit while you're behind, darling," I whisper, and her expression falls.

"I wasn't sure you'd come."

"Wolf of my word."

She tries to smile but looks away behind herself. I glimpse at the flowers again. They're beautiful with red, violet, and white flowers. Jealously rises inside me. The Cuorebellas prided themselves on their safe spaces, and I wouldn't blame her if she'd rather stay.

She starts to speak, "What happened was my—"

"No," I cut her off. "Not your fault."

"Rodney, they came because of me. I'm like a bad luck rabbit foot, continually bringing bad guys to your doorstep."

"They'd come with or without you around."

"But I wouldn't blame you if you did blame me."

"I don't, but..." my voice feels weak, looking at the quiet apartment, "...I understand if you want to stay here. If you don't trust me to protect you, because—"

"Wait, what?"

"Deal was to keep you safe, not to stay at *Mountain Edge*. You'd be safer here, the Cuorebellas are good at what they do. They have a better track record than me."

Her brows furrow, pursing her lips as her eyes search mine. She quickly inhales, crossing her arms. "How's your back?"

"What?" I tilt my head.

"Your back," she says again. "You took the brunt of the explosions when you saved me so...how's your back?"

My eyes widen as my hands begin to shake, unsure how to

respond. Pieces of the guilt and jealousy in my heart fall away, and I rasp, "Wolf, darling. Heal quickly."

"Maybe not quickly enough," she hums, then starts taking her apron off. "Carmen, can I take some fresh bread? I'm leaving with Rodney, and I know Delilah would love it."

"Of course, dear, but did you want to stay for dinner?" Carmen asks, walking out of the kitchen and wiping her hands with a towel. Her long dark hair, shaded with violets and blues, shimmers along her cherry complexion and sweet blue eyes.

I start to say, "Meg can—"

"We've got to head back," Meg finishes, hanging up her apron.

"Tavern's a mess, Meg."

"Then I can help spruce it up," she smirks, then disappears into the kitchen.

Carmen smiles warmly at me, approaching quietly. "She's a great florist, perhaps could give color to your place. Delilah always did want more flowers."

My eyes flick to the arrangement of flowers, realizing it was Meg who'd put them together. "I'm sorry for disrupting dinner plans."

"No worries, you'll just have to come back another time. I know you won't keep me waiting too long, right?" I look at her, nodding stiffly. She gently hugs me, patting my back as she whispers in my ear, "I'm glad you're okay, Rodney."

My throat closes up, hugging her a bit tighter as she strokes my head, sweet blossoms surrounding me. I look to see Alanzo at the kitchen doorway, arms crossed with a knowing smile. Right, as if I'd hide the truth from either of them. They could sense a hormonal shift in a ghoul five miles away.

Carmen steps back, smiling, and pats Alanzo's arm as she heads into the kitchen. Alanzo nods toward the kitchen, walking away. "Alanzo?" I ask, and he stops to glance back. "Is lil sis here?"

He doesn't reply, turning away down the hall. Meg calls out, "Rodney! Do you know Gunther's favorite pie?"

I walk toward the kitchen, pausing when I hear a door open, and hear Brenda's tired voice. Then I remember…I never called her that I was okay.

CHAPTER 19
ROM-COMS AND RYAN REYNOLDS

I cannot murder Clifford the Big Red Dog. I cannot murder Clifford the Big Red Dog.

"I'm just saying, boss, you two have been dancing around the other," Gunther says.

"More like weird square dancing," Zane snorts, leaning back in his seat. "Seriously, how were you not this awkward with me?"

"Look at you," I retort.

He presses a hand to his chest. "*Ow.*"

"And I wasn't afraid to throw you in the harbor. Twice." He shudders, bringing his drink in close. "Nothing grabbed—"

"A nixie grabbed my leg!" He counters, pointing at me. "I'm telling you webbed hands and all."

"They're long gone."

"Moved south or west my ass, I bet you fifty bucks they're still here." He holds out his hand, and I sigh before shaking it. "Mermaid, nixie, or whatever…those harbors are one big nope."

This is what I get for avoiding work.

We're in my office. It's been almost six days since I retrieved Meg, most of *Mountain Edge* has been repaired. Apart from clean-up, it's been quiet since Boston has "disappeared" somewhere on Staten. Some of the Wolf Mob has pushed to go after him, but I can't, even though I want to rip his throat out. He may be staying clear of the Underground and its mafias, but who knows if he's being protected by Freyja. Don't need a repeat on the tavern. There's been no movement from her either, hopefully, Alanzo's talk with her did the trick. Keep our distance and strategize, and make sure my tavern doesn't bring down the ceiling.

Zane finishes his drink and gets up to pour another. "You at least find out what's in that mystery cocktail of hers?"

"No," I say, looking at the whiskey on my desk, wishing it was that.

"I think Delilah knows, but she'll never sell out another bartender," Gunther chuckles.

Meg's been helping in every way she can, including bartending. Her laughter mixes with the others, becoming part of the Pack almost as if she was meant to be here. If she's not baking, painting, or nailing something in the tavern she's putting flowers in old liquor bottles, which Edward and Delilah love. And not just the tavern she's helped with.

A few days ago, we found an opening to check out *4D* and look through the rubble. Meg drew out the club schematics, informing us where DiNardi kept a safe and an underground compartment that might have held the hard copies of what he'd collected. Lastly, she told us where she input the information *she* found for DiNardi. The POS system of the club, a trojan horse within the system of some kind that DiNardi had created years ago. Small chance of it surviving the blasts, but better safe than sorry. I wanted nothing to do with human mobs, but I may have to resort to blackmail if we're threatened again.

We're waiting on Marcus to come back from *4D*.

"You asked for advice," Gunther says. I should've picked a different hobby to wait for them.

"I said thoughts."

"You need it, either way," Zane says as I rub my temple. "You two flirted at that last poker game, she gave you an in... then poof, nothing." I scowl at him as he throws his hands up. "She leaned in close! Seriously, it's 101."

"Careful, Perdie." He gives me an exasperated look. "Not in front of the others."

"Fine, when else you gonna do it? Or should I lock you two up in the kitchen?" Yup, I'm gonna throw him back into the water. I'll promote another alpha.

Meg and I *have* spent time together, without Larry, Moe, and Curly nearby. And there've been moments I thought of leaning closer to her, but something's always held me back. The fear still lingers, along with nerves, wondering if I should take Alanzo's advice. Just tell her, but the alluring, beautiful woman makes me lose my senses. She makes everything easy, and yet frustratingly hard.

I sigh, grabbing my whisky to knock it back. Zane places another in front of me. "She's your *Gaelach*. Your Mate. Don't make it complicated."

"Maybe I don't want that to be the only reason," I argue.

"Except, it's strung into your DNA. Fuck, I'd be howling for joy if I found mine. Myth debunked."

"She does fit in around here," Gunther comments, rubbing his wound a little. "Like it's supposed to be. Seems to like it here, too. Just tell her."

Yeah, *should* be easy.

Paranormals had Mates, someone you're with for life, joined in an oath in front of the Noctis Immortalis communities. Then there were Claimed Mates, giving an oath to the other through a ritual that binds you to that being until death. Those paths were for all Noctis Immortalis beings, ancient bindings, while were-wolves had the rarity of *Gaelachs*. They're your fated one, a connection that drives you toward the other. It's so rare it's believed to be a legend, gaining different titles across cultures of descendants like India, Africa, and Romania. For those of my bloodlines, Ireland, and the British Isles, it was *Gaelach*. Your Moonlight.

Neither anyone nor I in the Pack, that I know of, have met another wolf who's found their Moonlight. Legends state it's the one who shines their way through the night. The other part of your soul. There's no scientific confirmation or test, you just... know. It's why the others could sense it, even with a faint connection and her being human. Didn't know even that was possible. It's hard to believe in something you never thought real, let alone deserve.

I've been terrified, not wanting to believe it for fear of losing her. Failing her. I could fathom letting her go, giving her freedom, knowing she'd be happy, but not lifeless. Not empty eyes, which shake me to my core. I've failed before, what if I fail her, too? But a small bit of hope does grow inside me each time I'm with her. If the "fairytale" of *Gaelachs* were true, perhaps my fears are naught. And she's worth the fears.

"Fine, if you want space, go out with her." Zane's voice brings me back, sitting across from me. "Since you need more than fate to believe she's the one."

"Court her?"

"Did you really just say that?"

"What?"

"Try the word *date*."

"Look here, ya dope."

"Lickarse."

"Fuck off, Tramp." Gunther sighs heavily as Zane and I throw insults at each other like pups.

Zane points at my desk and says, "It'll help if you don't slip into outdated language. Besides, I've gotten more tail than you in the past five decades. You should listen to *Professor*."

"I don't want *tail*, you gobshite."

"You still need help, you—"

"Knock it off," Gunther intervenes, shoving Zane back into his seat lightly. "One day, he may actually yank your dick off, and I'm gonna laugh when he does." The grey wolf rolls his eyes as Gunther looks over at me. "Without the dumbass remarks, Zane's right on one point...go on a date. Get away from the Pack and the mob for once."

I scowl, sipping the drink Zane gave me. I start to scratch my head, stopping when I feel the sharpness. Another thing I should stop putting off. "Fine, ideas on dates?"

"Bakery?" Gunther suggests.

"Take her somewhere she can already make the stuff?" I ask.

"Art museum? Classic choice."

"Boring," Zane mumbles.

"Boring for you, *Marmaduke*," Gunther counters.

"You'd just be looking at stuff *we* lived through." Zane gestures to my one painting of a sunset over Ireland...of my grandfather's homestead. Okay, he's got a point. Museums can be like family albums for us. "Do an actual classic move, take her to dinner and a movie."

"What kind?" I ask.

"Rom-coms are your best bet," Zane answers with a wink. "Or Ryan Reynolds."

"For you," Gunther mutters.

"For anyone," Zane retorts, then waves him off. "Choose something that helps the mood. So, no documentaries."

"Oh...darn," I say deadpan.

"Just pick a movie with smooching. X-rated doesn't count."

Gunther gives me an exasperated look. "Throw him back to the nixies."

There's a knock on the door, and I call out, "Come in and please save me from Lady and the Tramp."

They look at each other, and say in unison, "You're Tramp."

Meg opens the door, holding a covered plate. She narrows her eyes at us. "You look suspicious."

"That hurts," Zane responds. "After every game I've let you win."

"Let?" Gunther and I ask. If I'm terrible at poker, it's because Zane taught me everything he knows.

Meg rolls her eyes, walking in to put the plate on my desk. She gives me a sympathetic smile. Warm delight spreads through me, making the dread the other two have been giving me disappear.

"Been up here for hours, figured I'd bring you some lunch," she says.

"Would've come down," I say, flicking my gaze to the others. "If just to escape these hounds."

"Well, when you *do* come down, there'll be a new batch of cupcakes."

"Champagne again?"

"No, scotch."

"You're upping your game."

"Adjusting to clientele." Her gaze flicks down briefly. "Since *someone* hasn't told me their favorite flavor yet."

"You'll figure it out, darling."

"Maybe," she muses, and I give a half smile. She winks playfully, turning to leave and I can't tear my gaze from her swaying hair and her ass. A heated want grows in my gut, wanting to push the other two out and say fuck it to the date.

As she opens the door to leave, the two wolves gesture at me and then at her, before she closes the door. Zane groans, looking at the ceiling as I ask, "What?"

"You're gonna be flirting until the end of time."

Gunther hums, raising a brow at me. "I've seen you handle a lot of shit, but a human woman makes you freeze?"

I growl, taking the cover off the plate to reveal a stack of burritos. I take one, tossing it at Zane and then Gunther. "Ya'll make me nervous."

Zane snorts. "Didn't seem that nervous when you were whispering in her ear that first day, not to mention touching her hair in front of Boston."

My expression becomes dark as a warning growl emanates from my chest. Gunther straightens, while Zane goes still. I don't need to be reminded how much of a territorial dick I was. Zane holds his hands up, saying softly, "Boundary found. Warning taken."

I grab my own burrito, leaning back in my chair as Gunther throws out more ideas. I completely tune out at some point, concentrating on past conversations with her. She's been so deep in the mob lately she's not done much. I can't take her out of the Underground, maybe something like a bakery wasn't a bad idea. She hasn't seen much down here.

Time passes with the conversation switching to other topics when there's another knock on the door. Marcus enters, narrowing his gaze at all three of us. "Meg's right. You're suspicious."

"Innocent as pomegranates," Zane teases.

Marcus grunts, crossing his arms. "You're why Brenda's weird."

I snort laughter as Gunther tries to hide his own smirk. Marcus gives me a look, and I shrug. I've thought to ask Marcus for advice, but he's kept to himself the past week, working without much talk. The only one he seems to tolerate with longer conversations is Meg.

"Victoria and Shannon are bringing down what we found," Marcus reports. "Got the safe Meg talked about but computers systems were gone. Police or the bombs got to them first."

"Can we get into the safe?" I ask.

"It's melted like it's been through hellfire. We'll try to get it open. Found old, melted drives in the underground compartments Meg mentioned."

"How'd the police not find it?" Gunther asks.

"Buried deep. Meg's details of the club's basement and how DiNardi arranged things helped a shit ton."

"With some luck, we may get the hard copies of what DiNardi collected, maybe what Ralph was trading for, too," Gunther comments.

"See if there's anything useful on those drives or in that safe. Anything that connected to him defecting or not, could use for leverage later," I tell Marcus, who grunts and disappears without another word. Gunther gives me a worried look, and I shake my head. "Would Louis be able to get into those drives, you think?"

"Could, but he's still going through footage and tapping into that thumb drive," Gunther sighs, standing up. "Brenda says he's working on it, but he's gotta be careful around the precinct, taking longer than either of them wants."

"What about sending it to Bill Midnight? The thumb drive or what they found at 4D?" Zane suggests.

"Not risking PSB finding any of it," I answer. "Not gonna chance sending *anything* over state lines, whoever is pulling strings could get wind of it. We'll have to hope the detective is good enough or one of y'all to hack into them." Gunther nods with a wave and leaves. "You should go see to checkpoints before dinner, make sure Marcus and the others weren't followed."

Zane gives a half salute as he stands up. "Got it, boss, and just so you know, didn't mean it about the lickarse thing."

I snort at him. "I know, and you're not a total dope." He smirks, but it falls quickly. "Anything else?"

"Just give yourself a chance, for her and you."

"You ever hate me for choosing the Pack over you?" The question slips out suddenly.

"Nah," he answers. "Shit was mutual, remember?"

"Yeah," I mumble, looking at the drink in my hands.

"Hey, Rod?" I look up at the tone of his voice, finding a warm gaze. "It wasn't your fault. Won't be with Meg either." I nod slowly, and he gives me a reassuring smile. "You'll figure it out, always have."

"Hope you're right."

Zane smiles as he heads for the door. "Course I am, 'cause Claw always said the same."

He closes the door behind him, and I walk to my closet, pulling out my grandfather's great kilt. I lay it out on the desk, brushing my fingers over the wool. I wish I could see what Zane sees. What any of them see, but all I continually feel is guilt and uncertainty.

You're not your father.

There's a soft knock and the door opens, bringing in the aroma of citrus and lavender which drifts under my nostrils. Meg stands silently at the doorway, tugging at her flannel shirt that used to be mine. "Got a minute?" She asks.

"Making sure I don't wither away?"

She scowls playfully. "No. Not yet."

I nod for her to come in, and she closes the door behind her. She tilts her head, looking at the kilt as she walks up. "That's the McLycan Pack tartan, right?" I nod. "I haven't seen it up close, apart from others wearing it."

I step aside, gesturing toward it. She traces her fingers over the lines, asking, "What does each color mean?" I raise a brow, and she shrugs. "Marcus mentioned tartans are designed specifically with meaning. I figured yours does, too."

I come closer, towering over her as my body brushes against her side. She goes still as I point, explaining my family's tartan. My history. "The main color is blue for the wilderness and my grandfather's favorite color. The grey is for the lineage of my grandmother, and the black is for the darkest nights we prowled and conquered as a Pack. Most of them were grey wolves back then. The green is for our Irish ancestry, dating back before it was ever a country ruled by humans. The wild and free side, filled with Paranormals of the night." She watches me, smiling gently and I give her one back. "Lastly, the red is the blood shed for our freedom. For those not with us anymore."

"Why is the grey surrounding the black?"

"My grandfather adored my grandmother, used to say her genes of the Irish Grey Wolf was the glue holding the McLycans together."

She presses her fingers against the wool, touching my hand. My finger strokes over her skin as I find tender brown eyes. Her mouth opens, while her eyes flick down then back up. My breathing becomes shallow, feeling myself ease closer to her side. Meg's breath skims over my skin, and I feel her shiver as I taste her scent on my tongue. *Tell me to kiss you.*

The voice jolts me. I inhale sharply, moving away toward my desk as the heat in my gut intensifies. "You needed something?" My voice feels rough as I sit down, trying to hide my hard-on.

Meg clears her throat loudly, sitting down across from me. "Yeah, um...well..." she pauses then shakes her head, "...actually it's not really anything that—"

"Meg." She stops, shifting in her seat and I'm reminded of the first time her being here. She's not as rigid, her legs bent underneath her as she fumbles with her sleeves. Her nerves are clear, and she averts her eyes from mine. "You can talk to me, darling."

She takes a breath. When her gaze meets mine, she relaxes and then admits, "They didn't find the computers with the POS system."

"Marcus already informed me. Either it was obliterated, or the police figured it was worth taking." She nods slowly, and I raise a brow. "Are you worried they found it?"

"More like if those agents found it first. Or this Freyja."

"How hard was that system to hack into?"

She shrugs. "Don't know. I always had a way in, which means I won't be much help with the other drives."

"Don't worry about that," I tell her, leaning back. "And more likely, those computers are long gone. Those explosives were meant to melt anything, including Paranormals." Her eyes go wide. "It was a precaution recipe."

She adjusts in her seat, and my gaze flicks down to her chest. I can imagine pressing my face—

Oh, fucks sake, back to being a pup again. I avert my gaze, trying to concentrate and keep my dick in check. "From what you told me, the feds *may* be able to get into that system, if they found it. I doubt they'll trace it back to you if that's what you're worried about."

"That obvious?" I smirk, and she gives a half-hearted grin. "Maybe you're right, and everything just melted. Just…it's been weird with how quiet everything has been."

"You and me both," I mutter. "I'd rather be Underground, but this Pack drives me up the walls sometimes."

"Aww, poor alpha." I narrow my gaze, and she smirks. Briefly, she looks around the office, then tilts her head at me. "Perhaps, it could be good to get out for a bit?"

"Oh, really?"

She nods. "I haven't seen that much of the Underground, and was hoping to see more, but you know I'd need an escort or whatever."

"Still somewhat dangerous," I murmur.

"Yeah, and could be back before—"

"Midnight?"

"Wouldn't want to worry that Pack of yours. Or you."

I lean forward on my desk, cocking my head at her. Somehow, this tenacious woman set up everything I needed to take her somewhere, and I have the perfect place to show her.

"Well, I'd be honored to escort you, get away from this quiet mess. On one condition, though."

"Were you serious about midnight?"

"No."

"There's not gonna be a pumpkin involved is there?"

"That's for another outing."

She crosses her arms. "Is everything gonna be a deal between us?"

"Maybe." She almost laughs, covering her mouth as I smile at her. She gestures for me to continue. "We could stay out past midnight, but I show you one of my favorite places."

"You drive a hard bargain, McLycan." She leans forward, and my throat goes dry as I get a full view of her chest as she takes my drink. Meg smiles over the glass and sips it. "Deal."

CHAPTER 20
A PARANORMAL IN CENTRAL PARK

I glower at a passerby, who promptly stops staring and walks away. Meg and I head down an alley late afternoon in the Underground. I've shown her places all day from the Underground Grand Central Station, what an Entrance looks like from below, Underground Times Square, to the edge of vampire territory. We even stopped at *Unbound Delights*; the newest coffee shop owned by the Cuorebellas.

The sparkling lights illuminate our daytime below, weaving through the crowds of Paranormals. Meg tries not to stare, especially at the shifters who show off their serrated teeth. She stays close as we head toward our last destination, pressing against me as a couple of vampires pass. One of their gaze flashes, baring their teeth. I snarl under my breath. They carry on without another glance.

Meg whispers, "I thought vampires can't bite without—"

"They can't, just like scaring people," I mutter, keeping a hand on her shoulder.

"How far until your *special* place?"

"Called it my favorite."

"Not much difference."

"There is when you say it like that."

"Like what?" She scoffs with a giggle.

"A sarcastic bloodsucker." She stops, and I glance back to her exasperated look. "What?"

She rolls her eyes, walking again. "Here I'd thought we *eased* on the bluntness."

"You haven't lived amongst them for centuries," I retort, and she sighs at me.

We pass by more pillars, bringing into view our destination, a wonder of the Underground. Meg gasps as we approach the tall steel archway etched with *Underground Central Park.*

I lead Meg into the beginnings of the sister park to Topside, a smaller version of above, but still huge. Thinner pillars are scattered about, imitating redwoods wrapped with weaving plants as they hold up the ceiling. Real trees intermingle among them, tall and lush. Bright lights above emulate the sun's rays in a muted fashion for the vegetation below. Multiple dark hues of green contrast the brick and stonework of the Underground, while the paths are ochre stones. No asphalt. Lastly, flowers bloom everywhere, sprouting along the paths, the small meadows, or against boulders left behind from the Underground's construction.

"How?" She gasps.

"Those lights replicate sunlight, helping everything grow. Can't rain down here, so there's a water system underneath. The water pools imitate the ponds above." She touches some branches, staring at the leaves. "Otherwise...just shifter magic." She gives me a look, and I smirk. "Another lecture for lil sis."

We walk through the park, her eyes filled with fascination as beings play in the distance. "This is incredible. Were you alive when they built this?"

"Yeah," I murmur, looking up at the "redwood" towers. "I remember when New York City was just that. Before Topsides... before Undergrounds."

I take her down a path near a fountain with a statue of a werewolf in hybrid form, looking out majestically into the distance. His ears are alert as he holds himself honorably while his kilt flares out in a nonexistent breeze. I smile softly.

Meg takes a step further, reading the plaque. *"Dominick McLycan. Father of the Undergrounds."*

"My grandfather," I say, touching the fountain edge as she looks up at him. "He was one of the longest-living werewolves, born on what would become the Isle of Ireland. He did a lot for the liberation of Paranormals in the British Isles centuries ago. Killed in 1953 by a stray bullet."

"I'm sorry."

"Learned to move on. He wasn't the same after my grandmother passed, but he'd lived a good, long life, and was the reason most of the Undergrounds exist. He started the ones in Europe, beginning in London, Paris, Dublin, and Rome. When he finally settled here, *Donny's*, my restaurant on Topside, was one of his first establishments in the U.S., before the Underground. He gave it to me before he died."

I start leading us down the path as Meg comments, "That's amazing. But why didn't he give the restaurant to your father?"

I pause, peering back at the statue. "They never saw eye to eye. My grandfather started the Wolf Mob, but my father made it his own. He took a different route in the...liberation of Paranormals."

Meg glimpses back before asking carefully, "Does your father hate humans?"

"No...I don't think so." My is voice soft. "He's just always had a firmer hand with everyone. And believes the Undergrounds should've stayed segregated when it was never my grandfather's intent."

"What was his intent?"

I look around the spacious park, noticing Paranormals, half-breeds, and humans who walk around. An old peace falls over me, watching them stroll and hear children laughing. My memory flicks back to centuries past, hearing Claudia laugh running through the meadows. Through the fields of Ireland.

"The Undergrounds became our safe-havens. Before we had to fight to keep territories, more than now. Even after decades, trying to get along, sometimes it's never enough for some. For any side. I won't say it was bad before, but I won't say it was entirely good either. No place is perfect."

"So, they became home."

My gaze catches hers, finding kind eyes and understanding. "Yes, for those who walk the night or not. To be who they are and...with."

She loosens a breath, peering out into the park. I gently grab her hand, and she startles, gripping me tight. Her hand is small against my rough one as I lead her down a path. She walks beside me as I take us down a path and around a corner to reveal a full, blooming garden. Meg gasps and lets go to rush toward the plethora of colors. I sit on a bench, watching as she explores the flowers. They're specialized plants, which can only grow here mixed with variants of primrose, lilies, gardenias, pansies, and nontoxic nightshade. Those are the only ones I can remember reading up on.

"None of these should be blooming," she says, touching a few. "It's winter."

"Park is climate controlled. It's warmer here, like spring or early summer all year round."

"Is the rest of the Underground like that?" I shrug. "Explains not needing a freaking coat," she mutters, and I chuckle at her realization. She sits down amongst the flowers, leaning back on her hands. "Do you miss snow or rain when you're down here?"

"You ask a lot of questions."

"Don't show me new stuff." She tilts her head teasingly, becoming a wonderful picture framed by the flower garden. Her dark sweater contrasts with the colorful flowers, blending with her fallen brown hair. A tender ache grows in my chest, calm as I look upon her.

I look up at the ceiling, humming. "Sometimes I miss it, especially when my inner wolf wants to run." I bring my gaze down to see her face scrunched. "What?"

"Are you serious?"

"You making fun of me?" I lean forward on my knees.

"Wait…what, no!" She waves her hands before her. "I just, you said inner wolf…and with humans, well…no wait—"

"Quit while you're behind, darling."

She throws her hands in the air, crossing her arms. "Oh, fuck off," she huffs.

I burst out laughing, throwing my head back. Meg begins laughing next, holding herself tightly as I struggle to breathe. How long has she been holding that in? I regain my breath, grinning as she holds a hand to her mouth.

"Do you want to take flowers home, I mean, to *Mountain Edge*?"

"Is that allowed? Or is flower snatching part of the mob now?"

"No laws down here about it, just don't take half the damn garden. A few shifters will be upset." A mischievous look crosses her face, glancing at some nightshade. "I'll bring you back for more."

She sighs, getting up as I pull out a knife and hand it to her. She furrows her brows. "You have claws, why do you have a knife?"

"To help humans steal flowers."

She snorts, taking it to forage as I sit back and watch her pick through the flowers.

I look around the park, relaxing against the bench, until I hear a sound of distress from Meg. I rush to her side, seeing blood on her fingers and catch her wrist, glancing at the small wound. "Five minutes, you've already cut yourself."

"I slipped." I examine the wound, thankfully not deep. "I'm not that clumsy, I swear."

"Clearly."

"I cut lemons and cook all the time, and…okay, maybe once or twice cut myself, but that's beside the point."

"Well, you're banned from my knives." I put mine away as she rolls her eyes. "No comment from the bleeding human."

"It's not nice to *taunt* bleeding people. Can I have my hand back now?"

"No, now hold still."

Her breath hitches as I bring her hand to my mouth, tracing my tongue over her wound. Meg shivers against the contact. I clean up the blood, and the cut begins to heal within a matter of seconds. She gapes at me, looking between her hand and me.

"Werewolves and vampires have healing abilities within our saliva," I explain gruffly, ignoring the coppery taste. I don't revel in the taste of it like my bloodsucker counterparts.

"Good to know," she whispers.

"Doesn't mean keep hurting yourself."

"I'll do my best not to." I let go, and she picks up the flowers she's collected.

"Is that all you wanted?"

"Well, you took my knife."

"'Cause you tried to use it on your hand instead of the flowers." She gives me a look of annoyance, and I don't hide my smile as she huffs at me.

"Are you done?"

"For now." I glance at the garden, gesturing toward some gardenias. "Do you want those?"

She looks then nods. I crouch, slicing through the stems with my claws, then hand them to her. Meg stares down at me as her fingers brush against mine. For a moment, we stay there suspended in time. Her warm, inviting scent mixes with the aroma of the flowers, belonging with their sweet scent. She blinks, then takes the flowers.

"Anymore?" I ask quietly.

She clears her throat, then points to some bluish flowers. "They'll compliment the pink and purple."

I grunt, retrieving them next. We spend time gathering flowers as she decides what to pick and I forage. She creates a large bouquet in her arms, almost spilling out of her arms. I rip off part of my shirt to wrap around the stems to keep them together. Meg watches me silently as I do, and I pause to find her gaze. Her brows are slightly furrowed, eyes searching my face. The warmth of the lights above shifts as night ascends the Underground; except I barely notice as I become lost in her brown gaze. Suddenly, I realize the hole I've felt doesn't feel consuming, and nothing has come to squeeze my existence. A light in the darkness.

"Thank you," she whispers.

"Course, darling." She looks up at the lamplight stars, and I follow her gaze, watching them pulse in violet and blue. "We should head back."

Meg follows me out of the park as the crowds dim, lamplights changing for the evening around us. We walk without a word, and before I know it, we're back at *Mountain Edge*. The tavern is dark, but there's noise in the back dining area.

"Fancy a game of poker?" I ask.

She shakes her head. "I'll let someone else win tonight."

I chuckle, heading up to the third floor and escorting her to her door. She stops, turning back to me. "Thanks for being my escort."

"Anytime, darling." Meg inhales deeply, and I swallow hard, begging her on the inside… *tell me to kiss you.* I fight my instincts, my breath shuddering as I gesture toward her door. "Get some rest."

She inhales sharply as I turn away, hearing her door open and close. My body trembles as I reach mine, frozen when I place my hand on the doorknob, unable to move. I press my forehead on the wood, frustrated. Tell her…*tell her.*

I let go, but fears come flooding back, remembering my mother fighting with my father and the flash of explosions. I tighten my jaw, not wanting to break that promise. To harm her. Voices clash in my head as I clench my hands. *–more blood on your hands, including hers. You haven't lived this long to not deserve some happiness.* The darkness comes back, gnawing at me as I shove it down. My throat feels tight as I try to loosen a long exhale, preparing myself for a long night drawing.

"Rodney."

I startle. My lungs burn as I turn toward Meg, who stands behind me with a primrose in her hand. It's light violet, striped with dark blue. She places the delicate flower in my hand, my heart pounding as I bring my gaze to hers.

"It seemed perfect for you," she whispers.

Her scent rises. I can sense her heart rate quickening, causing my own to flutter. My free hand twitches, wanting to reach for her. The silence stretches and once again the voice begs, *tell me what to do. Tell me.*

She gently smiles, and I nod once, turning away for the door. A snarl of desperation threatens to release as I put my hand on the doorknob again, and the door clicks open.

Her voice is a barely a whisper. "I want you to kiss me."

I freeze. "What?"

"You…you said no maybes," she says, placing a hand on my arm. "So…I want you to kiss me."

My head snaps towards her. Closing in on her gaze, I see tears forming in her eyes. She searches my face, and her expression falls a little as she swallows hard. My stomach drops when she takes a step back. "Sorry, if you don't—"

Every cord of restraint snaps.

I surge forward, grasping the back of her neck to tilt her head back. Her soft lips crash against mine as I finally taste her. She's everything I've dreamt of with the sweetness of springtime and wine. Meg's breath hitches, opening more as I trail my tongue over her bottom lip as she whimpers. She falls against my body with hands clutching my chest as I hold her. I never want the kiss to end as a thousand fireworks burst inside, and a moan releases from me as I continue kissing her. My hands grip tight like it's the last and not the first kiss. She sighs against me, pressing her chest against mine and I kiss her harder, wanting more.

I pull away, hating that I am, with my hand remaining on the nape of her neck stroking her skin tenderly. Her eyes flutter open as I murmur, "Took you long enough."

"Could say the same with you."

"Then I'll have to make it up to you."

"Start now."

"As you wish, darling."

I bring my lips back to hers, almost devouring her as I turn, pressing her against the wall. I encage her body with mine, feeling the heat of her as my own flares to life. Tingling sensations travel down to my groin, causing me to groan and shudder. I cup her face, careful not to crush the primrose. She moans, slipping her arms around my shoulders to pull me close. Meg holds on as we kiss with a bruising force, desperate to taste every part. She breathes heavily, and gasps as my hips brush against hers, my cock already hardening and throbbing for her. It strains against my pants and a deep groan releases from me as I push against her.

Shit. Not yet. Not yet.

I break away, heaving as I lean my forehead against hers. Her hand slips down to caress the side of my face, closing my eyes and inhaling the scent of her arousal. She glides her other hand down my neck, murmuring, "Rodney, do you not—?"

"Not tonight," I rasp, kissing her temple. "Ask me another night, and I won't refuse. I promise, darling."

She strokes her thumb over my cheek, and I lean into the touch. Her lips press gently against mine, kissing me tenderly. A whimper threatens to escape at the fond touch. "I believe you," she whispers against my lips.

I open my eyes, smiling at her small dimples and glistening brown eyes. She's flushed, and her lips are pinker than before.

"Go to sleep," I whisper. "I'll see you in the morning."

"Are you going to draw?"

"Maybe."

She hums, gesturing quietly for me to move and I do. She touches my chest, over my heart, then walks to her bedroom. I'm left standing in the shadows, speechless. Somehow, I'm able to tear myself away and head into my apartment. The next few hours I spend drawing the image of Meg sitting among the flowers with the moonlight, while the primrose sits upon my pile of charcoal.

CHAPTER 21
SHIFTER, SHIFTER

Light knocking wakes me up. Seriously?

I open my eyes with a scowl. Lifting my head, I hope there's some luck on my side they'll go away. Or it's Meg naked. They knock again, and I know I can't be that lucky. I grumble, getting up to stumble to the door and open it with a grunt. Meg grins fully dressed with coffee in hand.

Okay…I'm half lucky.

"Morning starshine," she greets.

I lean against the doorframe, smiling and watching as she struggles not to peek down. I'm nude again. "Reason for waking me up, darling?"

"You'll be thanking me soon."

"Am I?"

"It's past 9:30, and Brenda is downstairs." Shit, it's a brunch day. How the hell did I sleep that late? Meg chuckles, and adds, "Delilah said to let you sleep, no hurt in some extra hours."

"Lil sis angry?" I ask cautiously.

Meg purses her lips with confusion. "Josh said something about arm-wrestling, does that count?"

"Thankfully, no." She's in a good mood, that's a hopeful sign she's not pissed at me. Meg holds out the mug and I take it. "Thank you, darling."

Meg doesn't move, leaning across from me in the doorway as I sip the coffee. "You sleep at all?" She asks, and I shrug. "Drawing?" I nod. "Which memory?"

My smile becomes soft, and she reciprocates it. I begin to lean down to kiss her, but stop about halfway down, uncertainty bubbling up. Meg reaches for my head, pulling me down the rest of the way. I kiss her tenderly, both of us humming with content. I press my lips to hers once more, then pull away.

Meg winks and my heart flutters as she starts to head downstairs, pausing to flick her gaze down. "Maybe wear a kilt."

Heart still going pitter-patter I head into my apartment. I descend with an empty mug and wearing my werewolf kilt with a shirt, hearing muttering and grunts. I look over to see Josh and Brenda arm-wrestling with the werewolf straining against her. She barely bats an eye, before slamming his fist down. There's whooping through the bar, while Josh groans, tossing her some money.

"Okay, *my* turn!" Zane sits across from her.

"You sure, moon-moon?" She taunts, putting the money away.

"Half-daemon or not, you ain't taking me down, runt."

"Puppy chow."

"Dog pound reject."

He shouldn't have said that.

Her eyes glow, holding her hand out and Gunther counts them down as Delilah approaches. I glance at her, who glances at my kilt and smiles. "Don't."

"Didn't say anything."

"Your face did."

She snorts. "It's good having both you back."

"Never went anywhere."

"You don't have to leave physically to not be home," she murmurs. "And neither of you ever belonged on Topside." I give her a look, and she pats my shoulder. "Food's on the table, boss. And you deserved to finally get some sleep."

She walks away, teasingly consoling Josh on his loss, while I head over to the wrestling duo. Slowly, Brenda brings her arm down and taps his fist to the table. Zane howls in frustration. She laughs as she leans her head back, looking back at Marcus at the next table.

"You next, Balto?"

"No."

"Not enough coffee?" He grunts, ignoring her again. She lifts her head toward me. "Look what the cat drug in."

"Want food or not?"

She smirks, gets up as she puts her glasses on, then punches Zane on the arm playfully. He goes to wrestle her to the ground, but I grab his shoulder and shake my head. He rolls his eyes as I walk into the dining area, following Brenda. She sits in her old spot, next to me, and pours herself some coffee and then some into mine as I sit. She doesn't say a thing, putting food on both our plates. We haven't spoken since the argument on Topside. I'd forgotten about today. I wasn't sure she'd show.

I clear my throat and ask, "We good?"

"Course we are."

"Lil sis."

"We're fine."

"Brenda—"

"It's okay, Rodney." She stops, putting her hand on mine. "I was with Vinny when you called him...and when he dropped off Meg." I clear my throat. "And I know why...what happened in the park."

My thoughts ramble if I should tell her what I've wanted to. About what happened that night we blew the center. All I can say is, "I can't lose you, Brenda. I don't want to b-...bury you."

Brenda quickly wraps her arms around my neck. "You won't I promise." I squeeze her tightly, listening to her words. "I've got you to protect me, two brothers with personal space issues, overly doting parents, and a territorial vamp. We don't even need to include Beckham the Grey." I snort half-heartedly, and she hugs me tight. "Point is...I'm okay. You all have made sure of that. Trust me. And I'm glad you're okay, too."

"Okay," I whisper. "Just promise to be careful."

"Always." She pulls back, giving me a large smile. "Just know, I'll always have your back."

"Still coming next week?" I ask, feeling the heaviness of the words.

"Oh, yeah, my turn for beers," she says, clinking her mug against mine. "Two-pack? Been a long year."

"Maybe three."

"Well, I'll bring the booze, you bring the cards."

"Deal."

She kisses my cheek and then hands over some toast, she pauses to inhale a deep breath, quirking a brow at me. Oh, crud. We made up and now I'm gonna have her nosey ass in my business again.

"What did you do last night?"

"You are *not* that good."

"Well, you *do* smell of charcoal," she hums curiously. "Meaning up late, but I smell flowers, maybe…primrose?" I kick her chair, and she holds onto the table with a laugh. "Confirms it! You were K-I-S-S-I-N-G—"

"Quiet." I put my hand over her mouth. She mumbles as I glower at her. "Shush, some of them know out there, but…Meg and I are figuring it out. You know, privacy, the thing *you* want *your* brothers to give you?"

She glares at me. Ha! Got her.

Brenda huffs and nods against my hand. I let go, quickly wiping my hand off. "You like her then?"

I give her an exasperated look, and she smiles. Her clearly not moving on from the conversation, I reply finally, "Yeah, I do."

"Awww."

"Oh, for fucks sake."

"Hey, least you admitted it easier than Vinny. I had to shoot the bloodsucker for him to admit it, pro-tip, don't do that."

"Meg's not like that."

"Oh, I know," she chuckles. "Ma and she are like two peas in a pod, which, by the way, you better bring her back soon. I love baking with Ma, but Meg is *good* at it. Ma's been asking Pops to put more flowers in the house. Which now, I'm worried about him asking me about the botanical gardens on Topside, knowing him—"

"Okay, I get it, bring her to dinner."

"You try her whiskey cupcakes?"

"Wait, you have?" Before me?

"She's a keeper, don't fuck it up." I slam my hand against my face, grumbling as Brenda snickers at me.

"What are you doing to him?" I move my hand aside to see Meg walk in with more coffee.

"Sisterly talk," Brenda replies.

"Does that involve giving him a headache?"

"He'll survive."

"Or you could behave for brunch. I wouldn't want to tell your Ma that you left your manners at home." Brenda gapes as Meg walks out, and I start laughing.

Brenda shoves me as the other wolves start piling in, along with Edward who came back a few days ago. My right side is open for Meg as everyone puts food on each other's plates and talk. I catch Meg watching Brenda as she throws insults and jokes with the other wolves, almost fighting over a pancake with Edward. She acts like she's here every meal when it's been months. I glance at Delilah, who winks at me, looking smug.

"Hey, Brenda," Meg says.

"Uh huh?" Brenda mumbles with bacon in her mouth.

"Rodney showed me the Underground Central Park after visiting your brother's coffee shop yesterday."

"Did he?" Brenda flashes a look at me, and I frown, grabbing my coffee. I even catch Zane's excited eyes, and a small thumbs up. Privacy? In a wolf pack? Impossible. "What'd you think of it?"

"It's gorgeous, but he mentioned you could explain...shifter magic? How it created the park. I didn't know shifters had magic."

"Technically not magic, but—" The betas all make discomforting sounds, while Marcus growls at them to quiet. "Ignore the Toy Group, magic is just a fancy word for their abilities."

"Changing forms."

"Correct. The down and dirty version. Shifters change forms by rearranging molecules, the stronger they are the more they can rearrange. One of the strongest, Beckham, can shift into over seven forms. The average is three, but they can only create a form they've already studied, basically needing a blueprint. If they don't, something can go wrong like creating a new heart too large for an incubus or too small intestines for a vampire."

"Do werewolves have to do the same?" Meg quickly looks at Marcus.

"No," he answers next to her. "We're born with the three forms automatically."

"Second nature like succubi and incubi with their wings?"

"Or gargoyles shifting into stone."

"Oh, that makes sense."

"Yeah," he grunts, and Brenda gives me a curious, surprised look. I give her one back that I have *no idea* how Meg does it either.

Brenda clears her throat, continuing and glancing at Marcus. "Shifter abilities take more studying because the forms aren't strung into their DNA. They have a more scientific approach, passed down from generation to generation."

"All this goes into plants, how?"

"The more advanced, studied shifters can reform molecules *outside* their body. The vegetation growing in the park had DNA structures rearranged to grow underground, without the need for a hibernation stasis. All those plants constantly go through a specialized cycle of photosynthesis to bloom. Journals recorded from a century past discuss using similar reformations of fir trees."

"Could they do that Topside?"

"Best not to. Paranormals when building the Undergrounds had to create new ecosystems that could survive beneath the earth's surface, without natural light or air. Down to a science, like building a home for a reptile while living in northern Canada."

"Took a few times to get it right," I mumble, and Delilah grunts in agreement. Meg looks at me with confusion. "First few Undergrounds caused those below to go a bit insane," I shrug, and she gapes at me. "Time difference, no proper changeovers, air quality… partially screwed with some psyches."

"Not to mention shit falling," Zane snorts.

"So…this Underground, now, isn't what was originally here?" Meg asks.

"Technically it's the third one for New York," I say, and she gapes again.

"And *that's* where the shifter abilities really come into play," Brenda says excitedly. "Shifters can only rearrange molecules in a liquid state, and yes, there's debate about shifting bones and teeth, I'll have Beckham explain that one day." Meg gives me a look, and I grin, leaning back with my coffee. She opened the floodgates. "When the Undergrounds in the U.S. weren't staying up like those in other countries, a new plan needed to be implemented. The shifters discovered they could rearrange molecules within unpurified water that created a substance stronger than steel and titanium combined. Only the more powerful shifters can do this, due to the amount of concentration. It worked. After years and years of trial and error, they mixed stone and reformed water to create this new...well, element."

"Is there a name for it?"

"Shifter Stone," Brenda shrugs. "There's a long scientific name, but that's what construction calls it. It's what the pillars and main walls are made of here."

Meg glances at the wall behind her. Brenda chuckles, and briefly points at the ceiling, continuing her lecture. "The tricky part of this specific stone is that when it's done, turning that liquid into a solid state, can't be changed back. It's permanent. So, all the pillars they created long ago, won't and can't fall. Little to nothing can break them down. If we had an apocalypse, this shit would still be standing, and why most below aren't worried about anything taking it down. Each Underground is constructed differently, depending on the environment and part of the earth it was built into."

"They can't do that to people, can they?" Meg asks while Edward and Josh look up in worry. Maybe I should have Brenda lecture more often, start classes here.

"No," Marcus answers. "So, calm down, Milo and Otis."

"The frequency of the molecules in living things is different from plain water, *just* enough of that fraction keeps shifters from being able to. They can't even turn plants into it."

Meg puts her mug down, leaning closer toward Brenda on the other side of me. "How is each Underground built differently?"

"Oh, well there's those—"

"That may be enough for today," I interrupt.

"I could listen to Brenda for hours," Meg says, and I look into her curious gaze. "I was never taught any of this. School made it sound like it was normal brick and mortar."

"Well, wait until lil sis starts talking about Border Acts of the 1800s across Europe," Delilah muses.

"Or the Ghoul Outbreak that stopped World War II, you'll want a pen and paper," Gunther adds.

"Hey, it's interesting," Brenda protests.

"Not if you lived through it," Zane mumbles.

"Not my fault you're ancient, Rin Tin Tin."

"Wait until kids start talking about *your* childhood."

"I *wrote* about mine."

"She's got a point," Gunther mentions.

"Whose side are you on?" Zane asks.

"The one who can take you in an arm-wrestling match."

We all chuckle and Zane growls at them, then glares at Brenda who smiles smugly. He points at her chest, and says, "Rematch."

Brenda places her arm on the table, grinning ruefully. "Prepare to—"

"Go outside," I order, and she grumbles getting up and leaving with Zane. Others follow and make bets. Marcus gives me an exasperated look, leaving and grumbling about "pups." I look up at Delilah, and say, "Make sure neither of them breaks the bar again."

"You're kidding," Meg says.

"Oh, I've got more stories for you later," Delilah chuckles, getting up and tapping Josh's shoulder. "We'll clean up after the dynamic duo is finished out there."

They leave, and we're left alone. Meg comments, "Brenda really knows how to get under Zane's skin, huh?"

"You have no idea. Though kinda his fault, he's the one who play-wrestled her as a kid and gave her ideas for nicknames."

"Something tells me she hasn't changed much since then," Meg muses.

"Back then she was powered by curiosity, now it's coffee and stubbornness."

"I thought she'd be different at home, but she's just as wily with her brothers. Although it is kind of amusing seeing her stop when Alanzo says anything."

I chuckle. "Yeah, he always knows when to reel her in, unlike Cl—"

My words cut off as the old hollowness comes back. Brenda and Claudia would've been quite a pair. I stare at the empty table, thinking how Claudia would've taught Brenda to throw noodles on the ceiling, run around naked, or wrestle Zane. My heart becomes heavy, and I'm pulled out of the past when Meg places her hand on my arm.

"Rodney? You okay?"

"Yeah," I grunt, clearing my throat. "Just uh, don't tell her parents she wrestles with wolves. You know the whole manners thing."

"Uh-huh." Meg raises a brow.

I shake off the feeling, putting her empty plate on mine and stacking other dishes. "What's this I hear about whiskey cupcakes?"

"What about them?" She asks, helping.

"You holding out on me on flavors?"

"Perhaps, I didn't think it'd be your favorite."

"Oh, really?" I ask, leaning in close as I crowd her space. She backs up toward the wall, and I put my hands on either side of her head. "What do *you* think my favorite flavor is?"

She drops her gaze to my mouth. "Not whiskey."

"Something sweeter?" Meg lightly bites her bottom lip, grinning mischievously up at me. I lean in closer, tilting my head, and say against her lips, "'Cause, you may be right, darling."

I press my mouth against hers, tasting what has become my favorite taste. Her breath hitches, and I dive deeper into the kiss as my body presses against hers. Her hands rove down my chest, gripping my waist to bring me closer. A heated snarl emerges from the back of my throat pulsating through me. Meg doesn't falter, humming with satisfaction against the sound.

Suddenly, there's a loud howl from the tavern and we pull

apart, looking toward the doorway. Meg whispers against me, "I think Zane lost again."

Something cracks, echoing with a snap. "And now he's breaking things."

"No, he is not!" Meg dips down beneath my arm, escaping, and stalks out. "We just fixed everything! Zane, it is not nice to—"

There's arguing, laughter, and more chaos as it sounds like more wrestling. I look up at the ceiling for any help. None comes. But I do start laughing.

CHAPTER 22
AS JOKES GO BY

Zane grumbles, carrying out the table he accidentally broke to the back with Meg close behind. I sit in the tavern with Brenda, who looks proud at the mayhem she's caused. Watching Meg scold the tall grey wolf was a mood booster, especially with Delilah smirking the entire time.

"Know when you can bring her by for dinner?" Brenda asks.

"Next week, if things stay peaceful, maybe the…the night before?"

She cocks her head. "You sure that'll be okay?"

"Yeah, make sure you pick up the right beers," I retort, and she snorts, nodding her head. I sigh, knowing I'll have to work soon and start running numbers against all the changes we've made. The boring part of running a mob business: inventory sheets and accounts. I grimace, glaring up toward my office.

"Don't wanna work?"

"Got anything to keep my attention instead?" I ask.

"I'll give you two choices," she says, leaning on her elbows. "Cartoons or the update I got from Drauper."

Oh, how I wish I could choose the cartoons. "When did he contact you?"

"Late last night, hadn't contacted Gunther yet 'cause I knew I'd see you before Drauper woke up." I glance back at where Gunther and Marcus sit, sifting through papers between them. "Besides, I am Drauper's handler…kind of."

I scoff, and she smirks. "What he find?"

"So, to start, PSB won't state who's working the case," she lowers her voice. "They won't even tell the police or FBI who's working it. He contacted a buddy in the FBI, trying to see what was going on. They said not their department."

"Human mob was involved; FBI should at least be aware."

"Yeah, but I bet you two desert eagles that no one's investigating DiNardi's death."

"After DiNardi almost gave everything up? That doesn't make sense for the feds or police to drop it."

"Unless PSB didn't know, which would make sense given how airtight DiNardi's connections were with the NYPD for over two years."

"Then how'd those agents find out? DiNardi wasn't Paranormal, *no one* in his organization was. So, why'd they show up in the first place?"

Brenda shrugs. "Something else prompted them to investigate him?"

"Before using the explosives trail as an excuse to take over the case?"

"Makes them even more diabolical for planting them in the first place," she says. "They were making sure to control the case from the beginning."

"Doesn't answer why DiNardi or if they knew about him defecting."

"Well, wanna hear more fun news?" I grunt at her, crossing my arms. "Once Drauper hit walls with PSB and FBI contacts, I contacted Midnight. He says there are no open cases in New York for an investigation about 4D's bombing." Well, fuck me royally. "Rodney, they're making the case and DiNardi disappear on purpose, anything connected to him."

I swear under my breath. If they make everything disappear, it'll be harder finding those agents and who's involved.

"They *had* to know DiNardi was leaving, why else go after

him?" I whisper. "Maybe he found something that they didn't want found out."

"Perhaps," Brenda breathes out, flicking her gaze past me. "Either way, they shouldn't have that kind of pull. That's like…"

"Director level shit," I mutter. "And probably why PSB wasn't helping months back."

"Whose theory was that before by the way?"

"Does it matter?"

"Yeah, cause I think I owe a bottle of liquor to someone." I snort. "Explains how Freyja got involved, only a rogue Director would go to her. Knowing she'd keep quiet."

"Or she was helping DiNardi." Our eyes meet, and Brenda's jaw tightens. "She'd be the one to play both sides, you know how she is."

DiNardi could've been selling to her, whatever he wasn't giving to police and perhaps that's why Sebastian showed up. She could be pissed about a lot of things, so much so to help another mob boss attack the Underground. My brows scrunch, thinking about how Boston would've approached Freyja in the first place…or the other way around.

"Here's hoping nothing more disappears," I mutter.

"Don't worry," Brenda sighs, leaning back in her chair. "We'll find the fuckers who took your shit and messed with our 'mob ecosystem' and shoot their dicks off."

"I thought it was kneecaps."

"Thinking outside the box," she murmurs, looking at the bar. "They seem to."

My mind flits back to brunch, words connecting. *Outside the box. Diabolical.* A haunting feeling creeps up my spine, and my gut churns. "Lil sis." She hums, bringing her attention back to me. "Everything you said about the Underground's construction, that's public knowledge on Topside?"

"Mostly," she says. "Although I am a librarian and I've scoured sections of places that most people won't go near. I don't mind dust."

Or federal agents with a vendetta.

Brenda suddenly pulls out her 9-Mil, aiming at the front door. She keeps her attention on me as everyone goes still. Vincent walks in, brushes back his hair as he smiles, and approaches us casually.

"You're late, bloodsucker," Brenda tells him.

"A vampire is never late, we arrive precisely when we mean to," Vincent replies.

"That's wizards."

"I'd make a thoughtful Gandalf."

"Grow a beard first."

"How long?"

"Enough to braid, then strangle you with. I wanna see if you're into breath play, and I feel like blue could be your color." She puts her gun away as wolves snicker. "They think I'm hilarious."

"Oh, I know, sweet cheeks, but remember who you sleep next to."

"Don't bring my brothers into this."

Vincent presses his hand against his chest as he stops next to her. "You wound me."

Brenda pats his thigh, and retorts. "You'll live."

The vampire glances around the place. "Not bad with the rehaul, although I'd hoped you moved away from the western motif. Old habits die hard."

A few wolves snarl, but Vincent ignores them, smiling. Twenty years ago he would've never been able to walk in here or werewolf territory without catching some silver. Except, he's Brenda's Mate now. I'd like to wipe that smug look off his face, knowing I can't touch him, even in my own damn territory. My morning has been shot with just his cocky presence.

"I don't need advice from the one who owns a sleazy, cliché cigar lounge," I mutter.

"You should open your horizons more, think of what you could hang from the ceiling."

"Oh, I'm thinking of *something*."

"Okay, Thing 1 and Thing 2," Brenda interrupts, standing between us, patting his chest. "Don't make me point my guns at you two again." She looks at him. "Be nice. You're on probation."

He flicks his gaze to her. "Why am I on probation? I didn't lie to you or make your brother—"

"That's low," I growl.

"If the shoe fits."

"Well, not all of us are *Mr. Perfect*, are we?" I stand up, growling.

"It's quaint you have impossible dreams."

"Watch it, Nosferatu."

"Did you even apologize, *Airbud*?"

"Our relationship is none of your fucking business."

"She's my Mate, so yes...*it is*," he snarls.

I growl, claws becoming unsheathed as his fangs elongate. The wolves go still, barely making a sound. Brenda remains between us, muttering under her breath, "Not even two minutes."

"He started it," I growl.

"I need a hero," Brenda mumbles as she starts to back Vincent up. "Should have made you wait—"

"Vinny!" Meg's voice makes me freeze, and I sheathe my claws as she comes up next to me. Vincent detracts his fangs quickly. "Brenda didn't say you were coming."

Brenda and Vincent exchange a glance. I glare at them, "Don't you dare."

She sticks her tongue out at me.

Vincent straightens, clearing his throat. "Came to walk sweet cheeks home."

"'Cause the bloodsucker keeps starting fights, can't let him wander the streets alone," Brenda mutters, glaring back at him.

"What?" He asks.

"It'd be a shame if he got a black eye," Meg teases.

Brenda snorts, and it helps ease the last of the tension as Meg laughs with her. I flash a look to Delilah, who gives me an exasperated look. Okay, fine maybe I walked right into his little "bait the wolf" trap.

"Or he's gonna get himself mugged one day," Brenda jokes, jabbing her elbow into his stomach. He barely flinches, but a shadow of a smile appears. "Be terrible for his reputation."

"Speaking of, Vinny, I never got to thank you for helping," Meg says suddenly, and his red eyes swing to her. "Everything happened so fast, and you left, we never got to talk. I know you didn't have to get involved, but you did. Thank you. I'm grateful you're not what I was told you'd be, and I appreciate you getting me safely to the Cuorebellas. Brenda and her parents spoke highly of you, too."

I notice Delilah's shock, then Gunther's stunned expression. Marcus scowls at me, arms crossed with a look of "I told you so." Damn it, now I *kinda* feel bad for fighting with the vamp.

"No problem at all, Meg," Vincent answers.

"Well, Brenda, tell your Ma I miss her and look forward to seeing her soon," Meg says, and Brenda grins at her. "And that you behaved."

"You behaved?" Vincent asks, and she jabs her elbow into his gut again.

"Rodney will bring you to dinner next week." Brenda juts her head toward me. "They'll be ecstatic to see you and bring dessert."

"Sure, and will Vinny be there?"

Vincent's eyes flash for a moment, and he tells her, "Carmen would adore that."

"Well, Brenda, get him home safe," Meg teases again.

"Librarian enforcer at your service," Brenda says, giving Vincent a mock salute. "Can't let the bullies get to you."

He quirks a brow. "You're lively this morning."

"'Cause she beat two werewolves at arm-wrestling," Delilah calls over, grinning ruefully. "And lectured about shifters."

Vincent grins. "Your favorite hobbies, besides—"

"Time to go!" Brenda pulls him toward the entrance. "Until next round, Marmaduke!"

"I'm taking you down!" Zane calls out from the back.

"Will not!"

"Will too!"

"Quit it," I growl, and I hear him grumble through the doors.

"He's gonna be grumpy all day," Meg murmurs.

"I'll give him something to kill," I answer, and Meg looks at me with wide eyes. "Kidding." Kind of.

Brenda waves, leaving with Vincent in tow and I notice her smack his arm once they're outside. She gestures toward *Mountain Edge*, and he shrugs, which prompts her to start walking away.

Vincent quickly grabs her and kisses her, bringing her close before putting his arm over her shoulders as they disappear into the Underground.

"They really love each other, huh?" Meg asks softly.

I clear my throat and nod. Even seeing Brenda happy, I still have an old hate for the cocky bloodsucker. Guilt begins to follow the emotion and I look at Meg. "He didn't stay at the Cuorebellas?"

She shakes her head. "No, but her family talked a lot about him. I'm happy they have each other, perfect pair it seems."

Meg walks away as I stand still, the tavern going back to normal with a few beings coming in for lunchtime. I head for my office, beginning to think outside the box on leads when I see Marcus. He remains seated, alone and quiet as his gaze stays on the spot Brenda and Vincent were. His brows furrowed and the frown he always wears isn't of agitation but...longing. My chest concaves seeing those hardened eyes, empty and glistening with tears.

"Marcus, could you help me with something?" Meg calls from the dining area, and his head snaps toward her voice. He straightens and gets up, disappearing into the back.

I flick my gaze toward the bar and see Delilah with a worried expression. I shake my head, distracting myself from the pain I saw in his eyes.

CHAPTER 23
STRANGERS IN THE NIGHT, EXCHANGING FEARS

"We're in fucking trouble," Gunther rasps, staring at the chemical breakdown.

I spent all day working, then going off a gut feeling to look closer at the recipe we created for the explosives. The ones stolen. We'd made them to take out anything Paranormal, but never tested it on the pillars holding the Underground together, it never occurred to us. But looking back over the composition and what it *could* destroy, it's highly possible. Failure yanks at me, hating now that Marcus and I had made those explosives out of anger. Out of pain. We created them to kill the Paranormals who'd killed Claudia and Cassandra.

"They may not break down the pillars completely, but enough damage to one, and it can bring an entire section of the city down," I mutter, leaning over the paperwork next to him.

"How certain can we be that it may be their endgame? Could they know?" Gunther asks.

"It could be *why* they stole them, figured out what really blew up part of the Bronx. They knew it was us, and what the napalm could do. Intent on destroying us all."

"Rodney, it's one thing to blow up a club. It's an entirely different thing to potentially destroy half the city," Gunther argues as I sit down. "That's why we didn't even think about it, that's beyond—"

"They were stealing half-breeds off the streets for *years*," I say in a dark tone. "Hired a scientist that PSB tried to make disappear, turning beings into ghouls forcibly. What makes you think they aren't willing to do something like this?"

"Fine, it's a possibility," Gunther says, sitting down and rubbing his temple. "Why *4D*? Why use it on DiNardi?"

"Warn us. Practice. See what a handful could do."

"Trial run." Gunther hangs his head back. "By using the fucking mob."

My office becomes quiet as we sit in silence, realizing what could be at stake beyond pissing off Freyja and Boston or the entire human mob being handed over to the police—the entire Underground, our home. I brought Gunther up, needing just one being's voice in my head. My voice of reason and balancer to help think.

"Alright, best not to spiral," Gunther says, leaning forward on his elbows. "What's done is done. We gotta figure out next steps, without causing a panicked uproar. What Brenda told you about PSB's recent actions, it's obvious they're orchestrating this whole thing."

"Probably Freyja and Boston, too, for all we know. They got to DiNardi."

"Technically they got to us, too," Gunther suggests, and I furrow my brows. "Almost killed you in the blast, maybe we were part of the plan to die. Choose a mob at random and implode them. They're perfecting scenarios at pointing fingers."

"Don't remind me," I mutter, remembering the meeting where we almost started a fucking war with the NYPD and Topside.

"Inform the alphas and betas what could be at risk," I say. "Start searches to check major pillars and see if anything has been rigged. We'll start searching for the explosives again on Topside since PSB is pulling back along with the police. One good thing about that; fewer eyes."

"We haven't gotten anywhere in weeks, boss. It'd be looking for a needle in a haystack."

"We need to find those fuckers. Whatever it takes but not to raise any suspicions. Don't want to deal with Boston or Freyja's personal vendettas with this, too."

Gunther nods, letting out a long exhale. "Well, the drives were a dud, melted almost to nothing. We did get those safes open, but they're just documents for *4D* and DiNardi's other fronts. If he was alive, we'd have hit the motherload."

"Lil sis didn't mention anything about the thumb drive earlier."

"Louis called just before I came in," Gunther says. "Still working on it, but almost there. Whoever wiped those cameras, probably wiped that drive. He's trying not to accidentally destroy any potential digital footprints."

"Ralph could've been working for the agents, then."

"Why a con man as a deliver guy?"

"Half-breed and could get through both zones easily. Those agents would've known, given being's species status is public record and dug enough to see he'd worked for DiNardi in the past."

"Except, they didn't know about the price on his head." Gunther rubs his chin, tilting his head. "Still doesn't explain how the timing worked, from us catching Ralph to the bombing. How'd they know?"

I stare down at my desk and exhale sharply. I'm starting to think I owe Brenda the liquor bottle. She seems more cut out for this detective headache.

"We have a mole," I state.

Gunther slumps, nodding worryingly. "I'll keep everything on the down-low, see who shows themselves. Like Travis. Although I hope not."

I check the time, getting up and needing a drink. A splitting headache is beginning to form, and I need out of my office. "Inform alphas and betas tomorrow morning, let's not rock the boat just yet. Give ourselves the night to think. Hopefully, breathe."

He stands with a stretch and exhales sharply. "I'm beginning to think we should listen to lil sis' lectures more, what else have we missed from them? Maybe a way to keep ghouls at a further distance? Or vampires?"

"Doubt it." We walk out, leaning over the catwalk railing as the evening crowds come in, gathering at the bar. I watch Meg bartend, pouring down the line as wolves chat with her.

"You good, Rodney?"

"Fine," I reply and hear him sigh. "Why?"

"You want me to be honest or fluff your pillows?" Gunther asks, breaking my concentration on Meg. I give him a side glance, and he raises a brow.

"What?"

"There's never a right time for anything," he says. "Either from admitting what Freyja did, telling Brenda what happened that night, or who Meg is to you."

"Gunther—"

"I feel helpless knowing it ain't gonna be me, Zane, Delilah, or even Marcus to get you to open up again." I freeze as he holds my gaze. "You only started 'pretending' being the big bad wolf when… when Claudia died, but lil sis got you to be *you*, and then I don't know what happened." His eyes search mine, softening. "Unless Christine got to you more than I thought."

My stomach drops, trying not to remember the anger and hatred from her years ago. A failure I try not to think of ever. I swallow hard. "I can't change the roles I have to play, Gunther."

"Or you could say fuck it to those roles. Look at Vincent, he tipped everything upside down and made it work. Saved himself and a few others."

My stomach sinks, the jealousy rising again, and hating the bloodsucker for being able to do all that. Not all of us have his *luck*. Some of us don't like what's left us behind closed doors, riddled with failure, guilt, and fears. What was the point of surviving it all just to screw it up? And how do I tell my Pack that I don't…

I shake off those thoughts and put my hand on his shoulder. "If something was truly wrong, I'd tell you," I say, trying to convince him and myself. "I appreciate you caring, you're the best beta there is, even when your advice annoys me."

"'Cause I'm right?" I scoff at him, and he grips my hand for a moment. "You're the most stubborn alpha, so I gotta stay on my toes." He lets go, taking a few steps, but pauses to look back. "If you're not gonna open up with me, then maybe with her. She's your Moonlight for a reason."

I watch him walk away, my throat beginning to close as the

smell of napalm and fire throttle my senses. My vision is filled with watching *Mountain Edge* being blown apart. The Underground toppling as screams fill my head, dying. *You'll bring ruin to this Pack.* I picture Meg bloodied, and it feels like my heart is being pierced, twisting in horrifying images of her death. Gone.

I shake my head, rub it, and wince as my nails nick my skin. I huff in exasperation, heading for the stairs to the top floor when I pause to see Meg appear on the steps.

"You looked like you needed this," she says, holding up a light brown cupcake with vanilla icing, drizzled with caramel. "I would've brought up the cocktail, but the bar is busy."

I glance back at where I was standing, down to the busy bar, and then to her. The cupcake is dainty in my hand as I peel back the wrapping, taking a bite. It's rich in flavor with a hint of... "Whiskey?"

"Good wolf senses," she smirks.

I take another bite. Her brows scrunch, pursing her lips. "What?"

"Knew whiskey wouldn't be your favorite."

"Good bartender senses."

She shrugs. After watching me finish, she looks down at the bar. "You done for the night?"

"Yeah," I reply in a quiet tone. "Going back to bartend?"

"They'll be fine without me."

Shadows flicker over her face, her eyes still on those below creating all kinds of noise. A part of me wants to disappear into my apartment, hide away and be alone. While the other part yearns for company. Hers.

"Want a drink?" I ask, gesturing toward my apartment. Meg blinks, surprise flitting over her as she looks at me. "Just a drink, no hanky-panky." She cocks a brow. "Unless you ask."

She smiles, rolling her eyes then nods her head. I lead us up, quietly moving through the shadows. Meg stays close as I open the door, gesturing for her to enter. She does slowly, and I shut the door behind me as I turn on the low lights. She looks around, stopping in the main living area, and glances at my bed. Her gaze meets mine, brow quirking. "Large bed."

"Large wolf," I murmur, moving to the bar, and gesturing toward the couches. I grab whiskey, then a bottle of Cabernet I acquired from downstairs.

On instinct, I reach for a wine glass but stop. My hand hovers as I stare at the dust-covered glasses, unable to bring myself to use one. I pull out a brandy glass, pour the wine into that, and then pour my own drink. I turn, finding Meg watching me with her eyes flicking to the glasses on the shelf and then my hands. She smiles softly as I bring the drinks over, sitting across from her as she folds her legs underneath her. She settles, looking comfortable sipping the wine. Sensing how at ease she is, I relax a bit more.

"Nice place you got here," she comments.

"It's...home," I rasp a little, clearing my throat and taking a drink. My mind still flits to memories, emotions swirling with the weight of fear and failure. I stare at the amber liquid, suddenly feeling very alone as my mind spirals into oblivion.

"I want to tell you something," Meg says, breaking through my crashing thoughts, and I look up to see her gentle expression. "I know I haven't gone into much detail about my past, perhaps it's time that I do."

"You don't have to. I get wanting to keep skeletons in the closet."

"Yeah, but...some may not stay there even if I want them to." I go still, watching her sip her wine and look out the round window. "I want control over my own story. For you to hear it from me, no one else." My mind suddenly goes blank as I inhale deeply of her scent, easing into my bones, then nod for her to continue. "It's about what else I did for Boston."

"Meg—"

"I've appreciated you not pushing before, giving me that choice." She holds her hand up. "Except, this may change your mind about...whatever we are."

Mine. I shove back the inner voice, and say, "I doubt anything you've ever done will make me think less of you. Or change how I feel."

Her brown eyes meet mine. "You say that now."

"Darling." I put my glass down on the end table, leaning on my knees. "I ripped a wolf's head off less than two weeks ago. Before that, I shot Boston's guard without thought or remorse. The list goes on of the atrocities I've done, and we'd be here all night for what I've done in a *year*. I've got three centuries on you filled with decisions that have bloodied my hands and jaws, again and again."

Her gentle expression is gone, and I can practically feel her heartbeat quicken, but maybe it's mine. I try to remain calm, leaning back and taking my drink. My hands tremble as I struggle to keep my drink still. Fucks' sake, get your shit together, Rod.

"I killed the man who assaulted me." My chest tightens as I stare at the whiskey. "It's not centuries of mob work or survival, but…"

I'm unable to speak, looking up as she exhales sharply. She takes a drink and keeps her eyes out on the Underground. "When I first came to New York, I had nothing. My parents died abruptly, leaving me in their debt to clean up. I couldn't stay in that small town anymore, so I came to the city with a friend, hoping to start over. I learned how to bartend and loved it, especially after combining baking. Two loves into one. It was fun in the beginning, loving the nightlife, even after my friend went on to Florida. First few years were good."

She cocks her head, smiling like she's remembering.

"Growing up, I was warned *so much* to stay away from Paranormals. But it's New York City, and I saw so many kinds of beings, but never got close or crossed the neutral zones. Until one night, I just…ended up in a zone and saw an incubus. His wings were out, and I got scared. I ran away, ending up in another alley and a man was there. He grabbed me, and then…" her voice trails off, taking a moment to collect herself, "…there wasn't a piece of my clothing that was intact when he was done. I'd laid on the concrete, barely coherent when he was about to continue when that same incubus showed up and he ran off. I barely remember what happened next, but I do remember feeling safe with that incubus, who got me to the hospital. I never learned his name, feeling ashamed that I'd run from him in the first place after such…kindness he showed me."

"It wasn't your fault," I murmur.

"I know," she answers, meeting my gaze. "It's been four years now, and I've learned to move on. Still am. But I do wish I'd learned that incubus' name, thank him for saving me."

"Cuorebellas could help find him. Alanzo practically knows every incubus in the city."

She shakes her head. "If it's meant to be to see him again, I'll be grateful. I just hope someone showed him the same kindness he'd given me."

I exhale a sharp breath, taking a long sip. "You said you killed the man who did it."

"Less than a year later, I get a job at a new bar on Staten." Her eyes meet mine and my heart sinks, dreading knowing where this is going. "A few weeks in, I see the man. Long story short, one of the knives I used for cutting lemons ended up in his neck. So, I'm not *that* clumsy with knives." I snort as she smirks at me. "He was one of Boston's captains, his only mole in Antoni's operations. I owed him a captain and over a hundred thousand dollars, money the man was picking up the next night. And an intel drop."

Fuck, he didn't just want her back because of DiNardi, but everything else she'd lost him. "So, to pay your debt you became a mole? Replaced the guy you killed?"

Her gaze drifts down. "Later on."

A dark, possessive emotion spread through my chest. "Meg."

"Do you know what Boston does to those who cost him money?" She whispers, taking a shuddering breath. "Death is kind."

"Megara."

"I became *his*. Someone he could smack around, sell their body for, and use. So, when he needed another mole, I volunteered to replace what I took. He bought it." I want to tell her I'm sorry, anger rising in my gut with a snarl that wants to break free. I knew he was scum, but not like this. "4D became my safe haven, weird as it sounds, but Antoni wasn't cruel. And then I made the deal with him, trying to find a way out."

"Why didn't you tell me earlier?"

She smiles sadly. "I have a history of using mob bosses to get what I want. Maybe, you'd think I'd betray you next, and then

Boston attacked, and…even with Antoni dead, I'm using him. And you were right about me using you and the Pack as guards."

"Why did you? I could've just been like Boston. Like DiNardi."

"You promised to help me," she states. "And I'm finding it's better to trust Paranormals over humans."

"Why?"

"You have more humanity in you than them."

I finish my drink as she sips hers quietly, watching as I get up and pour another glass and sit down. After a few minutes, finally, I say, "Thank you for sharing with me. I honestly don't give a fuck what you've done, especially to survive, it's not my place to judge given my colorful background. You took hold of your own fate, be proud of that. And however, this…ends, you'll never go back to Boston, to *any* mob boss again. I'll keep that promise with you, no matter what."

"I believe you. And thank you."

I nod stiffly as Meg finishes her wine, getting up to refill it before I can. She moves around, pausing at the bar. "The one you leave a drink for downstairs…did they own the wine glasses?" My mind blanks out, and I turn to Meg and the dusty shelves. I swallow hard and nod. "Mind if I pour them a glass?"

I gesture stiffly for her to go ahead. Meg takes down a glass, cleans it, and fills it a little. She comes back to sit down, setting them on the coffee table.

"Window," I murmur, and she looks up. "She always drank at the window."

Meg moves the glass, placing it on the large windowsill, then pauses to look out at the twinkling lights. "Had good taste. Beautiful view."

My chest feels heavy as I breathe, staring at the glass reflecting the lights. I can almost imagine Claw smirking, giving me eyes to tell Meg she's pretty or something. I breathe in deeply, closing my eyes as I concentrate on the citrus and lavender, hoping to ground myself. Make the hurt and ache stop. I struggle with the words, trying to open up. Finally, I whisper, "They were my sister's."

"Brenda?"

I shake my head, feeling the tears pushing forward. "Claudia, but I always called her Claw."

"She like red wine, too?"

"Rosé." I smile sadly, opening my eyes to find her brown ones. "It's why I kept them up here."

"When was the last time they were used?"

"Thirty years." Meg inhales sharply and sits down quietly. "She was killed in an explosion. With my mother."

Meg's face crumbles. "Rodney, I'm so—"

"When *4D* blew, I was still inside until the last minute," I talk, letting the words tumble out unable to stop them as I stare at the wineglass. "Last one out, just like a Pack alpha should. But that's not why...all I could think of was...was Claw...mom...lil sis. Last words, and what could've been."

I put my glass down, rubbing my hand over my face, trying to keep the tears back. My breath is shaky. "I hate explosions. A shit ton. That's one of my skeletons. A mob boss...an *alpha* afraid of explosions. I'm fearful of what more they can take from me." My vision is blurry as I look at her. I want to tell her I'm sorry she had to go through those horrors alone. I want to keep her safe from everything that's happened. All I can say is, "Including you."

Meg sets her glass down, and comes over, surprising me as she sits on my lap to grasp my face. I lean into her touch, melting into her careful hold. She looks me in the eye, and I whisper, "I'm sorry."

"No," she shakes her head, gently kissing me as I caress her cheek. "I appreciate you telling me. It's okay."

I wrap my arm around Meg, holding her tenderly as we softly kiss. I breathe in, tasting the elegance of that intertwining of honey, lavender, and now wine. With each passing moment, the harsh pressure stifling me lifts. The guilt doesn't feel as wicked. The trembling stops as I breathe in, sighing against her. I place a gentle kiss on one of her dimples, and she smiles as she sweeps a hand over my hair. Her head lays against my shoulder, clutching me as I do with her.

"Don't...don't tell anyone," I murmur.

"I won't," she whispers. "Both our skeletons can stay in the closet."

"I'm sorry you went through all that."

"I'm safe in a wolf's den now."

The shakiness in her voice worries me. I grip a bit tighter, not wanting her to leave my embrace. Let alone my apartment. "Sleep with me."

She moves to look at me with wide eyes. "Your bluntness has gotten—"

"Just sleep," I murmur, kissing her other dimple.

"No drawing?" I shake my head. "No teddy bear on that large bed of yours?"

"You can just say no."

"That's not what—" She huffs, pursing her lips. "You gonna wear pants?"

"I'm a gentle-wolf." She raises an inquisitive brow, and I snort. "Yes, I'll wear pants."

She sighs, beginning to get off my lap. "I...I need to change."

"You can borrow mine," I say, standing up and moving to my closet to pull out a shirt and lounge pants.

"I'm gonna own half your closet at this rate," she comments, taking them.

"You look better in them than me." She bites her lower lip, and I pull out pants for myself. She smirks. "Bathroom is through there."

She disappears and I stare at the bathroom door, wondering what the hell I'm doing. Then again, fuck it. I don't want her far from me, for both our sakes. My inner wolf whimpers, not wanting her to be left or feel...unloved. Alone.

I shake myself, changing quickly and tossing the blankets back as she walks out. She's radiant with her hair braided, the shirt hugging her curves comfortably, and there's a rosiness to her cheeks. I nod toward the bed, and she gets in, narrowing her eyes at my chest as I slip in next to her.

"I promised pants." She scoffs as I lay my arm behind my head, staring up at the ceiling. Meg moves beside me, and I glimpse over to see her on her side, head propped up.

"This bed is big, even for you."

"You've seen me in my hybrid form."

"Oh, right," she hums, then asks. "How big are you as a wolf?"

"Pretty big but can't quite remember, been almost a decade since I've shifted into it, maybe longer."

"Is...is it the same inner wolf you were talking about in the park?" I side-eye her, and she grins. "It's a fair question."

I roll my eyes at her. "Yeah. It's that basic instinct, what we are at our core."

She hums again, flicking her gaze down. "Why haven't you in such a long time? If it's natural, that is."

"No reason to, although I should, given that it's not healthy to not shift."

We become quiet. The only noise is the background sounds of the Underground. I stare at the ceiling, then feel her fingers skim down my arm. I place my arm out on the pillows, and she scoots over to cuddle against my side. I hold her to my chest, placing my head over hers. Breathing deeply.

"Hey, Rodney," she whispers, and I hum back. "Thank you for making me feel safe again."

I swallow hard, kissing her head and holding her close as if our pasts couldn't touch us. Safe from fear and skeletons in the shadows. "Course, darling."

CHAPTER 24
WEREWOLVES AND DEMONS

Vast marble stonework looms over us, replicating palaces of old. *The Vault* is the largest building in the Underground, spanning blocks with four floors of history and information. A spiral staircase leads to the next levels, while larger staircases are further in the back. The library was created to hold pieces of history concerning the Noctis Immortalis, preserving books from those attempted to burn. Over the decades, it's become the safehold for all information regarding humanity or Paranormals.

"Is this library bigger than the New York Public Library?" Meg asks.

"Yeah," I answer.

"No clue by how much," Gunther adds.

"That would determine how you perceive size in generality." Beckham's voice floats from the shadows, the owner who prides himself on keeping the safety of knowledge for all. He's a shifter with light green skin, thin and tall with long white hair woven into a braid. His golden eyes shine as he buttons his usual cardigan, a presence that's ancient and misguiding to think he's frail. He's not. I've known him for two centuries, and he still sends shivers down my spine.

"Meg, this is Beckham, the owner and main boss for the shifters within the Underground Mafia," I introduce.

"I'm merely a librarian who enjoys a good book with tea," he says with a calm tone. "I've been told my library was chosen as a neutral meeting space."

"Appreciate you letting us," Gunther says.

"This is an open space for all, my permission is never needed for its sanctuary."

"Aren't those churches?" Meg asks.

Beckham smiles, showing his serrated teeth. Meg doesn't falter, holding out her hand and he shakes it delicately. "I've heard wonderful things of you," he says. "A pleasure for you to visit my library, are you interested in exploring its treasures?"

"Yes, I'm off 'informant' duty today," she muses, and I give her a look.

She's been "off" that duty the past two days while spending the nights in my bed. No talk of the mob, just her learning about my life and I hers. She'd stay cuddled against my side, providing a peace I've only gotten while drawing. I've finally slept, and so has she, because she wakes up with an adorable bedhead. Even with that small peace, those no escaping reality.

Gunther received a call from the detective the day before, and Brenda suggested meeting Underground. We've kept it quiet, only the Underground alphas and betas knowing about the potential napalm catastrophe. I hate keeping information from the Pack and Meg, but I don't want to start a panic. Not without something more concrete about what those agents want.

"Ah, what interests you today?" Beckham asks her. "I've heard you were quite intrigued by the construction of the Underground."

"I don't know much outside the main six Paranormals, how's that for a start?"

Beckham tilts his head, curiously. "For one who's not spent much time with our kind of the night, you are quite open to learning."

"Knowledge is good," she replies.

"Yes, it is." He turns to Gunther and me. "Little Sister is on the third floor."

"Little Sister?" Meg asks. "Brenda?"

"She's my protégé," Beckhams responds, gesturing toward the library. "Come, my new friend, I'll be your guide." Meg squeezes my hand, walking off with Beckham to disappear into the shadows of the library. The shifter's voice carries through the space, filled with calm excitement. "I'll have to tell you about my gargoyle friends, who quite love cabarets."

Gunther loosens a breath, while we head upstairs. "I don't know who makes me more nervous. Him or Alanzo."

"Beckham should," I whisper, remembering him in the mafia head meeting.

We make our way to the third floor, finding Louis and Brenda sitting in a reading nook. Her glasses are off, fingers moving over pages as she reads the braille books stacked near her. Louis watches her, drinking from his mug that's part of a tea set on a coffee table. The area smells of peppermint and chamomile. Someone's trying to keep things passive.

"Five minutes late, Lassie," Brenda says, continuing reading.

"Held up," Gunther replies as we sit across from her.

"Working?" I ask.

"I'm behind translating," she answers, then nods toward Louis. "He's all yours."

"Thanks," he says.

"I said I needed to work, and you were too chicken to meet them yourself." He sits back, frowning as I hide my smirk.

"Just ignore her," Gunther says, pouring the tea. "What did you find?"

Louis pulls out the thumb drive, holds it up and places it on the table. "It's empty."

Brenda should rescind his Sherlock nickname. "We know it was wiped."

"No," he says carefully. "I mean, it was empty *before* being wiped. Blank."

"What?" Gunther asks.

"I ran several different computer forensics to search for any traces of digital footprints. The only remnants were the program used to wipe the software clean. Nothing else. It was always empty, actually *can't* hold anything."

"What was the program used?" Gunther asks.

"Military grade. That's why it took so long. It was wiped while connected with a computer, not something you can do on the run."

I exchange a look with Gunther, a sinking feeling hitting me. I mutter, "He was bait."

"Who?" Louis asks.

"The guy who had it on him," Gunther answers.

"What was supposed to be on it? What DiNardi found or was trading for?"

"That's what we presumed when we found the connection with the agents," Gunther says. "A trade of some kind, a final intel drop or bait and switch, and he never made it."

"Where was this...*guy* found?"

I pick up my mug, looking at Brenda who remains quiet, which is suspicious. Gunther answers, "Edge of Manhattan, near the South Bronx."

Louis frowns. "DiNardi was making drops in Lower Manhattan though, near Soho."

Exactly where Meg thought, too. I ease back, and Louis meets my gaze as I keep a passive expression. He narrows his eyes slightly, and I can tell we're both treading forward carefully. I'm not sure I can trust him yet.

The detective states, "You think the agents sent him."

"What else did you find?" I ask abruptly.

"May help if I know all who's involved."

"Mob."

"Funny." He scowls, while I smirk.

"It's like listening to a bad scene from *Cops*," Brenda comments as Gunther groans lightly.

"Wanna join in, Batty?" I ask, and she lightly screeches with a hiss. I grin as Louis shakes his head.

"We'll share theories when you share what you've found. You know, physical trail?" Gunther says, sipping his tea.

Louis pulls out a folder, and sighs, "Fine...Clifford."

Brenda and I snort, while Gunther growls, "Careful detective, I keep *him* from overturning the coffee table."

"Not if he keeps calling you Clifford, I'll let certain things slide." My beta scowls at me, while Louis cracks a smile. "Go on, detective."

"When Brenda told me her inside contact in PSB said there are no open cases, I looked at our cross-logs at the station," Louis says, gesturing at the folder. "We have reports coming in about the bombing, saying PSB is looking into it. When in reality, they're not, and my superiors are believing them."

"Which Branch of the PSB are the reports coming from?" Gunther asks.

"All of them."

Gunther glances through the paperwork and pushes them aside. "This is just like months ago. Doing nothing, while saying they are."

"Could try getting NIIA involved," Louis says, and a chill runs down my spine. "Maybe they'll—"

"Whatever hooks PSB has on the FBI and the NYPD to accept letting this case go, they'll do the same with NIIA." My voice is rough, and Brenda flicks her gaze to me. "They didn't come when beings went missing, why would they come now?"

Gunther places a hand on my chest, and I ease back. "Agencies aren't gonna help us find these guys," he says carefully. "We've got to find them on our own. Those timestamps we gave you, did they help at all?"

Louis keeps his gaze on me, and I'm on the brink of growling when he pulls out pictures. "This is all I found," he says, pointing at a couple of cars, and two men getting into them. Faces turned away. "They arrived and left all within the timeframe you told me." Thank you, Meg.

"Plates?" Gunther asks.

"Stolen, from six months ago." The news about the drive being blank was the good news I'm realizing. The rest is bad. And then disappointing.

"If you wanted to see my face, just say so next time," Gunther says, grabbing his tea. "Otherwise, all of this could've been an email."

Louis folds his arms, settling into his seat. "That's just what *you* told me to look into. Ask nicely, and I may give what *I* decided to look into."

Someone got a backbone. I glare at him, and he does it back.

"Please share before my boss combusts," Gunther says while Brenda smirks from behind her book.

Louis nudges her side, and she grunts. "You said you wanted part of this."

"You're holding your own, Sherlock."

"Seriously?" She pats his knee. "Fuck you."

"Mated. Can't."

"What is it? Anything is better than dead ends," Gunther says.

Louis sighs, grabbing his tea and taking a long gulp. Hope he knows Beckham doesn't spike his tea.

"None of this can leave here," he starts.

Gunther waves his hand casually. "Obviously, but if you could stop doing the 'detective show' dramatics, that'd be helpful."

"I'm beginning to see where you get it from," Louis mumbles to Brenda.

"It takes a village."

He shakes his head, leaning forward. "DiNardi was planning to divulge more information than just the present mobs and operations."

"We knew that," I say.

"No...*more*." His voice drops. "He had information on players, bosses, and captains that left the game for almost *three* decades, somehow collecting information about those who'd been in charge before the currents. What happened to them, where they are now, shell companies, offshore accounts, etc. Not just New York's mobs, but he had a fucking *goldmine* on mafia operations all the way down to Georgia. They were planning to start here, and then continue joint ops with the FBI after getting him out."

"How'd they know he was telling the truth?" Gunther asks.

"Gave them a name and location. He was right, including all offshore accounts they were using."

I look at Gunther, a sickening feeling in my stomach. Meg doesn't know how deep the well DiNardi dug. He was using her for the other families. He would've been used by the FBI for *years*, there was no getting out of that. Neither would have Meg. She'd have gone from one cage to another.

"While investigating, there's another name that kept popping up," Louis continues. "DiNardi's handler thinks it was his contact for the older information, everything outside the city. Sebastian Crimsworth."

My eyes flash to Brenda, her expression neutral and not at all surprised. She knew.

The thoughts of Freyja being more involved come more into light, and the theory of DiNardi digging too deep may have been his downfall. Either Freyja was helping him or she wanted that information. And then the next horrifying thought...did DiNardi tell her about Meg?

"Maybe those explosives *were* meant for him," Gunther whispers, and I meet his gaze. "Stop all that from going out. That kind of information would've affected more than just the mobs."

"It would've crashed stock markets and bankrupted companies, that's just the start," I murmur.

"Those agents and their connections could've been on those rosters, protecting their own asses." Something gnaws at my gut, the *why* digging at my brain. For both DiNardi and the agents. The pieces were there, but not falling together.

"No one knew DiNardi was planning this," Louis interjects. "Only his handler and the main detective on the case knew. I've known them for years." I quirk a brow. "And maybe I had a drink with them, listening to their anger at all their work going down the drain. Can't blame them, they risked everything."

"That doesn't mean someone *else* didn't know," I say. "He was getting information somewhere, and they could've picked up the trail."

"And then what, told those agents?" Louis asks.

"Or those agents knew to go to them," Gunther murmurs, and I give him a look. "It was her center and *their* operation; the contact was already there."

"Why would she help them after—"

"She fucking helped Boston," Gunther hisses. "Sent armored vehicles..."

"Gunther."

"…and dozens of gunmen, it's not far-fetched she—"

"*Gunther*," I growl, and he shuts his mouth. I flick my gaze to Louis and Brenda, who watches wordlessly. Why is she quiet? She's never quiet.

"Want to tell me something?" Louis asks.

"It was handled," I reply gruffly.

"If it's part of whatever is going on—"

"Just mob business. Nothing you need to know."

"I think I *do* need to know. Handled or not. If other bosses are in on this, that toes Paranormal Laws, which could—"

"Be a way in for you?"

"No." His statement is flat as he points at me, making me sneer. "If things keep being swept under the rug by PSB, more people will die. Humans and Paranormals alike. My superiors are doing nothing. FBI gave up, losing the damn glory they wanted. And cops don't care 'cause they don't give a shit right now. In their heads, they lost. Time to go home, find another to implant, and do it all over. But I'm *not* gonna wait until someone bombs another building."

"Talking to me or her?" I ask, snarling.

"Keep her out of this."

"Oh, *now* you're trying to protect her?"

"Fuck off."

Brenda groans, closing her book. "Stop pissing in each other's cheerios," she says, leaning her head back. "Clifford, what happened to your beta skills?"

"Boss growled at me." I glare at the *big red dog*.

"Boo-hoo." She rubs her temple, grabbing her glasses. "None of the other bosses were involved, Topside and Underground alike, there's nothing that connects them. They all got caught up *after* DiNardi died. They're an outcome. We know those agents are the ones who planted the bombs, *you* have a witness." She glares at me, and I scowl at her. "But with all this bickering wondering of pointing fingers, who's involved, who got intel from who…have we thought *why* DiNardi chose to work with them?"

"They promised him something," I say. "Those were his last words."

"Did DiNardi know the bombs were there?" Louis asks. Gunther and I exchange a look. "You don't know."

"Didn't stay to ask," I retort.

"If he did, then he probably thought it was for a fake death," Brenda says, glancing at Louis. "Feds do it all the time, easy to presume the agents would suggest it. And maybe he *was* waiting on a messenger, to give it over and disappear. Except you showed up."

"With Ralph's head," I murmur. "He didn't know they were sending *him*."

"That doesn't explain why in baiting us there," Gunther remarks.

"Two birds, one stone," Brenda says softly. "Revenge for blowing up Traloski."

I place my elbows on my knees, thinking as I try to get every bit of confusing piece into the same bucket. "The one question I can't get out of my head is why DiNardi? Especially if they knew the kind of information he was gathering and doing it well. And if they didn't, again why *him*?"

Brenda trails her fingers over the book in her lap. "Maybe it was never about them."

I stare into her violet eyes, dread beginning to sink into my stomach. With one push of a button, DiNardi the main source of intel is gone, the Wolf Mob is gone, the mobs scramble for territory, and Freyja doesn't get the information she wanted *or* gave DiNardi for a price. But all fingers point toward the Wolf Mob, due to the explosives used, rumors suddenly planted DiNardi was selling. Chaos. Just like months ago with the police, the ghouls, and the missing half-breeds.

Were these fuckers the four horsemen of the apocalypse?

Fear starts to climb up my spine, realizing they may have gotten the POS system Meg talked about. Knew where DiNardi kept everything, killed him, and took it all anyways. Arsenal of secrets. And here's fucking hoping they have no idea what my explosives can do. "I need those agents."

"Trying," Louis says. "Using what I can to find their names, without getting caught sifting through their databases."

"Just get me photos. That's all I need to know who."

"How you gonna do that?"

"I can ID them." He glares at me, then at Brenda. "We get our hands on them, we find out what the hell their endgame is. I just need faces."

"What aren't you telling me?" I scowl, keeping my mouth shut. I don't trust him enough to give an *inkling* that Meg exists. He stands up, beginning to pace. "I can't help if you don't tell me how you'll ID the agents, especially ones so damn good at hiding. PSB is sealing *everything* on who's involved with the case. This is getting more dangerous, and if they're that many steps ahead, who knows what they're capable of."

"We're trying to safeguard our Pack," Gunther says.

"And I'm trying to safeguard a city," he argues. "If the mobs implode, the police need to know. Be there for the fallout. Federal agents doing deals with mobsters, blowing up buildings…Topside won't be safe. That should concern you." Gunther and I exchange a bored look. "Well, it concerns me."

"Thank you for sharing your feelings," Gunther states.

"Oh, fuck off." Louis leans over the couch, holding his head like he's going through his first mid-life crisis. He takes a deep breath. "I agreed to help because those agents, who've sworn to protect people *and* Paranormals, got away with stealing people off the streets. No one batted an eye, even me at one point. And right now, they're playing games with people who are ready to burn this city by the sounds of it, and if they do…innocent people will die. *Not* just your Pack. Trust me or not, but I'm trying to help stop them, too."

Okay, I'm starting to see what Brenda sees in him. The man's passionate I'll give him that.

Gunther looks surprised, looking at me with shrug, while Brenda's expression softens. "He fucked up in the past, but you can trust him. He's no snitch."

Louis looks at her, and she acts like she doesn't notice. I flick my gaze to Gunther, and he nods. I look at Brenda again, and she cocks her head. I sigh, "Fine. There was a survivor who worked for DiNardi, originally a mole for Boston but helped DiNardi, gathering that goldmine. They saw who planted the bombs and can confirm their identities."

"They're not a mole now?" He asks.

"No." Louis steps back from the darkness in my voice.

"Down, Lassie," Brenda comments.

"You had an inside man this entire time?"

"We promised to get them out alive if they helped," Gunther adds. "Couldn't risk anyone knowing what DiNardi had planned."

"As you said, all this is catching the attention of those with firepower no one wants to mess with. We're trying to avoid any more of that, including Freyja."

"I thought she was a myth."

Gunther snorts. "We wish."

Louis grumbles, coming back to slump back into his seat, and holds his head. "Just what we needed with this mess."

"We can all agree we need to find those agents. They're our key and the main catalyst to all our problems," Gunther says, flicking his gaze to me. "They've already caused enough chaos, who knows what they're planning next."

"Their endgame never changed," Brenda says in a low tone. Her jaw tightens, trailing her finger again over the book bindings.

"Lil sis—"

"Quit bickering and start working together before it's too late." She gets up and walks away, clicking her tongue as she disappears down an aisle.

I reach across, running my fingers over the binding to read the title. I clear my throat, sit down, and shake my head. Translating my ass.

"What was she reading?" Gunther asks.

"The Argenti Plague." He sighs, pouring more tea into all three mugs.

"What plague was that?" Louis asks.

"In the 14th century, there was a large werewolf scare across Europe," I explain solemnly. "It started because a man was killing children within a village, and they blamed the local family of werewolves. They murdered thousands in a twelve-year span, all on a rumor."

He stares at the book, and rasps, "Why the fuck was she reading that?"

"Because she's thinking the same thing we are," I sigh, taking the tea Gunther hands me. "If we don't stop these agents, put our shit aside, there'll be another...*plague*."

"Argenti means silver in Latin," Gunther whispers, handing Louis his cup.

"Traloski's dead. It'll take years before they find someone to finish what he started."

I stare at the tea in my hand. Maybe it's time I do open up and take help outside of my Pack, listen to Brenda and Marcus. "The explosives they stole could be strong enough to destroy the structures holding Topside up," I admit as Louis looks at the ceiling and I smell his fear rise. "DiNardi kept everything he found on the POS systems of the club. They're missing from the rubble."

Louis takes a long drink of his tea, and mutters, "Fuck."

"Take it from a couple of wolves who've seen the worst of beings. There's more than one way to create a plague."

Rosé Cupcakes

Flour
Butter
Sugar
Milk
Baking powder
Eggs
Salt
Vanilla
Powdered Sugar
Rosé Wine

CHAPTER 25

CAREFUL WITH STRAW HOUSES

There's icing on Skylar's shirt collar.

I raise a brow, watching as they swipe the icing off with their finger and I shake my head at them. Apparently, they visited *Mountain Edge* before I came to *Donny's*, and while Meg was in the kitchen. She's making dessert for dinner tomorrow at the Cuorebellas, stuck between a couple of flavors. Some of the Pack have been helping her, in more ways than one.

"You got icing?" Gunther asks, and they shrug.

Shannon shakes her head. "Y'all better bring cupcakes up next time."

I look at the dark grey wolf, and she nudges Gunther as he gives his fellow beta a knowing look. Yeah, he'll be sneaking some up later. You'd think I starved them or something.

"Update," I mutter, rubbing my temple.

"Zane's checking the last of the main structures," Gunther answers. "Finishing the last two tonight, down near Lower Manhattan Underground. No sign of tampering with the explosives."

"All Entrances are clear," Skylar reports. "Although I'd rather Gunther stay in contact with that detective of yours."

"Why?" I ask.

They glance at Gunther, who answers, "Louis is trying to be discreet, telling police there was an anonymous tip and to check certain infrastructures. If there's any sign of the explosives, he'll know first."

"I'm not sure how comfortable I am working with a detective, human at that," Skylar murmurs.

"We're gonna trust him," I say. "Don't need to trail him, Skylar, but Gunther will remain the main contact. His aid can help us keep an eye out for Boston and Freyja, too."

I'm worried about what some maniacal agents are up to; don't need those two screwing more shit up with their personal vendettas.

"No sign of him lately," Shannon reports. "Contacts haven't seen him in over a week. Think he went back to Jersey. As for Freyja, well, she seems to be busy with her *public* persona lately."

"Should I be watching human news now?" I ask.

"Some of her stock market holdings plummeted, connected to European flight lines. A couple of incubi were killed by a plane. Faulty GPS diagnostics didn't see them in time."

"Nights like this I'm glad I don't have wings," Gunther shudders.

"We'll use this time then to continue normal business and searching," I say, shaking my head. "It doesn't mean we're in the clear with them, but we'll use it to our advantage. Gunther and I will head back down to *Mountain Edge* later tonight."

I'm not hoping for a fight, but the stillness from the human mobs and Freyja put my senses on edge. I should be glad they've stepped back, allowing us to put all our efforts into finding these agents and our explosives, but the anxiety still ticks up my spine.

Shannon and Skylar nod, leaving my office as Gunther sighs, crossing his arms. "Detective got into the evidence locker of the police station involved with *4D's* bombing."

"And?"

"Everything was confiscated by PSB," he grumbles. "The chain of evidence is missing." Fucking great, probably means they did find the POS systems. "Informed him that all the profiles he found connected to the reports weren't a match."

Meg has ruled out every single profile we've shown. None of them were the agents. "Anything else?"

"I went off a hunch. Sent a couple of those names to Midnight, and he said they were agents, but work in D.C. or Atlanta. Sent him the rest, *none* of them work in New York."

"You're fucking kidding me." He shrugs, and I growl low. "And the police are just accepting it?"

"Midnight and Louis both think whomever these agents are, may not be active anymore. Someone else on the inside is pulling the strings, another with more power to do so."

"The director theory," I mumble, getting up to grab a drink. "Would make sense why other agencies are backing off, maybe getting phone calls instead of reports. We still need to keep trying."

"Will do." He starts to leave but pauses at the door. "Marcus left this morning to check on Garrick's supply chain. Garrick said he left hours ago, and Delilah hasn't seen him."

I sigh, leaning against the bar, and glance at the calendar. Two days until. "He'll show up but have someone cover his duties next few days."

Gunther nods, gripping the doorframe and I look over to see the concern on his face. "He gets more distant every year, boss. This time it feels...different."

"He'll be fine."

"You can't guarantee that." He frowns as my jaw tightens, swallowing hard. I've been distracted the past few days searching for answers, I haven't spent much thought on Claudia's upcoming birthday. A distant shadow, lingering with a hollow feeling.

"Give him space. That's what he needs every year. He'll be back." I force the words out, hoping they're true. Gunther sighs, closing the door behind him.

Dark feelings rise as I try to shake them off, knocking back a shot of whiskey. I blink, moving to the book shelving to distract myself again, revealing my maps to look them over. I pull down the transparent ones of routes and territories marked off, all mine and other mobs. My fingers trace over older routes, no longer in use after the police busts months ago. I'd planned to fully reinstate them, but it seemed futile at this point to go back to the Bronx.

I lean on my desk, folding my arms. Maybe it was best to steer clear of it and give it another decade before trying again. I tilt my head, staring at the lines and following them through neutral zones, melding into unspoken boundaries on Topside. Where are they hiding? And still, the question digs at me, why DiNardi? Everything points toward revenge, but it's left most of the Bronx empty. The neutral zones are free of Paranormals and mobs staying back until determined who owns what. I glance at the center we blew up and the several blocks we destroyed along with it. Empty.

I look closer, checking who owns what *before* DiNardi died and the surrounding area of the center, outside the neutral zone. DiNardi's green line brushes against the zone, and then next to his is mine to the east. Then it's DiNardi again on the west, and then Wolf Mob again.

Their endgame never changed, Brenda's voice echoes.

Mobs deal in revenge. Boston did it. Freyja isn't technically mob, but she most certainly thrives on it. DiNardi was turning everyone in, possibly for it, too. *You're dealing with someone who knows humans* and *Paranormals.* Gunther's right I need to listen to Brenda's lectures more often. Lil sis may be too smart for her own good, thankfully she's on my side.

DiNardi and my territories were the only ones still in place around the Bronx and inside it. Everyone moved, even me, but I still controlled access to the empty areas. Those turfs belonged to DiNardi and me. Once again, no one is in the Bronx neutral zones, including all Topside Mobs. It wasn't about revenge at all. They wanted the Bronx back. That's why we were baited there. *Two birds, one stone.*

"Those bombs were meant for *both* of us," I murmur out loud. They pulled a mafia move, making the other mobs respond in kind. Clearing the chessboard, willing to destroy the biggest mafia bust in history to do so. Fuckers were distracting us from the truth. And now they may have the information to keep controlling the mobs to stay out. *And* the explosives.

It's late, but I pick up my phone and dial. After a few rings, the detective picks up. "Hello?"

"It's McLycan."

There's some shuffling, and then mumbling, "Uh…usually, Gunther or—"

"Those agents are trying to take back the Bronx. Brenda was right. Their endgame never changed. The Wolf Mob can't get close, not without gaining unwanted attention. Start suggesting patrolmen go near the main neutral zone there, someone needs to have an eye on it."

Louis inhales sharply. "Yeah, sure, you think they'll try to start taking people again?"

"Let's not give them that chance." I pause, then say before hanging up. "Good job so far, and thanks."

Tossing the phone onto my desk, I rub the back of my neck and feel the sharpness of my nails. I bring my hand down, staring at the untrimmed claws. There's a knock, and then Victoria steps through with a bottle of scotch and folders. She smiles, puts the items on my desk, and says, "Figured you could use a drink."

"Good for now," I say, and nod toward the folders. "What's this?"

"I did some digging," she says, opening them to reveal lists of phone numbers. "This is *Donny's* outgoing phone records. Two calls were to dead-end numbers. The day before the bombing, while the other happened just before you left for *4D*."

"Someone here told them we were coming," I whisper.

"Didn't think much of the calls, until Travis was caught…and, well, maybe he wasn't the only one bent on revenge."

"Could you find out who made them?"

"I can try, we don't have cameras for precaution reasons, but I can ask around to see who came in. And try to trace the calls, see if they called Freyja or *4D*."

I exhale sharply. Maybe to DiNardi himself, thinking it was his messenger, and not us. I still had another mole to find. Or Travis was in more shit than we thought, at least he's dead. "Thanks, Victoria. What would I do without you?"

"Lose more poker games," she says with a wink, then her expression softens, flicking her gaze to the maps behind us. "You doing good, boss?"

"Yeah, why do you ask?" I straighten.

"You don't do well this time of year. And it's odd not having you up here, it'll be nice when things get back to normal."

I look around the office, noticing the dust collecting on the guns on the walls and other weapons. My mind flits to *Mountain Edge*, feeling a certain peace down there that hasn't occurred in years.

"May split my time more between the two," I murmur.

"Well, don't leave us alone too long up here."

Those blue eyes find mine, and I smile softly. "You'd always be honest with me, right?"

She smiles gently. "Of course."

"You ever hate me for breaking our relationship?" I ask, sitting on my desk's edge as she gives me a curious look. I shrug. "Been... pondering about past mistakes lately."

"Was I a mistake?" She teases, and I shake my head at her. A sad emotion dampens her scent lightly, and she lets out a long breath. "It wasn't meant to be, I think we both know that. And you were going through a...tough time."

I nod my head, and she exhales sharply, leaning forward to place a quick kiss on my cheek. "You'll always be my alpha and Pack leader. And I'll do *everything* to help you. So, no, I don't hate you."

"Thanks," I murmur. "Why can't the others be as nice as you? Never have to worry about you tugging my tail unless you're helping lil sis do it."

She chuckles and shrugs. "Gotta keep those wolves in line, and I'm still working toward beta." We both laugh and she starts to leave. "Staying here a while?"

I turn back to the other paperwork. "No, heading down to *Mountain Edge* in a bit. Hold down the fort for me."

There's a pause, and she responds, "Sure thing, boss."

The door closes behind her as I let out a long breath, sitting down and opening each drawer until I find the nail clippers. Finally, I start trimming my damn nails while my mind drifts as I do the very, very late task. There's another knock and Skylar comes in, and smirks.

"Finally, huh?"

"No comments. What is it?"

They place a small box on my desk. "She said you may need this, for…*precautionary* reasons."

Skylar leaves and I flick open the box, revealing three cupcakes with light pink frosting rosettes and pale wrapping. On the side is a note that says: *Your favorite, and don't blow down any houses.*

I grab one, looking over the delicate design. I hum as I take a bite and smile. Rosé.

She's right. They are my favorite.

CHAPTER 26
MY BONNIE LASS

Irish jigs echo from within the tavern as I watch the Pack dance and drink inside. Zane takes the lead, followed soon by Edward and Delilah. Gunther chuckles next to me, and I give him a look. "You knew about this?"

"Josh called saying they finished the repairs. They wanted to break in the *new* tavern."

"Same damn tavern."

"Admit it, boss, after the last few weeks, drinking and dancing is the smallest amount of damage they'll cause. What else were we gonna do, play poker and shit?"

I look at the joyful bunch. Yeah, he's got a point. All of us need to let loose, especially me if I'm gonna be grumpy about my Pack having fun. I pat his shoulder and nod toward the chaos. "I'll get you a drink, you pain in the ass beta."

"I thought I was the best."

"You're both."

We chuckle, entering the tavern filled with fiddle and pipe music. Delilah broke out the good stuff. Beings shout as we enter, starting another song. Walls vibrate as others dance, Edward and Josh taking the lead next. Relief floods me as I notice Meg behind the bar, mixing drinks and sliding them down the bar. Gunther heads to the other side as I approach. She grins upon seeing me.

Her gaze meets mine as I lean against the counter as she places a cocktail down.

"Get your cupcakes?" She asks, and I nod. "Well, was I right?" I smirk at her, and she touches my hand briefly. "Well, drink up... *boss*."

She winks as I take the drink, saluting her. The alluring flavors of her mystery cocktail play over my tongue. Meg disappears down the bar, mixing more drinks with glee. I watch her a bit, then the others as they holler and sing with the music. I chuckle at their rowdiness, feeling the weight of late lift, remembering older days. Just a pack of wolves, enjoying life.

Delilah grabs me, grinning wickedly. "Come on, boss, show everyone the *real* reputation of the McLycans."

"And what's that?"

"Dancing devils!"

She yanks me into the thrall, and I'm soon dancing with everyone else. I twirl Delilah out, catching another and spinning them. Zane catches up to me, dancing with me next until he heads off with Edward. My thoughts are drowned out by the sound of pipes, fiddles, and drums within a sea of twirling kilts and Paranormals. The bright, lively music switches from one song to another, none of the Pack missing a beat. I move around another, almost bumping into someone and freeze when I look down.

Meg stares up at me with a twinkle in her eye, curiosity on her face. "Didn't know you could dance, Toto."

"Toto?"

"Lassie is too formal."

"You've been hanging around wolves too much."

She puts her hands in mine, and smiles. "Maybe."

I pull her into a dance, and she laughs as I spin her, feeling her body brush against mine. Pleasure howls through me as we touch, her being electrifying my soul. The rest of the room becomes a fog, all my concentration on the human brimming with light as she dances with me. Her eyes glimmer, striking to my core, only her remaining in my mind. Meg's body presses against mine for a moment, and for that moment, it's only us. My breathing falters as

I breathe in her scent and realize…I love her. It wrecks through me like a howl in the late moonlight at the end of a long journey.

The moment is broken when Gunther sweeps in, taking her into the next dance as she goes smiling. I step back into the crowd, heart thundering in my chest, knowing it's not from the dancing. I swallow hard, trying to breathe. *Tell her. You deserve to—*

My gaze catches movement outside, and I weave through the crowd and slip out. Night shifts into full evening, small bulbs of light strung over the paths sparkle from the new exterior brick. Marcus stands silently, watching the commotion inside the tavern. Dark shadows cross his face, and I can't detect his scent. Like he's…gone.

"Marcus." His blue eyes don't stray, while his jaw grinds. "Marcus. Come inside." I reach for his shoulder. He turns away, sinking further into the shadows.

"I'll be back in a few days," he mutters.

"Wait, talk to me—"

"Will you ever tell her?" He suddenly asks, peering over his shoulder as I freeze. His hollow eyes, filled with emptiness peer into me. Words don't form in my mouth, and he frowns. "Then you can't help me."

He continues down the path and vanishes into the darkness of the Underground.

I look up at the shining lights, focusing on the pulsing glow as tears form in my eyes. I breathe deeply, listening to the music. The heavy loneliness comes back, straining the small peace I had. My mind replays the losses, each digging a hole deeper and deeper as I stare at where he disappeared. The screams come back, drowning me with burning flesh and blood, and my body trembles. *"Claw! No!" "Get below!" "Meg!" "Don't make me bury her! Don't—!"*

I gaze into the tavern, quickly finding Meg dancing among the rest. The only solace I've found, and the horror of losing that forever wrenches my insides. It hurts to watch what I could turn into, walking away from me. Like Marcus, what's left of me would be gone. And if I held her tight, kept her here out of that fear, how long until she hates me? How long until I become my father, watching the same anger in Meg as my mother? Until I fail her, too?

My eyes fill with tears, and I blink them away, staring at the Underground stars. I shudder, wishing it was Claw here. Marcus would laugh again. My father would have the child he wanted alive. I swallow hard and try to shake off the dark, haunting feelings.

I head back into the tavern, slipping through the crowd, everyone distracted with the dancing as I climb up the stairs. My inner wolf starts howling in pain as I stay in the darkness, gripping my door handle. My forehead presses against the wood, trying to keep my breathing level. I need her. I need—

I'm tired of feeling alone. I don't want…to fail again.

The stairs creak, and I inhale her scent, trembling from the warm aroma. I look over, seeing those eyes that give me peace. Less guilty for being alive. Her hand grazes my arm, keeping those brown, earthen eyes on mine as she turns me to face her.

"Meg," I rasp.

"One more dance," she whispers, taking one of my hands into hers. A small, gentle smile rises on her face. "Just one more."

I clutch her hand in mine, bringing her in close. The music changes to something softer and slower, and we sway to the melody. Her body becomes flush with mine, and I wrap my arm around her waist.

Reasoning leaves me, tossing away the crippling fears as she stays in my arms. Forgetting the fears. Forgetting the past and guilt. Forgetting the flames and anger. Forgetting the holes in my heart. I fall into a chasm of calm and love she's created. The anxiety dissipating as each moment with her drives it away. The darkness doesn't feel dangerous. Consuming.

"I shouldn't be surprised you could dance," she whispers, moving a hand to my chest.

"Could say the same with you, darling," I murmur, and she hums, placing her head upon my chest.

We continue dancing slowly, even as the music changes to lively beats again. I close my eyes, gripping her like it's the last time. *Tell me what to do.*

"Rodney."

"Yes, darling?"

She pulls back, looking up at me as she places her hands against my cheek. "Take me to bed."

"What?" I breathe out.

"No maybes, promise. I'm absolutely certain. I want you." She brings her lips to mine. The delicate caress against my cheek with the taste of her, I can't help a moan as I wrap my arms around her. A growing warmth forms in my core, spreading and shaking through me.

I break the kiss, breathing heavily as I look into her eyes. My body trembles, either from anticipation or fear, I'm not sure which. "Are you sure?" I ask.

Her brown eyes pierce something in my soul as she replies slowly, "I trust you, Rodrick Rowan McLycan."

I clutch her face, wanting to tell her everything about how I feel. Reveal the rest of the skeletons in my closet. Reveal it all as she stares up at me. The words are caught in my throat. I can't do it. Instead, I choose to give us this night. Anything to keep the darkness at bay and not lose this tugging of hope.

I murmur against her lips, "As you wish…Megara."

My arms dip down, grabbing her rear and lifting her against me. She gasps, holding onto my shoulders as I kick open my door and carry her into my apartment. The door slams shut as I press her against the wall, quickly locking it.

My mouth crashes against hers, and she moans loudly from the contact. My insides howl, wanting to dive deeper as she floods my thoughts. Everything becomes her, and I let go, wanting her… *needing* her.

Her legs tighten around me as I grip her ass and ample thighs. She moans again as I feel my cock harden against my jeans. My tongue slips over hers, and I groan at how wonderful she tastes and feels. My mouth leaves her, licking down her throat and trailing my tongue over her skin. I kiss her neck, moving us from the wall as her intoxicating aroma flourishes. The heat of her arousal, a sweet alluring scent, rises and engulfs me as I settle her down onto the bed. My chest heaves as I step back, watching her with a hunger that's been coiling inside me for weeks. There's a pink twinge to her cheeks, almost flushed as her chest rises breathlessly. Beautiful.

"You've seen me naked, darling...your turn," I rumble. Meg stares up at me, swallowing hard as her hands shake reaching for the hem of her shirt. I lean in close, trailing my hands over the curve of her stomach and towards her chest. "Show me what I've been dreaming about."

She gasps when I squeeze her breasts through the shirt and lets out a soft sigh. Her voice trembles, "Tear it off." I flick my gaze to hers, and she nods in confirmation.

I take the front of the shirt, ripping it down the middle and then her bra, the fabric falling to the ground in pieces. Her torso is revealed, and her ample breasts bounce as she falls back onto the bed. She lets out a yelp as I clutch both breasts again, groaning as my arousal builds seeing her fully. My cock throbs, while the rest of my body feels like it's on fire. The need for her writhes inside as I kiss her collarbone, moving down her body and licking over her nipples. Meg whimpers loudly as I suck gently, enjoying her across my tongue. I bite carefully and she jolts, gripping my arms as she bends her body toward me.

I continue sucking, rubbing the other between my fingers, and watching in delight as she wiggles under me. Meg grabs my hair, holding it tightly as I lick and nip at her skin. My free hand moves down her side, feeling the softness of her skin and curves, gripping her hip dips next. She gasps as I leave her breasts, going down to the hem of her leggings, and give her a wicked look. Her eyes widen and nod. I chuckle, tugging at the hem. The leggings are ripped next, and I get them off her in shreds. Her underwear is last, everything left in a pile of fabric on the floor.

"Some of that was yours," she rasps.

"Only you matter." Her skin is hot under my touch, and I groan as my hands caress her body. She shudders as I kiss her inner thighs, moving up to her hips. "Keep down on the bed."

I rip off my shirt, and she goes still watching me. I stare down at her dark hair gathered under her head, licking her bottom lip. Her chest rises heavily in anticipation. I come down to ravage her breasts again, causing her breath to hitch as she arches her back. My hand roves down over her stomach, her thighs, until it finds its destination at the heat between her legs. I find her entrance, teasing my finger over her clit as I lightly scrape my teeth over her collarbone. She brings her hands up, threading her fingers through the fur along my shoulders.

I come close to her ear, continuing to circle my thumb below. "It seems luck is on your side, darling," I whisper, nudging my nose against her jaw. "Guess who finally trimmed their nails."

Meg gasps as I push a finger inside her, and she moans, "Oh, fuck me."

"As you wish."

I slowly begin to pump my finger inside her, while circling my thumb over her clit. She grips my shoulders, pressing her head back into the mattress. I kiss her neck, inhaling her invigorating scent of arousal that drives me forward. "Tell me what you want."

"You. I want you." Her voice is a rasp and breathless.

"Need more than that, darling." I press my thumb and slide another finger in her as she whimpers. She swears as I scissor and hook them gently inside her. "Use your words, darling."

She glares at me, but her hips buck as I press my fingers further into her. I continue the sensual torture while massaging her breast with my other hand. Meg bites her lip, trying not to scream as her scent rises, covering me and the room. I kiss her neck in slow, languid movements. She whimpers again, and then relents, "Devour me. *Please*."

"Yes, darling," I growl in her ear, and she shivers.

I move, keeping my fingers thrusting inside her as I flick my tongue over her clit. She jolts as I pull my fingers out, plunging my tongue into her. Meg loosens a small scream as I taste the very heat of her, pleasure rolling through my body as I hold her under my mouth. She clutches the sheets, her legs squeezing around my head as I suck and savor her. I wrap my arms around her thighs, keeping her open for me as I continue to devour what I've wanted for weeks.

Fiery heat rages through me, roaring as my cock strains and aches.

Mine.

Meg moans, begging between strangled breaths as I suck harder, then press my thumb and circle upward. My fingers enter her again, licking up the cum that's begun to coat her. I hold her still as she tries to move, thrusting my fingers as I suck her clit. Meg lets out a sudden, quiet scream as her body shakes and I taste her orgasm on my tongue. I pull my fingers out as her legs tremble then clean my fingers. Massaging her inner thighs with care, I lick any remnants left on her thighs as she catches her breath.

I stand up, unclip my belt and take my pants off, all while Meg watches me closely. I walk over to the bedside table, and wink at her.

She snorts. "Cocky."

"Oh…that's coming next, darling."

Her gaze moves down, seeing my erect dick only a few feet from her and she blushes. She must've forgotten the first time she'd seen it because her eyes widen in shock. I chuckle darkly, taking out a condom and rolling it onto said dick that seems to be making her whimper now.

"Problem, darling?"

"You're bigger than I remember," she whispers. I open a bottle of lube, putting some on my fingers. "Oh, thank fuck."

I grin, walking back and leaning over her to slide the lube where my mouth was. She shivers at the touch, then I put the rest around my throbbing cock. I grab her ankles, pulling her closer to the edge of the bed. She squeaks, staring up at me.

"Tell me if you need me to stop," I say gently, and she nods. "Words, darling."

"Okay. Okay, yes," she answers.

I stroke my hands over her thighs, spreading them open as I nudge my cock at her entrance. My eyes meet hers as the heat inside me overpours, thrashing as my soul howls to be one with her. I want to devour her more, take her hard, and claim her with a crazed want. I can barely think as the softness of her skin beneath my hands makes me stop and see the want in her own eyes.

"Ready, darling?"

"Yes," she says, nodding.

My cock enters her slowly, and she throws her head back. A groan leaves me, shuddering at the intense feeling. Carefully, I thrust into her with short, slow movements, relishing being inside her and the heat of her body. I keep the steady pace until I come all the way to the hilt, letting out a moan mixed with a snarl. Her muscles contract around my cock, and I shiver from the sensation that pulses through me. Meg whimpers as I pull out then thrust back inside, the heat almost exploding and sparking down into my groin. My hands slide up her legs, gripping her hips as I continue to thrust harder.

I drive into her, moving a hand to her breasts and squeezing as she shuts her eyes. There's a tight line over her lips, and I pause. Meg grips the sheets next to her, shifting underneath me. Her eyes are closed tightly, and I watch her swallow hard. I move my hand over hers, stroking her hand before holding it. She breathes heavily, still not looking at me and her breathing is rapid. Too rapid.

"Look at me, Meg," I tell her softly, and she flings her eyes open. I bring my face close, kissing her tenderly then placing my forehead against hers. "We can stop—"

"No," she says. "Please, don't stop." She grips my hand, placing the other on my neck, keeping me in place. She raises her hips, pressing me further into her. She whimpers, moving her hips up again, and my breath hitches as her muscles contract again, pulling me deeper.

"Please kiss me," she pleads. I do as she says, kissing her with a force in hopes to make her own thoughts disappear. She moans, holding me tightly as we move our hips together, rocking slowly. Meg presses her hips up and a sudden growl emerges from my chest, and she goes still.

I quickly freeze as she pulls back. She stares up at me and flicks her gaze down.

"Meg, I won't hurt—"

"Do it again." I raise a brow, and she whispers. "Do it again... the growling."

I kiss her again, nipping at her bottom lip. My hands clutch her to me as I release another growl that vibrates my chest and hers. She shivers, wrapping her arms around my neck as I thrust into her again. She kisses my neck as another growl emanates from my chest, holding onto me as I drive into her.

"Harder," she pleads. "Rodney...harder."

I grip her waist, slamming into her at the plea. She shouts, throwing her head back as I continue. Fire wraps around my body with ecstasy building as I grip the sheets next to her, encaging her body with mine. Her breasts press against my chest, causing me to snarl with need and Meg pants hard. Still snarling against her skin, I nip at her skin biting carefully as she arches her back. I pound into her deeper and deeper.

Pleasure pierces through me and I won't stop the continuous growling that my chest emanates. I thunder forward as the pressure builds, throbbing inside and rising with a dark hunger. Meg wraps her legs tighter around me, bringing me closer as I feel the sweat of her skin against mine. I pant as her lips find mine, while my fingers grip her hair as I kiss her frantically. The crest of orgasm comes, tearing through like a hurricane.

"Rodney," she pleases, tilting her hips back.

"Let go, Meg...let go." My voice is hoarse, and she lets out a scream as I thrust forward.

I hold her close, slamming deep and the pressure builds into overwhelming pleasure. The bottom of my spine tingles and the rest of my body shakes. Every thought leaves me as the orgasm pulses and shakes me as Meg lets out a shout, her body tightening around me. She comes to the brink, pushing me over as the orgasm crashes through as I let out a thundering growl. My body shakes as I come hard, causing the bed to shake as I snarl into the blankets.

Sweat sticks to our skin as we breathe harshly, and I have to concentrate in not crushing her. I swallow hard, moisture gone from my mouth as I look down. Dazed and shining eyes find mine. I kiss her, humming as bliss replaces the fiery need moments before. I hold her close, falling into the peaceful chasm that's been formed like a protective shield.

Finally, I fall to the side, bringing her with me and refusing to being detached from her. She giggles against my throat, her legs staying wrapped around me. My breathing becomes steady as she rests her head on me.

Lavender and pine mingle together in the air.

"Sorry, if I scared you," she murmurs.

"Don't apologize, it's okay." I kiss her head, rubbing my head against hers. She hums, snuggling closer, which causes my body to jolt from the movement of still being inside her. "Careful, darling."

"Sensitive?"

I scowl at her, and she smiles, then bops my nose. I look at her incredulously and her grin gets larger, so I bite at her nose. She yelps, hiding her face against my chest.

"No biting," she mumbles against my skin.

"All together?"

She looks up, frowning with pursed lips. A huff of defeat comes out of her as she lies down. I chuckle, tightening my hold on her and nuzzle my face into her hair. The calm warmth she brings blossoms inside, promising peace. The darkness feels distant, unreachable as I lay there with her. Only us. Nothing more.

CHAPTER 27
THE CUOREBELLA FAMILY

"Are you nervous?" Meg asks.

"No."

"You…look nervous."

"I'm not—" She suddenly kisses my cheek, smirking at me as I look down at her. "Fine, only slightly."

"Why?"

We're about to have dinner with the city's most powerful incubi and succubus, and we finally had sex last night. I'm ashamed of nothing, but I don't want the fifth degree before I've even figured out my own shit.

"Brenda's brothers can be…invasive."

"You mean, Ricky?" I quirk a brow, and she pats my arm. "It'll be fine," she reassures me, and I can't help but give her a kiss on the cheek.

We head down the path to *Unbound*, most of the alleys dimmed for the evening. Meg brushes against me, and I glance down at the dark maroon button-up she's wearing. Another of my shirts and a small bit of pride does rise to see her in it.

"Is Marcus coming back tonight?" She asks suddenly.

I clear my throat as *Unbound* comes into view. "He's got some errands to finish next few days, he'll be back before you know it."

She eyes me, and I give her a half smile. After a few moments, she relents, and I breathe easier. Meg knows a bit about Claudia, but not that her birthday is tomorrow. I doubt telling her before this dinner is a great idea. I will after, maybe with lil sis around.

Ricky comes out of the club, grinning. "Just in time!"

"Hi, Ricky," Meg greets, hugging him.

He flicks his gaze between us as he slyly smiles. Yup, I have *every* reason to be nervous.

We walk into the club, filled with streaming lights and music. Lola and Mack are dancing on stage, twirling around the poles. Meg looks at me when Gina gives me a little wave, knowingly looking at Meg as we reach the apartment door. Ricky leads the way, heading up the stairs, but Meg pauses next to me and whispers, "Okay...should I actually be worried?"

"You remember their powers, right?"

"Yeah, but that..." her eyes go big, flicking to the dancers and Gina, who winks at her next, "...holy crap, they're *that* good?"

"Gina learned from the best," I mutter, gesturing upstairs. "Alanzo and Carmen will be respectful, but Ricky and Joey can be... *them.*"

"I can be pretty open, but..." she winces, stopping briefly on the stairs.

"We'll have lil sis rein them in," I whisper, putting my hand on her shoulder. "Unless you'd like a lecture on protection."

"I think we're good."

"How about kinks and safety releases?"

"Trying to tell me something, McLycan?" I smirk. "Not my usual dinner conversation."

"It is for them, but that's where Brenda comes in."

"Ask for a history lecture?"

"You're learning." We laugh under our breath, heading up the stairs.

I follow Meg into the foyer, greeted with the aroma of fresh pasta and bread. The air is warm within the Cuorebella home, and I notice Alanzo on the sofa reading a book. He sees us, closing it as Ricky disappears into the kitchen and Joey walks out. We nod briefly before he begins setting the dining table.

"Good to see you both, we appreciate you joining us," Alanzo says, hugging Meg. He glances at the container in my hands, raising his brow. "Are those the infamous cupcakes?"

Meg takes it from me, and replies, "Brenda said to bring dessert."

He smiles and the cinnamon aroma in the air strengthens. "She gets her smarts from me."

"And appetite, *mio cavaliere*." Carmen walks out, embracing Meg and kissing her cheek as she cups her face. "How have you been, dear?"

"Good. And the tavern is all fixed." Meg kisses her cheek, then holds up the cupcakes. "Rosé won for tonight."

"Those will go wonderful after dinner," Carmen mentions, hugging me next, then quickly kissing my cheek. She smiles, then ushers Meg into the kitchen.

"Need to talk?" Alanzo asks.

"No, things have been quiet lately."

"I know. Not what I meant." I glance at him as he cocks a brow. Really was hoping only the brothers would prod.

"Ricky!" Saved by lil sis. "Did you take my jeans again?" But wasn't expecting that.

"Not my fault your room is a mess," he responds, bringing out a pitcher of water.

There's a groan and tongue-clicking as I use the moment to move toward the dining table. Brenda comes down the hallway. She brushes past me, pointing a finger at her brother's chest. "I know you took them. They have the good pockets."

"Didn't take them. Pops—"

"You can play *Clue* later," their father interjects, placing a hand on Brenda's shoulder and Ricky's head. "Guests aren't here for two minutes, already bickering."

Brenda tips her head back at me, grinning as I smirk. "Hey, lil sis."

Ricky rolls his eyes, heading back into the kitchen as Joey snorts, setting out the plates. "You could help set the table, baby sis."

She frowns at him. "I've set up the last three nights *and* cleaned up."

"*You* had the time."

"Don't pull that shi—" Alanzo covers her mouth, shaking his head once. She mumbles her apology against his hand, and I try not to laugh. Alanzo kisses her temple, walking away as Joey smirks. Carmen hates swearing, and Brenda swears worse than all of us combined.

Brenda hugs me and then helps Joey set up without another complaint. I count the table settings and scowl as I realize there's one extra. Damn it, he's actually coming.

Dinner is set out and Meg comes over as Carmen directs everyone to their seats. Alanzo and Carmen are at the head of the table, while Ricky, me, and Meg sit on one side. The other is Joey, Brenda, and discount Aro.

The front door opens as we sit, and Vincent's voice emerges. "Apologies for being late."

I look over as Brenda points a finger gun at the vampire, and he kisses it with a wink. She nudges him away as he briefly kisses Carmen on the cheek.

"Good for you to join us, Vincent," Alanzo says, sitting down.

Vincent follows Brenda to the table, flashing a smile at Meg. "Hello again, Meg. Bring those cupcakes?"

"Hi, Vinny, and yes I did. They'll be dessert."

"What kind?" He asks, sitting down as Joey starts to pass the food.

"Rosé-infused cupcakes, they're Rodney's favorite."

The vampire's eyes glow, then grins. "Would've thought chocolate be your favorite."

I glower at him, wanting to wipe that look off his face when suddenly Meg's hand is on mine under the table. I go still as her fingers wrap around mine, squeezing them.

"Fascinatingly chocolate isn't that big of a fave with the Pack. But Rodney and Delilah have been wonderful letting me use *Mountain Edge's* kitchen to experiment." Her voice is heavy with sweetness. "I haven't had a proper oven in almost three years. Which by the way, don't bake with a half-working oven, everything burns and stinks for days."

I glimpse at her, catching her eye and she winks.

Ricky coughs suddenly, grabbing the breadbasket and handing it to me. I catch Brenda jamming her elbow into Vincent's side, who barely moves, which makes her mutter under her breath.

"That reminds me of Alanzo's and my first home in the city," Carmen says softly, patting Meg's other hand. "Do you remember, *mio cavaliere?*"

"Yes, *amore*," Alanzo answers, smiling. "You've always cooked the best food, even in that tiny place."

"It wasn't that small," she laughs, waving her hand at him. "Unlike that cottage you loved." His eyes glow, and it feels like the entire room is filled with joyful warmth.

"When did you move here?" Meg asks, keeping her hand on mine as I put food on both our plates.

"Oh, what year was it?" Carmen asks Alanzo.

His brows furrow then looks at Brenda. "Baby girl?"

"1788," she answers.

"How do you remember that?" Joey asks.

"They came after the human U.S. government made their Constitution," she says matter-of-factly. "Paranormals started their laws six months after, so in 1789 most Paranormals were traveling across seas. Pops chartered a good deal of those ships and came over in the summer."

Alanzo smiles gently at his daughter, and Carmen gives them a tender look before turning toward Meg. "Our baby girl helps us keep track of our history."

"Yeah, smarty pants of the family," Ricky murmurs.

"Cause all you remember are embarrassing stories from my childhood."

Ricky leans in front of me. "Hey, want to hear more, Meg?"

Meg tries to hide her smile, and says, "Maybe during dessert."

The dinner goes relatively normal for the first half, well, for the Cuorebellas that is. Within fifteen minutes, Brenda and Joey are arguing about laundry days, Ricky talks about some new sex harnesses downstairs, then Carmen shushes her children from telling Meg about the infamous lube story.

They're a lot like the Pack but may beat them on candid conversations. And there's something different, a longing I don't have at home. I watch Carmen and Alanzo speak with each other with no ounce of distaste for their Mate. I listen to Ricky and Brenda, joking and smiling with each other as siblings do. Joey talking business with his father, while Vincent leans in next to Brenda, stealing a kiss or two. A loving family.

The hole in my soul starts to gnaw again, flashing the past through me. Awkward family dinners. Watching Claudia who tried to get my parents to laugh, but they refused to be in the same room. Marcus, her, and I began to have meals with the Pack, finding happiness there instead. My mind drifts as Carmen and Joey bring out dessert plates, coffee, and cupcakes. There's a tightness in my chest as I come back to the present, hearing Ricky talk with Meg.

I blink and find Brenda watching me carefully. She mouths, "Are you okay?"

I tap lightly on the table in morse code, "Yes."

She narrows her eyes, and mouths, "Rodney."

I shake my head, forcing a smile, and tap again, "Fine."

"Well, Gina takes care of those who don't move on," Ricky keeps explaining, somehow coming to the subject of the club functions downstairs. "We hire any who decide to dance or do sex work, survivors or not."

"Survivors…would want to?" Meg asks.

Ricky smiles warmly at her, tilting his head. "Some do. They all find healing in their own way."

"Beings have a choice here," Alanzo says, leaning back as Carmen places a kiss on his head, pouring him a coffee. "For some succubi and incubi, whether in their DNA or not, they're not ready for such endeavors. The lifestyle downstairs isn't for everyone, and those who do stay, regain confidence and control over their bodies, powers, and other parts of themselves."

"I never thought of it that way," Meg murmurs. The softness of her voice makes me look over at her, finding her brow furrowed in thought.

"Healing is individual, Meg," Alanzo says gently, both she and I look over at him. His violet eyes flick between us. "How we decide to move on and survive, depends on one's needs. A lesson I learned many centuries ago and have continued to share. And it helps seeing other survivors sometimes, gives hope back."

Meg squeezes my hand under the table, and she nods lightly. An odd tug pulls at me, and I avert my gaze from the incubus.

"It's kinda why baby sis danced downstairs," Ricky adds, grabbing a cupcake and I get a scent of orange, sweet blossoms relaxing the air. "For herself, but for survivors, too. They could see someone who didn't fit societal norms, in most communities, on stage."

Meg turns to Brenda. "I didn't know you danced."

"Since I was, wait, when did I start?"

"I thought you were the historian," Ricky snorts.

"I will take your cupcake," she threatens. He yanks one to him, takes a bite, and hums a delighted sound. Brenda rolls her head and eyes at him.

"In general, since you were six," Alanzo smiles. "Fourteen for the pole." Meg's eyes widen as Alanzo chuckles again. "She was eighteen when she was finally allowed to dance *for* the club."

Brenda snags a cupcake, glaring at her brother. Joey sits down, shaking his head and chuckling with his father. "Pops would shut down the club to let me dance with Ma and Ricky before I was of age."

"Wait, I thought you worked at the public library before? And now *The Vault?*" Meg places a cupcake on my plate.

"I did and do. I stripped during college, then stopped when I lived on Topside. When I came back down here, I started dancing again and worked at *The Vault.*"

"Do you still dance?"

My gaze flicks to Alanzo, who's concentrating on his coffee, and I notice Vincent adjust in his seat. I clear my throat as Joey inspects the cupcake icing. Yeah, none of us want to think or speak about *why* she stopped.

"Focusing on my librarian skills now," Brenda replies nonchalantly, biting into her cupcake. She smiles, and it seems to ease both her family and Mate.

Meg flashes her gaze among everyone, then asks, "Were you good?"

"Oh, a damn good one," Vincent comments, putting his arm around her shoulders.

"You're biased," Brenda snorts.

"Hey, you were!" Ricky chimes in. "Learned from the best."

"And you're biased."

"And both correct," Vincent muses.

"Fine, then you can add poles to *The Lounge*, it'll spruce it up from being a backyard shack to a classy dungeon," Brenda taunts.

"The bar is intact again, including my office," Vincent argues. She snorts, eating her cupcake. "*You* keep wrecking it."

"Do not."

"Do too."

"Do not, bloodsucker."

"What about when we—"

"Does not count." She shoves a cupcake in his mouth. My mind flashes to Claudia having Marcus try her cookies, both laughing. "I'm tying you to a stripper pole."

"Promise?" He mumbles, licking the icing off his lips.

"Quit flirting," Joey groans.

"If that's you flirting, I don't want to see you fight," Meg laughs.

Brenda glares at Vincent but quickly loses the scowl as he brings her hand up to lick off the icing. He stares at her adoringly, eyes glowing with affection as he kisses her head. She rubs the arm across her shoulders, settling further against him, and it's like I've been punched in the gut.

My mind flashes back decades, Claudia and Marcus arguing playfully. Her green eyes filled with mischief and him letting her bait him. His growls always followed her laughter through the tavern. She'd push his buttons, but he always looked at her like she was the moon and the stars. He'd smile. He…laughed. Mated and happy, like those across from me.

Guilt draws me deeper into darkness as I loathe seeing them, not able to stop the emotion. I struggle to breathe, not able to stop seeing Marcus' hollow eyes and permanent scowl. A coldness passes over me as I hear screams and shattering glass. Ash and smoke choking me, reminding me what will never be again. Something tightens around my hand, but all I hear is the resounding question…*why wasn't I the one to die?*

"Rodney?" I look over at Meg, finding eyes reminding me of home. Hills of Ireland with the richness of the earth and its treasure all within one gaze. Through terrible darkness that fogs my mind, pushing me under, a guiding light. Moonlight. *Gaelach.*

There's no ease, only more guilt and pain as the thought of losing that light forever crushes me. *4D* blowing to nothing, teased by her scent like a cruel fucking joke, losing her before having her. Shots ring in my ears as screams echo, my head feeling like it's going to explode. Flames encase my back, while the taunting voice of Sebastian haunts me. Cars in flames, yelling, and flying bullets as I thought I'd lost her. *Failed* her.

My gaze flicks across, finding crimson eyes, and the sinking emotion worsens.

"Rodney, what's wrong, dear?" Carmen asks, and the burning flesh in my nostrils is replaced by sweet cherry blossoms. A different fog coats me, causing the haze to roll over my mind, choking me. I can't concentrate and my head begins to hurt. Although it should help release my fears, the scent of Carmen's powers only worsens the rising anxiety and hurt.

I rasp, staring at Brenda, and plead, "Please."

"Ma, let Rodney go," Brenda instructs, violet eyes staying on mine.

"Baby, I think—"

"Let him go, Ma."

The cherry blossoms disappear, slamming me with memories again. My chair falls back as I get up, heading for the door. "I need to…need to take care of something."

"Rodney," Meg calls.

"Stay here."

"Rod—"

"*Stay here,*" I command as my shoulders begin to shake. My chest aches, stopping at the doorway and fighting back the snarl in my throat. My insides howl, needing her as it fights against the horrors replaying in my mind. *Tell me to hold you.*

"Okay," she murmurs in a voice that makes my heart clench. "Okay."

"Rodney," Alanzo calls out.

"Pops, no," Brenda says, and I flinch when she touches my arm. She whispers, "I'll meet you there. Go."

"Take care of her," I snarl, forcing myself out of the home and running down the stairs.

I slam through the back door as the music in the club changes to a thumping beat, pounding into my head. I inhale deeply the outside of the Underground, barely feeling relief as memories and horrid emotions hound at me. I prowl down the alleys, stalking through backways and slamming my fists into the brick. Heat coils under my skin, throbbing and yanking at me in different directions, causing my claws to unsheathe. A dark growl leaves me, staying in the shadowed darkness as I head for my destination. Warring within myself as I start to run.

THE CEMETERY IS quiet as I approach. My chest aches as I breathe heavily, looking up at the archway, *New York Underground Cemetery*. My hands shake as I step in between the tombs. Most Paranormals wish to be cremated, not wanting to fall victim to potential ghoul outbreaks. Werewolves on the other hand...we're stubborn.

My feet drag against the stone as I flick my gaze to the headstones of beings laid to rest. Names and symbols are scattered among them. I weave through the maze of tombs, the lonely ache worsening when I see the large mausoleum.

It's constructed of stone and marble with a few steps leading up to the entrance framed by pillars. The name *McLycan* is etched in Connemara marble, brought over by my grandmother. A place to put our family, the Pack, and all those who wished to have their final rest here. My knees wobble as I approach, gazing at my family name. My chest rattles as I fall to my knees before the mausoleum, onto the steps.

"I promised to protect you...and..." My voice chokes, tears

streaming down my face. "You had a life. You weren't supposed... to...to..."

A sob escapes as I cover my face, letting the emptiness take over. Every ounce of me wishing for her to be here instead. Claudia wouldn't have failed. She'd have figured this shit out. She wouldn't have fallen into the shadow of a damn bloodsucker. She wouldn't have endangered the Pack with her decisions. Our dad's favorite would be alive, protecting the Pack, and not...

"When have you ever been good enough at keeping beings alive?"

I slam my fists into the steps, howling into the quiet cemetery. Wishing it had all happened differently, and that fate hadn't been so cruel.

CHAPTER 28
BATTLE OF THE BOSSES

Her name stares back at me in the dim light of the lanterns, flickering down the hall as I sit against the dark stone. The mausoleum is quiet. My feet scuff the floor as I continue staring ahead at the etching on the tomb.

Claudia Aisling McLycan. Beloved Sister. Cherished Mate.

It's been hours that I've been here, falling asleep at her tomb some time ago. Now I've just been sitting, allowing the numbness to take over and fog my thoughts. All that's left is an ache over my shoulders, weighing me down.

"I thought I was fine, Claw," I whisper. "But history almost repeated itself. *I* almost made it repeat. To lil sis...to Meg." I swallow hard, my throat constricting and burning. "I don't know... if I can do this."

Silence greets me as I hang my head between my legs. I inhale a shaky breath, finding only musk and stillness. There's no strength in me to get up, to fight. I lean my head back, closing my eyes but then I hear the scuff of boots. Brenda enters the mausoleum, carrying two packs of beer, setting them next to me.

"You bring the cards?" She asks, and I shake my head. "Tsk, I'll bill you for that." She pulls out a bottle of Irish beer, opens it, and hands it over before sitting down.

"Are you early?"

"No, besides, told you I'd meet you."

"How'd you even know I'd be here?"

"It's Claw's birthday, you'd never miss that," she murmurs. "And I run to *The Vault*, you run here. We all got our own spaces."

"Yours is probably more practical."

"Nah, you've got a better chance of becoming the next Tomb Raider." She pops off a bottle cap. "Too soon?"

I point my beer at Claudia's tomb. "She'd have said the same."

"Glad I'm not disappointing you, Claw." She salutes her tomb with brava. We sit in silence, drinking and opening new bottles. Brenda nudges my shoulder as we get to our third one, and I look at her. She pulls out a paper from her back pocket and says, "No judgment."

I open the paper finding a terrible drawing of a wolf and a small girl. I chuckle lightly, and she shoves me playfully. "It's not bad."

"Librarian one. Artist zero."

"Maybe stick with painting."

"Yeah, Ricky said the same."

"I'll get you big kid paints for *your* birthday," I murmur, putting it away. I place my arm over her shoulders, and she falls against my side, drinking. "Thanks."

"Figured if beers didn't help, I'd go old school."

Brenda has been coming with me to Claudia's grave since she was twelve. She insisted on coming with me every year on Claw's birthday as I had before. She always found time to sit with me. Through the years we started drinking beers and playing cards, some visits were easier than others and we'd laugh as I'd tell her about the days before her. Some days were hard, like today, and she'd just stay with me. Brenda always talked to Claudia like she was here. Like she wasn't gone.

"If you weren't okay to come to dinner, my family would've understood," she whispers. "You've already had some rough weeks, and I...wasn't exactly helpful with some of it."

"Not your fault."

"Rodney, I've been caught up with my own personal shit, but I should've been more aware. Knowing today was—"

"Again, not your fault."

"Fine, then finally say what's going on."

"Don't need to."

"Bullshit."

"There's *nothing* to talk about. It won't change anything."

"Double bullshit."

"Lil sis—"

"Like telling Meg she's your *Gaelach* won't change anything?"

I freeze. "How did you…?"

"As you've told me before, got a better sense of smell than a werewolf and a succubus combined." She shifts next to me, nudging my shoulder. "And, honestly, the way you act around her."

I grumble, exhaling hard before taking a swig of beer. "It's only—"

"If you say mob business or some stupid line that could be from *The Godfather*, I'm taking the beer back."

I glare at her, and she quirks a brow. I huff, knocking back the rest of it, giving her the empty. Brenda scoffs, opening another to hand over. She falls against the wall, drinking her own, then asks suddenly, "You hear him, Claw? Your brother takes a nice girl to the park, gives her clothes off his back, and brings her to dinner with *my* chaotic family, but won't tell her how he feels."

"Don't get snarky. And don't bring her into this."

"I need a partner in crime to keep you from destroying yourself."

"Am not."

Brenda gestures around us. "What's this then? You come here only when you want to remember or think you fucked up royally. Birthday or not, it's not why you're really here. What happened at dinner wasn't the first time this past month, I talked to Gunther and Zane." I groan and she gives me an exasperated look. "You've been growly, secluding yourself, and asking Zane if you fucked up?"

"I don't need to tell you everything."

"Yeah, we've already established that," she mutters.

My heart sinks, guilt rising again as she frowns at the tomb. She takes her glasses off and rubs her temple. "I didn't mean that," she whispers. "I'm just worried. Because you haven't been acting like yourself. I know with everything going on, it's not easy, but you've *always* been honest with me. The Rodney I know, the big brother I love, wouldn't string Meg along for *mob business*."

I put down the bottle. "You don't understand. I'm not."

"Talk with me before determining what I may or may not understand first."

I stare at the ceiling as my chin quivers, pushing back the relentless emotions. I whisper, "I love her, lil sis. Why would I string someone I love along?"

"Why not tell her? Stop destroying yourself—"

"Because it makes it real," I growl, getting up, and leaving my beer behind as I step away. The tears threaten to come forth while my head pounds and I rub my head harshly. I pause, noticing the lack of sharpness, and bring my hands down. "I'm keeping my word to her. She helps, and I get her out. End of. We move on."

"Rodney, don't make that decision for her. Trust me, that never works out and you'll realize how dumb it is until it's almost too late. It's okay if it's real."

"No...no it won't be."

"But going on living unhappily is? What's the point of living like that?"

I exhale softly, realizing how much she doesn't know how lonely I've already been. There were good days, and good times, but I'm always soon wanting myself to be in that tomb instead. Locked away in dark rooms. *"You must get used to moving on while the rest of humanity just…well, leaves."* The guilt *always* comes back. *"Long life also means you hold on a bit too tightly to things you shouldn't."*

Brenda interrupts my thoughts. "Do you think Claw would want you to be unhappy? Your mother? Your grandpappy?"

"Don't."

"They'd want to see *you* happy, including Meg."

"Stop."

"Rodney, just—"

"I don't want to lose anymore," I state, facing her. She stands next to Claudia's tomb, and I wince remembering her voice over the radio again. I shake my head, trying to keep the memory away.

"The Pack will help; they obviously adore her. My family, Vinny, and I included. You won't lose her—"

"Yet I almost lost you," I snarl, pointing at Claudia's grave as my frustration starts to rise. "You were almost buried next to her. Gone. *Forever.*"

"Rodney," she says gently, reaching for me. "I'm right here. I'm fine—"

"I didn't know that for over four hours!" I yell, and she goes still. "I spent *hours* thinking I'd sent you to your death, repeating what happened to Claw! *I* strapped you with those explosives. *I* fucked up. *I* agreed to send you into that center! I didn't even argue with you. If it wasn't for that fucking vampire, you'd be ash along with the rest of those ghouls. And it's my fault. *My* Pack had silver bullets rained down upon them, almost killing Meg, too. It was *me.* Everyone close to me *dies.* She's fucking safer away from me because all I do is repeat history. So why should I tell her she'll be *strapped* to someone who gets his family killed? That she'll soon be buried next to them!"

"It's not your fault, Rodney."

"Yes. *It is.* I've proven I'm not enough to keep anyone safe."

"You're wrong."

"Am I?"

"What about me then?" She asks and I furrow my brows. "Pops trusted *you* first with me, and you were the first one to hold me outside of my family." She gestures outside and then to me. "I was safe with *you.* You helped keep me safe during college, checked up on me, bought my first guns, and a shit ton more. That's over twenty years, which is a damn good record. We all make mistakes, but blowing that center was *my* idea. *My* fault. Not yours."

I breathe heavily, trying to listen, but my mind continues to spiral. Perhaps I had helped her, but not always. It was Vincent who taught her how to use the guns, escorted her everywhere, and taught her how to navigate without sight. *He'd* done it right. Protecting her. The playboy bloodsucker who spent over a century doing nothing didn't fucking fail. While I lost.

"Your Pack and the rest of the Underground Mafia respect you," she continues. "They will help you, so you don't continue destroying yourself. We've got your back, I swear it because none of it was your fault, Rodney. You deserve to be happy."

Do I? A stabbing feeling hits my chest, and I rub at it, leaning against the wall. "I can't do it again. I can't risk it...I can't, Brenda."

She sighs, chugging her beer, and the bottle clinks with the rest as she tosses it. She opens another, and I hear mumbling as I look over to see her talking to Claw's grave.

"Tell me what to say to him, Claw," she murmurs. "Because Meg loves him, too. The way she looks at him, it's just like my parents. The meant to be kind of thing. Pretty sure she adores his growly ass, and he's here thinking of the past that won't help."

"You're talking to the past. *My* past."

She turns toward me, tilting her head. "Then take it from the librarian who spends her days *listening* to history and the past. It only repeats when we don't give ourselves a chance to change the outcome." My expression falls and hers becomes gentle.

"I can't risk it."

"Why not? I understand being scared because, fuck, I was terrified when I thought Vinny would come back to me dead. But you can't let that fear control you."

"That's...that's not it."

"Then what? She's in the past." She points at the grave. "They're all in the past, along with *your* past decisions. It's not now, so what's holding you back?"

"He doesn't want to become me." Marcus' voice echoes through the mausoleum. He walks in holding a bottle of wine, wearing the same clothes he'd left with, and his face looks ragged. His gray skin appears darker against the dim lights, and his blue eyes faint. "You're earlier than usual."

"Needed to think," I reply, and he grunts. He comes forward, stopping a few feet from Brenda who hasn't moved from next to Claudia's tomb. "Marcus—"

"If I could tell Claudia that I loved her, I would," he says, planting his gaze on me. "I'd tell her over and over again. Hear her say it, too. So, you're a fucking idiot for not telling Meg."

I snarl, not in the mood anymore for "life lessons" from him or Brenda. "You don't get to tell me—"

"Meg had a shitty fucking life on Topside, did you ever talk to her fully about it, or were you too busy self-wallowing?" I freeze as he snarls back at me. "She found good here, in the Pack, and in you when she didn't have to. She could've thought about only herself, instead, she listened and believed in you. The least you could do is tell her the truth."

"And then what? What happens when others find out she worked with DiNardi? You know Freyja will find out. They came for her for a reason. They'll do it again."

"Then you protect her."

"And you've seen I *can't* guarantee that. You were there!"

"You don't need to guarantee it."

"Yes, I do."

"No, you don't."

"Yes—"

"No. All Meg needs is to be supported, respected, and loved. That's it. *That's* what you guarantee."

"I *have* to keep my word in protecting her," I snarl stepping forward as anger, fear, and hurt mix into a whirlwind. "What kind of Mate would I be if I kept her in danger? If I got her killed?"

"Like me?" Marcus' face darkens as my eyes widen, shaking as he gestures toward me. "*There* it is."

Brenda clears her throat, keeping quiet as Marcus looks at her and then carefully bends down. He places the bottle of wine in front of Claudia's grave, staying crouched and murmurs, "I may be a surly son-of-a-bitch now, but I don't regret loving her. I don't regret being her Mate and having the life we had, even if it was taken from me. If you want to live with regret, fine...but don't you fucking dare drag Meg down because you were too cowardly to admit you needed her."

I swallow hard, trying not to cry or throttle him as the trembling worsens. I avert my gaze from them, staring at the ground as the minutes tick by in silence. All while I'm screaming inside, unable to let go.

Brenda grabs another beer, walks over to Marcus, and holds it out to him. He scowls up at her. My body stops shaking, going on alert as Marcus' hollow gaze lands on her, slowly standing. He towers above her, glowering with a coldness that's worse than the cemetery air. He glares down at the bottle in her hand, and I ready myself to grab her if finally snaps. He stares over at Claudia's tomb.

"I never hated you, Brenda," he says abruptly, and she goes still. "I just hated you weren't her."

My throat constricts as the grey wolf confesses, while Brenda lets her arm with the beer fall to her side. "For the longest time...I wasn't sure if I did hate you. Growing up, you were just like her. Strong-willed, loud, and stubborn. It felt like a cruel joke, losing her suddenly and then you came along. You became this fucking band-aid for the Pack, a piece of patchwork Rodney and they needed...their little sister. But never for me."

Brenda deflates a little, putting the beers down. She starts to say something, but he stops her. "I didn't lose a sister; I lost my Mate...my best friend. You couldn't be any of those for me, never mine in *any* way. So, I thought I hated you because you reminded me of pain and who I would never have again. I was prepared to live like that, to *endure* you and your antics. But then you did something." Brenda begins to tremble as Marcus nods toward Claudia's tomb. "She'd call me Balto, too."

What?

Brenda rasps, "Why didn't you tell me? I'd have stopped—"

"That first time, I wanted to strangle you in the park, to not have you take that, too. But then, somehow it felt like a part of her was back," he whispers. "No one knew she called me that, not even Rodney. She'd call me Balto because she believed I always seemed to save the day last minute, giving everything to the Pack. Yet, I didn't save her." He touches the etching of her name, and his breath hitches. "When that sting happened in the Bronx, you begging me to leave ...I realized only Claudia would send someone like you to harass me, make me keep my promises to her. Even when I didn't want to."

"I...I couldn't let you die," she whispers.

He turns away from the tomb, and the hollowness in his eyes is a bit less. "I know," he murmurs. "I don't hate you, Brenda. I just hate you're not her. And I don't know how not to feel that way anymore."

Lights flicker as the mausoleum becomes quiet. The guilt comes crawling back, hating listening to Marcus like this. Not wanting this.

Brenda grabs the beers again, and asks, "What did you promise her?"

"Not always be a grouch." Brenda snorts suddenly, then tries to stop herself. His mouth turns upward a little into a sad smile. "And to stay alive."

She inhales sharply. "I'll stop calling you that, and I'm sorry—"

"Don't stop." Pain laces his expression; his eyes glistening with tears. "She feels less far away when you do. And...I'm learning I'd rather feel, than nothing at all."

Brenda nods gently, then grabs his hand and puts a beer into it, clinking it with hers. "Okay...Balto. You gotta make a new promise with me and Claw. Rodney, you're our witness."

He looks up at me, and I almost flinch before he looks back at Brenda. The agony lessens on his face as tears escape my eyes.

"What's that?" Marcus asks.

"I'll keep calling you Balto, but you can't stop growling at me. It'd hurt my feelings and Claw's." He snorts. "I gotta keep my sarcasm up with Vinny somehow, and you're the best wolf for the job. You've got experience."

"Ever tell him he smells like a chihuahua?"

"No, but now I want to."

"You should put cherry jello on his pizza."

Brenda chuckles. "What did she put on yours?"

"Puppy chow."

I listen to them as my mind drifts as the agony writhes inside me like a quiet volcano. The pressure over my shoulders pulls down, and more and more I hate that it's not me inside there. It rises in my gut, towards myself. And the truth, hearing Marcus' words, roars in my head. *Like me.*

Marcus may hate Brenda for not being Claudia, but I hate myself for not being Vincent. Not confronting my father, when he did. Not saving whom I love, when *he* did. I soon find myself filled with turmoil, replacing the ache that once was there.

"Rodney." Brenda's voice feels far away, but her hand drifts over my arm, and I shudder at the touch. "He's right. Don't live regretting not saying anything. At least you'd know you were honest with yourself."

Something snaps inside me, and I growl, "Fine."

I prowl past her, and Marcus goes to grab me. "Rod—"

"*No.*" The order is absolute, and they both go still. I storm out, aiming to whom I want to give my *honesty*.

———

I SLAM through the door of *The Lounge*, stalking past the deconstructed booths and bare walls. Vampires hiss and snarl at me, and I growl back, baring my teeth as I throw open the back doors toward Vincent's office. Samuel appears in front of me, blocking my way.

"What are you doing, McLycan?"

"Out of my way."

"Not until—"

"*Move.*"

The vampire's ruby eyes flash, snarling with elongated fangs as he pulls his gun out. It clicks as the safety goes off, and I take another step forward. His eyes widen, and warns, "Don't try it, *wolf.*"

I shout, "*Dracultelli!*"

His office doors slam open, and Samuel is gone from my vision. Vincent replaces him, inches from my face, crimson glowing as his fangs elongate.

"He's a proper guard, and sweet cheeks is fond of him. Careful how you tread, *pup*," he snarls in my face.

"Oh, yeah," I laugh maliciously, and shock comes over him. "Fuck...*you.*"

My anger explodes, pulsing through my body as I bring my arms back and thrust my fists forward. I hurl the vampire back into his office, crashing through the doors as I shift into hybrid form, unable to control my anger and hate. I run at Vincent as he quickly gets up, meeting me head-on.

We slam into each other as I bite at him, but he swiftly punches my jaw, tossing my head back. I throw him against the desk as it cracks. The vampire snarls, thundering through the office as he runs and hits me. Again. And again. I pivot, causing him to miss as I punch him next, clawing at his chest. He jumps back as blood drips down his face, snarling with bared fangs.

He takes a step forward and growls, "What the fuck are—"

"I hate you," I state, pointing a claw at him. "I hate you for staying, not fucking leaving. I hate that you spent *decades* doing nothing, apart from causing mayhem and whoring yourself, only to be praised after three damn years of being boss." I stalk him as he watches me with wide eyes. "I hate you for protecting Brenda, saving Meg and my Pack when I couldn't! I hate that you saved her from that explosion when I couldn't save my sister! Even from your damn psychotic father, you got to save her again! And I especially hate you for having the life Claudia should've had! That Marcus should've! When you did *nothing* to deserve it. Why did it have to be *you* who didn't fail!?"

His expression falls, and my fury snaps making me see red as I see the emotion on his face. Pity. I throw myself at him, but he doesn't fully fight back. He dodges attacks, slams me back down, and spins around. He punches me, forcing me to run into walls as I snap at the air. Furniture shatters, splintering across the torn carpet. He grabs my head, tossing me against a wall and I loosen an enraged snarl, baring my teeth.

"I stayed for Brenda, not to spite you—"

"Yet, I became the forever second to Vinny the *fucking* Vampire, savior of the damn Underground. A reminder of what—"

"What the fuck are you talking about?"

"*You* saved her!" I shout. "It just had to be you! To be you saving her from explosives while I'm—" I breathe heavily. *Scared of them.* I snarl, "You just had to save lil sis from everything to bloodsuckers, your father, and then Meg—"

"I didn't save Brenda."

"Why did you get to succeed? After I couldn't protect my sister...my mother...my, my..." the words trail off, not able to say *Gaelach* into the roaring void.

"Rodney."

"Fuck you. Fuck you for not failing. For being the damn hero."

He steps back from me, but all I see is carnage. Blood drips down the walls, and wrath encages me, cornering me like an animal. *Get below! Claudia! The place is rigged! Meg! Scatter!* I clutch my head, growling at the memories as they slam into me, over and over again. *Rodney! No!*

"Brenda saved herself." Vincent's voice sounds far away. "From the center. My father. If I hadn't intervened, she'd have killed Bruno herself. And I'm pretty sure the one who taught her how to fight with her bare hands was you." I meet his ruby gaze. "She saved *me*. So...who do you actually hate? Me? Or Brenda?"

I falter a step back. "I'd *never* hate her."

"So, then yourself," he says softly.

His words shake me to my core, and a snarl breaks from my throat, half whimpering. His gaze darkens, bringing his hand up to gesture for me to come at him. "Hate whomever you want but do something about it instead of whining like Courage the Cowardly Dog. So, come on then, you *yapping* Shih Tzu."

His taunt flips the anger back on and a growl rips through my throat. Vincent matches the sound, goading me. We slam into each other, and he grabs my neck, throwing me to the ground. I bite at him, but he easily deflects, kicking me away. I get around, slamming him into the wall as pieces of it fly. Glass shatters as he throws me into the cabinet, and the lights flicker as we fight, turning the place into nothing but a mangled mess of blood, fur, glass, and wood.

We collide, fist to fist as I snap my jaws at him, and he roars in my face, blood trickling down both our heads. I plant my feet down, keeping from sliding back as he pushes me. All I feel is rage, coursing like lava. I feel myself let go, falling into a chasm of blood and anger until there's a shout through the chaos. It's distant as I roar at the vampire before me, but we're broken apart abruptly. My body is flung backward. I skid and turn my attention to the intruder.

I find blazing violet eyes. "Keep your hands *off* my Mate."

"No! Brenda!"

I surge forward, not thinking straight on *who* I'm attacking.

Vincent slams into me instead. He's thrown against the wall hard, and there's another shout as metal snaps. Something hits my back, and I tumble forward, crashing into what's left of the desk. My head spins, and I shake it as I get up, lunging for the fallen vampire. Someone jumps on my back, putting me into a light chokehold.

"Stop…Rodney, stop," Brenda gasps against my head.

The rage doesn't relent, showing images of flames, death, and pain. The void consumes me, hoping for an end that never comes. I growl, tossing Brenda off my back, and hear her grunt in pain before I'm slammed into another wall. I stagger, baring my teeth at the two. Brenda stands, snarling back like a wolf in a challenge, standing between me and Vincent. "*Stop.*"

I roar and she does in return, causing me to do it again, thundering against the walls. Her eyes widen suddenly, and then her scent hits me. The darkness diminishing enough for it to ring through. Citrus, honey, and lavender.

My head pounds as I breathe it in, almost staggering at the weight of it. Blinking, I see Brenda and Vincent more clearly than before, both still. There's blood on her.

Brenda. My lil sis. What have I done?

Horror develops me as I turn slowly, seeing Meg next to Marcus, who holds her close. She stares at me with large eyes as her scent begins to dissipate, but I can still smell it. Fear. Pain, like I haven't felt in decades, hits me. I let out a choked snarl, losing the final hold over myself, and howl in agony. My body shifts, changing into its full wolf form, ripping apart my clothes as bones creak and groan. Another howl leaves me as I race out of the destruction I've created.

DAY ONE

DENIAL

DAY TWO

ANGER

DAY THREE

BARGAINING

DAY FOUR

DEPRESSION

DAY FIVE

....

Irish Cream Cupcakes

Flour
Butter
Baking powder
Vegetable oil
Heavy cream
Eggs
Salt
Chocolate
Espresso & espresso powder
Cocoa powder
Powdered sugar
Irish Cream

CHAPTER 29
FULL MOON

I can't shift back.

I've been in my office at *Donny's*, licking my wounds as it were, although the physical ones have all healed. My eyelids droop, staring at the wall unable to think. Gunther, Shannon, and Victoria have all tried to get me to come out, to shift, but I just...can't. I don't have the will to, including eating or drinking. Even with Gunther informing me that Boston has been sighted up north, coming out of hiding...nothing.

Apart from the Pack, no one knows I'm here, all under the assumption I'm still below. Those who do know have been told I'm mourning Claudia, which technically isn't untrue. Although all I feel like is a jackass. Hating parts of myself as I continue to lay here in silence. Unable to shift back like some pup. I'm supposed to be there for the Pack, be a leader, an alpha...yet here I am, fading away. I wouldn't care if I did. Kind of deserve it.

I glance at the phone cords ripped from the wall, tired of the ringing a day ago.

"She's okay. Lil sis is just worried about you. She's not mad." Gunther's words echo in my head. *"We'll give you time, but...we still need you, boss. We need—"*

Everything hurts.

I huff, adjusting and wincing at the pinching in my back. I get up on all fours, pacing in a circle, and slump back down from a different kind of soreness. My head drops to the ground, wishing I could draw the eyes that haunt me, plaguing my soul which remind me of morning pastures and golden light. Warmth. Moonlight.

I shake my head, getting back up and try to shift, at least, into my hybrid form. I groan and growl, but nothing. It feels like I'm being blocked, like an old memory I can't quite recall. Huffing, I fall back to the ground in defeat. Instinct has taken hold, the churning emotions keeping me within animal form. Not eating for four days isn't helping either. It could be longer, maybe weeks before I can shift back. The alphas and betas could handle shit, but I knew realistically, I can't be gone long. Not without someone trying to take advantage to hurt us. Again. The thought of failing the Pack should get me back up. Shake it all off and shift. Do what should be done. But…I just *can't*.

My eyes close slowly, imagining the fields of Ireland, my grandfather walking me through wheatfields. The moon shines in the large sky as stars sparkle above, while his hand lands on my shoulder, smiling down at me. A whine escapes me. *I'm sorry, grandpappy.*

I drift, barely remembering the scent of citrus, lavender, and honey.

*W*HELP, *she found me.*

Claudia's face comes close to mine, and I snap my jaws at her. She smirks, then bops me on the nose. I sneeze, scrunching my face in annoyance.

"Grandpappy said what would happen, should've listened, Rod," she says, sitting beside me. I sit on my hunches, grumbling low in my throat. She chuckles, scratching my neck softly as we gaze out at the unfamiliar hills. "You can't keep ignoring your emotions, otherwise you'll keep shifting into an oversized sheepdog. Although running after you ain't that bad." I whine, groaning as I fall to the ground in frustration. "Not helping yourself there."

I glare at my sister, her eyes shining in the early dawn. I take a deep breath, concentrate, and shift into hybrid form. I lean back, breathing hard as she rubs my back. "I'm the older, wiser sibling, not you."

"Stop being so stubborn then," she retorts.

We sit a moment quietly as the sun rises, and I finally say, "Things were easier in Ireland. Didn't feel this hard, and the hills aren't the same here."

She continues rubbing my back, and murmurs, "I know."

"I didn't want to worry you."

"Far too late for that, tis my duty to worry over you."

"Sure, Claw." She bumps my shoulder, and I bump her back. Her easy expression pains me suddenly. "I don't want to disappoint you, too."

"You don't. And never will." I pull her into my arms as she sighs against my chest, stroking my fur, and then starts to scratch behind my ears. "You always try to help everyone, but yourself. Can't become an alpha if you don't believe in yourself."

I exhale deeply, and say, "I just want to make dad proud. Make all this change work."

"By acting like him?" I shrug. "Him and grandpappy aren't the same, practically opposites. Why should you be like dad?"

"Grandpappy gave him a choice. I haven't really-...what if I don't get one?" I murmur, and she stops. I stare at the grass, wishing it was the fields of Ireland. Home.

"You always have a choice," Claudia whispers, scratching my head again. "I'll make sure of it. I'd rather you be like grandpappy anyways."

"While petting me?"

"Perhaps when you stop acting like a temperamental poodle."

I shove her, and she laughs, jumping on my back and trying to wrestle me. I stand, and she falls off with a grunt. I look down as she frowns up at me, so I help her back up. Patting off the dirt, I tell her, "Thanks, Claw."

"What are cute sisters for?" I give her a look. "Help get yer thick head outta yer ass."

"Now who's trying to be grandpappy?" She grins broadly, then jumps on my back as I start walking back toward the city. "What would I do without you?"

She hangs over my shoulders, rubbing my head vigorously. "You'd be left alone to wander the streets of New York!" She says dramatically, and I stop to give her an exasperated look. "Fine, more likely lost in the woods some-where." I snort, and she jumps off me, taking my hand. "Come on, let's go home."

I look at the city of New York in the distance. She tugs at my hand, smiling as the rays of morning come over the horizon. Brilliant warm light blinds me and suddenly I don't feel Claw's hand in mine anymore.

No…please don't leave me. Please.

I'M AWAKEN from knocking at the door. That's it, I'm cursed.

I glare at it as Gunther comes in, and I growl low. He puts a hand up in defense, and says, "Someone's here to see you." I snarl, shaking my head once. "Boss, I think you should—"

I bark, getting up as my hackles bristle and he lets out a frustrated sigh. He shakes his head, then murmurs, "It's Meg."

A half-whimpered bark leaves as I stagger back, shaking my head. He narrows his gaze, raising a brow. "Taking that as a no?" I bare my teeth, and he sighs, closing the door as he leaves.

The ache devoured by this crushing depression starts to come back, and I snarl angrily at myself to make it stop. I pace, wondering if there's a way to break down the walls and run for the hills. I've already made my bed, might as well add another damn blanket or two. There's another knock, and I snarl *hating* the damn sound at this point.

It opens, and I let out a dark, rumbling growl, but the sound is choked out when Meg steps through. She carries a covered tray as Gunther behind her smirks, shutting the door behind her. She walks in, places the tray on the bar, and takes the cover off. Steaks and cupcakes, all fresh. Meg then places the steaks on the ground before me, and then crosses her arms.

"They said you haven't eaten," she says, and I flick my gaze to the cupcakes. I sniff the air, finding their sweet scent. Screw the steaks. I lick my lips, moving toward them. "Oh, no you don't." She stands in my way. "Water and steak first."

I growl low, taking a step toward her. As a full wolf, I'm still taller than her. I bare my teeth as I attempt to appear menacing. She looks up at me with a quirked brow and comes closer. I continue growling, instinct taking over in wanting the damn cupcakes and the fact I'm being defied.

"You're not gonna hurt me," she states, and I falter, blinking rapidly. She smirks, coming within inches of me. "See? Boop." Two fingers lightly bop my nose.

My head shakes and I sneeze. Blinking rapidly, I stare at Meg. A soft expression comes over her and she orders, "Steak first, McLycan."

My stomach suddenly growls, and for the first time in four days, I want to eat and am willing to. Meg glimpses at my stomach and then gestures to the food again. I huff, relenting to let her and my stomach win as I head over to the steaks. Meg remains near the bar, keeping me from snatching the cupcakes as I devour the food, then drink some water when she puts down a bowl. Once finished, I nudge away the empty dishes. I drop, laying down to wait for her to leave.

Instead, she comes over, settling on her knees before me, and places a cupcake between my paws. I stare at the cream frosting with white chocolate shavings, smelling sweet rosé. My favorite. I look up, and she tilts her head. "Deal is a deal. You ate."

Guilt gnaws at me, and all of a sudden, I don't want the cupcakes anymore. I look away, putting my head down to stare at the wall. A part of me wishes she'd leave, let me suffer in this darkness. While another piece of me, deep down, begs, *please don't leave me.*

"I talked to Brenda," she murmurs, and my heart starts to thunder in my chest. "She's upset, but not mad. She just...doesn't know what to do. And you didn't hurt her, not really. She mentioned grappling sessions worse than that, and something about a Dracula reject." She touches a paw, and I shudder. "Rodney, she told me a lot of stuff because she loves you." I try to back away from her. She clears her throat, gets up, and grabs the entire tray of cupcakes. She kneels back down, putting it on the ground.

"I also spoke with Marcus, Gunther...and then Zane," she sighs softly. "Some things finally made sense after I spoke with Carmen. She seemed to understand where I was coming from. She gave some good advice, better than anything I've heard. I guess, six hundred years does that, huh?"

I huff, not removing my sight from the wall, but hear a cupcake wrapper crinkle. My ears twitch as I look over as she picks off a shaving. She sighs, looking up so her brown eyes meet mine.

"So, I'm going to listen to Carmen and you're going to listen to me, Rodrick Rowan McLycan. First, I love you." My breath becomes shaky, eyes widening. "Second, being your *Gaelach* or not...I can't imagine coming back to Topside like we never happened." She smiles, looking up at the ceiling and around the office. "Brenda gave me some books, though, I hope I said it correctly. I think I preferred her lecture on the different kinds of Mates and how it all works, but Vinny did make coffee."

I involuntarily snort, scrunching my nose confused by the sound. Meg holds the cupcake up and my stomach twists. But I take the offering from her hand and the sweet taste covers my mouth as I lick the last of it from her hand.

"Thirdly, I want you to know I wasn't scared of you, but *for* you. You looked hurt and then you growled at Brenda, and I know you'd hate it if you hurt her, because you love her. She's your friend... your sister, and..." she stops, settles more onto the ground, and touches my paw again, "...I realized something after talking with everyone. That, perhaps, they didn't know fully. Certain skeletons."

I cock my head, unsure where she's going with this. Meg reaches forward, stroking my muzzle, and smiles sadly. "I've bartended enough, Rodney, to know traditions for some people. Who does what, and why. Those who set aside a drink for the dead are usually veterans, missing their buddies and wanting to remember them." Her eyes start to glisten with tears. "Or they feel guilty they came back alive."

A whimper leaves me suddenly. She swallows hard as I try to stop the whine in my throat, not wanting to hear the truth in her words. To hear them out loud. And the shame that follows. The self-hatred.

"I can't imagine the loneliness you had to have felt, and then had to continue protecting your family. Your Pack. I can't imagine the guilt and shame you felt because it was enough you didn't tell anyone about the explosions. How they make you feel. What happened in 4D. And then Brenda told me about the center. What you blamed yourself for. Scared of." She moves forward, taking my head in her hands. "I am *so* sorry you've suffered in silence. I'm sorry you don't have your sister or your mom anymore. And that your father should've stuck with you when it got hard, not blame you. And I'm sorry you've put so much pressure on your shoulders, trying not to...go through all that again. But it's not your fault. What happened with your sister and mom is not your fault."

I grumble, trying to shake my head away from her. She grips onto me, looking me straight in the eye. "It is *not* your fault."

The words sink deep, and I whine at the back of my throat as my shoulders feel heavy. Meg puts my head over her shoulder, hugging my neck close as I bring my head down to pull her to my chest.

"You kept me safe and—" I grunt, trying to pull away from her, but she tightens her hold on me. She clutches me, speaking against my fur, "It was *you* who called Vinny to help. *You* saved me from Boston. And then Calhoun. I had decided to make that deal with you, to stay, but I'd be dead if it wasn't for you. Getting help isn't failure, Rodney, it's the smart thing to do. It's the brave thing to do. Not to be blamed for."

Meg's words slam into me and the darkness that's covered me starts to shatter. The screaming in my head doesn't come, and those voices of shame...distant. She holds me tight as I breathe heavily, trying to decipher my thoughts and emotions.

"I know we had a deal," she whispers. "I'll help keep my end of the bargain; you know that. But I *do* want to try with you." I whine again, fear creeping back again. "I believe in you, even if you may—"

I pull back, and she lets go as I start to pace, trying to keep myself from snarling in old pain. Tears form in my eyes as I push away the horrific images, wanting them to disappear. I growl, trembling as I continue to pace. I shake my head wanting to hurt to leave but freeze and drop to my hunches when she says, "I'm glad you're alive."

Those words surge through me as I blink through tears.

"I'm proud of you for surviving, trying when you probably didn't want to," she continues gently. "And...and I think Claudia, your mom...Donny would be proud of you. For trying and living. I can't take away your pain, and I wish I could. The same as I know you wanted to for me. To take away those fears...the skeletons in the closet. But I can't, so all I can do is tell you I love you, and I won't let you be alone. Because I am glad, *you're* here. That *you* made it."

My entire body shudders as my chest rattles and my throat constricts. I take a deep breath, and the shift happens. I land on my knees, clutching the carpet as tears stream down my face. I try to swallow down the sobs, rasping, "I hate that I didn't follow her...I wanted it to be me, it should've been *me* in that building. Not... not..."

Meg kneels before me, grabbing both of my hands. Through my blurry vision I try to focus on her as the sobs break out. "They can't know...that I wanted to leave them...my Pack... wasn't... wasn't enough—" I choke on a sob, and Meg cradles my head against her shoulder. She holds me as I sob, clutching her as I cry into her hair. "I'm scared...fuck, I'm scared...I can't—"

She hushes me, stroking my head. "You're not alone. I'm right here."

I squeeze her tighter as she kisses my cheek, rocking me gently as I cry. Every ounce of pain comes out in those sobs, years waiting to be held without guilt. My muscles tremble as she hugs me, whispering soft words against my skin. It feels like hours, being wrapped in her arms as I cry clutching her. When the tears finally stop, I remain where I am, glued to her as she strokes my back. The tears dry as the weight on my shoulders lessen, along with the ache in my chest.

"You can be scared," she whispers. "I am, too."

"Because of me?"

"Because of losing you. I've known you for, like, a month and the idea of not having you around...it scares me. And I know that sounds insane—"

I pull away, placing my palm against her cheek as I gaze into her deep brown eyes. I take a shaky breath. "I love you."

She smiles, and then whispers, "Well, *that* wasn't so scary, huh?"

"No," I murmur. "But you're a scary human."

"Me?"

"Only you'd poke an alpha wolf's nose in a form that could… devour you."

"Being cheeky there, McLycan?" I shrug weakly, and she smirks.

I swallow hard, and say, "I'm scared of losing you, too."

Meg inhales deeply, then leans forward and I meet her halfway for a tender kiss, brushing our lips against the other. I breathe easier, inhaling her scent as it develops my aching bones with ease and safety.

She breaks the kiss, then places one on my cheek, and exhales sharply. "Well, any idea what we do now? I don't think this was in the contract."

I shake my head, threading my fingers through her hair to feel the soft strands. The dark feelings leave me slowly, replaced by thoughts of her as she gazes up at me. "I don't know, darling."

"Well," she sighs. "I guess we'll figure it out, but with a bit more honesty. From *both* of us."

I smirk. "Deal, darling."

"And, well…" she starts, then strokes my cheek, "…maybe not right away, but you could talk to Alanzo. I think he'd understand your fears, from what Carmen told me and their past, um, I think both may be able to help." I stare at her, unsure about the request and she quickly adds, "Only if you want to. Or just me if you're more comfortable. But just a suggestion."

I tighten my jaw. "Maybe."

"Where's that absolute wolf of mine at?"

"He's tired and wants more cupcakes." My stomach growls, and Meg looks down. She quickly brings her gaze back up with narrowed eyes. "You have a habit of always finding me naked."

She rolls her eyes. "You're having more food before cupcakes. Not letting you *wither* away in your very…very dusty office."

"Not that dusty." Meg gives me an exasperated look, putting her fingers against the desk. She makes a smiley face, and I give her my own tired expression. "Fine."

I yank her back to me, nuzzling my faze against her shoulder.

She rubs my back, kisses my head, and whispers, "I love you and I believe in you, Rodney. Even if you don't."

"I love you and I trust you. And I'm sorry for not telling you the truth."

"You don't need to apologize. I understand." I hug her tighter, and she hums lightly. "But thank you."

I inhale her scent, feeling the unfamiliar emotion of safety with her. She holds me and the voice that's cried out for her for weeks is quiet, sated with love and compassion. Untouchable from the darkness.

She kisses my cheek, pulling away. "Come on, time to get dressed and more food. *Then* cupcakes," she says, taking my hand as we get up. She averts her eyes and turns toward the door.

"Don't want to add anything to that list...darling?"

"Oh, nooo, get your pants or kilt on," she says waving a hand at me. "It's been a long four days, and I need a drink or something." She opens the door. "Shannon! I need more dinner!"

I quickly swipe a cupcake from the floor, turning toward my closet as she gasps behind me. I glimpse over my shoulder as she grabs the tray off the ground, a smile breaking through as I shove the cupcake in my mouth. I open my closet, coming face to face with the dusty great kilt.

Meg laughs behind me, and I flick my gaze to her at the bar. She holds up a bottle of vodka, old and opened for some time. "Want a martini?"

I smile softly at her, the crushing weight and screams gone from my head. I'm still fucking scared, but I don't feel as alone, and those fears don't seem as monstrous. Not when my *Gaelach* has a spine of steel, willing to stand between me, dessert, and my shadows.

CHAPTER 30
PEAKY PARANORMALS

"Call her," Meg insists.

"I will later," I argue.

"She's worried about you. Stop being so stubborn."

"I don't have time—"

"You did for a plate of cupcakes." She crosses her arms.

"Priorities." She quirks a brow in disbelief. "Want me to say I don't like them?" I crowd her space, backing her up against the wall and placing my hands on either side of her face.

"Don't twist my words—" I cut her off with a kiss and she gasps. She clings to my chest as I press my body against her, fervently kissing her. Days without her and it was hell for more than a few reasons. It feels like I can finally think and breathe clearly. I cup her face as she wraps her arms around my neck.

She breaks the kiss, scowling at me. "Don't distract me."

"I'll talk to her when we get below. Promise." Meg sighs, placing a quick kiss on my lips before lightly shoving me back to walk around.

It's been a few hours, and I think I've eaten enough for four wolves. Meg wouldn't let anyone else into my office, giving me the time to sort myself out. I'm relieved to have the time to breathe. And she's fucking sexy ordering them around. She's tried to get me to call Brenda, but I'm not ready yet. Fuck, I'm barely ready to face my damn alphas and betas for the shit I pulled. Fully prepared to get scolded.

Meg pauses near my desk, looking at the maps I still have out. I join her, leaning against my desk as I pull her towards me. She asks, "Is that everything you own up here?"

"Yeah," I answer against her ear. "Mine are the dark blue, DiNardi was green, and Vincent's red, of course."

"I didn't know Antoni was that close."

"Yeah, we were right on the edge of the other," I say, and she hums, leaning back into me and holding my arms close around her. "What is it?"

"I really didn't know you were that close to each other," she murmurs. "That's why Ralph went through yours, I guess."

"Yeah, figured. But he didn't know routes changed, got caught."

"Is that how that other mole got through? Knew the routes?"

"Freyja's mole?" She nods. "Probably."

"So, they were Wolf Mob?"

"Ex-mob."

She turns, scrunching her brows at me. "If they were ex-mob, how'd they get through your territories?" I blink slowly, looking back at the maps. "I mean, Gunther said something about how Skylar tracks ex-mob for precautions, but how would they've gone unnoticed?"

I stare at the maps, and a sinking feeling hits me. "They knew our current routes. And borders."

Her breath hitches, and she looks back at the maps, too. "Help on the inside."

More than just the inside, not all Wolf Mob knows the routes. I breathe deeply, keeping that piece of information at the back of my head. "Knew I kept you around for a reason. Keep my head clear."

"Oh, is that what I do?" She smirks back.

"What? Compliment, darling."

"Almost...*darling*."

"Getting sassy with me?" I growl low, and she shivers, tightening her grip.

"Rodney," she warns. I chuckle at her reaction, already smelling her arousal that tickles my nostrils. I growl again and she glares at me, rubbing her thighs together as her breath hitches.

"I love you," I murmur, kissing her neck.

"I love you, too." She moves her head, allowing me to kiss her fully as she hums at the contact. I move a hand down her stomach, caressing her hip dips, reaching for—

There's knocking. I break away, snarling at the potential intruder. Meg giggles, trying to move away, but I refuse to let go. She snorts as they knock again.

"Go away," I growl.

"Warranty is overdue, boss." Zane peeks in and then leans against the doorway. He looks at Meg, wrapped in my arms. "She bribed you with cupcakes, didn't she?"

"No."

"Yes." I scowl at her, and she grins smugly. I can't help my own smile.

Zane grins, then calls out, "They're alive and look like a Hallmark picture."

I groan, burying my face into her hair as she rubs my arms. Gunther, Zane, Shannon, and Skylar fill the space looking relieved, while Marcus hangs back by the doorway.

"I'd ask if you'll quit being stubborn, but that's impossible," Gunther comments, nodding toward us. "Good thing she's here."

"Our own *wolf* negotiator," Skylar smirks.

"Hey, the best part of all this was the boss taking Dracultelli on his own, almost whooped his ass if lil sis hadn't shown up," Zane says with a wink.

"Could go for round two, boss. Let us watch," Shannon comments.

Meg was right to keep them out.

"Enough," Marcus warns. "Leave it be."

Gunther and Zane exchange a look, then to me. I try not to make eye contact with Marcus, not ready for that conversation either. Meg gives me a reassuring squeeze.

I sigh, then say, "We're heading down to *Mountain Edge* soon, so get your shit together and tell Delilah we'll be there for lunch." Apparently, it's mid-evening on Topside.

"Thank goodness," Zane mumbles.

"Saying something about my cooking?" Shannon jabs him.

"No," Zane responds, not sounding too convincing as he leaves.

"You know what, get food from the bodega next time, mutt."

"Oh, come on!" She follows him out with Skylar close behind, shaking their head. Gunther and Marcus stay behind, watching me as I remain wrapped around Meg. She goes to step away, but a possessive snarl leaves my throat.

"Rodney McLycan, you will let go of me," she states. I grumble, dropping my arms as she steps away and adjusts her shirt. She kisses my cheek, and whispers, "The kilt looks good on you."

"Another good thing out of this, you two ain't dancing around each other anymore," Gunther comments.

"Shut it," Marcus warns. I glance over as he watches Meg, who walks up to him and murmurs under her breath. His gaze softens a little as she touches his arm.

Gunther gives me a look, and I ignore it. "We need to—"

"Boss, we've got trouble!" Shannon calls. All three of us bristle as she comes slamming through. "Vehicles incoming. Streets are clearing out. It's Boston."

Meg spins to me, eyes wide as I straighten. "Put wolves in defensive positions. Ready for an attack and give warning below."

Shannon rushes out as Gunther says, "He should be north. He shouldn't be here."

"No shit," I grumble as Meg comes to hug me, trembling.

"I mean, he shouldn't know either of you is here." I finally meet Marcus' gaze, and his expression hardens. The sinking feeling in my gut comes back.

"What if someone saw you come up?" Meg asks.

"They wouldn't have waited over four days," Marcus answers, then looks at me. "And I brought Meg up through the tunnels."

I flick my eyes to the map, something scratching at the back of my mind as I look at my disorganized desk. Slowly, the pieces fit together and my heart sinks. Please let my gut be wrong this time. I can't chance it to lure them out or be wrong, not with Meg here.

"Marcus." His blue eyes meet mine. "Keep her safe." His eyes harden and then nods.

"Rodney," Meg whispers.

"Stay in the backrooms with Marcus," I tell her, grasping her face as I keep my fear in check. "I'll distract Boston, and Marcus will get you back down into the Underground. Once below, contact the Cuorebellas."

"You are not sending me away again," she says harshly, holding onto my wrists tightly. "I'm not leaving you—"

"Meg." My voice is faint as her chin quivers, eyes searching mine. I kiss her gently, then let go as she steps back. "I love you. *Go* with Marcus."

Tears build in her eyes, her fear rising as Marcus touches her shoulder, beginning to lead her out. "I love you," she murmurs.

It takes everything within me not to chase after them as they disappear. I snarl, moving to my desk and tossing on a dark flannel, and adjusting my kilt.

"You gonna finally kill him?" Gunther asks.

"If not me then you will," I answer. "But we need a fucking opening, we'll be surrounded by his crew, no doubt carrying silver."

"We'll follow your lead. Need a damn good distraction, drop their guard."

I load two .45s, then ask, "You sure only Pack knew where Meg and I were?"

"Yeah. Didn't want others prying. Give you time."

"Thanks." My voice is rough, and I pause. "Who's out there now?"

"Don't like that tone." Gunther moves quietly, shutting the door completely. "Only some inner crew from below, *Donny's* immediate crew, and a few of Skylar's. All Pack. You're not saying—"

"Someone ratted Meg out."

"Shit."

"I've been up here a few times, and each time, he doesn't show. He ghosts for weeks, and just now comes when Meg is here? How he know?"

Gunther clears his throat, looking at the doorway. "I know we thought it could be another but…any idea who?" I swallow hard and nod. "Alright, got your back, boss."

I secure my guns and head for the door. "Here's hoping someone doesn't stab it."

"That's what you got me for," he says as we head out the door. "Although I'm starting to miss when humans ran from us."

"Fuck that, it was worse back then."

We walk down the hall, coming out into the main area with wolves spread out with rifles cocked and claws ready. Cars are lined up outside, boxing us in, and I see gunmen. The Pack looks over at me, most seeming relieved. I scan their faces, coming upon one and my breath becomes shallow, hoping I'm wrong. I tear my eyes away as my gut yells at me that I'm right, not to listen to the denial or blame at the back of my head. But I can't ignore the growing emotion of betrayal.

"We're not turning this into the O.K. Corral," I say, seeing Boston leaning on a hood of a car. "We talk, distract, and then fucking kill them for burning the Underground."

Everyone loosens a growl, echoing low in the restaurant. I stalk to the front, take a deep breath, and slam open the door as I stride out. Zane, Gunther, and Skylar stay close behind as Boston's people raise their weapons, but he holds his hand up.

"McLycan, heard you've had a rough couple of days," he says with a smug smile.

"What's it to you?" Wolves station themselves along the sidewalk as Boston's men watch them, guns cocking.

"Thought I'd cheer you up."

"Doubt it," I growl.

"Aw, come on, McLycan, is this about the Underground?" He opens his arms, stepping forward. "Business is business, and you didn't give back my property. You should understand that."

Oh, look, there's the anger from days ago, it's back and there's no vampire to fight.

Zane snarls behind me, along with Skylar. "Watch your words," I warn.

Boston's smile falters as I bare my teeth. His gaze meets mine, and I can tell we've both made our decision. "She owes me," he hisses. "I need what she has. What she knows. You think I'm giving up *two years* of investment?"

I glance at the men he's brought. "You replaced those we slaughtered below pretty quick. Bartenders aren't that expensive, Boston. Invest in a new one."

He frowns. "She's mine. She was *my* mole and knew where DiNardi was selling—"

"Whining is a bad look on you," I taunt. "I told you she belongs to—"

"Give her back!" He yells suddenly and his crew raises their weapons. His men rustle along with my wolves. I flick my gaze, knowing I need something else to shake them up.

"How'd it feel knowing a woman outwitted you?" I say darkly, and he fumes. "Fucked up your shit so easily, that now you're whining like a newborn baby?"

He sneers and raises a hand. "Then maybe *you* should be brought down a pedestal, see how it feels," he threatens. I clench my fist, ready to attack when there's a shout.

"No!" I straighten, hearing Meg's cry as she comes between me and Boston. I snarl, seeing Marcus come out, not looking unperturbed as Meg faces Boston. "Leave them the fuck alone, Charlie!"

"You little—"

"DiNardi wasn't selling to the Wolf Mob, but he was selling out *you* to the FBI and the NYPD," she spits at him, and Boston visibly stumbles back.

The wolves who didn't know murmur behind me. Gunther growls at them and they quiet as Boston's crew relaxes their aim, staring at Meg. Boston glares at her, sneering, "And *why* didn't I know that...*sweetie?*"

I'm tearing his fucking spine out.

I bristle, keeping my gaze on Meg, not understanding what she's doing.

"Because I was helping," she states. Why is she outing herself? "I gave him *everything* about you Charlie, and any other fucker you pushed me toward. Who abused and used me!"

"You fucking bitch—"

"And guess what? That information has made it to the police, so you better start counting your days. They'll be coming for you. All of you!" What?

Boston looks at his gunmen, more of them lowering their weapons as they back toward their vehicles. Wolves snarl behind me, growling low.

"How?" I ask her.

She turns toward me with a steady gaze. "You were gone, and I wanted out. I thought you left me. And I wouldn't go back to him. I wasn't taking a chance."

I cock my head, and that determined look on her face doesn't falter. No. She'd never go behind my back. And then it clicks as her mouth tightens. *Were you going to sell me? Distraction, darling.* Smart woman.

Boston's men step back, looking at each other in shock and worry. Boston sputters, looking around as if the police are coming around the corner now. Almost there.

"You left?" I rumble, stepping closer. She doesn't back away, keeping her ground. "We had a deal, Meg."

"See?" Boston intervenes. "She's a betraying bitch who will drag us *all* down! Who knows what the police know?"

"Sounds like a you problem. Police are for humans," I say, flexing my hand three times. There's a grunt behind me, and Zane shifts his weight.

"Until she goes to PSB!" Boston spits, pointing at her frantically. "What then? NIIA?"

Meg shakes her head, "I would never—"

"She's already gotten DiNardi killed, who's next?" Boston screams, and more of his men look at him in shock. "Get rid of her or we use her, McLycan! Play this smart, for all of us. Of course."

I take another step toward Meg, noticing Boston isn't carrying. Gunther grunts once as Boston tries smiling. I look back down at Meg, and she whispers in Noctora, *"I believe in you."*

My head tilts like a predator assessing their prey. Carefully, I bring my face close to hers. I clench my fist for Gunther and Zane, and whisper to Meg, "Drop."

She goes to the ground as I leap forward, landing on Boston. The rest of the wolves descend upon the stunned crew, ripping forward as they shift into hybrid form. Zane slaughters the gunmen alongside Skylar and Marcus, shots ring out as I shift into hybrid form. Boston cringes beneath me as limbs from his men are ripped off and the air is filled with broken screams. Most of his men are killed within seconds, all we needed was that small window.

I bare my teeth at the mob boss, who pleads and begs beneath me. "Look, look…you-you heard her—"

"You fucked with my Pack, Charlie," I growl with saliva dripping down onto him. "I warned you. No more games."

He tries to fight me. "W-wait, no…no-no—!"

I bare my teeth at him, and snarl, "And you're replaceable."

I tear into his windpipe as he flails beneath me. His scream is cut short as I snap his neck, making the last of his crew pause and scramble. I roar, grabbing his body and tossing it against a vehicle into a mangled mess. The Wolf Mob tears apart what's left of the men that try to flee.

"Take out whoever's left!" I thunder.

I turn back to Meg and walk toward her, but suddenly there's movement in the chaos as someone aims for Meg. Marcus plows forward, ramming into the assailant as they go flying back and he releases a menacing growl staying between them. I look over to see Victoria getting up, snarling, and running toward Meg again, but Skylar reaches her, pinning her to the ground. Victoria thrashes under the alpha's hold, while the rest of us watch as she screams.

"No! She betrayed us! What are you doing?!"

Others and I shift back into human form. I stare down at the white wolf who snarls at Meg, Gunther coming up next to me, touching my arm briefly. My stomach drops, hating I was right. It was her. The reports, tracking, phone calls…she was covering up her involvement.

"She admitted to outing us! Going to the police!" Victoria screams.

"She was lying," I rasp.

Blue eyes meet mine, and I swallow hard as my heart cracks. She goes still, breathing heavily. No…

"She was distracting Boston," Marcus says, staying in front of

Meg. "She knew he'd start scrambling if he thought police were after him. Including his men."

"No," Victoria bites back, shaking her head. "No, she was… was—"

"Victoria," I say softly, and she looks up at me. "What did you do?"

"Protecting the Pack! Not her! She's a liar and deceitful, use you as she did with the others. She's already used two bosses, you were next!"

"How did you even know that?" I never told Victoria. She wasn't a beta yet.

"I was helping. They were going to destroy you, and I had to help the Pack. Listen to me, Rodney, I'd never betray you—"

"But you did."

She shakes her head vigorously, then screams furiously, tearing out of Skylar's arms to run forward. Zane gets in her way, snarling and she stops before the large alpha.

"Very few knew I'd killed Ralph that morning," I say quietly. "And most were with me at *4D*. You found the info on Travis, helped with the warehouses, and knew all current routes. How to get through without being noticed. Getting the explosives without being noticed." She goes still and her eyes begin to fill with tears. "Why, Victoria?"

All the wolves are silent, watching her with deep hurt and betrayal. Pain writhes inside me. She breathes heavily, almost too loud within the horrified silence.

"They…they took from us," she says. "I was helping you get it back. For *you*. I was helping to regain—"

"By almost getting us killed?" Zane asks with a shaky voice. "A death trap?"

"They were only supposed to grab *her*." Victoria points at Meg. "They take her back and the Wolf Mob would get the Bronx back, everything we lost! No more busts, no more police."

"I was talking about *4D*," Zane murmurs, and her eyes widen. The agonizing truth sinks deeper.

"Only the Underground alphas and betas knew about Meg's full involvement," I say, glancing at the other wolves who keep strict expressions. "How did you know, Victoria? How?"

She starts to shake, and then her expression drops, filled with horrified eyes. She steps toward me, and the others snarl at her to stop as she says quickly, "Freyja. Rodney, she wants—"

A gunshot echoes and Victoria's head snaps back, red blossoming on her forehead. She slumps to the ground as all breath leaves me, horror screaming in my head. I shake with sudden rage and agony as Shannon screams. Skylar holds Shannon back while Zane yells at the body of the white wolf.

"There, helped with the trash." I turn toward the sickening voice of Sebastian, who stands far enough away from us with a singular car, gun still raised. He grins. The wolves snap, ready to pounce. "Attack me, and this place will be crawling with NIIA and PSB in minutes. *Or* I could take out more wolves, perhaps, your boss," he says, cocking his gun. "Your choice."

I stop the others, snarling with rage as the ache in my chest worsens. I frown at him, and he continues grinning, bringing the gun down. "We'll have to make this quick since the feds are already on their way. You caused quite a ruckus."

Bloodsucker has me cornered and he's already killed one of my wolves. I can't lose more. I focus on breathing, trying not to spiral over how much shit my Pack may be in if I don't listen to him.

"Why?" I question him.

"She served her purpose. And was about to blab."

"Fucking monster!" Zane yells.

"Admit it! She was on the chopping block." I glimpse up, sensing more gunmen waiting for Sebastian's command if we move wrong. "She betrayed you, whether she did it with good intentions or not. Wouldn't be enough though, huh? Don't you have that Pack Law of no mercy or some shit, hound?"

I want to strangle him. Hating that he's right, but I could've saved her. And if not, she'd at least have died by a wolf's hands and not this rotten fucker.

"What do you want?" I ask.

"The girl," he says, nodding toward Meg. "Give her to me, and you get 45 minutes before the feds show. Don't and you get... seven."

"No," I snarl.

"Think about your—"

"*No.*" Whatever Boston had planned for her; Freyja will do worse.

Soft hands grab my arm, pulling my attention away from the vampire. Meg's eyes find mine, and I shake my head at her. She looks back at Sebastian and whispers in a shaky voice, "Rodney, you can get everyone below. Please. It's okay."

The fuck it is okay. A friend of decades was just executed before me, and now I may lose her, too? No. *No.*

"I go with her," I snarl at Sebastian, finding his crimson eyes. Meg grasps my arm tighter. "You get us both or no deal, bloodsucker."

He tilts his head. Thinks a moment, and then grins with a singular nod. I quickly turn to Marcus, who looks at me in horror. "Make it look like *Donny's* was attacked. Boston takes the fall. Get *everyone* below."

"Rodney."

"If I don't come back, it's yours." His expression hardens, beginning to shake his head. "The Pack is yours. You keep them safe, no matter what."

"Rod."

"I trust you...Balto."

He frowns, inhaling sharply and nods once as he turns to bark orders. Gunther flashes a worried look at me, then follows Marcus. Zane shakes his head, his chin quivering, and I give him a look to follow. He swallows hard, before ripping himself away to collect Victoria's body. My heart aches as the other wolves start moving, feeling their worry and uncertainty.

Meg takes my hand, and I take a deep breath. I look toward where Sebastian waits, and whisper, "Come on, darling...we've got a date with the devil."

CHAPTER 31
SHE GOT TOPSIDE LOCKED UP

The car is quiet as I keep Meg against me. Sebastian drives with the divider up. Thank fuck. My mind keeps replaying Victoria's head snapping back while I stare ahead.

Meg squeezes my hand. "I'm sorry, Rodney."

"Not your fault, darling."

"I know, but…she was your friend."

I press my forehead down against hers and whisper, "I hate it, but she made her decisions, and that bloodsucker was right…she broke Pack law."

She strokes my face, letting out a soft exhale. "Still…I'm sorry you lost a friend."

I tuck her under my chin, closing my eyes as I struggle against the warring emotions of betrayal and fear. I trust Marcus to protect the Pack, getting them below, safe from the feds and Freyja's goons. I can't say the same for Meg and me.

"How worried should I be about Frejya?" Meg asks.

I open my eyes, glaring at the dark divider. "You trust me?"

"Yeah."

"Don't agree to any deals with her," I say, moving back to give her a serious look.

"Only make deals with you…right?" She tries to lighten the mood, but she swallows hard. I give her a half smile.

"I'm the only devil for you." She scoffs, leaning against my shoulder. "She won't hesitate to get rid of you. She'll pause with me." Probably not, but maybe luck is back on my side.

"Who exactly is she?"

"She's—" The car stops, and the door opens suddenly.

We're in Lower Manhattan, but not many people are milling about this evening. I stare up at the tall, mirrored skyscraper, my heart thundering as I remember the last time being here. I glimpse at the building's plaque. We follow behind Sebastian as Meg stares at the plaque, entering a lobby lined with silver, paintings of the city, dimly lit by fluorescent blue lighting. Meg shudders next to me, a natural reaction to the eerie ambiance of the coldness that describes the woman we're being handed over to. We approach a platinum elevator, and the vampire gestures for us to get on. He smiles, ruby eyes glowing as the doors close, leaving us.

"She owns the building, doesn't she?" Meg rasps, and I nod as she tightens her grip on my hand. "That means...holy *shit*." Yup.

Christine Veldastein AKA Freyja is a well-known billionaire who owns most of New York City, Atlanta, Charleston, and Topside cities near the Mississippi. She's twenty-nine, inherited her father's law firms and real estate businesses when she was nineteen. Since then, she's created her own empire that revolves around information. Anyone who isn't part of the mafia knew her as Christine. Billionaire. Tycoon. While some knew her as Freyja— the fucking "Godfather" of Topside. The She-Devil.

"I've seen her in magazines. Even on television in Vermont," she whispers. "I'm guessing she's more powerful than the media says? More influence?"

"Vincent's believed to be dead by all federal agencies, Paranormal or not, because of her," I answer. "She wiped his existence, erasing him into myth. Most Paranormals believe it's his sister controlling the Blood Mafia, that he died with his father, or... Sebastian is the Blood Mafia Boss."

"Oh, well...that explains a few things."

The elevator stops and we walk into a lobby with barren grey walls and dark marble floors. The ebony doors open before us, and a familiar face walks out.

"Alfred," I greet the dark brown werewolf, who smiles pleasantly with amber-yellow eyes. He's wearing a white button-up with a black vest, slacks, and hair coiffed. He's older than me by fifty years but holds himself like he's in his 500s. Years ago, I tried to bring him back to the Pack, but he declined. I'd take him over Sebastian any day. He wasn't cruel, just loyal.

"She'll be a moment," he says, glancing at Meg before disappearing through the door.

"His name is *Alfred?*" She asks, and I nod. "Please tell me she's not also Batman."

"No." More like fucking Penguin and Catwoman combined.

We wait silently as my hair rises with each ticking moment. Anticipation makes my stomach tighten, knowing she's making us wait. Meg holds my hand tighter, and I look down to see her lips pursed and brows furrowed. I inhale her scent, grounding myself. I'm about to enter a poker game with a long-time nemesis, and I'm out of good cards. Any help from the other families won't be optional here, we're on our own. My best hope is to stall and get Meg out.

The door opens, and Alfred gestures for us to come in. We enter her office, a large space with a gigantic window as the back wall, overlooking the city. Lights outside trickle into the cold, blue-tinted monochromatic office. One side is just shelves of alcohol, cigars, and imported vices, the other side is books and ledgers containing who knows what. In the middle, by the window sits a large ebony desk, papers stacked neatly, behind it stands the she-devil herself.

My spine stiffens. It's been years since I've seen her, and she's not the young girl I once knew. Christine Veldastein is shy of five feet tall, smaller stature with long reddish-blonde hair that hangs past her shoulders. Her fair skin shines against the dark suit she wears, plunging deep with tight sleeves. She picks up a glass of white wine with her right hand adorned with silver claw rings. My gaze meets hers, finding the only familiar feature —hardened hawk-like green eyes, which pierce into you. Just like her father.

She walks around the desk, stopping just past it to bring the glass to her bloodred lips, showing no emotion. She barely comes to my torso, yet she stands like she's twelve feet tall. The most fearsome human on Topside.

"Rodney, what a surprise."

"Christine," I murmur.

Her eyes darken. "It's Freyja to *you*." She moves her gaze to Meg, her voice cold. "You're whom I wanted to speak with, but since the dog came, we can settle other business."

Meg goes to move, but I hold her back, and whisper, "Don't get close."

Freyja smirks, holding her hand up for the silver claws to shimmer. "Careful getting attached to hounds, they'll bite back."

Meg crosses her arms and raises her chin, asking, "What do you want?"

Freyja puts her glass down, grabbing a folder. She takes out two photos, holding them up for us to see. Headshots of two PSB agents. Meg inhales sharply, and whispers, "That's them."

"You don't have to whisper," Freyja taunts, putting the photos back into the folder. "I already knew it was them. Since it *was* my building in the first place that was blown to nothing."

"You knew this entire time?" I snarl.

"Not entirely," she says, picking up her glass and walking to the wall of ledgers. "Federal agents, politicians, government officials always want anonymity. I guarantee that, prepared to give it. What people decide to do with what I give them is their own prerogative, not mine." She slides her gaze to me, and I scowl. "The consequences are theirs to handle. But when I heard from a certain white wolf that you made a deal over these men, it presented a perfect opportunity for me."

I flick my gaze to Meg, my jaw tightening.

She traces a finger over the bindings, and states, "This is how it shall go. I give Rodney the names and location of the agents he wants so badly, and Meg...you stay here. Your deal is completed, your welcome."

"No," I say.

"I wasn't talking to you," Freyja hisses, turning toward us. "Although I should thank you for taking care of Boston. He was becoming a loose cannon, especially after my warning to you."

"She's not staying."

Freyja glowers, putting her attention on Meg, who's breathing shallowly. "You have something I want. You saw what will happen to those mutts. So, I advise you not to try taking away what I am owed."

Meg shakes her head. "I don't even know what—"

"You worked with Antoni, helping him obtain information. I want it. Whether you willingly give it to me or not, I *will* have it."

"Fine," Meg says, trying to keep her composure. "I'll tell you where to find it."

Freyja chuckles darkly, walking back to her desk, and putting her drink down. "No, you stay here on Topside, help me get what I want."

"Or just tell me what you want," Meg argues. "Antoni didn't share everything."

"I wonder why?" She taunts. "With your reputation of betraying people?" Meg straightens, dropping her arms. Freyja smiles like the cat who's caught the mouse, and my heart pounds. "No, I want to confirm *everything* you know. Just like how *he* kept you below, I assume."

I snarl a little at Freyja, who smirks. Meg stays quiet, and I see her pursing her lips thinking. She flashes her gaze to me, and I shake my head once. Don't you dare.

"Will you leave Rodney and the Pack alone?" Meg asks, stepping toward Freyja. I grab for her, but she shrugs me off. "Will you leave them be?"

"I'll guarantee that he'll leave unscathed, what he decides next will determine the fate of the Wolf Mob."

"No," I say, grabbing Meg's arm and she spins toward me as I stare into those brown eyes. "No...no deals."

"Rodney—"

"She will make you disappear. Use you worse than Boston or DiNardi."

"Or you?" Freyja asks, and I glare at her annoying smirk.

I look back at Meg, clutching her shoulders. "You'll lose your freedom with her, even when you've given everything. She will take and take until there's nothing left. And then give you to the feds, you'll never have a life again."

Her gaze stays with mine, swallowing hard as she murmurs, "Deal's a deal. I identified the agents."

My heart cracks as her jaw tightens, determined to see this through. She's trying to save me, the Pack, and everyone else who's helped her. Protected her. My hands shake, knowing I'll lose her forever once Freyja's claws are in her, caught in her web. A damn deal or not, I'm keeping her safe and *alive*.

"Take me as collateral," I state, and Meg gasps. I step past her, pointing at Freyja. "She writes everything down she remembers, then takes the names of the agents to the Wolf Mob, and I stay here. If she lies about the information, do whatever the fuck you want with me."

"Rodney, no." Meg yanks at my shirt. "The Pack—"

"Marcus will take over." She goes still as I glance down at her. I look at Freyja, who tilts her head. "Come on, Christine. It's me you want, not her."

"Don't flatter yourself."

"Then why'd you come to me a decade ago? Too much politics with Vincent? The alphas would've told you no instantly, but me... you had a chance." Her eyes begin to blaze as I continue to taunt her. "And I turned you down. You gave up. I must've meant more to you than you thought."

"No," she says coldly. "You were worse than I thought."

"Then you should be delighted to have me on your leash."

She narrows her gaze, steps behind her desk, and pulls over the phone, looking directly into my eyes. "As satisfying it is to see you beg and grovel over a *human*...I decline. I have no need for a washed-up alpha, who can't keep his wolves alive."

"Hey, you *bitch*!" Meg yells, pointing at her. Freyja quirks a brow at her, unperturbed. "You don't know anything about him!"

"Don't I?" My chest tightens, watching her expression darken. "Since you're so willing to give up your freedom for her, then you won't mind me selling you to the highest bidder. Agree to my terms or NIIA will be here to collect."

"What?" Meg gasps.

"Or perhaps PSB, since someone wants certain people to disappear, including you. I'm sure they'd love to have you under their thumb, Rodney. People will be owing me favors for the next decade when I hand you over," she sneers. "*That* will bring me delight, you *never* seeing the Underground again or your Pack."

Meg gasps as I stare at Freyja in shock. The anger and fury in her eyes. The kid I knew was long gone.

"Fine, I'll—" I spin, covering Meg's mouth with my hand. She struggles in my grasp as I hold her close, tears forming in her eyes as she shakes her head at me. My chin quivers as she stares up at me.

"No," I whisper. "When they come for me...run."

I gently release her, stroking my thumb over her cheek. "Let me agree, please."

"Darling, I promised you freedom, with or without a damn deal." Alfred moves near the door, and I glance at him as he quickly averts his eyes.

"What will it be, Meg?" Freyja asks.

Meg's chin quivers, her scent becoming weak as she clutches my wrists. She then says loud enough for her to hear, "No—"

There's a shout from the foyer, and I pull Meg around to shield her. She clutches my shirt as gunshots echo with shouts and snarls, glass breaking. I inhale, finding a scent that doesn't belong here. A smile pulls at my lips as Alfred growls, noticing who it is, too. He moves, but the doors slam open with two bodies thundering through with a shaking force. I watch Sebastian get slammed into the carpet, dragged through the flooring, and pinned as his arms and legs are broken. He screams, left on the ground as the other vampire stands, adjusting his leather jacket.

"Vinny!" Meg gasps.

Alfred moves toward him, but two shots ring out, hitting his knees. He hits the deck, bleeding as Brenda walks through, smiling ruefully. "Heard you needed a librarian enforcer."

CHAPTER 32
TOWER OF GLASS

"This is what happens when you don't call," Brenda says, shooting Alfred in his feet and he groans. She shrugs at him. "You'll heal, unlike some I don't use silver." She puts her gun away. "Anyways… I get worried, yell at wolves, and have to storm buildings with my territorial bloodsucker."

"Admit it, sweet cheeks, it's the best date we've had in weeks," Vincent says.

"That bookstore was fun."

"You sat in romance for three hours."

"Taking notes."

"I prefer demonstration."

"Can't tie myself up, that's what I have you for."

Vincent trails his tongue over his fangs. "Very true, sweet cheeks."

"How the *fuck* are you two worse?" Freyja spits out. So, we agree on one thing.

I look to Freyja, whose hand is still on the phone. I whistle twice, and Brenda pulls out her Glock and shoots the phone off the desk. Freyja glares at me and then Brenda. "Your aim has improved."

"I was aiming for your head. Oops." Brenda comes up, lightly punching my shoulder. Relief floods me, seeing her okay. And that she's here at all. "You good?" She whispers.

"Been better."

"Told you, Lassie. Always got me," she murmurs, then winks at Meg as she heads for Freyja. Vincent joins her, crushing a few of Sebastian's ribs first. The vampire hisses at him, and Vincent snarls low which causes the lights to flicker and crystals of liquor to shatter. Sebastian goes still into submission.

"Freyja…darling," Brenda says, walking around the desk. "You smell like cheap wine and candle wax. Found the Phantom did you, Christine?"

"Fuck off, *baby sis*," she sneers, glaring at Brenda who leans against her desk. "Here for another deal? Sorry, but I'm in the middle of something."

"Nope, just keeping your hands off my family." Brenda points at me and Meg. "That's my family."

"That *mutt* isn't your—"

"Careful," Vincent warns, trailing fingers through broken glass. "She's been touchy lately, and that phone will be the least of your problems. And he's not a mutt."

Did the vamp just defend me?

Freyja hisses at him, "I *own* you."

Vincent smiles, chuckling while looking at Brenda who gives him a tired look. "Father's dead. Your little scheming won't work on me and if you send feds after *my* ass, I'd love to see your…little claws against hers."

Brenda grins, waving her fingers.

"She was going to call NIIA and PSB on Rodney," Meg tells them, moving around me, but keeping her hand in mine. Brenda's expression darkens. "Unless I gave myself over to her, she was going to lock up Rodney. And she has the agents' information right there."

Freyja laughs coldly. "Oh, aren't you a fucking snitch? I see why Antoni was worried. You chose *perfectly*, Rodney."

Meg points at her. "Brenda is *my* friend, along with Vinny. You aren't."

"As if they have *human* friends," she ridicules.

"Coming from the one in her lonely glass tower," Meg retorts.

I pull Meg back to me, saying gently in her ear, "Darling, I love you, but don't taunt her."

All three look at us, each with a different expression. Brenda is smug, Vincent impressed, and Freyja is pure disdain.

Brenda grabs the folder from the desk, and Meg nods as she opens it, then places it inside her jacket. Freyja goes to claw her, but Brenda steps back and Vincent snarls.

"Give it back. I'm fucking warning you."

"No," Brenda says, staying near Vincent. "Here's how this is gonna go. We all leave, and the feds never know we were here. Meg comes with us, and I don't shoot you in the kneecaps."

"You wouldn't dare."

"Try me."

"You're a bratty, bitch but you…" Her gaze flicks to the side, and something shuffles.

I click my tongue twice, and Brenda pulls out her .45, tossing it to me. I catch it easily, and turn, shooting Sebastian in the legs as he tries to move. He groans, falling to the ground and I walk over to kick him in the stomach.

"Leave him be!" Freyja screams.

Another gun clicks, and I see Vincent aiming at her. I glare down at the vampire who killed Victoria, rage fills me as I once again see her head snap back. I snarl, putting a foot on his chest to keep him still. He stares up at me as I aim for his head. It's not silver, but a headshot will do it. He's not a pureblood.

"Accidents happen," Vincent murmurs, and I see him nod once, giving me permission.

"Rodney." Meg's voice catches my attention, and I look at her. "It won't bring her back." I falter and my mind flashes to decades ago, killing those who murdered Claudia and mom. Only pain followed. I swallow hard as Meg's gaze softens.

"You kill him, Rodney, and the moment you leave I tell PSB, NIIA, CDC, every *fucking* medical center that Brenda exists," Freyja threatens.

I freeze and then see the horror on Brenda's face. "You wouldn't."

"How fast do you think it'll take for them to grab her?" She straightens. "Obtain the last *living* experiment of Traloski, his creation they tried to stop. To learn she's immune to everything. Oh, they'll do *anything* to have her."

Vincent intervenes, "Her parents—"

"Except, Brenda would never let them destroy the city," she sneers, glaring at Brenda, who's gone very still. "No, she has a heart. How many would die, innocents, for her? Or instead, I could contact some daemons who'd *love* to know she exists. There's a colony up north—"

Something primal inside me snaps, enraged. I shoot Sebastian in the groin, and he screams. Freyja's eyes flare, and I aim the gun at her head as I move toward her. She steps back as I snarl, and Vincent joins me with his gun trained on her, too.

"You wouldn't fucking dare," Vincent warns.

"Give me what I want, and they'll never know." She flicks her gaze between us. "Or shoot me. *If* you can."

Meg gasps, and I glance over to see lightning at Brenda's fingertips. It's red. My gaze moves up to hers, finding the large scars across her face. There's a tightness around my heart, imagining her becoming an experiment again. Chained. And then I look at Meg, who watches us with wide eyes. The constriction in my chest worsens as I imagine her locked away somewhere for good. Caged. Both their fears coming to life. Including mine.

Gone.

I tremble with rage. Freyja doesn't flinch as I step toward her, barrel aimed at her temple. "Give me what I am *owed*," she threatens. "Or kill me."

"Don't," I snarl. "Because for them Christine, I will become the monster you think I am. For *them*, I'll do anything."

A flash of hurt crosses her gaze, hardening again as she steps forward, pressing the hot barrel against her forehead. I keep my hands steady, staring into her green eyes and seeing the hatred in her. The woman who almost got Meg and my Pack killed. Ordered Victoria's death. Betraying old friends, creating a rift that can't be mended. I should pull the trigger, and say fuck it to morals to protect them, but I see the young girl from years ago suddenly.

Hurt and anger, lashing out in pain. Grief. And a part of me understands. *"It was the mercy in your eyes."*

I whisper, "What are you so willing to die for? To hurt us. To turn your back on us completely?"

"You. Blowing up that center caused DiNardi to get killed because you pissed off those agents. *You* killed him."

"I pressed the button, not him," Brenda says.

"Doesn't matter!" Freyja argues. "Antoni had what I needed, then was blown up before I got it. All because of you."

"People were being snatched from the street," Brenda growls. "Turned into ghouls against their will, and it was done in *your* building. Blame yourself for helping the wrong beings."

Freyja glowers, keeping her piercing gaze on me. I don't want to pull the trigger, not have it end this way, but the fear of losing Brenda or Meg screams in my head. Their names etched in stone. I glimpse at Vincent, whose expression is harsh and menacing. I can't…I can't pull the trigger. I swallow hard as his gaze finds mine as I barely nod and step back.

"I know where Antoni kept everything," Meg says suddenly, stepping forward as Brenda tries to keep her back. "It was embedded in the POS system at *4D*. I don't know what you wanted, but he had everything on there. Lists, names, accounts, and more I never saw. If you want what he had so badly, go get it yourself."

"And I should believe you, even with so much rubble left behind?"

"Yes," Meg states. "Because I have no reason to lie, and I'm not letting either of them kill you. They'll hate themselves for it, and I won't let you do that to them. You may be cruel and unfeeling, but they're not." I look at her, finding steady brown eyes. "Password to get through are the coordinates to his first club, *SkyRoll.* Then input the year, 1923. Whatever you want will be on those computers."

"Where?" Freyja questions.

"PSB got hold of them," I answer. "Go to them since you seem to have a habit of helping the wrong people."

"And I should believe you? Let you all go? I don't think so."

"Then let's make you a believer," Brenda speaks suddenly. "You want to play, Christine? Fine. Let's up the damn ante."

"What are you—"

"Out me, and I out your real name to every federal agency, government official, and major business in and outside the U.S. I will tear down your carefully crafted *secret* identity and bring the courts to *you*. You may have ties, but so do I. I've learned to play nice the last couple of months, and Midnight has been cranky. Especially because half-breeds went missing, and you're partially to blame."

"Midnight wouldn't. He owes me," Freyja argues.

"He still works for me," Vincent adds.

"Yet, *she's* threatening me," Freyja says, looking between the two of us. "Look at you both. Chained at the neck by them. The degenerate bloodsucker and the simpering mutt."

My gaze meets Vincent's, and he smiles wickedly, turning toward Brenda. I follow his gaze to her and Meg, both ready to strangle Freyja if she doesn't shut her mouth soon. Brenda's eyes glow and her hands clench. A small grin forms on my face as I realize something.

Not everything had to be on my shoulders, not when two of those I protect are willing to take on the challenge. And are good at it. Leashed or not at least I'm not in a lonely glass tower. Alone. And thankfully, those two females are on *our* side.

"Call me mutt again," I say, keeping my gun steady and meeting her gaze. "Go on."

She sneers, "Mutt—"

Brenda's claws punch out, and Freyja's eyes widen as red lightning flickers at her hands. Her voice is filled with menace and warning, "Threaten me all you like *Christine*, I'll take on the damn challenge, but do not insult my family. Or I'm gonna give you a history lesson as to why you don't fuck with the Cuorebellas." Freyja's breath hitches.

Well, wouldn't Alanzo be proud.

"Take the damn intel Meg is giving," Vincent says. "We're telling the truth. Walk away."

She cocks her head at me, then looks at Meg. "Fine. But *you* stay in the Underground since you seem to love it down there. Otherwise…word may slip out about Antoni and his helper." Brenda growls, the lightning sparking more. "She stays below, I won't come for her. Promise."

I flick my gaze to Meg as she says, "Deal."

Warning twists in my gut as Freyja glares at me, but I pull my gun back along with Vincent. I walk away, quickly getting to Meg, who lets out a shaky breath. I wrap an arm around her shoulders, breathing in her scent, and hope it eases the trembling in my chest. Something doesn't feel right, but none of this does. Brenda retracts her claws as Vincent adjusts his jacket, moving away from Freyja.

"Good luck grabbing the agents," Freyja taunts. "They're nowhere near neutral zones."

Brenda chuckles, jutting her head toward the collection of liquor. "I have human friends now, remember?"

The she-devil growls as Vincent grabs some scotch, handing a bottle to Brenda, who says casually, "You owe us for a Mating present. And ruining my day."

"And she's drunk half my supply," Vincent adds.

"Have not."

"I have cameras, sweet cheeks."

"Ricky made a bet."

Vincent grabs a box of cigars, holding them up as Freyja scowls at him. He looks at Brenda. "Interested in fire play?"

"I don't want to taste you crispy, bloodsucker," Brenda scoffs.

I look down as Meg tightens her grip on my side. She watches the other two in disbelief. Yeah, they handle situations weirdly. I grunt at them to hurry up, heading for the door. Vincent starts to walk out with his "prizes" and shoots me a look. "He Pack?"

"No."

He pulls out his gun, shooting Alfred in the legs again. Vincent smiles ruefully, heading into the lobby as Alfred groans and watches with harsh eyes. I lead Meg out, pausing at the door as Brenda turns to Freyja.

"One last thing…Christine." She cocks her head, and her tone darkens. "I do still have my heart, but if I find out you knew the entire time what those men were planning, what they were doing…you'll realize some secrets even *you* can't keep."

She slams the doors just as glass shatters and there's a muffled scream.

We get on the elevator and Brenda opens her bottle to take a long swig. She slumps against Vincent's chest, and she mumbles to him, "We should've run away."

He kisses her head. "You had homework, sweetheart." She scoffs.

I hold Meg close to me, and she looks up as I give her a faint smile. She leans her head against my chest. "Thank you both," Meg whispers.

"No problem," Brenda says as Vincent puts an arm around her. "Just another fucking Tuesday."

"It's not Tuesday," I say.

"Close enough" She waves me off.

"Does this mean…its over?" Meg asks.

Brenda smirks mischievously and I give her a look. She takes another swig, handing the bottle to Vincent as she pulls out her phone. "Better late than never to collect."

"You mean the agents?" I ask.

She dials and it rings a few times before she says, "Rise and shine, Sammy! You owe me twenty bucks. I didn't kill anyone."

CHAPTER 33
THE "GOOD" GUYS

A distant horn goes off, echoing as I lean against the dock seawall and look up as Vincent opens a warehouse door. He drags chains behind him, prepping for our "guests" that are on their way. As another horn blares in the late night, Brenda sighs beside me. Meg is back at *Mountain Edge*; she didn't need to be here for this next part. I glimpse over at Brenda, who adjusts her jacket as a cold breeze comes. I put my arm around her shoulders, pulling her close.

"So…you talked to Meg?" I grunt, nodding. "What's the plan?"

"Take our time, figure shit out," I murmur. "Hopefully get Mated in the future." She hums, and I let out a long sigh. "I'm sorry for being an ass."

"Don't be. Vinny needed the workout."

"Brenda, I fucked up."

"Yeah, and so did I," she says, poking my chest. "It's okay. I mean, don't make it a habit crashing through doors and grappling, but it's okay. And I'm sorry for not realizing, and practically having you send me to my death with your explosives after everything you went through."

"You were…hurting and wanted to stop others from hurting. I get it. Cause so did I." I kiss her head. "Just don't make it a habit." She gives me a thumbs up and I chuckle, tightening my hold on her. "You know, you were pretty scary earlier."

"Learned from the best."

"So, your father?"

She snorts, snuggling closer as another cold breeze comes. "Well, Ricky's too much like Ma to be the next 'Kraken,' and Joey's the 'Diablo of the Underground.'"

"Please tell me you're not serious."

"Please help me make fun of him, so he drops the idea." We laugh softly as something clangs inside the warehouse. Bringing out all the stops, good.

Brenda breathes in deeply, pushing closer to me. "What's gonna happen to Victoria's body?"

My throat constricts, and I take a shuddering breath. "Not sure yet."

The winter breeze gets worse, and I bring Brenda into a full hug, shielding her from the wind. She wraps her arms around me, and whispers, "I'm so sorry, Rodney."

"Me too, lil sis."

I hold her close, breathing deeply as I look out over the freezing water. The hurt turns into a numbness, but the screams don't come. After all that's happened, Brenda still helps keep some shadows away, but not all.

"Meg suggested," I start, clearing my throat. "She...uh, suggested I talk to Alanzo about things to...to help. But I don't know if...would he?"

"Course he would, but I'll talk to him." She hugs me harder. I nod against her head, taking a long breath. "Always got your back."

"I love you, lil sis."

"I love you, Lassie."

She reaches up to kiss my cheek, snuggling back against me as some snow is picked up from the wind. She grumbles about the cold, and I chuckle at her. I see Vincent leaning against the doorway, watching us.

"Want me to lighten the mood?" She asks.

"Do I have a choice?"

"How would the Pack feel about rebuilding *The Lounge*? Cause, y'all are fucking fast. Vampires suck at remodeling apparently. Could give you a discount on Scooby snacks."

"I'm throwing you into the harbor."

She yelps as I act like I'm going to toss her in, but headlights appear at the end of the dock. I let go as Vincent approaches, and she adjusts her glasses, sticking her tongue out at me. The car moves slowly, and Vincent mutters, "About damn time."

"They were in Upper Manhattan, shush," Brenda says, poking his shoulder. "And he had to smuggle Gunther through the zones."

The car comes and turns around, parking next to us. Louis gets out, wearing his usual jacket. Well, now I feel left out. He folds his arms, looking at me. "How the hell you ain't freezing?"

I glance at my kilt and dark flannel, then smirk, "Wearing it traditionally, too."

He raises his brows, shakes his head, and turns to Brenda. "Never have me do that again. Even with Gunther, that was a bitch."

"Aw, come on Sherlock, admit it, you had fun. Even got to see Clifford the Big Red Dog."

He scoffs. "Not that much fun after finding out Christine Veldastein is Freyja. Are you fucking kidding me?"

"I wish," Brenda grumbles as Vincent pops the trunk, and there are muffled voices. I join him, snarling at the two agents tied up and gagged. Vincent slams the trunk close.

"This is the part where I look away...right?" Louis asks, stepping back.

"Uh-huh." Brenda pats his shoulder. "And where you and I get midnight margaritas. There's a cute bar down the harbor."

The vampire and I exchange a look. "Sweet cheeks."

"Pops would ground me for months if he found out I helped you...*acquire* information. You've got this, bosses," she says, kissing Vincent quickly. "And you two need bonding time. Aside from practicing MMA."

She is *not* leaving me alone with the bloodsucker after the long-ass day I've had.

"You buying?" Louis asks, zipping up his jacket.

"Oh, yeah, I owe you for helping Oliver and Company, but I still get my twenty bucks." She begins to walk away, leading him down the dock. "Call when you've tossed the leeches into the harbor."

She *is* fucking leaving me with the bloodsucker. "Lil sis."

"Sweet cheeks."

"Kiss and make-up, I don't need pictures!" She calls back. "Get your anger out on the fuckers and get along before you drive me batty. Have fun. Love ya!"

Louis smiles, following her as they disappear down the dock. I'm left alone with the vampire as horns blare in the distance and the water laps against the dockside. I take a deep breath, looking over to meet his crimson gaze.

This is punishment.

"Your fault she's conniving," I say, pointing at him and slamming the trunk open.

"I'm the charming best friend and Mate who gives her coffee," he counters. "You're her brother, what's your excuse?" The men mumble, trying to move further into the trunk. "Left or right?"

"Does it matter?"

"I'm trying to be courteous, given sweet cheeks thinks we need a buddy cop moment…Lassie."

This is *no way* how I saw my day going. I could be cuddled up with Meg right now. "Fuck off, I'll always despise you." I grab the left one, dragging him toward the warehouse.

"I thought it's because of my good looks and dental plan," he says, carrying his human. "No idea it was jealousy—"

"Shut up." I drop the agent, spinning on him. "It's not jealousy. It's your fucking cocky, sarcastic attitude like you're some fucking know-it-all."

"You dropped your human."

"Like that!"

"It's called humor, which sweet cheeks and your *Gaelach* seem to think you have."

"I do. You just annoy me." I pick up the agent, throwing him over my shoulder as he garbles under the gag. I stalk into the warehouse with Vincent close behind. "Want to know why?"

"Oh…yes, please…enlighten me," his deadpan tone makes me growl.

"You never fully deal with the consequences of your damn actions and somehow people don't fault you. They don't hold you accountable because it's you…fucking Vinny. You're like the annoying younger brother who gets away with everything, smiling over a lollipop. Oh, wait…you *are*."

I toss off the agent, pulling over a metal chair. The few lights hanging from the ceiling swing a little, next to some chains and hooks. There are a couple of tables with rope and other tools.

"You *honestly* think that?" Vincent asks, drops his agent in a chair, and then yanks a chain down to wrap around their torso.

I grab mine and plant him on the seat. "You never had responsibilities until Brenda showed up," I talk while tying them up. "Before that, you lounged about and caused trouble like a spoiled aristocrat. You whored yourself, gorged on blood, and let your older sister do all the work. How many times did she bail you out? How about Samuel saving your ass? And then when you could've walked away, leave…you didn't. You supposedly stayed for her, the only damn being you've ever given a shit about apparently. Fuck the rest of us."

"So, what if Brenda is?"

I turn, gesturing to the outside. "Some of us had family to provide for. A family to protect, along with every other Paranormal in the Underground. We worked and fought to keep it safe below, *earning* that shit. Losing beings along the way who deserved to be here."

He watches me with a frown. "And you don't think I did? Work or fought?"

"No. You suddenly got to succeed, and no one batted an eye. None of that time you wasted mattered, and then you got to protect *everyone*. Suddenly, you're who they call, even fucking me. While I spent my entire life trying to do the right thing, only to fucking…fail." I look away, taking a deep breath. "So, fine maybe it is jealousy and I'm angry at myself…because I find it unfair *you* got the happy ending."

"And not Claudia."

Anger coils in my gut as I shove my shirt off, tossing it onto the nearest table. Vincent quietly takes his jacket and shirt off, neatly folding them onto a table. I roll my eyes, then slap the agent to wake him up. He mumbles, going wide-eyed as I tighten his hands against his thighs.

"You didn't fucking fail," he says, and I stop. "We can't save everyone, even those close to us. But you, no…you didn't fail." I look down and see fearful eyes, snarling at him as he flinches. "And did you ever think I was trying to atone for my mistakes?"

"What?"

"I knew what the fuck I was." Vincent moves over, grabs the other end of his chain, and starts rising the agent off the ground. "I knew I was a degenerate to everyone. I made myself that way, so my father would leave me the fuck alone. Give up on me."

I scoff. "Try having one who doesn't give a damn about you. Almost killed several times in the past month, and he only showed up to yell, blame, undermine me, and no 'Get Well' card."

"I'll raise you…" he pauses, and then does it with the agent who squirms, "…try having a father who tried to kill you and your Mate."

"Try watching your sister die."

"Try watching your *mother* die."

"I *did*."

"But at least Fredrick didn't kill her in front of you," Vincent argues, locking the chain and shoves the man, making him swing. "Even though your parents hated each other, he didn't kill her. Mine *was*. And then I was left alone with a monster for two centuries."

"You had Anita! Unlike me, you got your sister, be grateful for that." I take some frustration out by jamming my claws into the agent's arms, who screams against his gag.

"Sure," Vincent scoffs. "The sister who cares *so* much that she tries to lock me up. Cage me like an animal? You lose your cool, no one bats an eye. *They* forgive you. Me? My own sister becomes terrified, waiting for me to become Bruno or my fucking grandfather. *Now* who doesn't have to deal with consequences?"

I stop and stare at him as he heaves, glaring at the man before him. "The rumors were true, then?"

"Yeah." He looks down at his hands, sneering at them. "Anita is all I have left of family, and she's waiting for me to snap. So, tell me, was Claudia ever scared of you?"

"No," I murmur.

"Then I'm fucking jealous you had a sister who loved you, unconditionally."

I huff, looking over at the agent who watches me with scrunched brows. "What the fuck you looking at? Forget who you stole from?" They shake their head, mumbling against the gag.

"Sounds like he's got shit to say," Vincent comments.

"Probably." I jut my head at his. "You think yours will? I want my explosives back before they blow up the damn Underground next."

Vincent's brows furrow, glaring at the man as he grabs his collar, and snarls, "They don't need fingers to talk, right?"

"Right."

"We'll start there." Both men thrash against their restraints. I unsheathe my claws, slice down, and cut off three fingers as the man screams and shakes. Vincent's man screams next, and I look over to see blood dripping down their body and his.

Vincent pauses, staring at the ring on his hand, covered in blood. "Brenda was the first to not look at me like I was a monster. I was raised to be used, become a prop and a replacement. Everyone kept their distance. Until Brenda. I won't apologize for finally being happy, but I'm sorry you lost part of yours. And at least you still have your family. You've always had the Pack, who are loyal to you and care. They stuck with you, even in the bad times, following you out of respect, not fear. So...I doubt they ever blamed you for what happened to Claudia or Cassandra."

I let out a long exhale, noticing both agents have gone quiet. They've passed out.

I look over at Vincent, and ask, "Anita really tried to lock you up?"

He nods, dropping his hand to his side. "Yeah," he sighs, running his bloody hand through his hair. "It's felt like all I ever had was Brenda in my corner, so I did everything I could to keep her safe." He looks over at me, giving a sympathetic look. "And from one fucked-up son to another, we're not failures because we choose not to become our fathers."

We hold each other's gazes and realization dawns on me. We're jealous of each other, one having something the other didn't have a chance to possess. A couple of sons with fucked-up fathers with god complexes. A typical Greek tragedy or some shit. Aren't we a damn pair?

"I'm not getting mushy with you," I state.

"Aw, did I bring a tear to your eye?"

He just *had* to ruin it. "You know what? You hit like a kitten."

"Right, and you're a real *danger floof*."

"Brenda had to give you backup," I retort, slapping the agent awake, who groans under the gag.

"I was *letting* you win."

"Yeah, fucking right."

"You're like sweet cheeks, needed to let out some steam," he says, punching his man awake. "She destroys my gun range; you destroy my office. Maybe I should turn *The Lounge* into a rage room."

"I'll ask Meg to make cupcakes as reconciliation."

"Chocolate ones?"

"Oh, so *those* are your favorite?" He slides his gaze to me. "Whatever you want, just don't let lil sis hire my damn Pack to rebuild your place."

"Deal." His agent garbles, and Vincent cocks his head at him, and then over to mine. "Want to chain yours up, too? Something tells me they'll squeal quickly, and I want to make this fun. Not shooting Freyja has worked me up."

"Same," I grumble, kicking the chair over and the agent grunts against the ground. "Not as kinky as you, but..." I grab a knife and tilt my head at him, "...they don't need legs to talk either, right?"

Both men start yelling, trying to thrash and get loose. Vincent plunges his claws into the man's arm, and he starts screaming louder against the gag. Vincent smiles, and says, "Limbs aren't required to talk. And I think we deserve some fun tonight."

I thrust my knife into the agent's leg, listening to him shriek. "Agreed."

———

"Explosives secured," Vinny says, hanging up the phone. "Gunther and Zane passed them off without a hitch."

I exhale, tapping the cigar on the wall next to me. "You sure about keeping them?"

"Lounge is already a shambles, if it blows, it'll add character," Vinny talks around his cigar.

I lay my head back against the brick, taking another long puff of the cigar Vinny acquired from Freyja. I stare at it, and ask, "Where did we go wrong with Christine? She was a good kid."

"She made her own decisions, and now we're stuck with a woman with grudges the length of the Mississippi River. Fingers crossed she finds what she wants and leaves us alone."

We sigh, sitting against the warehouse, covered in blood from the now, dead agents. They're wrapped in pieces, waiting to be tossed into the harbor. Vinny suggested a smoke break, waiting for the explosives to arrive in the Underground. He was right about them speaking quickly, little too quickly. It was the truth at least, everything was accounted for, and hidden in the rubble of the center we blew months ago. Smartasses. Damn place is gonna be the bane of my existence.

It's quiet in the late evening up here, the moon shining with waves lapping at the docksides. Serene almost with snow fluttering over everything. Staggering difference from fifteen minutes ago.

I think of Meg as I stare at the moon, how her brown eyes would shimmer. There's an ache inside, realizing with the deal she agreed to, she may never see the moon again. But she'd be safe below away from Freyja, the human mobs, and police. I want to put it all behind us, except I'm not sure what to do next.

I glance at Vinny, watching the water and puffing his cigar. "We're not friends."

He flicks his gaze to me, and says, "Thank goodness, I have a reputation. Friends with a werewolf? What would grandma-ma say?"

"How has lil sis not killed you yet?"

"She missed." He taps his thigh.

"Bullshit."

"Must be the adorableness, then."

"Only to her."

"That's all that matters." He smiles softly, his comment serious. I huff, and he raises a brow. "Question, Pongo?"

I look at my cigar, feeling the rolled tobacco between my fingers. The question bubbles in my throat, wanting to ask, to know. That old part of me tells me to keep my mouth shut, don't talk about it, and yet...I've opened up about other things. Why not with him? Even if he annoys me.

"Brenda was right, when she told me she could hold her own, and she can," I murmur. "Probably our fault, teaching her everything, but...do you worry about losing her?"

"Every fucking moment." I stare at him, and he takes a long draw of his cigar. "That's the thing with someone owning most of your soul, you always worry you'll lose them. I don't know what it's like losing a sibling, but I imagine the hollowness doesn't truly leave. Never filled again. That's a terrifying thought, centuries of emptiness."

"What do you do about it?"

"Keep protecting her, believe in yourself," he smirks. "Even if it's not enough. And tonight was...almost not enough."

I inhale sharply. "If Freyja hadn't agreed—"

"She'd be in the bags with them," he answers bluntly. "Fuck the past, and what we had before."

"Yeah, was almost on that edge, too."

"The fear of losing a loved one makes you do crazy ass shit; I should know. So, fighting with me, I get it. Just give me a five-minute prep next time."

I snort, then ask, "How'd you know it was Brenda? That you loved her?" He quirks a brow. "No funny business, just asking."

"Isn't Meg your *Gaelach*? Some automatic thing?"

"It's not exactly like that." I scratch my head, wincing, and glare at my claws, then smirk as I look up at the moon. "But when I realized I couldn't fight it, it felt like a train wrecked my body. Dancing with her, every time she touched me it was like those damn fairytales humans talk about. She felt like home, warm and inviting and free. She's like this light, comforting which puts you in this trance and I don't have to keep putting walls up. Moonlight shining through the darkness."

"You're more romantic than me."

I snort, and he shrugs. "Your turn."

"Her and I getting drunk when I found out I was boss, that's when I realized." Laughter erupts from me, and he joins. "See? Not romantic. Even asked her to get naked with me, and she declined."

"Imagine that."

"Truly appalling." He grins, staring into the water as his expression changes into something fond. "She's a blazing star, filled with dangerous light and knowledge. No matter when, she's shining. A wonderous creature with a heart and hope for the world. And my entire being feels alive with her, keeping me breathing and making the darkness not so secluded as before."

"Bullshit on me being more romantic."

He snorts as he stands up, flicking his cigar away. "Well, if that's anywhere close to how Meg makes you feel, I promise to help you protect her. From one Mate to another."

"We're not Mated."

"Oh, please you'll be Mated in like six months. Can I be best man?"

"No, and we're gonna…take it slow."

He sighs dramatically, and nods towards the bodies. "Should dump them."

"Hungry?"

"Not after what they revealed." He looks in disgust. "I've hoped in the past century fewer humans would become villainous wretches. And better codenames. *Agent X*, seriously? That's who they were taking orders from?"

"Humans suck at nicknames." And club names. I stand up and toss my cigar. "We know *someone* is controlling some of PSB's actions now, too bad not black ops. Easier to deal with. Now we've got politics."

"We'll have to be careful, there may be more than this Agent X, trying to recreate that serum or worse," Vinny grumbles, grabbing a bag. "A fucking Bond movie scenario."

"We'll find them," I say, grabbing the other bag. "You don't think they're the same ones who caused all those issues twenty years ago?"

Vinny pauses. "Long time for humans."

"Not if this X guy just started in PSB, that's enough time to get to a director position if human," I explain. "Start accumulating people after finding Traloski, those with mutual interests."

"And someone erased most of Traloski's records." Vinny scrunches his brows. "We'll need more help, Midnight's too far. Perhaps get another contact on the inside of PSB."

I think, and suggest, "Contact Beckham. He'd know who'd be able to handle it."

He looks at me with surprise, grinning. "Look at you Lassie, giving good suggestions and working outside your Pack."

I snarl lightly, rolling my eyes as we continue dragging the bags to the water. He tosses his in first, and it begins to sink. Suddenly long-fingered, webbed hands grab it. Pale hair vanishes into the darkness of the water.

"I thought the nixies left," I murmur, exchanging a glance with Vinny.

"So did I."

I toss my bag next, and another nixie grabs it, yanking the bundle into the depths. Fuck, I owe Zane fifty bucks.

"Maybe Brenda's fear of water is warranted," Vinny mutters. "Remind me never to go fucking swimming."

We stare at the quiet water a moment longer, and back at each other and say in unison, "Shared dumping ground?" We shake hands, backing away from the edge. I'd rather deal with hoards of ghouls than nixies.

"Speaking of sharing," Vinny says as we walk back to the warehouse. I watch him carefully, wondering where the fuck he's going with this. "With the prospect of agents determined to kill, control, and destroy it may be good if we combine our forces."

"Oh?"

"We help protect the Underground, share resources...more willingly than before, and perhaps we won't have to keep blowing up buildings. The city is a delicate creature. With more than a few humans up here playing Dr. No, it'll be beneficial not to fight with each other."

"You trying to make a deal with me?"

"Being smart." He stops and cocks his head. "And perhaps, undo what our fathers have done."

I work my jaw, knowing he's right and don't want to admit it. We've broken down some barriers, but working with him? Except, I know I'd have suggested the same damn thing. Lately, I've realized I'm not cut out for this detective, mystery bullshit. And Vinny knows the beings who are.

I sigh, hold my hand out, and shake his. "You still annoy me."

"We can talk about it over tea." He picks up his clothes. I groan at him, moving to grab my own. "This could be the start of a beautiful…"

"Don't say it."

"…partnership. Remember, we're not friends."

I scoff but hide a smile as I put on my bloody shirt. Vinny stretches and mutters, "I'm starving."

"Nothing like a long day of making deals with the she-devil, getting shot at, and torturing humans to work up an appetite." Vinny grins wickedly, and I know he's gonna make a crude joke. Suddenly, there's a shout in the distance.

We turn, seeing Brenda and Louis run for us. She yells, "We've got a problem!"

Oh, what *else* can happen tonight?

Vinny gets to her quickly. "What's wrong?"

"Got a call from a buddy," Louis says between breaths. "Police have been called to collect a human from the Underground, it's Meg. PSB liaison will be with them, and if she doesn't come back to Topside, they'll send more."

I growl, "How the fuck—"

"Someone sent an anonymous call," Louis says, typing something on his phone. "Saying she was kidnapped and held hostage, warrant is being pushed now."

"What? She agreed to stay."

"Doesn't matter," Brenda says. "She's human and won't be able to claim asylum below. She's not claimed, doesn't have Paranormal blood, or ties to the Underground. It's like foster parents not being able to keep foster kids because bio-parents claimed custody."

"Who the fuck are the parents then?" I ask.

"Don't know, anonymous tips are protected," Louis answers. "Buddy called cause he's working late and thought I could go, but I don't have jurisdiction access with the PSB Human Liaison Branch."

I look at the other two, and Vinny grumbles, "We should have killed her."

"She wouldn't have broken the deal," Brenda argues, and we look at her with exasperated expressions. "Fine, she was gonna turn Rodney and me in, all that jazz, but we all know she holds her deals. Her reputation means everything to her. Maybe another loophole—"

"Agent X," I mutter, and Vinny scowls.

"Agents disappeared, got fidgety," Vinny suggests. "Probably knew Meg's involvement, not risking her to reveal PSB fucked up the operation with DiNardi."

"Getting rid of loose ends," I murmur. Brenda looks between us. "Later."

"Didn't you say Meg was part of the Pack?" Vinny asks.

Brenda and I shake our heads. "Honorary, not officially."

Louis chimes in, "How long does it take? I can ask to hold off until morning."

"Weeks," Brenda replies. "She has to go through a tribune."

"Mating then?" He asks, pointing between Brenda and Vinny.

"Official Mating takes days, needing to be approved by the Pack and the courts," I explain. My mind spirals as I try to think of something. If Meg comes back to Topside, Freyja will send the human mobs after her. The Underground Mafia can't protect her up here.

"We've got a couple of hours to think of something," Louis says.

"You're being quite helpful," Vinny comments.

Louis looks at him, moving closer to Brenda, but keeps his voice level. "From what McLycan and Brenda told me, if the mobs or police get a hold of Meg, she'll either die or have as much freedom as a caged sparrow. And it sounds like she's already been through enough."

"Even if it means the intel she knows could take down the mobs?" Vinny asks, and Brenda jabs his side. He continues frowning at Louis.

"Yes," Louis states.

I glimpse at Louis, who meets my gaze and doesn't flinch.

"We can smuggle her out of the city," Vinny suggests. "Make sure she doesn't land in any of their hands." His eyes meet mine, and his soften. Gone. She'd be gone.

"We can wait until things calm down," Brenda adds. "Joey can get her to Keir's ranch, out of the state. They'll never find her; you know Keir will take care of her. And then we—"

"What?" I ask, turning toward her. "I wait months to see her again, *maybe*? We both know the Pack won't initiate her unless she's in the Underground, Keir's not Pack. And if we try to go the adopted route by Paranormal, Freyja will come for her the moment she comes back to make it official. Or worse, Freyja will bar it, sending police back down to grab Meg on the same grounds of kidnapping and coercion."

"Beckham can help," Brenda says.

"It'll be months, maybe years," I whisper. "She'll become a fugitive every time she tries to come back, and I can't do that to her. Not when there's no guarantee there'll be an end to it. Unless... Joey makes her disappear with the other survivors."

Her face crumbles at my suggestion, and my own heart feels like I've cracked it. She grumbles, scratching her head, starting to pace. "There has to be a way around..."

She talks out loud, while Louis and Vinny watch wordlessly. We all know she can't stay in the Underground; she'll always be on edge as we try to hide her. Or PSB will use her to arrest me or the Pack next, and that would break her heart. She'd give herself up like tonight.

I look up at the moon shining down, swallowing hard, knowing I'll have to let her go. I promised to keep her safe, never to go back to another mob boss. Joey taking her would give her that, freedom. Never caged again. *"Give her a choice,"* Alanzo's words echo in my head. I stare up at the moon, almost seeing her among the flowers out in Montana, all that wildlife. Free and she wouldn't be locked in the Underground forever from Freyja. I could do it, let her go. But then, I remember her arms around me, holding me. A strong gentleness I've craved for centuries, safe from the shadows.

I don't want to let her go.

Vinny catches my attention, flicking his gaze down to his hand, and I see the ring on his finger. I go still, realizing what he's implying. *She isn't claimed.*

"She's human," I rasp.

"So was Brenda," he whispers, and my heart pounds mercilessly as the idea takes root. There's one way she could stay, overriding the courts and law, keeping her with me in the Underground. "Do you have to bite her?"

I shake my head. "Hybrid form."

"Would that hurt her?" I give him a look, and nods once. "If she says no, we'll get her out of New York. We'll figure shit out later."

Brenda stops, looking between us. "What are you—"

"You explained Claim Mating to Meg, right?" I ask, and her eyes widen, nodding. "Call the tavern that I'm coming and about the police. How much time do I've got?"

"Couple hours," Louis answers. "I can try to get more."

"You'll need a third party to confirm her scent," Vinny says quickly. "Can't be Pack, who knows who PSB will bring."

"I've got that," Brenda says, taking her phone out. "Fucking go, Rodney, we'll take care of it."

"Counting on you, lil sis." I start running toward the tunnels.

"Run, McLycan, Run!"

I sprint down the dock, racing for *Mountain Edge*, hoping with every fiber of my being I don't have to send her away.

Tell me you're mine.

CHAPTER 34
I'M YOURS TO TAME & LOVE

I arrive at *Mountain Edge,* slamming through the doors barely noticing the relief on the wolves' faces as they get out of my way. I pass Marcus, Gunther, and Zane, racing up the stairs as they prepare the tavern for the police's arrival. Delilah meets me at the second landing.

"She's in your apartment," she whispers. "Knows they're coming."

"If she decides to leave, be prepared to get her to Joey," I speak low.

"What? But she's your—"

"I know, but she fulfilled our deal, and then some." My gaze meets hers, and she nods stiffly. "I'll give her a choice, but I won't make her stay this time."

She grasps my shoulder as I struggle to keep my composure. "I'll keep everyone below. Give you time, no matter the decision. Gunther will come up when they arrive."

I nod as I move up the stairs, trying to breathe as my lungs tremble for air. *Tell me I'm yours.* I pause at my door, then walk in, and lock the door behind me.

Meg stands at the round window, staring outside as lights create delicate shadows across her face. I begin to memorize every detail in case I have to draw her from memory next. Remember her. Suddenly, those long nights feel hollower.

She turns, hugging herself close as we meet each other halfway. Her gaze flicks over my face, pursing her lips in thought. I inhale her scent, trying to calm myself as it wraps around me, calling for home.

Her brows scrunch, staring at me as she steps forward. "Rodney, I..."

"Let me say something first," I rasp, taking her hands. "You've got a choice. I won't force you to stay or leave. It'll be difficult trying to stay, they'll keep trying to come for you unless you agree to Claim Mate with me." Her eyes widen as her breath hitches. "I won't force you to do that. I won't force you to stay Underground, away from everything above for me...but deals a deal, darling. You kept your promise, and so will I, even if that means you must leave. Wherever you choose to live, I'll help grant that."

"But...I could come back, right?"

I swallow hard, placing my hand against her cheek. "I know we agreed to try, but it won't look like what we'd hoped. If you wanted to leave, try in the future...it'd be months. Maybe years."

"You'd wait that long?" I nod stiffly. "But...but wait, they said being separated from your *Gaelach* is agony. I'd be...gone, and you'd be—"

I cup her face, looking into her earthen brown eyes, and find clarity. All that matters is her safety, by my side or not. The warmth from her steadies me, and I speak gently, "I swore weeks ago I'd make sure you'd be free. If you'd asked, truly, to go I'd have sent you to the other side of the country. I'd have sent you wherever, safe and happy. That's all I cared about. You alive." I come in close, breathing in that warm scent that reminds me of spring. "I will not be my father. I will not make you stay where you don't wish to be. No matter how much pain I'd be in, it'll never compare to knowing you'd be gone from this world."

She reaches up, stroking my cheek and I lean into her touch. In her gaze, I see home. The hills of Ireland that once gave me strength. Gardens and pastures, cascading through twilight and freedom. Her gaze pierces my soul, giving a final comfort from the darkness.

"Understand this, Megara," I murmur, smiling affectionately. "I love you with every piece of my soul, and you'll always be my Moonlight in the darkest nights. When I feel the loneliest, you will be the colors I can never draw. Every long night, I'll remember your gentleness in the dark. You will be the first light of my mornings, and the scent of fresh pastries made with lavender, citrus, and honey. And if I have to, I will wait a thousand years more for you. *You* own your freedom, not me."

Tears form in her eyes, spilling as she tries to blink them away. I swipe my fingers over them, kissing her forehead tenderly as my throat constricts. "You gave me safety from my shadows, my darling. I will love you wherever you desire to be."

"I…I love you, Rodney."

"Whatever your decision, it's yours."

She pulls back, searching my face as her hand traces down my jaw to my throat. Her chin begins to quiver and my heart thunders fearfully. Finally, she says, "You said I'd see spring."

Something clenches my chest, making it hard to breathe. She tilts her head, then softly pulls me down for a kiss. I suppress the sob forming in my throat as I cradle her head, kissing her for the final time. Every piece I won't forget, searing her into my soul as she presses her body against mine. Meg's tongue trails over my lip, and I open to taste her fully. My breathing becomes ragged, clutching her as she kisses me for what may be the last time.

She breaks it, and murmurs, "And I want to see spring here with you."

My heart stops. "What?"

She pokes my nose lightly. "I'm not leaving you alone ever again."

"Meg—"

"You were going to let Freyja imprison you, so I'd be free," she says, tears streaming down her face. "You've given me a sense of home here, a family, and safety. You have a heart of gold and are kind, and patient. I love you, and I found my freedom here…with you, skeletons and all. Why would I not choose you?"

My heart swells, catching my breath as I embrace her, trembling. She wraps her arms around my neck, allowing me to bury my face into her neck as tears fall from my eyes. They tumble onto her shoulder as she clutches my head.

"I'm staying, why are you crying?"

"Relief. Joy...fucking name it," I murmur, moving to kiss her and she laughs against my mouth. The sound makes me grin, then reality hits. I break the kiss, glancing at the clock. "Meg, we don't have much time and I apologize if this next part feels... unromantic."

"Oh, *this* wasn't romantic enough for you?" She points at my shirt and kilt, and I look down to grimace at the blood. "Looking like a rat dragged you from the sewers?" I eye her, and she grins. I pick her up, and she yelps. "Rodney, put me down."

"No, you said yes."

"That's not how this works."

"It's exactly how this works." I kiss her neck, and she sighs as I walk us into the bathroom. "Not Claim Mating you covered in... work."

"Not even gonna try saying paint, huh?"

"I work with charcoal."

"Could've tried."

"It's paint," I say deadpan.

She almost falls out of my arms laughing, and I nuzzle her neck, biting softly. She bats at me as I set her down and go to turn on the shower. I need to wash this damn blood off me, and I need a precursor session before the actual Mating. She was reactive to my growls before, but it's an entirely different thing being fucked in hybrid form.

The large shower heats as the water falls from the ceiling, creating a rain effect. Meg starts to undress with me, flinging bloodied clothes to the hamper and dropping my kilt. It falls to the ground, and Meg pauses in her underwear. I smirk as she asks, "You weren't wearing underwear since *Donny's*?"

I shake my head, gently turning her around and unclasp her bra, kissing her shoulder. She shudders, bending over to take her underwear off. I don't keep myself from staring at her ass, moving my eyes over her curvaceous body and dimples on her thighs.

Excitement thunders through me, knowing I get to worship her soon for forever. She turns, quirking a brow as I step into the shower, gesturing for her to follow. The water falls over my skin, watching it stream down her own as I start washing the blood off. The crimson disappears down the drain. Halfway through, I kiss her briefly, sweeping back her wet hair.

"Few things with Claim Mating," I say, then start sliding the washcloth down her breasts. "One, no condoms."

She swallows and nods her head. "I got a shot six months ago, good for another four. Unless werewolf sperm—"

"It'll still work. For both reasons." I kiss her nose quickly, and she scrunches it. "Second, when I tell you to, repeat a phrase after me." I switch to Noctora. *"My eternal, Claimed Mate."*

She tries a few times, and then gets it. "I'm taking more language lessons."

"Who taught you the other phrase?"

"Carmen." She winks at me, and I smile, helping wash more of her body and rinsing the last of the blood away. "Anything else?" She hums when I touch her breasts again, moving my hands over her stomach and hips.

"One more thing." I tilt her head up, gripping her to become flush against me. "I have to be in hybrid form." Her brows shoot up.

I've only had sex in my hybrid form with other werewolves, no idea what it's like with a human or how dangerous it could be. I'll be damned determined not to hurt her.

I watch her carefully, and then slowly Meg's scent shifts, reminding me of the first time she saw me naked. Arousal. She stares at my chest, flicking her gaze down. Interesting.

"Darling," I say, stepping forward for her to back against the wall. She swallows hard, biting her lip. "Want to tell me something?"

She places her hands firmly on my chest, keeping her gaze from mine. I take her chin gently, making her look at me as her mouth becomes a thin line. So, it's not just the growling she's turned on by. Oh, she's fucking perfect.

"Here I thought it'd be a problem." I place my hands above her head, water streaming down my back.

"I didn't say anything."

"Your face did."

"Aren't we in a hurry?"

"Not that much."

"Rodney."

"Meg," I whisper against her ear, and she shivers. "As much as I adore your *curiosity* for the main event, you'll need help adjusting. It's not just my height that gets bigger...*darling*."

She whimpers, her breath hitching as I nip at her skin. She grabs my shoulders, arching her back as I lick the water from her skin, moving down her chest. I circle my tongue around her nipple, sucking, and moving to the other as I bring my hand to massage the other. She moans and carnal desire wraps around my spine into a hot, needing want. Her nipples harden as I bite gently, pinching the other as I move further down.

I get on my knees, gazing up at her with a smug grin. She grips my shoulder as I lick my tongue over her sex, and she gasps. Flinging her head back, I circle her clit with my thumb, careful with my nails. I haven't trimmed them, so this calls for other means of getting her ready. My tongue is perfect.

I clutch one of her breasts, squeezing her nipple as my tongue flicks, entering her. A groan leaves me as I taste her, pressure building as my cock throbs. My body aches for her, wanting to take her, but I continue to suck harder, wanting her to come first. Sparks fly down my spine as she tugs at the fur on my shoulders, pushing herself close to my mouth. I press her against the wall as my tongue thrusts inside her, tasting the heat that pours from her and a snarl bubbles up in my chest. Her legs shake, and I lick upward, nipping at the folds lightly. She groans again, yanking at my fur as her mouth opens in ecstasy. Grinning wickedly, I know what will undo her. I press my mouth against her, holding her firmly against me.

I growl.

Meg lets out a scream, pushing herself toward me as I pin her against the wall with my arms. I do it again, the growl vibrating against her sex, and she yells, "Fuck! Rodney! Fu—!"

She cums on my tongue, almost bending over me as she orgasms as I keep her upright. I lick up the last of her cum, humming and smiling to myself. I leave kisses over her skin, moving up her thick thighs, the curves of her stomach, ample breasts, and finally her lips. Completely divine.

"That was the warm-up, darling."

She pants slightly, holding onto me to stand. "You better hurry up before I lose feeling in my legs then."

"As you wish." I reach under her, grab her ass and lift her. I press her back against the wall, wrapping her legs around me. Keeping an arm under her rear, I position my cock to enter her and kiss her neck. My tongue trails through the water and sweat across her skin. She moans as I slowly enter, her muscles tightening around my dick and the pressure in my groin twitches with need. I groan from the pleasure that already threatens to wreck me, her heat surrounding me.

"Rodney," she rasps.

"I've got you, darling," I murmur, thrusting myself into her.

I pull back and plunge forward, driving deep as we both shout. I snarl low, parts of me pulsing, raging with desire down my spine. Fuck. The heat snaps through me and I pull back, thrusting into her. She grasps my shoulders, clutching me as I drive my hips forward. Her muscles clench, and I groan against her shoulder, shaking. Meg's nails dig into me, and I grunt, trying to maintain control as ecstasy begins to surge from my core. The wave of pleasure starts to crest, and I stop abruptly, ceasing the oncoming pleasure before it throws me.

"Hold on," I tell her. I turn the shower off and walk out while keeping her attached to me. She holds on and I groan as she moves a little. Damn, she feels too good.

"Trouble…Sirius?" She bites my ear.

"You'll pay for that."

She does it again, tightening her legs which makes my cock sink deeper inside her. I almost stumble, surprised at the shock-wave she's caused. I bite the top of her breasts, and she yelps as I drop her on the bed. The loss of her warmth is jarring, but it's enough to put me back in control. I still have to fucking shift.

Meg looks up at me expectantly, opening her legs a little and I want to fall back on my knees for her. I grasp her ankles, moving my hands over her calves, dimpled thighs and hips. I lean over, placing a kiss in the middle of her chest, trailing my tongue to her throat.

"You ready?" I ask.

She nods her head, and I quirk a brow. "Yes, Rodney."

"Turn over, darling." She pinches her brows, and I gesture for her to do so. She huffs, turning over, getting on her hands and knees as I grab lube from the bedside table. I cover my throbbing dick with it as she eyes me, and I wink at her. I stare at her ass a moment once I get behind her again, admiring the view that is the length of her back and fallen wet hair.

"I want to see you," she whispers.

"Giving you time to adjust first," I answer, lining my cock up with her entrance. "And for other precautions," I mumble to myself as she wiggles under my touch. I rub the back of her thighs, feeling her soft skin.

"Is it really that...oh, fuck me," she moans as I enter her again, clutching the sheets.

I chuckle darkly, watching her writhe a moment before she pushes her hips back against me. I thrust into her steadily, stroking my hands over her back. My hips pound into her as she stays on her knees, leaning onto her elbows. Pleasure and heat mix as I breathe in her scent, growling at the sensual aroma that strike through me. My body begins to thrash inside, needing to be released as my skin tightens.

My inner wolf howls, ready to devour her as I thrust deeper, and she lets out a loud moan. It feels like I'm going to burst for other reasons, itching to be let loose. I dig my nails into the blankets, tearing through the fabric. Meg whimpers, pushing her hips further against me and I let out a loud growl.

"Meg, I'm gonna shift while inside you." My voice is a mixture of snarls and groans. "Tell me if I need to stop." She doesn't reply, groaning loudly into the blankets as I thrust into her again. "*Meg.*"

"I will!" She cries. "Please, don't stop, don't stop…please."

At the sound of her pleas, I shift. A growl echoes from my chest as I change into hybrid form, shouting at the tightness around my cock. I choke out a strangled snarl. Oh, fuck me I could cum right now.

My body shudders as I tower over her, straightening my back as I look down, noticing how much smaller she feels now. Meg gasps, whimpering beneath me as she presses her face into the bed. Worry flickers through me. "Meg, are you—?"

"Why do I feel like you're piercing my stomach? Is that even possible?"

"No," I chuckle low, my voice deep and dripping with hunger. She wiggles, and I groan at the movement. I trail my wide tongue up her spine, and she freezes at the contact. I breathe in deeply, pressing my nose against the nape of her neck, giving her a moment to get used to the size difference and feel. I move my hand up her back, careful with the long claws as it covers so much of her. She relaxes around me, breathing deeply as I nudge her shoulder.

"You weren't kidding," she gasps.

"You okay?" I ask, rubbing my head against her back. And she shivers. "Meg? What is it?"

"I forgot your voice…it gets deeper."

I chuckle again, and she shudders as I bring my mouth close to her ear. "Ready for more, darling?"

She nods. "Yes, keep going, Rodney."

I pull back, then thrust forward gently and she responds with a groan. Meg buries her face into the blankets and seeing her come undone makes my body shake with want. I drive into her again, deeply and as safely as I can without breaking her. I pull her hips up, and she lets out a soft scream as I pump into her, both of us breathing erratically. Pleasure drives up my spine and throbs into my groin, aching as the orgasm begins to rise again. She trembles beneath me as sweat glistens across her skin as I snarl, one of my hands thrusting into the sheets, shredding the blankets and mattress.

"Meg, you remember the phrase?" I snarl.

"I want to see you."

"Meg—"

"Rodney, I want to see you when you Claim me! Damn it!"

I growl, grabbing one of her legs, flipping her onto her back, and sinking into her with a rumbling snarl. She lets out a scream, arching her back as I bare my teeth and growl in pleasure from the position change. My hands land on either side of her head, and I stare down at her with my wolf eyes.

Her face is flushed, sweat covering her body with a sensuous gleam. Her lips are parted, wet hair framing her face as her brown eyes meet mine. I pant heavily as she reaches up, threading her fingers through my fur and up to my ears. She kisses the tip of my nose and I lick hers back. Suddenly, she grips my scruff tightly, pressing her hips forward and I jolt, snarling in want.

"Mate me," she states.

"As you wish, darling," I growl.

I pull back, thrust into her, and let the raging need take over. She throws her head back, screaming as I kneel, grabbing her hips and pulling her toward me. I drive deeply into her, pounding mercilessly as the pressure builds deep in my gut. My cock throbs as I inhale the aroma of lavender, honey, and citrus which drown out every other scent, apart from mine—pine and charcoal.

I growl, pushing into her as she screams as I grab her hands, pinning them above her head. She clutches me as I hover over her, thrusting myself closer to orgasm. I glance down and her eyes come to mine, a different warmth filling me with a calmness I've chased for decades, reaching me finally. And for a moment, time stills. Mine.

"My eternal, Claimed Mate," I declare.

Meg pants, and repeats, *"My eternal, Claimed Mate."*

Abruptly, the pressure explodes inside, and I let out a thundering roar as I feel myself snap. I thrust one last time and Meg gasps as her own orgasm reaches its peak. It shakes through us, pulling every bit of strength out of me as I let go of her hands. I snarl into the sheets above her head as I rip into the blankets. She clutches me, letting out a quiet scream as the wave pulses through us both, shaking the bed as the lights flicker.

Her scent clings to me, engulfing me as I breathe in our Mating scent, and relief washes over my senses. My scent now covers her skin permanently, and I exhale with bliss. Meg breathes heavily, gripping my fur as her body trembles against my chest. "Did it work?"

"Yes, darling," I murmur, nuzzling the top of her head. "I'm forever yours."

CHAPTER 35
WHAT BIG TEETH YOU HAVE

Meg snuggles against my chest, and I glance at the clock. I doubt we have much time before they come knocking. I shifted back into humanish form, now just holding my Mate and kissing her head.

"Should get dressed," I mutter.

"What happens when they get here?"

"PSB has to follow certain Paranormal Laws created before them, which includes no separating Claimed Mates; it falls under the human claim laws. They'll bring someone, a third party, to validate the Mating scent. Lil sis is sending someone else to be on our side in case who they bring ain't honest." She nods stiffly, and I cup her face, kissing her. "No matter what they're not taking you."

Meg smiles against my lips, wiggling her hips. I squeeze her side as her breath hitches. She breaks contact, averting her eyes. I tap her shoulder as her brows scrunch, and she looks at me, biting her bottom lip. I quirk a brow at her.

She asks, "Do you think we could...do that last part again?" I tilt my head, and she sighs. "I really like your hybrid form."

"No...really?" I say deadpan.

She smacks my shoulder, and I grin, flipping her onto her back. Meg scowls at me but loses it when I touch her nose with mine, then kiss it. She hums, the sound centering me after the longest damn day of my life.

"Don't have to hide from me, darling," I whisper against her ear, kissing the underside of her jaw. "I'll come in any form you want."

"You... Rodney!" She sputters, pushing me over, and I laugh. "Not that funny."

"Yet, you think I'm hilarious," I smirk at her, getting out of bed. She rolls her eyes, smiling and my heart skips a beat.

I head over to the closet, pushing some clothes aside to find her. I go still when I see my first great kilt of the McLycan Pack, given to me by my grandfather in Ireland.

"Grandpappy, I'm not old enough."

"I believe in you, Rodrick."

My throat constricts and I smile gently, and then I see Claudia's next to it. I stare at them, looking back at Meg, who's braiding her hair. I take a deep breath, my hands shaking as I grab both kilts and a long-sleeved shirt. Walking back over, she stops when I put down my kilt on the bed.

"How many kilts do you have?" She asks.

"A few," I smirk, glancing back at the bathroom. "They get beat up sometimes." I give her the shirt, and ask, "Do you know how to pleat?"

She puts the shirt on, looking at the kilt in my grasp. She grabs my hands, helping stop the shaking. "Are you sure I can wear it?"

"I'm the head alpha and main lineage of the McLycans, you wear whatever I say," I say roughly, and she smiles, rubbing her thumb over my skin. "This one was Claudia's, but I think she'd have wanted you to take care of it."

Meg gives me a caring smile, taking the kilt from my hands. "Okay and thank you. Marcus started showing me, but I may need help."

I nod, then gesture to the floor, helping lay hers out. She starts to pleat pretty well but needs a few pointers as she continues, then I grab one of my extra belts to slide under hers. I have her lie down, helping fold hers properly, and tuck the extra around to her back. Once I'm satisfied it's on well, I do mine, laying down and putting it on as she watches me.

I grin at her, standing as I cross mine over my shoulder. "Thoughts, darling?"

She crosses her arms, about to say something when there's knocking. I head over and unlock the door to reveal Gunther. His eyes widen, then he clears his throat. "Really making a statement, huh?"

I ignore his comment. "They here?"

"Yeah, and their third party is Alfred." Fuck. "One agent and one officer with a fucking warrant to search the place if she's not down in five minutes."

"Lil sis' witness here?" He shakes his head. Well, double fuck, gotta stall.

"Could just bottle your Mating scent to convince them," Gunther smirks. "Fucking strong enough, did you two meld together?"

I growl, a possessive side rearing its head as I debate tossing him over the railing. Meg grabs my hand and I stop as she gives a sympathetic smile.

"Gunther, he's had a long day, quit teasing before he throws you over the railing." Maybe we did meld together.

He looks her over quickly, eyes getting teary. "Welcome to the family, Meg."

"Thanks, Gunther."

"I'll be down in a few," I say.

"Making an entrance?"

I glimpse over the walkway, noticing the PSB agent wearing the signature dark suit. She has dark copper skin, black hair pulled into a tight bun, and wearing sunglasses. The officer next to her wears a badge, guessing detective, given he's wearing a tweed jacket that doesn't compliment his freckled fair skin and blonde hair. Both frown as Delilah tries to talk to them, while other wolves watch from the side. Alfred stays near the door, somehow standing with the number of bullets Vinny and Brenda put into him. Always did heal fast.

"Fuck it. Entrance."

"Stretch before you do," Gunther chuckles, heading down the stairs to clear the room as Meg looks at me confused. She glances down, realizing what Gunther is doing and her eyes go wide.

"You are not...Rodney, you can't...what do you—"

"Quit while you're behind, darling."

"You're not wearing underwear." I grin ruefully as I shift into hybrid form. She gapes as I poke my nose against her cheek, and she hisses low, "Rodrick Rowan, you'll scare—"

"Still a mob boss, *Megara*," I murmur, turning and jumping over the railing. I fall toward the tavern floor and land roughly on my feet, barely falling into a "superhero" landing. Lil sis may be right, I'm getting too old for this shit. I stand fully, looking over the two humans who seemed to have stopped breathing. The ache in my knees was worth it.

The agent collects herself, while the other shakes slightly. His fear drifts under my nose, and I show my teeth, kind of smiling. The agent takes her sunglasses off, pinning me with a sharp gaze. "Rodney McLycan?"

"May I help you?" I ask as a few wolves move casually to defensive positions. Alfred flicks his gaze at them.

"Agent Dawson and this is Sergeant Kelp." Close enough in guessing. "That's Alfred Withersby, a volunteer from the PSB Alliance Branch."

"We know each other," I mutter. Probably heard through the grapevine they were coming for Meg. How convenient for his moonlighting gig.

"We've been told you're harboring a human down here," Dawson continues. "There's no claim on her from any Paranormal. She's not attached or adopted by anyone, and we've been informed she's been here for over a month. She needs to come back to Topside with us until paperwork is submitted and finalized."

"Except, she *is* claimed," I say, crossing my arms. "She's my Mate."

"Paperwork?"

"Claim Mated, don't need it."

She narrows her eyes, looking past me and I glance over my shoulder to see Meg at the bottom of the stairs. She remains close to Marcus, who keeps a hand on her shoulder. Dawson addresses her next, "Ma'am, I need to speak with you."

"Ma'am?" Meg scoffs. "I could be older than you, but not that old, especially with these ruffians who are pushing their next century."

Some wolves chuckle, while I try to keep my composure. Delilah finds my gaze and smiles.

"Fine. Ms. Brunswick." So, that's her last name. "Were you manipulated into Mating or staying with this werewolf?" A few others grumble and growl.

"It's a valid question," Kelp says.

"We believe in consent," I say. "Is that not normalized on Topside?"

"Watch your tone," he replies, moving his hand toward his gun.

"And watch your trigger finger," Delilah says softly, flicking her gaze and he moves his hand away. "You're not on Topside…*officer.*"

"I'm still the law," he sneers. "And *she's* still human, which gives me the jurisdiction to provide safety and order so she's not in danger. Such as being coerced into a wolf's den." Not gonna tell him how we met then.

Dawson sighs, "Ms. Brunswick, again, were you—"

"No," Meg says defiantly. "I came here on my own accord to get away from an abusive work environment, and they offered me sanctuary. Then they gave me a job bartending, and I met my Mate and decided to stay. Including to help take care of this…*wolf's den.*"

"Yeah, right," Kelp grunts.

"It's true," Meg states. Mostly.

"None of you can fool me, I know who you are," Kelp says, pointing at me and I bare my teeth a little. "You're the fucking Wolf Mob of the Underground, and *you're* the Wolf Boss in charge of them."

"That's a pointed accusation," Zane mutters. "What if I was? My feelings would be hurt."

"Or me? All those years wasted," Edward adds, leaning in his chair.

"Maybe, it's me," Gunther says. "That's even *if* we were the Wolf Mob, sounds like a nice gig."

"Enough," Dawson interrupts, bringing her gaze to me. "I still need proof of the Mating."

"We can all smell the Mating scent," Marcus says gruffly. All the other wolves grunt, agreeing. The officers exchange a look, just had to get a fully human PSB agent and a *prejudiced* volunteer.

"This could be a ploy," Kelp insinuates. "Tricking and lying to us."

"Unlike you, we don't need to," Zane grumbles.

"You have a tan around your finger, sarge," Josh says, leaning on the counter. "Wife recently left or did you have plans after this?"

Kelp pulls out his gun, and Dawson yanks it back down. She hisses, "Keep your fucking cool."

"You heard—"

"They're baiting you. Shoot them without provocation, I have to arrest *you*."

"*He's* in monster form," he points at me.

"We're Underground," Delilah snarls. "Not on Topside where we have to follow *human* laws because a shadow scared you."

"Please let me handle this," Dawson says carefully.

"I'm clearly not under any duress," Meg speaks, stepping away from Marcus. "There's no need to worry. I'm even wearing their Pack…Clan tartan."

Dawson looks over, agreeance on her face, but then Kelp says, "So what if you're wearing a skirt."

All the wolves stand up, growling low along with me. Zane crosses his arms, showing off his great kilt and snarls, "It's a *fucking* kilt."

"Agent Dawson, you should know Paranormal Laws well enough that *no one* can be forced into Claimed Mating," I say, trying to keep Zane from ripping the sergeant's guts out for calling them that. "It has to be mutual. You have a werewolf not part of this Pack, ask him. He'll scent it."

She turns toward him, and I pin my glare on Alfred. He brings his hands in front of him and a sinking feeling hits me. He's always been honest, but he *will* lie for Freyja. A loophole in getting Meg back on Topside, helping her. He presses his lips into a thin line, then levels his gaze with me, almost apologizing for what he's about to do. The others sense it, tensing behind me as I start to snarl.

"Alfred?" Dawson asks. "Can you confirm they're telling the truth?"

He sighs and looks at her. "There is n—"

The doors open abruptly, and in walks the most unexpected being Brenda could've sent.

Carmen smiles wide, shining brightly wearing a tea-length dress patterned with flowers, while her hair is pinned back, and carrying a picnic basket like she's off to a garden party.

"Oh, it seems I'm interrupting something," she says, walking past Alfred and the officers as cherry blossoms mingle in the air.

Dawson visibly relaxes, and says, "Ma'am, we're just—"

"Rodney, you should've told me you were back, I was worried," Carmen speaks like the police aren't here, placing the basket on the bar. She pats Delilah's hand, coming to me. "You missed dinner last night with Meg."

I cock my head at her. "Apologies, I've been busy."

"I kept telling Alanzo that you—"

"You are imposing on—" Kelp tries to argue but shuts his mouth quickly when Carmen looks at him.

"Imposing what?"

Dawson interjects, "Ma'am, we've come to escort Ms. Brunswick to Topside, she's been kept here illegally for—"

"Illegally?" Carmen asks, her tone still bright. "That's absurd, she lives here."

"No, she doesn't," Kelp argues.

"I don't think he heard me, dear." Carmen rubs my arm lightly, and I relax a little. "Officers, she's my new daughter-in-law, so how would she be here illegally?" It's not her powers that wash over me, calming me, but adoration for the succubus who barely comes to my chest. "She's Mated to Rodney."

Dawson looks between us, then asks, "He's…your son?"

Carmen scoffs and gestures for Meg. "Family doesn't have to look like you to be family, dear. That's very rude of you to assume otherwise. Although I'm not Pack, some loyalties of mine had to stay in certain communities."

"Ma'am—"

"I don't know why they're arguing with me when your Mating

scent is so strong." Meg approaches us, scrunching her face. "Sorry, baby, but it is. It reminds me of Alanzo and I when—"

"Ma'am!" Dawson calls.

The room fills with more of the sweet scent, and Carmen takes Meg's arm, linking it with hers. The succubus is calm, but there's something odd about the growing aroma. She raises her brow at the officers.

Dawson clears her throat, and says, "We've been informed that she may have been forced into staying here."

Carmen laughs, kissing Meg's cheek. "I don't think they know you."

"Apparently, by the way, what do you think of the kilt?" Meg asks, stepping back for her to see.

"It looks lovely on you." She holds their hands out, and I can hear some of the wolves snickering. I glance over, and yeah, the annoyance on the officers' faces is close to hilarious. I get why Brenda called her. "You pleat better than my baby girl."

"Rodney helped."

"Oh, look at you being a good Mate," Carmen tells me.

"Learned from the best," I murmur, and she smiles gently.

"Can we *please* stay on topic?" Dawson interrupts, all three of us look at her.

Carmen looks at us both, then winks, and turns toward the officers. "Agent...?"

"Dawson."

"Agent Dawson, Meg is a *very* capable and strong female, who loves Rodney very much. Anyone with a Paranormal nose can sense their Mating scent. Here in the Underground, we follow *all* Paranormal laws and Mating etiquette, and your insinuations of her mistreatment toward these wolves are appalling. Rodney lives here, so...Meg lives here. Wouldn't you agree Alfred?"

He watches Carmen carefully, eyes widening when I almost taste those cherry blossoms, noticing the change. An overly, sweetness follows them...something tainted. He finally answers, "Yes."

"There. Now, Meg, I wanted your opinion about a recipe with pralines and pecans, not sure what liquor to use. I'd like to surprise *mio cavaliere*, pecan is his favorite."

"Oh, sure," Meg answers, looking at the officers. "Unless you need anything else? We have to start dinner."

Kelp looks to burst a blood vessel. Dawson loosens a long breath, shaking her head. "No, we're done here."

"Appears so, Agent Dawson," I say.

"McLycan." She puts her sunglasses on and walks out with Kelp close behind. Alfred gives me a look, disappearing through the door. Once out of sight, everyone shouts in relief.

I loosen a breath as Meg hugs me, and I hold her close as the weight on my shoulders lifts. I bend down, whispering in her ear, "I think you fibbed a little."

"What?" Meg looks me in the eye, scratching behind my ear. "Every bit was true...*McLycan.*"

I nudge her with my nose, and she giggles then turns toward Carmen. The rest of the wolves start a round of drinks, while Delilah grabs others to start dinner. Long ass day equals a long ass meal with drinks and poker. For once in a long time, I look forward to it.

"Will you stay for dinner?" Meg offers.

"Oh, thank you, baby, yes I will," Carmen answers, and Meg goes to join Delilah.

I watch her disappear, shifting out of hybrid form. Carmen pats my arm, and I look at her as she smiles. "Thank you," I murmur.

"I'd do anything for my family."

"I think I owe Brenda quite a bit after tonight."

"No, this wasn't for her this time." My stomach flips as I stare into those caring blue eyes filled with grace and love. I swallow hard and nod stiffly. "Oh, baby," she murmurs, hugging me tightly as I do with her. "You're not alone. And our door is always open."

We embrace for a moment longer as I take a deep breath. She kisses my cheek, pulls away, and rubs my shoulder. "Now, I expect you both for dinner in a few days, and next Thursday. I'm making tiramisu. I'll talk to Meg about discussing details for your official Mating Ceremony. Ricky will be delighted in helping, after Brenda's birthday party here. Don't worry, Alanzo said no sex swings."

I laugh as she walks away, while Gunther joins her. I shake my head and walk over to the bar, while Zane leans against the counter.

"Remind me never to piss her off," he comments as I walk around and open the cash register, taking out fifty bucks. I'll restock later. I put it down before Zane, and he gives me a puzzled look. "What's this?"

"New dumping grounds," I mutter. "Harbor. Next to Dracultelli's warehouse."

Zane takes the money, then freezes, staring at me. He blinks quickly in stunned silence, and I start chuckling heading back to join the others. Finally, he's fucking speechless.

CHAPTER 36
MEMORY...

I place two white roses at Victoria's tomb, setting them next to what I'm certain are two whiskey glasses Brenda left. I sigh heavily, staring at her name etched into the new stone.

Victoria Carmichael. Loyal Friend and Wolf.

She wasn't supposed to be buried here in the mausoleum, but I couldn't burn her. Not like Travis. She'd fucked up, costing her life, but she'd done it to protect the Pack and to help me. Victoria tried. The tomb meant for Brenda was given to Victoria, since lil sis and I agreed she'd probably never be buried here anyways.

I walk down the silent hall, pausing briefly at my grandfather's tomb next to my grandmother. My hand presses against his name, and I continue past mom's until I reach Claudia's. Taking a deep breath, I close my eyes, allowing myself to remember.

"I'M MATING MARCUS." I look up from the dining table, staring at Claudia with bewilderment. She stands at the doorway, arms crossed with a serious expression. "I told him yes."

I blink slowly. "Are you asking for my blessing?"

She groans, rolling her head back. "No, that's...isn't that what humans do?"

"Apparently, but that would be dad's job."

"He doesn't care long as I act like a 'respectful wolf' and be worthy." She mimics our father, and I smile at her. "I just wanted to tell you first."

"Well, I'm happy for you." I stand up, opening my arms for a celebratory hug.

"You're not mad?" Or not.

I drop my arms. "Why would I be?"

"He's your best friend, practically your second, not to mention he's over a hundred years older than me."

"Age difference? Really? It's rare when we're within a decade of each other," I answer, crossing my arms. "Those are all excuses, so you trying to convince me or you about this?"

"I'm just, you see worried, well…Rod…you see, I mean—"

"Quit while you're behind, Claw." She blows a raspberry in my direction, and I smirk.

"I love him," she states. "But…is it really okay if I'm Mated before you?"

I drop my arms, saddened over her confession, and gesture for her to come over. I sit down, and she sits next to me. Her worried eyes watch me, reminding me she's barely a hundred, still pretty young for a werewolf. But she's plenty old enough to make her own decisions.

"Claw," I start. "You said you love him?"

"Aye, a lot."

"That's all that matters. Although, how you love his grumpy ass I have no idea."

"He's not grumpy." She rolls her eyes, pushing my shoulder. "He's… misunderstood."

"I've known him for over a century, Claw. He's grumpy."

"Marcus just doesn't like loud beings."

"Coming from the loudest wolf in the Pack."

"I am a delight, and extremely adorable," she counters.

I chuckle. "Aye, you are." I hit her jaw lightly. "Claw, I want you happy. If he makes you happy, that's all that matters to me."

She smiles, takes my hand, and asks, "Can I tell you something?"

"Not something for me to be worried about, is it?" She shakes her head, and I nod for her to continue.

"He's really sweet with me. His frown lines are precious, and he always seems to know when I need a hug or to get my favorite drink. He loves hugs, too, by the way. Marcus may be strong, and gruff all the time, but he's got *this gooey center. When he does laugh, he's got the best smile. It makes me feel like…everything will be fine. So, yeah, he makes me happy."*

"Then I'm really, really, happy for you, Claw."

She throws her arms around me, hugging me close and nuzzling against my neck. I laugh at her, holding her close. She breathes deeply, and I can feel her smile against my skin.

"Do I get your blessing then?" She teases.

"Wholeheartedly," I smirk, sitting back. "Besides, he's the only one who has patience for your heathen arse."

"Am not!"

I give her an exasperated look. "Kitchen. Last week. Exploded."

"I was experimenting."

"How does that—"

"Not my fault the butter caught on fire!"

I start laughing, and the door opens with Marcus slipping in. He flicks his gaze between us as Claudia grins at him, and he seems to relax. "She told you?"

"About her blowing up the distillery or causing the cave-in near the construction down south?"

"Not me!"

"Uh-huh." Marcus glowers, apparently not finding it funny. "Yes, she told me. Congratulations."

Claudia runs over to slam into the large grey wolf, who barely budges. She reaches up to kiss him, and he reciprocates. My heart swells a little, happy for them. A small want tugs at me but feels faint like it's too soon. To wait.

Marcus looks fondly at Claudia, stroking her long hair back as I see a hint of a smile on his face. She looks at me, then points. "When you find your Mate, I'm gonna tell them every embarrassing thing about you."

"Never mind, no blessing."

Claudia lets out a fit of giggles, and Marcus scowls again. I wink, and he grumbles as Claudia starts to yank him out of the room. "Come on, cutie."

"Not in public, Claw."

"Fine. Scrumptious." Marcus lifts her, throwing her over his shoulder. "Marcus!"

"Talk later, Rod," he says, waving a hand as they disappear.

I lean back, grinning at the two. They've rarely been separated for the past ten years. About damn time. Pride and joy spread through me, but that little ache is still there. Impatient almost. I rub my chest, going back to work. "One day, Claw…one day."

I STARE at Claudia's tomb, and then pull out the parchment from my bag. I open the charcoal drawing with shaking hands. It's of Meg sitting in the park, amongst the flowers. I set it behind the bottle of wine still here and place my hand on her tomb.

"I miss you, Claw, a shit ton," I whisper. "But I'm figuring out how to be happy again, find some light in the darkness. Not sure when I won't hate myself so much, and not be so scared to lose others…but with Meg, it doesn't feel as crushing or hollow. Someone to help me face all that. Quit being alone. Even fearing losing her."

My throat constricts, swallowing hard as a few tears tumble. I smile gently. "I promise I won't hide anymore, be more like grandpappy like you said. He's who I looked up to, not dad. But…just know I'm taken care of, and wish you were here with us. Every damn day."

There's noise, and I turn to see Marcus walking through the dim light. He stops a few feet from me, and we stare at each other. He looks at the picture I've placed down, and I whisper, "Figured she'd have liked it."

He clears his throat, and states, "Your father called." I raise my brows. "Complained about the Pack and that we should go back up to Topside, but then Meg took the phone." I snort suddenly, and he looks at me. "I don't think he's gonna be around for a bit. Again."

I grin a little. After seeing Meg take on Boston, Freyja, the police, and me all in one night…she's not a woman to be challenged. Another thing I love about her.

I glance at Claudia's tomb, and murmur, "Like I said, Claw. We're taken care of."

Marcus clears his throat again, shifting his weight. He gestures toward her tomb. "She'd be proud of Meg, and not just cause she can use an oven without it exploding."

"More like amazed there's not flour everywhere."

"Or egg."

"We ever figure out how Claw got so many noodles on the ceiling?"

He shakes his head. "Blamed magic, and that it gave the place... character."

My chest hurts a bit, and I close my eyes, taking a deep breath. "You remember the day she told me you two decided to get Mated?" He nods. "She kept telling me everything she loved about you." His gaze meets mine, glistening with tears. "Said you weren't grumpy, just misunderstood with a gooey center. Being sweet with her and that you secretly loved hugs. Claudia always saw the best in you."

I pull out another drawing, setting it beside Meg's.

He looks over and his eyes widen. It's a portrait of Claudia and Brenda together, what I imagine they would've been. Claudia's arm is over Brenda's shoulder, who's holding a book and smiling wickedly with my younger sister. Tears fall down Marcus' face.

"I'm sorry I wasn't there enough for you," I murmur. "And I'm sorry Brenda couldn't have helped you like she had with me. I do hope Meg can. I hope she can become the sister you always needed to help find that gooey, loving center of yours that Claw saw in you."

He takes a shaky breath, rubbing his hand over his face as he stares up at the ceiling. A sob releases from his throat, and I'm tempted to grab him, when he says, "I don't blame you for not wanting to turn out like me. Even I wouldn't have wanted to wish this on anyone."

"Marcus."

"I wanted to die...so many damn times," he whispers, and my heart cracks. The words I'd told Meg, strike deep as my vision becomes blurry. "But I couldn't do that to you. I promised her... and she believed in me. But every damn day it got harder...and harder without her...and, and the hope of that empty feeling leaving...left. I couldn't..."

My hands shake as he frowns, chin trembling as he shuts his eyes. "It's not your fault," I rasp, and he shakes his head. "It's not your fault, and I'm glad I had you all these years. Because I didn't want to live either."

His gaze meets mine, blue eyes filled with sorrow, but not hollow. "What?"

"You're not alone," I whisper, and he shakes his head and I finally yank him into my arms. He clutches at my back, trembling violently as he tries to keep the sobs at bay. I hold onto his head, whispering what I had needed to hear, too. "I want you here. I need you. And you're not alone...I've got you. You're not alone..."

Finally, he sobs against my shoulder as I hold onto him tightly. His cries echo through the mausoleum as his claws dig into my back, bawling against my skin. I keep my friend safe in my arms and let him mourn his Mate in safety. And not alone.

Mystery cocktail...

Did you think I'd let you have it that easily?

CHAPTER 37
NOT ALONE IN THE MOONLIGHT

We stop outside *Mountain Edge*, noticing the activity inside with Delilah and Josh taking charge of decorating the place for Brenda's birthday in a week. Marcus grumbles next to me, back to his usual scowling expression. Both our tears have long dried.

"Just had to make a deal with her," he mutters.

"Bloodsucker pissed me off," I answer. "Maybe lil sis will *acquire* some good liquor from Vinny. He imports the expensive stuff." He snorts, almost grinning. My phone rings, and he prowls into the tavern.

I grab my phone and stare down at the Chicago area code. "Who's this?"

"Oh, I'm hurt, after everything I've done." The voice is smooth, but slightly obnoxious and cocky, much like Vinny. I wait, and they say, "Bill Midnight, McLycan...it hasn't been that long."

Oh, right *that* cocky vampire. "You still sound annoying if that helps."

"And you sound like Vincent." One more thing we can agree on. "Not a compliment, unless—"

"Is there a reason you're calling me, and not Brenda?"

"Because I have a favor."

"Have? Don't you mean—?"

"Tomato, tomato." I'm remembering why I'm glad he left. "Anyway, I need assistance in finding this *Agent X*, since they've been thrown into my court to search for." His fault for choosing to work at PSB. "Meaning your help."

"Oh?"

"Careful with your excitement, you may burn down the Underground with it."

"Fucking tell me what you want," I grumble rubbing my temple. This is why Brenda usually deals with him. Or Gunther. Because I'll find a way to throttle him through the phone.

"I need you to ship me some of your explosives that were stolen, so I can run forensics and scan them for any DNA traces." He's fucking kidding. "With any luck, Agent X may have handled them, perhaps not, but best to cover all options. Or find anyone else who may have been involved in trying to kill you, while succeeding in killing DiNardi." He's not.

"No."

"But I—"

"You really think I'm gonna send explosives strong enough to destroy Undergrounds, across city *and* state lines for you to use PSB's equipment to run tests on them? I'm not taking a damn chance like that, not if Agent X is as high up the chain as those fuckers thought he was."

"I can be sneaky."

"No."

"I'll wear gloves, too."

"Not happening. Don't care how it may help, not risking it. If you honestly think it'll…"

"I do."

"…then fucking come to New York, you negative O prankster."

There's a pause, and he comments, "Did you learn that from baby sis?"

"Fucking call her next time. Not me. That was the damn agreement, Midnight. So, don't think groveling will get your hands on my explosives. Answer's no. And don't even try it with Gunther either."

I hang up, letting out an exasperated sigh. Small relief when he left for Chicago years ago, and I just invited him back. I shake my head, heading into the tavern.

I step over a box of streamers and balloons, heading to the bar as Meg comes out of the dining area. She carries some bottles of whiskey, stopping near Marcus who's sitting near the back. She smiles, murmuring something and I watch his shoulders relax as he nods. He smiles a little as she comes to the bar.

I sit down as she gives the bottles to Delilah and goes to make her signature cocktail. "Ever gonna tell me what's in this?" I ask.

"Even I don't know," Delilah mutters, then smirks as Meg rolls her eyes as the wolf walks away.

"She just wants my recipe," Meg whispers, pouring the drink and placing it in front of me and another beside me for Claw. I half-smile, leaning forward and she takes the hint. She kisses me and I close my eyes, inhaling our Mating scent and ease soon follows. Her touch swallows up the past hour or so of tears and pain, and I open my eyes as she strokes my cheek. "You okay?"

"Should ask you that," I say, taking a sip. "Heard you spoke to my father."

She scoffs, "He's an ass."

"Did you tell him that?"

"Among other things," she mutters, not making eye contact as she cleans some glasses. I narrow my gaze, reaching across to poke her arm. She sighs heavily, "I may...have told him he's not welcome here until he learns how to be a better father, otherwise I'm making him take etiquette lessons from Beckham."

I stare at her in disbelief. She actually scolded him.

Meg puts down the glasses, and continues, "I know that...you and him, well the...Pack, but...you know, okay I may have crossed a—"

I howl with laughter, holding onto the bar for support. Meg gapes at me as I continue laughing, then finally tell her, "Quit while you're behind, darling."

"Rodney—"

"You can scold my father anytime," I speak as my laughter fades. "Just next time let me be in the room."

She lets out a sigh of relief. I reach across, pulling her toward me as she gasps as I kiss her. Meg lightly pushes my shoulder, laughing against my lips. I kiss one of her dimples, cupping her jaw.

"So, you're not mad?"

"Never, darling."

She kisses my nose, pulling away as Gunther enters the tavern and sits next to me. He glances at the extra cocktail, looking in need of alcohol. I push it toward him, and Meg winks at me.

Gunther takes the drink as Meg walks away. He takes a long sip, and I snort at him. "You must have great news."

"Well, first, the warrant was dropped on Meg, they've dropped the investigation," he answers, taking another drink. "Damn that is good. Anyway, Beckham's contact in PSB completed the process, and Megara Brunswick is now officially claimed by the McLycan Pack."

"That was fast." It's been ten days since the longest damn day of my life, but that's quick even for the courts.

"He's...good." His voice sounds tired, and I quirk a brow as he takes another drink. "Talked with the detective. Louis won't snoop around PSB just yet, treading lightly. Doesn't want anyone to get suspicious, so laying low, watching from the sidelines. He also didn't take recognition for the information we gave him, which surprised me."

"That reminds me, Midnight may call you, tell him no." Gunther looks at me puzzled. "Called and tried to convince me to send our explosives to him."

"Is he insane?"

"My thoughts exactly, so just send his ass to lil sis or something," I mutter, drinking the rest of my cocktail.

"Police are crawling through Manhattan and Staten, making everyone go ghost," Gunther says. "Including Freyja and her lackeys. I'll admit meshing our routes with Vincent was a smart idea. Keeping us out of the spotlight." I grunt at him, and he looks at his drink. "You ever gonna tell me what happened with Freyja in that tower?"

"No." He watches me carefully and then nods.

I hope she pushes her obsession into PSB, and maybe take out

Agent X for us for whatever she wanted. Leave us alone down here, but only time will tell in the next coming months. Meg and I compiled everything she remembered from undercover, hiding it in *The Vault* with Beckham and Brenda. Lil sis said she'd handle the rest as a failsafe, mentioning "adding" it to her collection of secrets. Not sure what she's thinking, but she's got my back and Meg's. I'll trust her conniving ways.

"Louis still gonna work with us then?" I ask, pushing thoughts away from Freyja.

"Yeah," he grumbles, and I eye him. He grunts, finishing his drink. "Long as he quits calling me fucking Clifford."

"Thought you loved nicknames."

"I should growl at him more."

"Welcome to my world."

"Great, lesson learned."

"Maybe he's flirting." Gunther snorts. "Or spending too much time with lil sis." He glares, and I smirk at him. "He helped get those agents, owe him for that. He's officially dirty cause of us."

"Yeah, yeah," he mutters, and I chuckle at the frazzled beta. "And he's a reliable inside source for the NYPD, smart and careful, got a knack for cybernetics, and finding information. Perfect inside cop."

"Convincing me or you?"

"Can we change the subject, before I rethink staying as your beta?" He complains, pushing his empty glass away. Meg comes back as I chuckle. Something about the cop is really getting under his skin, and it's interesting seeing him shaken up.

"Trouble in paradise?" Meg asks.

"Please say we're playing poker tonight, so we can whoop his and Zane's ass at cards," Gunther says.

She laughs, pours both of us another cocktail, and smiles at me before walking away. I grin as she goes, tilting my head to get a better look at her—

"You good being back down here?" Gunther interrupts my thoughts. "Might be a while before we can open *Donny's* again."

Killing a mob boss has its perks sometimes, like other mob families staying far away and scrambling for what's left of their shit. We made a deal with Louis. Meg gave him everything about Boston's operations, and the police have been arresting surviving members, confiscating warehouses, and "investigating" his death. I made the decision to shut down *Donny's* for a bit until things settled down, keeping Topside Wolf Mob in Lower Manhattan. And me living in the Underground again.

"Where I belong," I say taking my drink and furrowing my brows. "Wait, did you say earlier he *didn't* take the credit? We said he could."

"Apparently he sent everything in through an anonymous email," he answers, taking his drink and standing up. "May hate him calling me Clifford, but I'm starting to see what lil sis sees in him."

Yeah, he'd have been set for a damn promotion or some shit. It wasn't as much as what DiNardi promised the feds, but it was a lot on Boston's operations, connecting to other human mobs. Huh, guess he wasn't for the glory after all.

"You meeting with Joey tomorrow?" Gunther asks.

"Uh-huh, a new group of survivors to send out to Keir. I'll have a meeting with Vinny on using his tunnels to get them out." Gunther pauses, cocking his head and furrowing his brows. "What?"

He shakes off the look. "Didn't say nothing."

"Your face did."

He smirks and goes to sit down with Zane, who's taking a break from hanging pin-the-tail on the werewolf. I stay seated, staring at my drink and the ache in my chest starts to grow. I sip some of the drink, but my chest feels tight suddenly as it feels like something creeps up my spine. My hand clenches the glass, trying to keep myself from rubbing at the ache and sudden hurt when someone sits next to me.

I glance over as Meg smiles, placing a white cupcake with dark frosting in front of me. My arm goes around her shoulders, and she rubs my chest lovingly and the ache starts to subside. I press my face against her hair, taking a deep breath.

"Tried peppermint schnapps with dark chocolate," she murmurs. "No vodka ideas yet."

I chuckle, stroking her hair back, and hum to myself. There's still one last promise for me to uphold with her.

————

MEG YAWNS, leaning against my shoulder as we walk through the park. The lights cast a faint glow, mimicking starlight and moonlight.

"Jet lag?" I tease her.

She bumps my shoulder. "Is there a reason you wanted to come this late? Brenda's party is tomorrow."

"Won't be long. Had a promise to keep with you."

"What else is there?"

"Showing you spring."

She scrunches her face, looking at the lush colors of the park. "It's always spring or summer down here, though. The comment I made when we Mated was a euphemism, Rodney."

"Well, I wanted to show you...*my* spring." I smile, leading her up a hill and stopping at the top. "What my grandfather fought for. And so will I." Meg looks out and gasps.

Below is the sibling of Sheep's Meadow above, smaller and filled with blooming wildflowers. The grass is tall, imitating green pastures sprinkled with color, much like those I grew up with in Ireland. Trees surround the area, hiding the dark walls of the Underground, looking like a fantasy retelling of where the sun shines. The Underground moonlight glows over everything, casting a deep blue ambiance.

Meg tightens her grip as I pull her down the hill. She stares at the vast space, stopping to look at flowers, and running her fingers over the grass. Her laughter echoes into the silent night, making my heart soar. I watch her in adoration, a ray of light in the way she inspects every plant and flower, touching them gently as she handles the petals. A calming peace takes hold of me, the darkness vanishing out of reach.

Suddenly, she pulls me down to the ground and we lay side by side, staring up at the ceiling of stars. She breathes deeply as I place my arm under her head, cradling her next to me.

"What do you think?"

"Beautiful," she whispers. I find her brown eyes, shining with delight.

"Claw and I would sneak out here," I murmur, and she listens with a soft expression. "She'd shift into wolf form, run around like a pup through the grass. And try to eat the flowers. Some nights, I'd have to chase her down to get back home."

"She sounds mischievous."

"Oh, she was. Worse than Brenda."

"Hard to believe that."

"Claw had this way of always having pranks ready. Not sure how she thought of half of them."

"Smart and diabolical. Just like the rest of the Pack," Meg laughs.

"Careful, you're part of that Pack now."

She hums as she cuddles closer to me, placing her head on my shoulder. I close my eyes, inhaling our Mating scent. *Mine.*

"Hey, Rodney."

"Yes, darling?"

"I know we haven't talked about it, well...it doesn't, okay well I was thinking—" I open my mouth and her hand covers it, eyeing me as I raise my brows at her. "I was thinking of being changed into a werewolf."

I blink slowly. She purses her lips, getting that determined look on her face. I move her hand from my mouth, and ask, "Really?"

She looks at our hands, intertwined. "I want to stay with you, for as long as possible. Why settle for fifty years, when it could be centuries together? Besides, it seems fun being one. Healing fast and all, but I may miss silver jewelry, but I like gold more anyways...well, who cares, but I could help keep—"

"Stop while you're ahead, darling."

I crush my lips to hers, sinking her body into the grass. My tongue sweeps over hers as she opens her mouth. I breathe deeply as I taste her, clutching her face. Passion burns through me as I kiss her fervently. She wraps her arms around my neck, and I moan moving a hand down her side and gripping her thigh. I break away with a rasp, "You'd make an amazing werewolf."

She hugs me as I roll over so she's on top of me. Meg leans her elbows on my chest, grinning down at me. "And I get to choose who, right? Can't be you, we're Mated."

I furrow my brows. "Who taught you that?"

"I can read, McLycan."

"You can?"

She smacks my shoulders, rolling her eyes at me. "Very funny."

I chuckle up at her. "I'm guessing you had someone in mind?"

She nods, rubbing her hands down my chest. "Yeah, I've been thinking who'd I'd like as a…wolf sibling."

"Please don't say Zane."

She smirks and shakes her head. "Marcus." I go still as she takes my hand, tracing her finger over my skin. "He's already been like an older, protective brother. Someone I trust and could count on. And I think he'd like to have a sibling…he was an only child. Help him feel part of the Pack again," she murmurs the last part.

I smile softly, feeling relief as she talks about him, realizing how much he's opened up with her. Her hair falls over her shoulders as the lights shimmer in her gaze, and I reach up to stroke her cheek.

"Perfect decision." She smiles, tilting her head. I take her hand, placing it over my heart. "You ready to be stuck with me for a long time?"

"Oh, I'm counting on it, Toto."

"One more deal then."

She groans, "Seriously?"

"It's a good one."

"That's ominous."

"Don't trust me?" She gapes at me in fake shock, and I grin wickedly.

"Devious werewolves," she mutters. "Proceed with the ominous deal."

I pull her down closer to me. "When you change, you have to learn one thing," I say, bringing her closer to bring my mouth against her ear. A rumbling growl vibrates from my throat, and she gasps, her body shivering.

"You sneaky… Rodrick Rowan McLycan! Behave—"

She falls into a fit of giggles as I kiss her neck. Our laughter echoes through the meadow as the lights flicker above, the moonlight shining down. Happiness warms my soul, and the weight of loneliness is gone as her laughter mixes with mine—a wolf boss and his darling.

AUTHOR'S NOTE
SURVIVOR'S GUILT

I was eighteen when I was deployed to Afghanistan. It was probably the best time I had while I was in the Marine Corps. But I was still within war zones and the reality it brought.

Before I even left what we called "The Sandbox," I was showing signs of PTSD and survivor's guilt. Over the months after I came home, I struggled like many veterans, with the heavy weight of loss and the hollow feeling that never truly leaves you. It's been over a decade since those days, and the weight is still there. The crying still happens. The tightness in my chest comes back when I see certain sunsets. The ache in my heart still throbs when I hear *Wagon Wheel* by Darius Rucker. There's a punch to my gut when I get thanked for my service, wishing it wasn't me. In those small moments, I wish I had never come back. That perhaps, it should've been me coming home under a flag. Not those we lost.

Rodney was written for every veteran who has suffered that loss. For those who've locked themselves in rooms with the dust of the past. He is for every veteran who refused help when they thought they were better off alone. He is for my Marines who growl at every person who's offered a helping hand, trying to be that "perfect" image they told us we needed to be. He's for those who've tried to shoulder every burden in attempts to erase the past. For those who struggle, trying to find purpose again. And he's for the buddies we wished had picked up the phone...but didn't.

He is the reminder that vulnerability isn't weakness, but strength. That asking for help is brave. That our fears do not control us, but we control them. That our purpose does not revolve around perfection or duty, but our honor, loyalty, and joy within our own lives. And for all whom we've lost...would want us to find happiness again.

I wrote his story, in the beginning, to help through my own trauma and guilt. To help with healing and it did. Until it became my only solace during a dark time in my life. He became my guiding light as I struggled with loss again, losing another friend to the dreaded 22. (For those who don't know, there is an average of 22 veterans a day who take their own lives, losing that internal struggle.)

Rodney, the McLycan Pack, Meg, the Cuorebellas, the Underground... all of it became my lifeline. And suddenly, it became more important than ever for me to share his story. I *had* to convey the anger and frustration and desperation. I couldn't pull back punches of how loss tears us up and how guilt can fester if we're not careful. And I couldn't sugarcoat the shadows that linger in our minds, whispering words we shouldn't believe. But even with *all of that*...it's not hopeless. There's still happiness to be had. There's love and joy and peace that can be found with the right people and support. Even in our hardest moments, we can continue, and that someone, somewhere, wants us here.

You are not alone.

You deserve happiness. And I'm glad you're here.

I know the days get hard without them. Don't give up. Don't you dare give up. Not yet. The McLycan Pack has your back and believes in you. Even on the days when you may not have that belief. From one survivor to others...get back up.

Semper Fi to all my U.S. Marine siblings & brethren.

May we all find a bit more peace in our hearts before our time is done. And that we don't cut it short.

And lastly to Evan...I wish we had more time, my friend.

Good night Chesty, wherever you are,
Elm Jed

BOOKS BY ELM JED

Mafia, Murder, and Mayhem Series

Vinny the Vampire & Me

Sweet Cheeks & Her Mob Boss

The Wolf Boss & His Darling

The Werecat & Her Lone Wolf

Memories of the Underground: Volume One

Contemporary Mafia Series

My Dear Watson

My Forgotten Demons

My Emerald Fire

My Dear Leo

ABOUT THE AUTHOR

Elm Jed is an award winning author, who mostly writes mafia, paranormal, and suspense romance. They are a disabled, queer, Marine Corps veteran, who's been writing since they were ten years old with a degree in Theatre. Their books focus on mental health awareness and giving readers a space to feel seen in different ways from disabilities to understanding their queerness.